MW01119006

The Secret of the Dragon

Path of the Ranger, Book 17

Pedro Urvi

COMMUNITY:
Mail: pedrourvi@hotmail.com
Facebook: https://www.facebook.com/PedroUrviAuthor/
My Website: http://pedrourvi.com
Twitter: https://twitter.com/PedroUrvi

Translation by:
Christy Cox

Edited by:
Mallory Brandon Bingham

DEDICATION

To my good friend Guiller.

Thank you for all your support since day one.

MAP

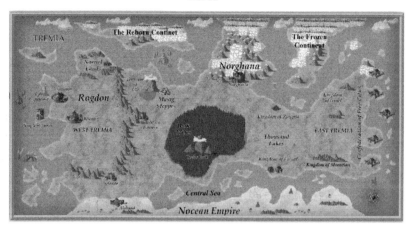

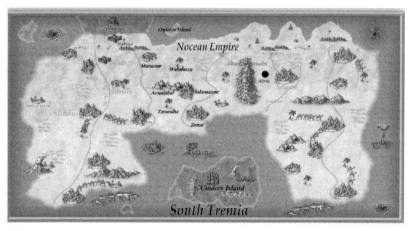

Chapter 1

The Panthers entered the Throne Hall of the Royal Castle with uncertainty in their hearts and guilt weighing heavily on their shoulders. They walked slowly, almost dragging their feet, trying in vain to delay their meeting with the King. Thoran had summoned them, but not only the Panthers; he had also summoned Gondabar and Raner. And if, as a rule, when the monarch requested their presence it was not usually for anything good, the fact that their leaders had also been called indicated that the meeting was not going to be a pleasant one, especially after what had happened at the Royal Wedding.

Gondabar was leading the group down the long corridor toward the throne. His steps were unsteady and he moved slowly, almost as slowly as the Panthers. Raner was walking behind the leader of the Rangers, watching in case Gondabar stumbled and required his assistance. The Healer Edwina had been performing her arts of healing magic on the afflicted body of the octogenarian leader and he had improved substantially, although he still wavered, as was the case today. Magic had its limitations, even that of the expert Healer.

Behind them came Nilsa, who was more used to these situations than the rest of the group. She knew the great hall well, although she could not help being a little impressed by the magnificence of the room and by the number of soldiers of the Royal Guard on watch in front of the columns and along the walls. She was troubled, wondering what the King might want with them. With every step she managed to control the restlessness that churned her stomach a little more. By the time they arrived before the King, she was sure her nerves were under control.

The redhead was followed by Astrid and Lasgol, who were exchanging troubled looks. Astrid was sure the King was going to hold them accountable for what had happened during the wedding. Thoran might be a brute, but he was intelligent, and he was not going to let conspiracies, murder attempts, or covert movements from the shadows go unpunished. Lasgol breathed deeply. He was more worried about everything that had to do with Eicewald and the

Immortal Dragon. He was sure the King would want to know what had happened and would not be satisfied with the initial account Gondabar had given him. The implications of revealing to the King what they knew at such a late time, added to the consequence of his Royal Mage's death, were going to be terrible. He could almost anticipate the shouts and accusations they would hear. He was sure they were going to reach even the Nocean deserts in the south.

Ingrid and Viggo were walking in the middle of the group. The blonde Archer had warned Viggo to keep his mouth shut, since the audience with the King was going to be conflicting enough, and they could all end up in the Royal Dungeons. Ingrid was concerned with the murder attempts on the King and on who was now their Queen, and whether the matter might stain their reputation. Viggo, as usual, had promised Ingrid that he would be on his best behavior, and that regardless he was not worried at all. He did not think they could be involved in the attempts—there was no evidence against them. As for Eicewald's death and the problem with the Immortal Dragon, well, Gondabar and Raner would have to deal with the consequences, not the Panthers.

He shrugged and then strained his neck to see who was in the throne room. He glimpsed King Thoran sitting in his. Of course his unpleasant brother had to be there, Duke Orten, standing on the right of the throne. On the left was Ellingsen, Commander of the Royal Guard, and beside him the Ice Mage Maldreck. Viggo's face twisted at the sight of the Mage. He did not like that treacherous viper at all, and the fact that he was present was not a good omen.

Gerd and Egil brought the rear of the group and had also glanced at the throne to see who was waiting for them. Gerd was holding his fear back for whatever might be going to happen to them. He had it under control. He knew it was best not to imagine things before whatever had to happen. They were likely in a big mess, of that he was well aware, and he feared the consequences, but he also knew he had to keep his fear at bay and was doing so successfully. Egil, on the other hand, was calm, as calm as the situation and his alibis allowed him to. The dragon problem would have repercussions or not, that remained to be seen. The matter of the murders, the most fishy business, he had well tied up and was not expecting to be found involved, either him or the Western League. That was what he was hoping for, even expecting, but he could be wrong. Kings, and

6

especially Thoran, could act irately and unexpectedly.

Gondabar reached the throne and stopped. Raner and Nilsa stopped behind him. The rest of the group stood in a line behind the redhead so the leader of the Rangers and the First Ranger were in front of them.

"Your Majesty, we have come in answer to your summons," Gondabar said and bent over in what was meant as a deep bow but was not because he nearly lost his balance.

Raner missed nothing and reached out to help his master. Seeing that Gondabar was able to recover, he bowed deeply and the Panthers joined him.

"Gondabar, your looks aren't improving. I had understood that the Healer had examined you and performed her healing magic on you," King Thoran said by way of a greeting.

"And so she has, Your Majesty. I assure you that, in spite of my fragile appearance, I feel well," Gondabar replied.

"Perhaps the old Ranger is in no condition to serve his King as his position requires," Duke Orten said to his brother, raising an eyebrow. Lasgol caught the threat at once. They were questioning Gondabar's capacity, which upset Lasgol deeply. Gondabar was a pillar, not only for the Rangers but for the Kingdom of Norghana. The meeting was not beginning well, as he had feared. He had the clear feeling that it was going to get even worse.

"Age is heavy on the body, but I can assure my lords that my mind is as lucid as my first day on this job," Gondabar replied defensively and tapped his temple with his finger, smiling.

"Well, it doesn't look it," Thoran said.

"In fact, it would appear the very opposite. I'd say you've lost your mind," Orten added, now glaring at Gondabar.

"Your Majesty? Duke Orten? May I ask what you mean?" Gondabar asked, bowing his head as if he had indeed done something wrong and was going to be chastised for it.

Thoran beckoned Commander Ellingsen, and he handed the King a scroll.

"I mean this report you have written detailing the incident that led to my Royal Mage Eicewald's death," the King replied angrily, showing the report to Gondabar.

"Your Majesty, I wrote it with the information I was given. I know it is hard to… believe…"

"Are you telling me that you stand by what is written in this report?" Thoran asked him, and his words carried not only the weight of a threat but were contained and seemed to put a brake on the rage behind them.

"Your Majesty…"

"Think carefully about what you're going to say, old leader," Orten threatened, folding his arms and standing with his legs apart in a clearly unfriendly gesture.

Gondabar straightened up and looked at the King and his brother. He took a deep breath and in an elegant, quiet tone said, "The content of my report might be difficult to believe and digest, but I can assure my lords that it is what happened. So I believe and so I have communicated the fact to my lord King because of the threat inferred from the situation and against which we must prepare the Kingdom."

"Prepare the Kingdom? Against what? Against a bloody dragon? Have you completely lost your mind?" Thoran exploded, yelling at Gondabar at the top of his lungs.

"Your Majesty …"

"Only a lunatic can affirm that a dragon killed Eicewald," Orten added. "He's wrong in the head, brother," he told Thoran.

"I thought that once the Healer saw you, you'd recuperate your sanity. I see that hasn't been the case," Thoran said, shaking his head and looking furious.

"You're in no shape to lead the Rangers," Orten said.

"I swear the dragon is real and he exists," Gondabar insisted, gesturing with his hands but maintaining as calm a tone as he could.

"If you believe in the existence of a dragon that measures over a hundred and fifty feet long, with magic capable of killing the leader of the Ice Magi, you're delirious!" Thoran shouted so loudly, that for a moment it looked as if he were going to blow Gondabar along the whole corridor back to the entrance of the hall.

"That's nonsense! The old man is senile!" Orten shouted.

"Your Majesty, the report has been verified," Raner said, standing up for Gondabar.

"Verified? By whom? By you?"

"Among others, yes…" Raner replied.

"You're not even capable of stopping two murderers from escaping the castle! What can you verify!" Thoran yelled at him, jumping to his feet, beside himself.

"You'd better shut up, First Ranger. You've already proven yourself useless by letting the assassins escape disguised as Rangers!" Orten joined him, jabbing an accusing finger at Raner's chest.

The situation was getting worse by the moment. The Panthers had already guessed something like this might happen. All they could do was weather the storm. If they said anything they would get the same treatment as Raner. The King and his brother would blow their heads off with their roars.

"A dragon! Do you think I'm an idiot? Is that what you think?" Thoran asked, pointing at Gondabar and Raner.

"Very much the contrary," Gondabar replied. "Your Majesty has a very lucid and intelligent mind."

"And yet you come to explain the death of the leader of my Magi with a fallacy? With a children's tale?"

"With a mythological fable, rather," a voice said suddenly.

All those present turned to see the Queen enter, accompanied by her bodyguard Valeria and the Druid Aidan.

"What fable are you talking about!" Thoran protested, still beside himself.

Queen Heulyn walked up to the throne. Ignoring everyone present, she sat in her throne beside her husband, the King.

"Dragons appear in fables based on mythology. There are dragons in many regions of Tremia. In Irinel, for instance, and among the Druids too, isn't that so, Aidan?"

"It is, my lady," Aidan replied. He had stayed beside Valeria at the foot of the Queen's throne.

"You too believe in that utter nonsense? Don't tell me you do, because that's stupid!" Thoran said to his wife rudely.

The Queen looked at Thoran with narrowed eyes. It was clear she did not in the least appreciate Thoran's tone with her.

"I haven't said that. I'm saying that dragons are mythological beings with a wide representation in fables throughout Tremia."

"I don't care! They're children's tales, whether they are widely spread or not! Dragons don't exist! Have you all lost your minds? "Thoran shouted, waving his hands in the air.

"They've never existed," Orten stated, joining his brother.

"Commander, do dragons exist?" Thoran asked Ellingsen.

"No, Your Majesty, they don't."

"Do they exist, Maldreck?" he asked the Ice Mage.

"Of course they don't exist," Maldreck affirmed seriously.

"Thank goodness. I was beginning to think I was surrounded by lunatics," Thoran said, sitting back in his throne.

"Or under a spell," Orten added. "That would make more sense."

"Are you under the influence of any spell, sorcery, witchcraft, or similar?" Thoran asked the group of Rangers before the throne.

"No Your Majesty, we are not," Gondabar replied.

"Then you've lost your minds!" Thoran yelled, enraged.

"Husband, there's no need to yell at them until they go deaf," the Queen said, covering her ears with her hands at the loud shouts.

"I think so! And what are you doing here anyway?"

"I'm your wife, and your shouts could be heard from Irinel. I came to see what was going on."

"You may withdraw. It's an internal matter."

"I'm interested. It's not every day you hear of the existence of dragons," Heulyn said, nonchalantly looking at the Rangers. "Although if they're involved I'm not that surprised," she said, indicating the Panthers. "I told you I didn't want them assigned to my protection. But since they are, it gives me the right to be here and listen to their explanations, in case they affect my personal safety."

"My Royal Eagles have nothing to do with that, isn't that right?" Thoran looked questioningly at Gondabar and Raner.

"Your Majesty..." Gondabar began to say.

"Only me," Lasgol said, stepping sideways to be seen.

"What are you doing?" Astrid asked him in a worried whisper.

"Don't do this," Ingrid whispered as well.

The rest of his comrades stared at him with surprise and concern.

"You, what's your name and what do you have to do with all this?" Orten pointed his finger at him and asked unpleasantly.

"I'm Lasgol Eklund. I was with Eicewald when he died. The report is based on my sworn affidavit as a Ranger."

"Sworn affidavit as a Ranger?" Orten said, who from his look did not know the concept. He looked at Raner.

"A sworn affidavit as a Ranger cannot be refuted or questioned. It's accepted as the confirmed truth, since it is sworn on the tome of *The Path of the Ranger*," Raner explained.

Orten wrinkled his nose.

"So, we accept the fact that Eicewald was killed by a dragon only because of the statement of this Ranger. That's absolutely ridiculous. If a Ranger swears he's seen an elephant flying, are we also going to accept that as the truth?" Orten said mockingly, waving his arms.

"Of course not," Gondabar said. "There's more than only Lasgol's statement. We've been investigating the possible existence of this dragon for some time. It has to do with two secret sects we've discovered and which worship him as an all-powerful lord."

"This is getting even better. Now it turns out that there are secret sects   that worship dragons in Norghana," Orten waved his arms angrily again. "This is not only ridiculous, believing in all their nonsense is of utter simpletons."

"I wouldn't have said it any better, brother," Thoran joined in. "Sects that worship dragons? A dragon killing my Royal Mage? Do you know how stupid you sound? How idiotic you look right now? I feel like throwing you all into the pigsties so you can cavort with the swine. They are undoubtedly smarter than you, seeing what we're witnessing."

"Say the word and I'll order it with pleasure," Orten hastened to say.

"I have a question," Queen Heulyn said.

"Go ahead, ask," said Thoran.

"If these sects worship an all-powerful dragon and this dragon has killed the First Ice Mage, where has such a creature come from?" the Queen asked with honest interest in her tone, not angry or mocking.

Gondabar took a deep breath.

"It's difficult to explain... we discovered that the spirit of the dragon, his essence, his power, had survived inside a very special orb. He accomplished that by remaining frozen for several thousands of years. We don't know the exact time period. It thawed a short time ago, we believe by the orb's own actions. There are indications that the spirit woke up, although we don't know the reason behind that either, and forced the ice to melt by using his power. Once freed of his icy prison, he searched for a body in which to be reincarnated and found a fossilized dragon inside a volcano. With the help of his adepts, he prepared a process to liberate the fossil from the rock wall, revive the body, and the spirit of the dragon transferred itself from the orb to the body of the dragon, thus coming to life. This dragon is the one that killed Eicewald," Gondabar explained as seriously as he could.

"I see..." the Queen said, staring at Gondabar with narrowed eyes.

"You see?" Thoran turned to her with eyes open wide. Then he looked at Gondabar and began to laugh with loud guffaws that echoed throughout the throne hall.

"That's an awesome fable!" Orten joined him, also laughing with tremendous guffaws.

Gondabar and Raner stoically bore Thoran's and Orten's mocking laughter as it grew in volume. They laughed as if this were the funniest thing they had ever heard.

The Panthers bore the mocking, looking at one another, puzzled by the situation. Lasgol remained firm where he was without showing whether the mocking was affecting him or not. They had known this might happen, they had talked about it, but it was one thing to imagine it and a very different one to suffer it.

The King's and his brother's guffaws went on for quite a while. Tears began to run down their cheeks from laughing so hard. The guffaws were like blows they all felt. The King and his brother were laughing at them mercilessly, revealing themselves for the rude, brutal bullies they were.

"My Rangers... have become court jesters..." said Thoran, breathless from the laughter he could not control.

"The best jesters," added Orten, holding his stomach with his right hand from laughing so much. "All they need is to set music to the tale and make it into an ode."

"You don't like the joke? You're not laughing?" Thoran asked Ellingsen and Maldreck, pointing his finger at them.

"It's a pretty incredible story and... entertaining... yes," the Commander said and smiled.

"Hilarious," Maldreck laughed. "No doubt taken from some mythological tale from some faraway corner in the north."

"I'm glad to see it's not only my brother and I who think so. I'm sure my Royal Guard and even my Royal Rangers here on watch and protection duty are also laughing their heads off, although they don't dare to show it," Thoran said, who was on his feet and gesturing at them encouragingly. "Laugh! Laugh at leisure!"

A few of the Royal Guards laughed and the rest followed so that the whole room filled with laughter. The Royal Rangers smiled but did not laugh. Mocking their leaders made them feel very uncomfortable. The Queen, Valeria, and Aidan were not laughing. They were not even smiling. They maintained a grave expression, watching what was unfolding.

The laughter and the mocking continued a while longer, until Thoran sat down in his throne again and his face became serious. The laughter died out and was replaced by a tense silence.

Thoran took the report and tore it in small pieces.

"This is a bunch of lies and an offense which I will not tolerate in my presence!" he yelled in a new bout of rage.

"You make fun of the law with your behavior, you buffoons!" Orten joined him, reaching for his sword and taking a step toward Gondabar and Raner.

Lasgol prepared to act, led by the need to protect their leaders. He could not let the crazed Orten harm them. If Orten took another step toward them, Lasgol would jump on him.

Chapter 2

Thoran pointed his finger at Orten.

"Stop, brother! Don't shed blood!" he shouted like someone giving an order to a bulldog not to attack.

His sword already half-unsheathed, Orten's face was red with rage. He looked unable to hold back; he was not going to listen to his brother. He was going to attack them.

"Incompetent cretins!" he yelled, glaring at Gondabar and Raner.

Lasgol began to slide forward stealthily and gently.

"Stop! I'm ordering you!" Thoran shouted at this brother.

Orten stopped. He was struggling to control his rage. For an instant everyone watched tensely, hoping he could control himself. Finally, he took a step back and sheathed his sword.

"They deserve a severe punishment for their stupidity and foolishness," Orten said to his brother.

Lasgol returned to his previous position with another swift move. He hoped no one in front had seen him; it seemed as though no one had. They were all too concentrated on what was happening with Orten to notice him. Everyone except Valeria, who was smiling at him. She had seen him, and she gave him a knowing nod. Lasgol replied in turn.

"I know, brother. Let me remind you of the situation we find ourselves in with the Zangrians. I don't need any more problems right now."

"I'll take care of the Zangrians, don't worry."

"I do worry, brother. Don't underestimate them. They're dangerous, very dangerous."

"They're mere brutish dunces."

"That too. But they have a strong army, and we're weakened since the war with the West."

Orten made a disagreeing face but said nothing more.

There was silence again. Everyone was aware the King would not let this pass without some severe punishment.

"Our intention is always to serve the Kingdom. The explanation we have presented to you is what we believe to be the truth…"

Gondabar started again to explain.

"Shut up," Thoran said, raising his hand to stop him from saying anything else. "The day a dragon appears before me and I see it with my own eyes, that day I might believe you. Today I believe you are all fools who have been tricked with a children's tale. This is something I can't tolerate from someone of rank in my service."

"Remove him! That way he'll learn!" Orten shouted, pointing at Gondabar.

Thoran raised his hand to calm his brother's temper.

"Gondabar, I want you to know that if it were not because we are about to start a war with the Zangrians and I need the Rangers, I would remove you right here and now like my brother rightly demands."

"Your Majesty…. I'll abide by your decision."

"Which infuriates me even more, because I want to remove you from your post, but right now isn't a good time at all. I swear I'm only keeping you in it because I need someone with experience for the job and I don't have time for your Grand Council or any other Ranger rituals to choose a new leader."

"We'll manage without him! Throw him out! We'll make anyone we want the leader without the Grand Council!" Orten raved, intent on removing the leader of the Rangers.

Thoran waited a moment for his brother to stop shouting. He turned to address Gondabar.

"This isn't the best time to remove you, and because of that, and only that, you're safe for now," he told him. "But, no one escapes the King's punishment for their foolishness or failure. So I'm sending you to the Royal Dungeon until further notice. Let everyone know that whoever fails their King ends up with their bones in the Royal Dungeon."

"Good!" Orten cheered his brother, jabbing the air with his fist.

"As Your Majesty wishes," Gondabar replied, bowing his head. He looked saddened.

"Your Majesty…" Raner started, trying to defend his leader.

The Panthers murmured in surprise and protest, which Orten quieted at once.

"Silence! The King's will is unquestionable!" he shouted threateningly, and his hand reached again for his sword.

"The fact that you're in prison doesn't free you from your

responsibilities," Thoran continued telling Gondabar. "You'll lead the Rangers from there until I reinstate you, if I ever do that, which I doubt, seeing your deplorable behavior and the poor judgment you've shown regarding this matter."

"Yes, Your Majesty…" Gondabar nodded, downhearted.

"You, Raner, will act as his intermediary, handing down the orders to the Rangers. I choose to believe that your leader has led you down the wrong path and that you've followed him out of loyalty and honor. But, you've already failed me twice. If you do so again, there won't be a dungeon for you, I'll let Orten deal with you."

"Yes, Your Majesty," Raner said, bowing his head.

"It'll be a pleasure to deal with him, I look forward to it," Orten said with a sadistic grin as if he really wanted Raner to fail. He was rubbing his hands. It was no mere threat. He wanted the First Ranger to fail so he could let out all his cruelty on him. He was a sadist without any scruples, and he did not mind who saw and knew it. On the contrary, he took pride in it.

"You, my Royal Eagles, will abandon all efforts that have to do with this colossal folly of the dragon and will continue with the mission I entrusted you with," Thoran ordered, looking at his wife, Queen Heulyn. "You'll be the Queen's protectors. That will be your job. I'm not confident that the danger is past. The Zangrians might try to kill her again."

Heulyn looked at her husband and seemed about to say something. But then she appeared to change her mind. Her usually surly, haughty face softened a little.

"As my husband, the King, wishes," she conceded.

Thoran looked surprised. And if the King was surprised, the Panthers were even more so as they exchanged looks, not understanding why the Queen was not protesting this order as much as usual, as she had done repeatedly on prior occasions.

Lasgol looked at the Queen and he thought he saw a calculating look in her eyes. This was premeditated and measured. She was not accepting the King's order just because, or because she did not want to enter into another argument with the King. There was something else behind it all. Lasgol could not begin to imagine what Heulyn was up to, but he guessed it would be good for them to know as soon as possible. The Queen's plans and intentions were still a mystery to them, one they needed to understand. He looked at Valeria before he was aware of doing so. If anyone had any inkling as to what the Queen was plotting and the reason why she had not complained about having the Royal Eagles as her protectors, it would be her without a doubt. Valeria noticed that Lasgol was looking at her and she smiled. Then she looked at the Queen and made a surprised face. She had also been having the same thoughts as the Panthers.

"I see that my Queen is accepting my commands gladly. I like that," Thoran smiled at Heulyn triumphantly. The Queen acquiesced with a slight nod.

"I am."

"As for the Royal Eagle who has had such an inappropriate performance in all this," Thoran said, pointing his finger at Lasgol, "he is as of now demoted from my Royal Eagles. Let him return to the tasks of a Ranger, and substitute him with someone with a better head who is less capable of being influenced. Someone who deserves to belong to my Royal Eagles."

"Whatever Your Majesty wishes," Raner said.

"I never liked you," Thoran said to Lasgol, looking at him with narrowed eyes. "I remember who you are, whose son you are. I'm not surprised you've been deceived like you have."

Lasgol said nothing. He bowed his head and accepted the King's decision. He knew that defending himself would lead to nothing—it would only infuriate Thoran further. The King and his brother would not listen to him. He did not have the support of Ellingsen either, and certainly not that of Maldreck. Thoran had mentioned his father, and that upset him greatly. A fire began to burn within him, and he had trouble holding back the urge to tell the King a few home truths, but he had to; it was the most intelligent thing to do. Lasgol did not want to risk the rage of the two brothers; things might end badly, much worse than they were already going. Better to be smart and let the insult pass. There would be time to collect on it later on.

The Panthers were focused on Lasgol and were throwing him glances of support and small signs of encouragement unobtrusively. Astrid's face showed a mixture of rage and frustration. Egil made him a sign with his hands to calm down. Lasgol knew that Egil was going through the same emotions. It was not the time for confrontation; he would find the way to turn things around. Viggo had a look that clearly said: *don't heed this moron.* He made a sign and winked at him. Ingrid and Gerd had more serious looks on their faces and were troubled, he could tell. Nilsa was wiping the sweat of her hands on her thighs and had a look of disgust on her face.

"As for the matter of covering Eicewald's position as Leader of the Ice Magi, after consulting with Orten, I have decided Maldreck is to take over."

"Your Majesty, it's a great honor," Maldreck said, bowing elaborately. "I will not disappoint you."

"You'd better not. You are the most powerful Ice Mage, but not one with the most illustrious background. If you make one single mistake, you'll face the same punishment as Raner. I'll find someone who serves me better."

"That won't happen, Your Majesty. I have learned from my past mistakes. I will serve you faithfully and with intelligence. I'll lead the King's Ice Magi. We'll be a magical force to be reckoned with in the continent," Maldreck said and looked at Orten out of the corner of his eye; the King's brother was glaring at the Mage.

"You promise a lot, Mage…" Orten said in a disbelieving tone.

"I swear you won't have any complaints about my disposition and competence," Maldreck said, bowing his head and bending almost double.

"I want the Ice Magi ready for combat the moment I need them," Thoran said. "If the Zangrians move forward we'll have to push them back, and one of our advantages is the power of our Magi which is much greater than theirs, am I right?"

Maldreck nodded.

"It is, Your Majesty. Their Magi are no rivals for us."

"All Magi believe they are superior to their rivals. We'll see what happens. If you fail, you'll hang from the battlements," Orten threatened him, jabbing his finger at Maldreck.

"I will not fail. I will prove the superiority of the Ice Magi over any other Magi," Maldreck said with conviction.

"I also want you to keep training the young ones and find me more magi to train. I want to have more magi available than any other rival kingdom," Thoran told him.

"Your Majesty, that is more complicated… finding people with the Gift is not a simple task. Not because we are not searching for them, but because the Gift is found in very few people. We've tracked Norghana up and down and we've only found a couple of potential pupils who are already at the Tower with us."

"So, track Norghana all over again, from down up this time!"

"Yes, Your Majesty, of course."

"Brother, there's something else we can do about it," Orten suggested.

Lasgol was worried. He did not know what Orten was going to suggest, but knowing him it would not be anything good, that much was certain. He put his hand to his chest where he felt his pool of magical energy. He hoped that whatever the Duke suggested would not affect him or those who were like him. He felt a restless tingling in his stomach.

"Do tell, brother, I'm listening," Thoran said.

"If we don't find magi here, we could bring them from abroad," Orten said, beginning to pace in front of the throne. Thoran and Heulyn watched him, interested.

"What do you mean 'bring'?"

"We can bring them in, offer them gold, and search in other kingdoms. And if we find candidates, young or not so young, we'll bring them here to train at the Tower. That would give us an important advantage in the fight. Imagine having twice the Ice Magi we now have?"

"Magic is of different natures in different people," the Queen intervened. "I don't think what you are proposing can be done. What do you think, Aidan?"

Thoran and Orten turned toward the Druid.

"What my Queen says is correct. The Gift manifests itself in different ways in different people. Not everyone can become an Ice Mage, even if they have the Gift. My case, for instance," he said, spreading his arms open. "I am a Druid—my magic is in tune with Nature. It's not magic based on one of the four elements like that of an Ice Mage."

"Is that so, Maldreck?" Thoran asked.

"Yes, and at the same time no, my lord. If the Gift has manifested in the person already, this person will lean toward the magic more in tune with their Gift. That is correct. But, this might be altered if it's found in a young person whose Gift has not yet manifested or has done so recently. In that case, we could redirect their tendency toward the type of Magic we want, in this case the Elemental Magic of Water, and from there specialize them in that of Ice," the Mage explained as if he were teaching a lesson to his pupils.

"What does that even mean? Yes or no?" Orten was glaring at Maldreck, not seeming to fully understand.

Heulyn intervened.

"He means that if you find someone with the Gift and they're very young, they might be led down the path of magic the expert decides. Isn't that right, Aidan?"

The Druid nodded.

"It's not recommendable, or accepted in most of the communities of Magi, who believe we must cultivate the magic in the manifested tune, but it is true."

Thoran's face stretched in a smile of triumph and greed.

"We'll search for young ones with the Gift in other territories, and if we find them, we'll bring them to the Tower," Thoran said. "I want more Magi in my ranks."

"It's very likely they'll refuse to leave their lands…" Maldreck said.

"So we bring them by force!" Orten cried.

The Queen made a disgusted face.

"Although I share my husband's view regarding having more Magi to defend our interests, I don't think kidnapping foreign children is a good policy. It will be discovered and rumors will fly across Tremia. We'll be accused of abducting infants and our reputation will be sorely damaged. My father wouldn't approve and neither would other kings."

"What does it matter what others think, we can do whatever we want!" Orten replied.

"It does matter," his brother said. "We can't antagonize our allies with actions that call us into question. My wife has good judgment and understands politics," he said with a grateful nod toward Heulyn. "We must be careful."

"We could do it secretly," Orten suggested.

"We could offer the possibility of being trained here with the Ice Magi and reaching a position of power. Many peasants and plebeians would take the opportunity without thinking twice. Their parents as well, since it would mean a better future for their children," Heulyn said.

"I like that idea. We'll offer gold and a position. That will persuade most people," Orten said.

"And what do you think about those who are already magi?"

"We can't turn them into Ice Magi if their Gift has already developed in another type of Magic," Maldreck warned.

Thoran was thoughtful.

"It doesn't matter what type of magic they have. If it can be used against our enemies, we want it. We'll offer them gold and position too."

"Understood. I'll organize it," said Orten.

"Remember, brother, we don't want to look like children traffickers," Thoran warned Orten with a stern look.

"I understand, don't worry," Orten replied reluctantly.

"Maldreck, you'll be in charge of preparing a discrete but honorable funeral for the late Eicewald," Thoran ordered.

"Discrete, Your Majesty?" the Mage asked, raising an eyebrow.

"Yes. I don't want to fail to honor someone who's died serving the Kingdom, and least of all the leader of the Ice Magi. That would not go down well with the Magi. But I don't want everyone to know we've lost our most powerful mage either, especially the Zangrians. It puts us at a disadvantage and it shows weakness, things I don't need right now."

Maldreck made a sign that he understood.

"It will be a solemn but secret funeral."

"Perfect. That pleases me," Thoran said.

Lasgol felt sad hearing the King's wishes. Eicewald deserved a great funeral with everyone present to show respect and gratitude. He would love to be able to say goodbye to the Mage, paying him tribute and all the honors he was due, which is what he deserved for everything he had done for the Kingdom and for so many people, among them the Panthers, and also Camu and Ona. Camu was going to be distraught by the news. He wanted to say goodbye to the Mage as much as Lasgol. It was a very sad thing. Lasgol looked at his comrades and saw by their faces that they felt the same way.

"And now let's focus on what's really important, which are the Zangrians and their intentions for war," said Thoran.

"There's no movement on the border," Orten said. "We have every inch of it under surveillance since the murder attempts at the wedding."

"Which is significant…" Thoran said.

"Significant?" Orten raised an eyebrow.

"It is. They should have made some movement by now, knowing

them. They're up to something, and I can't figure out what," Thoran said thoughtfully.

"I think they don't dare to attack. We have their great General Zotomer in the dungeon and we've expelled all the Zangrians from the kingdom, so that means they're out of spies here," Orten said.

"Ellingsen, has everyone been expelled?"

"That's correct, Your Majesty. It started right after the murder attempts. There isn't a single Zangrian in all of Norghana, my lord."

"Has General Zotomer spoken? Or any member of his retinue?

"No, Your Majesty. They deny any implication in the attempts… they say the Zangrian assassin wasn't working for their kingdom, that it was a ruse to implicate them… that they had nothing to do with what went down…"

"Oh sure, and I'm a little damsel!" Orten cried. "It was them for sure!"

"The fact that the assassin who tried to kill me was a Zangrian doesn't necessarily mean that Zangria was behind the attempt on my life," said the Queen.

"As a rule, the most obvious things are also true," said Thoran. "I'm inclined to believe it was Zangria."

"Too obvious. My father shares my observation. He thinks it's too elaborate an attempt for the brute Zangrians, and too obvious."

"Did the King gather any additional information when he returned to Irinel?" Orten asked.

"Nothing so far. But, now that my family is back in Irinel, he'll be better able to help us with this situation. Here his resources were limited."

"Yes, I told your father to go back to Irinel at once so we could prepare for whatever might come," Thoran said.

"If he finds anything that might shed light on those murder attempts, he'll let us know at once," Heulyn said.

"Raner, have you found out anything else about the two cooks who managed to escape?" Thoran asked in an annoyed tone.

"We followed their trail to the border with the Masig. They crossed the river Utla in a boat they had ready and waiting. Then they went into the steppes. There their trail was lost," Raner said.

"Hellfire! That's right below my castle!" Orten exclaimed angrily.

"And your men watching the river did not see them. Small favor you do me, brother, if I trust you with the surveillance of the borders and assassins cross them at will and without impediment!" Thoran said accusingly.

"I'll hang them from their toes for being useless!" Orten yelled, enraged at the insult to his abilities.

"Did you find out how they got their posts in the kitchens? With whose help?"

"No, sir, but it was very well organized," Raner replied.

"I'd say it was well organized! They managed to escape under your nose, among your Rangers!" Thoran said, pointing at the Rangers present.

"It'll be difficult to know who helped them now that they're gone…"

"This is wonderful! They try to kill me and the assassins escape! They try to kill the Queen and we kill the assassin, and now it turns out it's not what it initially seemed to be! This is inadmissible! Shame on you!" Thoran yelled, beside himself.

"Your Majesty…" Ellingsen tried to apologize.

Raner joined him. "Your Majesty…"

"Leave! Everyone, leave and bring me evidence! Irrefutable evidence!" he yelled and waved his arms for everyone to leave the hall.

Lasgol marched out with the rest of them, and he could not shake the feeling that the matter was going to get even more complicated. So much so that it would affect them terribly.

Chapter 3

"That went great," Viggo said bitterly as the Panthers walked into the room they all shared in the Tower.

"We already knew something like this might happen if we went to the King," Astrid replied, coming in after him and shaking her head, saddened. "A sorry spectacle."

"That's why Gondabar and Raner didn't want to go to the King without solid evidence. Now it's clear they were absolutely right," Lasgol said, coming in with his head down.

"I wasn't so sure about not informing the King of what we had found out," Ingrid said, following the others with a crestfallen look on her face. "Whenever Gondabar and Raner opposed telling the King, I thought it was risky. I thought it would be worse once they found out about the existence of the dragon and that we'd be accused of having hidden what we knew. I have to admit though, after what we've witnessed, that I was wrong. Now I understand our leaders' fear. Their worst expectations have come to pass. I had guessed it might go badly... but it was a lot worse than I expected. A spectacle as embarrassing as it was regrettable. I can't believe what we've just witnessed. I'm ashamed of our monarch and his brother. Their behavior is unforgivable. The outrage to good old Gondabar, a wise, prudent leader, who's always been at the service of Norghana, it's unpardonable. I'm more disappointed than ever in who rules Norghana and rules us."

Nilsa, who was coming right behind Ingrid, had a face that said it all: red eyes, moist cheeks, and a runny nose.

"I can't believe the King has sent Gondabar to the dungeons, it's horrible. More than that, it's a tragedy. I feel so bad for him," she sobbed, unable to hold back her tears. "He doesn't deserve such treatment after all he's done for the Rangers and the Kingdom. A man who's given everything for the Corps and for Norghana, who's sacrificed his whole life, always putting his duty to his country first. He doesn't deserve such ill treatment and humiliation," she sat on her bunk and put her hand over her eyes to cover her tears.

Gerd strode to the end of the room, where he hit the wall with a fist in frustration.

"That was shameful. He didn't deserve that treatment. Not him, nor any of those present. That was a despicable act. Just thinking about it makes me feel sick," the giant said, hitting the wall again.

"I've always believed our beloved monarch was a cretin and his brother an even greater one. Any day now Orten's going to lose it and kill someone right there in the Throne Hall. Just wait and see," Viggo said, sitting on the window sill with a light leap and drawing out his black knives. "Egil, whenever you wish, just give me the order and I'll deal with them," he told his comrade as he passed his thumb along his throat.

"Viggo! That would be regicide! Don't even think about it and least of all mention it out loud!" Ingrid said, looking around everywhere, as if fearing that someone might have heard. Luckily, it was only them in the room. "If anyone heard you, they'd hang you. You can't talk about such things so lightly."

"Fine, lightly or not, I mean it," Viggo turned to Egil and winked at him.

Egil smiled at Viggo with bright eyes.

"Nothing is as simple as we'd like it to be in this life. We must always look for the right time and place to make the correct covert actions to pursue a glorious goal," was his reply in a tone of intrigue and secrecy.

"So, look for that time and place. I'm more than fed up with those two and their charming manners," Viggo replied.

"We're not going to do anything in that direction, least of all now, after two murder attempts. Don't you see that the King has everyone with their eyes peeled, watching around?" Ingrid said. "We have to tread very carefully. One false move and it might be misinterpreted. Rest assured that Thoran and Orten never forget who Egil is. I bet they watch his every move, and our own by proxy."

"I'm very good at hiding my movements," Viggo smiled at Ingrid.

"No matter how good you are, you won't be able to fool the whole Royal Guard, besides the Royal Rangers," Nilsa told him. "That's not counting Ellingsen, Maldreck, and the spies the King might have around."

"With Astrid's help I believe I could," Viggo said. "Are you up for a night mission?"

Astrid smiled.

"Thanks for the invitation. I'm not saying it might not be possible for the two of us, but I agree with Egil and Ingrid on this. It's neither the time nor the place. Too many vigilant eyes, too much protection. There'll be better occasions."

"I also agree with Egil on this," Lasgol said. "Our goal has to be to find and destroy Dergha-Sho-Blaska. We can't lose focus here and go for different and risky goals. We have to finish off the Immortal Dragon. That's the greatest danger and our goal. I know he's planning something, something that will be horrible for everyone, I guarantee it. Besides, we owe it to Eicewald, who gave his life fighting against the Dragon. I still can't believe the good Mage is dead."

"Lasgol's right. The Dragon has to be our top priority. The rest will have to wait," Ingrid agreed.

"I'll wait," Viggo smiled at Ingrid. "I'll wait impatiently," he added, and his eyes showed a lethal gleam.

Ingrid understood at once what Viggo was insinuating and signaled him to not get into trouble with one of his schemes.

Gerd snorted, leaning on the far wall.

"The problem is that we can't do much now that we're assigned to the Queen's protection. We won't be able to go in search of the dragon…"

"Very true. That's going to complicate any course of action," Astrid said. "Besides, we'll have to deal with the little blonde, who I trust less than anyone."

"Val? I don't think she'll be a problem," said Nilsa.

"How's that?"

"We have an agreement… an understanding, to collaborate, she and I," Nilsa told them. "I trust her, at least regarding anything to do with the Queen and the Druids. I don't think she'll play us."

"Well, you're wrong," Astrid said, making a face. "I don't trust her one little bit, regarding anything. I swear she'll betray us again."

Ingrid folded her arms across her chest.

"It's good for us to have Val as an ally, considering the love the Queen has for us. I was really surprised she didn't refuse our protection, honestly. Weren't you?"

"Yeah, I was surprised too," Lasgol said, nodding.

"I had expected her to flatly refuse and that she would start insulting us and asking for our heads again," Nilsa commented, opening her eyes wide.

"Yeah, the usual when it comes to her regarding us," said Viggo.

"And yet it wasn't like that. Why? I wonder…" Gerd murmured. "Doesn't it seem weird? She insulted me without even knowing me, just because I'm part of the group. It's odd. I think she's up to something for sure, and it has to do with us."

"Irrefutable, my dear friend," Egil confirmed.

"We need to understand what it is she's looking for and what it has to do with us," said Lasgol.

"Keep your agreement with Valeria," Ingrid told Nilsa. "Don't trust her completely and don't tell her anything about us that might be incriminatory. Try to find out what's going on with the Druid Queen, what she's planning and how we're involved."

Nilsa nodded. "I don't know how much I'll be able to find out. Valeria's smart, and she's not going to let me dazzle her like the Royal Guards and Rangers…"

"A pity that your charms don't work on her, Freckles," Viggo said sarcastically.

"At least I have some charm. Unlike others," she replied with a mocking gesture.

"Good counterattack," Viggo smiled. "The best way to get information out of Valeria is to send her Lasgol."

"Me?" Lasgol asked, jerking his head back.

"No way. Lasgol, don't you dare go near that trickster," Astrid said with a look that meant she loathed the idea.

"As a rule Viggo's ideas aren't usually the best, but in this case I admit it's not such a bad one," Ingrid said with her hand to her chin and eying Lasgol.

"I'll talk to her and get whatever it is with my knives," Astrid offered, unsheathing them.

"I'm afraid that's not going to work with Valeria," Egil said. "Threats or even physical pain won't have any effect on her. She's already survived that. Nilsa's approach, one of friendship, is more adequate in my opinion. First, because it was Valeria herself who looked for it in order to get close to us. Secondly, because she trusts Nilsa, even if only a little. The idea of sending Lasgol isn't bad," Egil went on looking at Viggo, who spread his arms wide in triumph. "The problem is that Valeria would see through Lasgol."

"She would?" Lasgol asked, raising one eyebrow.

"My dear friend, you have many qualities, but lying isn't one of them. Besides, Valeria knows you well. She'll read you like an open book."

"She'd better not touch the book, not even the cover to close it," Astrid said with a frown.

The group settled in their room, most on the beds, some on the windowsill. They remained thoughtful, trying to bear the frustration, rage, and indignation of what had happened. They pondered about the situation and the repercussions and the next steps to take.

"I'd like to go to Eicewald's funeral…" Lasgol said suddenly, "it saddens me to not be able to give him the proper send-off he deserves."

"I'll try to find out what Maldreck's planning," said Nilsa. "The Ice Magi aren't exactly the most subtle or covert. They usually act as if the Norghanian ground they tread on belongs to them, and Maldreck is no exception."

"Thanks, see if you can find out how they're going to carry out the funeral," Lasgol said to Nilsa.

"We're all going to miss him," said Gerd. "It's uncommon to find such a good and kind mage as Eicewald was, as well as a loyal friend. What happened to him is awful."

"And the fact that he was willing to help, even teach," Lasgol added. "I'll never be grateful enough to him for all he's taught Camu and me."

"Yeah, I liked the traveling 'Don Juan' mage," said Viggo.

"*Don Juan mage?* Where did you come up with that?" Ingrid said, staring at him wide-eyed.

"The Turquoise Queen was crazy about him, don't you remember? And in order to woo her he had to be very good in the art of seduction, the Queen of the Turquoise waters had quite the character," Viggo said, shaking one hand.

"That doesn't make our dear Mage a 'Don Juan,'" Nilsa said. He was an adventurer and a good mage. It seems he also experienced some romance during his journeys, but don't add things you don't know."

"I'm glad he enjoyed life," Astrid said, looking thoughtful. "Indeed, in this life we should enjoy every day, because we never know if it'll be the last," she said, looking Lasgol in the eye.

"Our friend was a pretty uncommon combination, and a very

worthy one," Egil said as he wrote something down in one of his notebooks. "A scholar, adventurer, loyal to Norghana and the King, teacher and leader of other Magi. I enjoyed the conversations we had so much… I'll miss them a lot. He was a learned man with much knowledge, a rarity."

"Has anyone any idea of where he might have hidden the twelve silver pearls Dergha-Sho-Blaska is looking for?" Ingrid asked.

They all looked at one another, shaking their heads. All looks converged on Lasgol in the end.

"I'm afraid not," he said. "The place that comes to mind is the Forest of the Green Ogre, but if they were there, Dergha-Sho-Blaska will have sensed them and found them like he did with the great pearl."

"What do you think he wants them for?" Gerd asked, scratching his head.

"We don't know, but it has to be important if he's gone to all the trouble of reappearing and revealing himself," Egil said. "He's been in hiding, shrouded in secrecy, and the only time he's shown himself has been to get the Pearls. That's why I'm guessing they must be very important for him, to further some goal he's after."

"Why is he in hiding? We know he's recovered. He fought against Eicewald, Camu, Lasgol, and Ona and defeated them easily. That indicates he's strong," said Ingrid. "Why not reveal himself if he intends to rule over Tremia?"

"I'm wondering the same thing," Nilsa said. "If he's so powerful, why doesn't he show himself and crush the Norghanian forces?"

"There must be an important reason," Astrid said.

"Of course there is! If I were him, with all that power, I'd already have razed some kingdom or other," Viggo said. "Even if it were only for practice. He must be very rusty after being frozen for thousands of years."

Ingrid glared at him.

"Would you really do that?"

"Well, you know what I mean, if I were a dragon and unable to control my killer instincts and my thirst for burning kingdoms," he said with a shrug.

"I think that, once again, we find ourselves confronted with a situation where Dergha-Sho-Blaska needs the right moment and place to make a covert move in order to reach a very important goal,"

Egil said.

"He's waiting for something?" Lasgol asked.

"That's what I think, yes. He doesn't want to show himself because he still doesn't have something or because the moment he's waiting for hasn't yet arrived. It could be both."

"And we have no idea what either of those things might be," Viggo stated.

"One of them could be the Silver Pearls," Astrid guessed.

"It could be indeed," Egil nodded. "The question is what he wants them for, and I'm also afraid it won't be for anything good, for us or our kingdom. Perhaps even all of Tremia. We have to find out what it is and deny him the Pearls."

"All right. Now we have a tangible goal," said Ingrid optimistically. "I like that."

"The problem is that we have to protect the Queen..." Gerd insisted.

"Lasgol's off the hook," Nilsa said. "He's no longer a Royal Eagle. Sorry, Lasgol..." the redhead apologized with a shrug.

"It's okay. We're Snow Panthers. I'm not worried about the Royal Eagles. To tell you the truth, I never really felt much like a Royal Eagle," Lasgol said, smiling.

"Well said," Astrid said encouragingly.

"Well, being Royal Eagles does have its advantages too..." Nilsa commented. "Look how well everyone treats us and how respectfully, even the Royal Guards."

"Not only that, but we're allowed to go anywhere in the castle at our leisure, which is good for us," Ingrid added. "We don't have to give explanations to anyone and we can give orders to the rest of the Rangers and even the Royal Soldiers."

"You love giving orders," Viggo said with a mischievous grin.

Lasgol thought for a moment.

"It's a small advantage. Now that I'm free, I can take care of whatever we need to investigate outside the capital with Camu and Ona."

"That's a great advantage," Egil said. "By the way, how's Camu?" he asked.

"Recovered. He's a lot tougher than we are and he also recovers faster from injuries. That's what Masters Esben and Annika say."

"Wonderful!" Gerd said, clapping his hands happily.

"Camu wants to 'deal with the dragon.' He's very mad at Dergha-Sho-Blaska, I've never seen him like that," Lasgol told them.

"It's only natural… after what happened…" Astrid said. "Eicewald's death must have affected him pretty badly."

"It has affected him indeed," Lasgol said, crestfallen. His friend had suffered tremendously—not because of the wounds received in the fight but because of the death of the Mage.

"And what'll happen if the little dragon suddenly reappears when he sees Lasgol nosing around where he shouldn't?" Viggo asked.

"You can't face the dragon on your own," Astrid told Lasgol. "Not without us, it's too risky."

"Astrid's right, if by ill fate you cross paths with him again, you have to run," Gerd told him. "Don't fight that monster unless we're all there to help you."

"I know I shouldn't confront Dergha-Sho-Blaska. It's obvious we're not rivals for him," Lasgol admitted with contained rage.

"We have to find some kind of weakness in that beast, something to exploit in order to defeat him," Ingrid said.

"We've already found the weakness," Egil intervened. "It's one Lasgol confirmed—the great, immortal, all-powerful dragon is vulnerable to Aodh's Bow."

"But he only scratched the dragon with the Bow, didn't you?" Viggo asked, frowning.

Lasgol nodded, bowing his head.

"That's right. And that scratch proves that the Bow can hurt him, that he's vulnerable to it even if he's not to all the rest."

"Let's see if I understand. He's vulnerable to the weapon but it barely does anything to hurt him. I don't see where we win."

"We have the possibility. The vulnerability is there. We just have to learn how to exploit it, as Ingrid has just pointed out."

Viggo seemed to understand what Egil was trying to say.

"Ahhh… now I see."

"I'm lost," said Gerd.

"Me too, a little," Nilsa said, wrinkling her nose.

"What he's trying to say is that we have to make the scratch become a deadly wound. We have to find the way," Lasgol explained.

Nilsa and Gerd nodded.

"We'll find the way," Astrid said confidently.

"You can be sure of that," Ingrid joined, her putting a hand on

31

her friend's shoulder. "We'll find a way."

Lasgol glanced at Egil unobtrusively. He had more doubts. It did not seem like it would be so easy to find the way to kill Dergha-Sho-Blaska. The battle they had lost had left a deep mark. The wounds sustained and especially Eicewald's death weighed heavily on his heart. He knew they were not ready to face the dragon again, and this knowledge did not let him rest. If Dergha-Sho-Blaska decided to appear again, many lives might be lost, including the Panthers'.

Chapter 4

The atmosphere in the Royal Dungeons was as lugubrious as could be expected of such a place. Many were the stories that ran throughout Norghana of what this place had witnessed. All of them were horrendous tales about nobles, traitors, and beggars who had entered the place to never come out again. The poor wretches who had suffered the ill fate of ending up there died screaming in the cells with rock walls, windowless, cold, and damp. Their screams did not even reach the upper levels. It was as if the dungeons had been built for that purpose, to drown out the prisoners' cries of despair.

It was a place with an atrocious reputation in the kingdom. Just the mention of it made people cringe. It was said that illustrious people had vanished in there, from nobles to princes and even kings, both Norghanian and foreign. A lot of the talk was exaggerated, but part of it was true. The soldiers and executioners who had served in the dungeons had let their tongues run on more than one occasion at a tavern or inn after too much beer, wine, or mountain firewater.

The Panthers were going down the stairs that led to the dark world of terror in the underground, below the castle. They were coming to see Gondabar, who had summoned them. From what they had understood, the Royal Dungeons were made up of two underground levels below the castle. They were as wide as the base of the main building of the Royal Fortress. A whole enemy army could be locked up in there. In fact, it gave off that impression since the cells of the first floor were brimming with prisoners.

"Wow, this place is enormous..." Gerd commented, looking ahead, all the way to the back, "and horrifying..."

"I find it quite cozy," Viggo said nonchalantly. "Look at all the guests our glorious king has accommodated in here."

"Have you noticed that the majority are Zangrian?" Ingrid said, realizing the fact.

"Yeah, and those who aren't must have had something to do with the murder attempts," Astrid guessed as she eyed a couple of prisoners who looked like informants or perhaps spies.

"I don't see Gondabar, do you?" Nilsa asked, trying to locate him. She craned her neck, staring into the dark surroundings.

"No, I don't see him here. Maybe he's further back," said Egil, who was also looking for him all around.

Lasgol was taking in this underworld of pain and suffering. The torches on the walls and oil lamps the guards had beside their posts were the only light in the place. They gave enough light so as not to stumble on the irregular cobblestones but not so much as to see the whole space clearly. The barred cells and locked dungeons were in shadow. There were many guards—surly, unfriendly looking soldiers. They were talking among themselves and harassed the prisoners at the least noise or plea or lament. Most carried punishing clubs and whips instead of war axes.

The Panthers went on toward the far end, passing by the cells. In a locked dungeon they saw the eyes and part of a man's face staring out of the peephole.

"That's General Zotomer of the Zangrian army. He was at the Wedding and the King locked him up," said Nilsa.

"Well, at least he's still alive," snorted Gerd.

"They must be keeping him hostage," Ingrid guessed. "It's common practice in these kind of situations between nations when they go to war."

"Hey you, Viggo… come closer…" General Zotomer whispered in Norghanian with a strong accent from the rival kingdom.

"Well, well, I'm popular even in the filthy Royal Dungeons. Though I really don't know why it surprises me. My reputation is beginning to be legendary and reaches even these places." Viggo straightened up and walked over to the General.

"Be careful… don't do anything…" Ingrid whispered as she looked around to see what the guards were doing.

Viggo motioned her not to worry.

They stopped and watched what Viggo was doing as they looked around trying to keep the anguish the place oozed from flooding their bodies.

"I see that the decorated and illustrious general of the Zangrian army remembers my name," Viggo whispered to Zotomer.

"I remember you. You were the Ranger assigned to protect us during the wedding."

"You honor me, General," Viggo said in his usual ironic tone so that you never knew whether he was being sincere or laughing at you.

"You are a Specialist Ranger, are you not?"

"I'm the best Specialist Ranger," Viggo noted.

The general's eyes looked out of the peephole sweeping the room.

"Good, they can't hear us," he said, referring to the guards who were chatting not far away. "I want you to take a message to Zangria."

Viggo raised both eyebrows.

"That's an odd request. Being as I'm a Ranger, I don't think I can do that. Because of the matter of treason and hanging and other related things."

"I'll cover you in gold if you do this for me."

"Hmmm, now we're speaking a language that interests me."

"I'll tell you who to deliver it to in the village of Durgosten, a few days after crossing the border. Do it and you'll have a life of luxury. You'll be able to buy yourself a duchy."

"I'd like that, indeed I would, I've always known that I was born to be noble and rich. This is nothing but proof of that."

"Do you accept?" the General asked with urgency in his voice as his eyes looked in every direction.

"He accepts nothing," Ingrid said, standing beside Viggo.

"But, my quarrelsome blondie… he's offering gold, nobility, a duchy…" Viggo whispered in her ear, trying to persuade her.

"And our King offers you the noose or decapitation by axe," Ingrid snapped.

"Yeah, that doesn't sound good at all," Viggo admitted.

"No one needs to find out," General Zotomer said.

"We refuse the offer," Ingrid said cuttingly. "Come on," she told Viggo as she grabbed his arm and dragged him away.

Viggo made a sign to the General that they would continue the conversation later.

One of the soldiers noticed something was up and came over with another guard.

"You can't speak to the prisoners, King's orders," he informed them.

"Understood. We're moving on. We're not here for him," Egil said in a pacifying tone.

"Very well. Continue, Rangers."

They went on looking for Gondabar, whom they still had not

seen; it was not a good sign. The further back they went, the more difficult the circumstances they would find their leader in.

At a table beside an armory with tools sat four huge executioners. They were as big as Gerd but flabby. Whereas Gerd was muscular and lean, the four executioners had an additional layer of fat. But they still looked strong and capable of tearing a person apart with their huge hands. They wore the dark clothes of executioners, and just the sight of them made Lasgol shiver. Those men were in charge of torturing and executing the prisoners. As far as they knew they worked for Duke Orten, who frequently came down to conduct personal interrogations. It was said he enjoyed causing pain.

"I don't want to know what they're up to," Nilsa commented, looking away from them.

"I bet they're very good at playing hide-and-seek in this gloomy underworld," said Viggo. "See how they're all dressed in black?"

"They're here to cause pain," Astrid said, watching them with narrowed eyes.

"Let's hope we never make their acquaintance," Egil said, looking at them out of the corner of his eye. "Yet, it's good that we see them and are aware of the dangers we're in. We could very well end up down here in a cell with a couple of them besides Orten. Don't you ever forget, the risks we sometimes take can have nefarious consequences."

"We'll keep that in mind," Lasgol said. "And you do the same. You're in more danger than any of us of ending up down here."

Egil smiled and shrugged.

"I'm aware. The warning is for all of us and particularly for myself."

"I see two officers ahead," said Ingrid, nodding toward them, "let's talk to them."

The Panthers approached and introduced themselves to the officers in charge of that level of the dungeons.

"We're the Royal Eagles, we're looking for Gondabar, leader of the Rangers," Ingrid said curtly.

The two officers looked her up and down.

"He's at the back," said the tallest, a veteran.

"We're keeping him separated from the others… for his safety," the other one said. He was younger and shorter.

"Safety?" Lasgol was alarmed.

"There are lots of objectionable people in here," the veteran said.

"We don't want anything to happen to him," the younger one went on. "Sometimes strange things happen here."

"Nothing can happen to him. If anything should happen to him, I'll make you responsible," Ingrid told them sternly, threatening them with her finger.

"And you'll suffer a painful death," Astrid joined in opening her cloak and showing them her knives.

The most veteran raised his hands.

"You don't need to threaten us. We're just doing our duty."

"Well, you'd better do it a lot better," Viggo said. "I know your faces, and if you don't, I'll have to come down on a nocturnal visit."

"We're all on the King's side," said the younger officer. "That won't be necessary."

"We're on the side of our leader, whom the King has sent down here unjustly," Egil clarified. "It's not the same thing, and you'd do well to remember that. It's not a good idea to get on the bad side of the Royal Eagles. In fact, it's very bad for one's health."

"Listen carefully to what you're being told," Gerd threatened as he leaned toward the officers with all his brutal presence.

The two men stepped back.

"Nothing will happen to him. We promise," the veteran one said.

"Make sure he has an exquisite stay," Ingrid told them.

"We'll make sure he lacks nothing," the young one said, nodding at Ingrid.

"Gondabar had better remember his stay here as a comfortable vacation," Viggo said.

Both officers nodded.

"Come on, let's continue," Ingrid said, and they moved on through that lugubrious place of suffering.

The dungeons were brimming with prisoners, and in several nooks they saw wretches chained to the walls without cells or bars, like animals, with guards watching at a distance.

"I don't understand how they're allowed to do that," Nilsa said, shaking her head. "That's inhumane."

"It is. They've filled the cells and now, since there's no more space, they chain them to the walls," Astrid said, shaking her head as well.

At last they saw the cell where they were holding Gondabar.

Raner was at the door, so it had to be that one.

"Thank goodness he hasn't been sent to the lower level," said Nilsa.

"Why's that?" Lasgol asked.

"From what I've heard tell by the Royal Guards, whoever is sent to the second level underground never sees the light of day again," said Nilsa.

"I've also heard something of the sort," said Egil. "The King's enemies are locked up down there. I'm sure there are Western Nobles imprisoned in there."

"I can slip down and find out," Astrid offered. "It's very dark, I wouldn't have much trouble blending in with the gloom."

"It's risky..." Egil thought for a moment. "We'll have time for that later. It has to be carefully planned."

"Okay, as you wish," Astrid replied.

They reached the cell. It was only four walls of rock and a door with a lookout. The door was open and Raner was in front of it. He greeted them.

"Welcome," he said, his face showing disgust and sorrow.

"Sir," Ingrid said with a nod.

"Is he in there?" Nilsa asked as if afraid he would say yes, although she knew that was the answer. She simply could not believe it.

"That's right, unfortunately. I still have trouble accepting it," Raner admitted.

"It's a disgrace," Egil said, looking carefully at the place as if he were memorizing it to later draw a detailed plan.

"Go on in, they're expecting you," Raner said with a wave of his hand.

"*They're* expecting us?" Lasgol asked in surprise. "He's not alone?"

Raner shook his head.

"You're expected for an important meeting."

Lasgol looked at Egil who looked back, interested. Astrid and Viggo frowned.

"Let's not keep them waiting," Ingrid said, ready to enter the cell. Nilsa followed swiftly and after them Gerd, then the rest entered the cell.

It was bigger than it looked from the outside. They had shown the decency of assigning Gondabar to a cell with room enough for six people. It was badly lit though. There was a bunk bed on one side and a desk on the other where a small oil lamp gave off the little light available. The furniture was of good quality, so they must have brought them especially for the leader of the Rangers who was sitting at the desk, working as usual. He had several messages on the desk and was writing another one. He looked the same, no better or worse than when they had seen him at the Throne Hall. If they did not know they were at the Royal Dungeons, they might have said the leader of the Rangers was keeping up with his usual work at the Tower of the Rangers.

A little further back, standing, were two figures. The shadows hid them so the Panthers could not see their faces, although by studying their clothes they could tell they were a woman and a man. This surprised everyone because they had expected Gondabar to be alone. The two figures stepped over to the desk when the Panthers walked in. When the light shone on them the Panthers recognized the occupants: Mother Specialist Sigrid and Dolbarar, leader of the Camp. They both looked very grave and troubled. They said nothing, looking at the new arrivals, then smiled, welcoming and greeted them with brief nods which the Panthers returned.

"Sir, you called us?" Ingrid asked.

Gondabar looked up from his writing and at the Panthers and Raner, all in front of his desk, filling the cell.

He smiled with evident joy at seeing them.

"Indeed, I need to speak with you about important matters. Please close the door and have someone keep watch so we're not heard from outside."

"I'll keep watch," Gerd volunteered, and he left the cell, closing the door. After making sure there was no one near enough to hear anything, he put his ear to the lookout so he could hear what was said inside.

"It's horrible that they have you in here, sir. It breaks my heart to see what they're doing to you," Nilsa said with moist eyes.

"Take it easy, Nilsa, this isn't the worse that might have happened," Gondabar said in a kind tone.

"That's true. The meeting went very wrong…" Raner commented. "Worse than we had anticipated," he said, looking at Sigrid and Dolbarar, who nodded. "We knew they might not believe us and that would lead them to dismiss us. We thought they were likely to ridicule us even. Getting angry and showing their malcontent and fury was also within the predictable outcomes—we were counting on that too. Yet, there were dangerous… instances… we never thought they'd go this far."

"You don't deserve what happened and least of all to be here. It's unforgivable," Ingrid said, deeply offended at seeing her leader there.

"We all feel it's a terrible punishment, disproportionate and inhuman," Astrid joined in.

"At least I've kept my post. I'm still the leader of the Rangers. That's a small victory I'm proud of."

"For a moment I thought he was going to take that away too," Raner said with a snort. "Thank goodness he didn't," he added, relieved.

"That's comforting for all of us," Dolbarar intervened with a snort and a nod. He looked good, much better than Gondabar. "We need the leadership, wisdom, and brightness of our leader to face the coming dangers, which we foresee will be terrible."

"I also thought the same. I'm glad that wasn't the case. I feel I can still be of service to the Rangers and my Kingdom," Gondabar admitted.

"He didn't dare take away your command because of the complicated situation the Kingdom finds itself in, not for any other reason," said Sigrid, shaking her head with her arms folded over her chest. Judging by her tone, she was furious.

"As Raner said correctly, the situation was tense and difficult, but we're still here, and that's what matters. We can keep working for the Rangers and the Kingdom, that's fundamental and the only truly important thing," Gondabar said, trying to bring some optimism to the meeting.

"It is, but seeing the leader of the Rangers here, the treatment he's receiving, isn't honorable. It's unacceptable, and it makes our blood boil," Lasgol said, clenching his jaw. He felt awful seeing the cell they had Gondabar in, and seeing him in it overwhelmed him with rage. He was having trouble keeping calm. Seeing Dolbarar and Sigrid there helped though. Between all of them they would manage to get out of this big mess.

"I appreciate your words. I know it hurts you to see me here like this, but you mustn't let this hinder your tasks, clouding your minds with thoughts born of rage and frustration."

"We'll try…" Lasgol conceded. He did not want to add to Gondabar's worries; the man already had many serious concerns to deal with.

"Let's look on the bright side of this unpleasant incident," Gondabar said. "His Majesty didn't take my work away, due to the complicated situation the Kingdom finds itself in, like the Mother Specialist has correctly said, and we must take advantage of this. That's why I called you all here, so we can see how to solve the problems that beset us."

"Yes, sir. Whatever we can do, we're on your side, absolutely. You can count on us and our loyalty," Ingrid said.

"And I'm grateful for it. Keep in mind, after seeing the way they took our report, of all the possible punishments, this one isn't that bad. I've been in dungeons before, when I was younger. Not these, but similar ones. I survived then and I'll survive now. You shouldn't worry about me but about the Kingdom."

"On this occasion, perhaps you should consider your own life before the Kingdom," Egil said compassionately. "Spending time in places like this takes its toll on the body and soul."

"Never that," Gondabar shook his head and hand. "The Kingdom must always come first, no matter how delicate or risky our personal situation might be. The same with the Corps of the Rangers, we lead by example. Our comrades' eyes are now on us and on how we solve this situation. The integrity and determination we show will mark the path to follow."

"We understand and accept that. We'll act with integrity and honor," Ingrid promised.

Viggo's face as he stood silent behind Ingrid was not so devoted.

"I must speak to you regarding several important issues," Gondabar announced.

Sigrid and Dolbarar leaned forward.

"We're listening, what do you wish us to do?" Sigrid asked him.

"We're at your command," Ingrid said, and they all listened carefully.

"First and most important is that we keep working as if I were at my study in the Tower of the Rangers. Nothing must change. It's already been established that my personal assistants act as messengers with the Tower. They'll be coming and going from the dungeons carrying messages back and forth."

"I've spoken to the dungeons' officers and there won't be any problem," Raner said.

Wonderful. If for any reason they're forbidden to come and see me, which might happen, I'll inform Raner and we'll have to come up with an alternative plan."

"I'll take care of it," Raner confirmed.

"Good, now I want to discuss two things…" Gondabar had started to say when the door of the cell opened and Gerd came in.

"Ellingsen's coming, with soldiers," he said urgently.

Gondabar put his finger to his lips.

The Panthers stiffened. Raner made a sign to Gerd to let him receive them and they exchanged positions.

Lasgol frowned. This might mean bad news.

Chapter 5

The door opened and Ellingsen walked into the cell, followed by two large Royal Guards. Half a dozen more waited outside. The Panthers had to step back to let them in, the cell could not fit any more. Ellingsen realized this and made a sign to the two guards to wait outside. Then he turned to Gondabar.

"Leaders of the Rangers, Royal Eagles," he said with a brief nod.

"Commander," Gondabar greeted him. The others nodded in turn.

"Is there a problem?" Raner asked suspiciously.

"Not as such. I was informed of this meeting and sent down," Ellingsen explained.

"The King doesn't mean to stop the leaders of the Rangers from meeting to plan their work and missions, does he?" Gondabar asked, but it sounded like a statement instead of a question.

"He doesn't oppose the leaders meeting, no," Ellingsen confirmed. "I'm here for another reason."

"What reason has made you come to such an inhospitable place?" Raner asked him.

"I come to inform you that the King doesn't want his Royal Eagles visiting the leader of the Rangers in the Royal Dungeons," he said and looked at Gondabar, then at the Panthers.

Lasgol jerked his head back in surprise. Nilsa was blinking hard. Ingrid folded her arms over her chest. Gerd and Viggo muttered words of surprise and discontent under their breaths.

Sigrid and Dolbarar looked at each other and commented something in whispers that no one else heard.

"Why? He's their leader, they have to be able to talk to him," Raner said, voicing what they were all thinking.

Lasgol looked at Astrid, who looked back at him with a gesture that meant she did not like it. Egil was watching Ellingsen with narrowed eyes, calculating the reasons behind that order.

"The King doesn't want his Royal Eagles to neglect their duty as protectors of Queen Heulyn."

"You can assure his Majesty that they don't and won't, not while

I'm First Ranger," Raner told him dryly. He did not seem to like the King's intromission one little bit.

"And yet, here they are…" Ellingsen commented with a wave of his hand at the Panthers.

"The Queen is safe in her chambers, resting," Nilsa told him. "Valeria and Aidan are with her."

"That may be, but her protectors are here, in the Dungeons."

"I called this meeting. They are here because I called them," Gondabar said, defending them.

"Whichever way it is doesn't change things. I've been ordered to inform you that the Royal Eagles are forbidden to come down to the Dungeons."

"But that is entirely unnecessary," Ingrid protested.

"We always do our duty," Gerd protested.

"We are sharing important information with our leader. That can't be forbidden," Astrid added.

"I'm merely transmitting the King's orders," Ellingsen said, but what he meant was that they should shut up and obey, since they were the King's orders and could not be ignored.

"I don't see the need to stop us from seeing our leader," Lasgol said angrily.

"If you don't obey the order, you'll be arrested," Ellingsen warned them. "I've brought the guard with me. The King won't take it kindly."

"That won't be necessary," Gondabar said, raising one hand in a conciliatory gesture. "The Rangers always obey their King's orders. They won't visit me again. You can tell his Majesty."

"Very well," Ellingsen nodded but did not move.

"Anything else…?" Raner asked him, seeing he was not leaving.

"Yes, there is a second order I must transmit to you."

They all looked at the Commander, thinking it would be something bad.

"Go ahead, what's this new order?" Gondabar motioned him to speak.

"This affects Raner and the Royal Eagles," Ellingsen started. "His Majesty wants the First Ranger to take over the training of the Eagles as Royal Rangers to thus improve the degree of protection they might offer the Queen and other members of the Royal Family."

The Panthers stared at him blankly. If their surprise had been great with the first order, with the second one they were nonplussed.

"The King wants us to train as Royal Rangers?" Ingrid asked blankly, not quite understanding and wanting clarification.

"That's correct. Raner will be in charge," Ellingsen told them.

"We're already Specialist Rangers, some of us with several specialties. We don't need any more training," Astrid said, making a face.

"I definitely don't need it. I'm ten times better than a Royal Ranger," Viggo said with his usual bluntness and lack of any sign of humility.

"You can be whatever you want. That's irrelevant. The King's order is clear and isn't to be contested," Ellingsen warned.

"We're already Royal Eagles…" Nilsa insisted.

"Yes, and his Majesty wants you to be trained as Royal Rangers whose function is to protect the King and the Royal Family," Ellingsen clarified.

"It's really a very good idea," Egil said all of a sudden, leaving them all frozen. They looked at him, but by his tone and look he was serious and not joking. "If we want to be efficient protecting the Queen, we must learn the best way to do so. We have never been trained in protection or serving as bodyguards; it'll be a good addition to our skills."

"If you say so…" Viggo did not agree and was shaking his head with his arms folded over his chest.

Astrid did not look convinced either. Gerd and Nilsa seemed more surprised than anything else. Lasgol was trying to understand why Egil thought this was a good thing.

"I'll make sure they're trained at once so they can serve their King and Queen," Raner assured the Commander.

"Very well," Ellingsen began to turn to leave.

"Does this mean we'll become Royal Rangers?" Nilsa asked before the Commander was out the door.

"That's up in the air and depends on Raner," Ellingsen said with a gesture at the First Ranger.

"If I train them to become Royal Rangers, they'll receive the merit and position," Raner said, looking at Gondabar for his acceptance. The leader of the Rangers nodded slowly in agreement.

"It's all clear then. I take my leave," Ellingsen gazed at all the Panthers. "Make this last visit with your leader here brief," he told

45

them as a warning.

"It will be," Gondabar promised.

Ellingsen saluted with a brief nod and left the cell. A moment later Gerd opened the door and put his head out to watch them leave.

"They're gone. We're alone," he told the rest.

"So, what's all this about?" Lasgol said, feeling surprised and puzzled.

"This is going to be a pain," Viggo protested.

"It doesn't need to be," Ingrid said. "Look on the bright side, as Egil has done already. We'll learn new functions and obtain a new rank. I see it as a positive thing. It'll help us in the future."

"Aren't we a little short and lacking muscle to be Royal Rangers?" Nilsa asked.

"Not me," Gerd said, grinning at her and flexing his biceps.

"Well, you'd fit in as Royal Ranger, but the rest of us… not at all."

"As a rule we choose people Gerd's size, that's true," Raner said. "But size and strength aren't always necessary. The Royal Rangers are chosen because they're good, the best, able to kill a man with their hands without ruffling their hair. You are all skilled, so you won't have any trouble fitting in."

"But we won't have to be Royal Rangers, will we? Protecting the King and Queen all day must be so boring," Gerd said mournfully.

"I know them well, and the truth is that their job is very boring, all day on watch duty around the castle," Nilsa joined him.

Gondabar smiled.

"No, you won't have to be. We need you for other missions that only you can carry out. Royal Rangers are trained when necessary, and we can replace them as needed. It's more complicated to replace you. You're more special."

"Thanks. We are. Me in particular," Viggo said confidently.

"The King is making things complicated for us," Sigrid said with a look of disgust on her face.

"Serving the throne has never been an easy task," Gondabar told her in a calm   tone. "This monarch and his new wife will mean some difficulty or another, which we'll have to deal with as we've always done, with diligence and without creating any conflicts."

"They're the ones creating the conflict, not us, and be assured

46

we'll have a lot more in the near future," Sigrid said.

"But, they haven't stopped us from maintaining our structure of command and rank, and we can still meet and communicate," Gondabar told them, once again looking for something positive in the chaotic situation they found themselves in.

"I'd never had thought that the leaders of the Rangers would have to meet in dungeons.... We're living in strange times," Raner shrugged and then shook his head.

"This isn't the first time the Rangers have lived through complicated situations," said Sigrid.

"It's also not the first time a king of Norghana is at odds with them, or even hangs or decapitates them. It's happened in the past; it might happen again."

Dolbarar looked at Sigrid and put his hand on her shoulder.

"I hope none of us have to witness it, my dear friend," he said. "Although I do admit we're living in strange, turbulent times."

"I'm glad you're here today. Your presence gives me strength," Gondabar told them.

"You know you can always count on our support," Sigrid said firmly.

Gondabar nodded and smiled gratefully.

"Now, we must talk about matters of importance. First, the matter of the Immortal Dragon. I want and demand that, although the King has dismissed it as nonsense, we continue our efforts to find and destroy it. I'm still convinced it's a real danger, more so now that he's appeared and killed Eicewald. We must protect the Kingdom and its people."

Sigrid looked at the Panthers with narrowed eyes.

"Those of us who haven't seen that dragon must blindly believe your word..."

"The dragon exists. We've all seen it," Ingrid assured her.

"I've fought against it," Lasgol replied. "I can swear it exists. He's real, very powerful, almost invincible, possibly immortal, and he killed Eicewald. He wants something, something that'll bring about Norghana's doom."

Sigrid nodded and then heaved a sigh.

"I needed to hear it from you. More so now with everything that's happened with the King. If you say so, I believe you. You have my support."

"We promise," Ingrid said.

"I swear he exists," added Lasgol.

"In that case, he exists," Dolbarar sentenced. "I believe you, Panthers, no matter what, no matter how unlikely it might sound. I believe you because I know you and I trust you and your good judgment and criterion."

"The Camp Leader honors us," said Egil, bowing slightly.

"We won't be able to investigate," Raner said, indicating himself and the Panthers, "with the exception of Lasgol. The King's made sure of that."

"I won't be either. I'll be under constant watch, and if the King finds out that I'm still searching for the Dragon, this time he wouldn't hesitate to cut my head off," Gondabar said. "But you can keep searching," he said, indicating Sigrid and Dolbarar. "Sigrid from the Shelter and Dolbarar from the Camp. I want both of you to continue the search."

"We'll have to do it discretely," said Dolbarar. "It'll have to be a task carried out secretly, or rumors of it might reach the capital."

"Let it be so, Dolbarar. I want you to carry the weight of the search from the Shelter. Choose the Rangers you involve in the search carefully," Gondabar told him.

"So it will be," Dolbarar nodded, looking at Lasgol and winking at him.

"What do you want me to do?" Sigrid asked.

"I want you to deal with the White Pearls. They'll be your responsibility. They trouble me."

"I will. We're already watching and studying the White Pearl at the Shelter."

"I was going to tell the King about the danger they pose…" Gondabar started to say and then sighed deeply, "but I couldn't. After what we witnessed, trying to explain what they are would be a mistake. I'd lose my head, and that wouldn't help Norghana."

"No, it wouldn't," Sigrid said. "We need you alive. Don't take any more risks."

"How many are in the know about the White Pearls and what they are?" Gondabar asked.

"All of us here in this room, my brother Enduald and Galdason who are studying it, and Loke who's watching it," Sigrid said.

"The Master Rangers?" Gondabar asked Dolbarar.

"They don't know. You asked for discretion until we had a good understanding of the problem, and I haven't told them anything," Dolbarar said.

"It's the same with the Elder Specialists. I haven't told them what's going on, although they suspect it's something serious, hence our interest in the Pearl. So far they haven't asked me anything and I haven't explained."

"Very well. They are discrete and wise. As they should be," Gondabar congratulated them. "For now I want the matter of the Pearls to be handled very carefully and in secret. The others wouldn't understand. They're not prepared to understand what a Portal is or what it can do. It's too dangerous. If they knew, they might even want to use it."

"That's not possible right now. Only Camu can use it with his power."

"Yes, but who can tell whether Maldreck or another of his Ice Magi might want to use it for their own benefit? After all, it's an Object of Power, grand and magical. The Ice Magi will want to take possession of it, and they'll be in their right. They can take over any magical object in the realm."

"That could be dangerous," said Raner.

"That's why no one else must know of their existence, at least until we can control the Pearls," Gondabar said.

"Control them?" Sigrid asked, frowning.

"Yes, that's the mission I want you to take on. The Pearls must be controlled and watched."

"How? Why?" Sigrid asked with a look of concentration, trying to understand what Gondabar wanted.

"Create a group of Specialists to watch over the Pearl. The reason is simple. It's a gate that will allow the Dragon to reach the Shelter, and therefore Norghana, without being detected. Him, and whoever travels with him. He might be accompanied by sectarians and lieutenants. It's a huge risk we have to keep in mind."

"I understand. I'll take care of it," said Sigrid.

"As for everything else, keep training Rangers and Specialists as usual. We're going to need them."

"Because of the war with Zangria which appears inevitable?" Dolbarar asked in a troubled tone.

Gondabar nodded.

"It's something I hope can be averted. Nevertheless, we'd better be prepared in case it isn't."

"We'll be ready," Sigrid told hm.

"When do you leave?"

"Tomorrow. The others have already left and are taking care of their responsibilities," Sigrid said. "Dolbarar and I stayed because we wanted to see what happened at the King's audience…"

"Will Edwina also leave with you?" Gondabar asked, interested.

"I'm afraid not…" Dolbarar said with a look of annoyance.

"What's wrong?" Gondabar asked him.

"King Thoran has asked her to stay here in the capital. After seeing that she was able to heal Orten, he doesn't want her to leave."

"But Edwina is a Healer of the Order of Tirsar. King Thoran has no power over her, not even in Norghana."

Sigrid nodded.

"He knows. He used the excuse that he needs her to treat you since your health is frail."

"Edwina has already treated me. I'm as well as I can be. That's an empty excuse."

"Even so, the King has insisted that she stays to look after you. Edwina did not dare refuse."

"More so after hearing that you're in the Dungeons," Dolbarar added.

"Poor Edwina. She must be free to go wherever she wants," Gondabar was shaking his head mournfully.

"For now, this is the situation," Sigrid told him.

"We'll find a solution for Edwina," Dolbarar promised. "Don't worry. She'll recover her freedom to travel."

"We'll work on all this. We have much to do and I'm afraid very little time to do it," Gondabar told them.

"Do you know something we don't?" Sigrid asked him.

"I know the bones in my feet hurt. That means trouble is coming," Gondabar said.

"A most reliable and proven method," Dolbarar chuckled.

"It's never failed me," Gondabar joined him with another chuckle. "Now leave and take care of business."

The Panthers left the cell while Gondabar finished discussing things with Dolbarar and Sigrid. Raner stayed guarding the door of the dungeon.

As they were heading out of that grim place full of hurting souls, Lasgol pulled Egil aside.

"Why did you say before that it could be a good thing to become Royal Rangers?"

Egil glanced at his friend and smiled.

"Being a Royal Ranger gives us access not only to the Queen, but also the King. We can access the Throne Hall and Thoran's and Orten's private chambers," said Egil with a gleam of intelligence in his eyes.

"That's true," Nilsa confirmed. She had been listening carefully. "It gives us access to any room the King goes to, since we must protect him and make sure they're all safe. Only the Royal Rangers and part of the Royal Guard have access to the whole castle."

"That's going to be convenient," Vigo commented. He had also been listening and grinned at Egil.

Lasgol had the feeling the new situation they were in now was going to be difficult to manage and dangerous. He left the dungeons with a bitter aftertaste.

Chapter 6

Lasgol went over to the Royal Stables. His heart was divided. On the one hand he was feeling sad, and on the other he was feeling happy. A stable boy with platinum-blond hair and skin as white as milk came to greet him as soon as he saw Lasgol approach.

"Needing a horse, sir?" he asked, willing to help.

"No, thanks, not today."

"Can I do anything else for you?" the boy offered, seeing that Lasgol was entering the stables anyway.

"Yes, I have a horse being cared for here, a pony…"

"I'll come with you."

"Thank you," Lasgol smiled at the boy, grateful for his good cheer.

"Of course, sir. Follow me, please."

The boy led him to a small enclosure behind the great sheds. There were several horses and ponies resting there. They all looked healthy; they were well fed, rested, and groomed, their coats shining from a recent brushing. They had hay and fresh grass and were all quiet and content.

With pain in his heart, Lasgol had come here to say goodbye to his faithful friend and partner. He entered the enclosure and very slowly, to not frighten the other animals, went over to Trotter.

How do you feel, my dear friend? he transmitted to him using his *Animal Communication* skill.

The Norghanian pony saw him and immediately neighed with joy and came up to Lasgol, who welcomed him, stroking his forehead and muzzle.

Have you missed me during the time you've spent here recovering? Or has the good life they've given you made you forget all about me?

Trotter licked Lasgol's face and hair repeatedly and neighed again.

Okay, okay, I see you've missed me and haven't forgotten me. I've missed you tons, he transmitted, throwing his arms around the pony's neck, hugging him.

You look great, Lasgol walked around Trotter, inspecting him. The other horses moved away to give them space.

Trotter snorted and shook his head up and down.

I know you want to go back out on adventures. But how's that leg? Lasgol transmitted, stroking the pony's right front leg where he had suffered that ugly fracture.

Trotter raised his foot and brought it down again to show he was all right, but he did not lean hard on it.

Does it hurt? Lasgol was worried and stroked Trotter's mane.

The pony shook his head sideways as if he were saying "no."

Where am I going to find another faithful mount that'll understand me the way you do? Lasgol's eyes moistened.

Trotter nibbled at his cloak. He wanted to go on more adventures.

You can't come with me anymore, Trotter. I'm so sorry, but you have that nasty fracture in your leg, Lasgol transmitted, stroking it. *If I take you on an adventure, there's the risk of it breaking for good and never healing.*

Trotter half reared and neighed, wanting to show Lasgol that he could still go with him and be his faithful mount.

I'm deeply sorry, my friend. It can't be. I can't take the risk. It would kill you. Your days of adventure are over.

Trotter bowed his head and made a noise as if he were sobbing. Tears ran down Lasgol's cheeks. All he could do was stroke him for comfort. For a long while the two friends remained together in silence, Lasgol's head leaning on Trotter's back and the pony's head on Lasgol's shoulders as he nibbled affectionately at his clothes.

I have to leave now, Lasgol transmitted at last. He did not really have to go anywhere urgently, but this parting was digging a hole in his chest, and he did not want to make Trotter any sadder by letting him see how it pained Lasgol to part from him. *You'll be taken good care of. You're going to be moved to the big corrals south of the city where you'll have a glorious retirement. I've made sure of that.*

The good pony nodded, shaking his head up and down. He had accepted his fate.

Ona and Camu send their love.

Trotter snorted, showing his teeth.

I know that Camu has been a pain for you, but deep down I know you love him. And Ona has always been good to you, even if panthers and ponies don't get along well.

Trotter licked Lasgol's hand and he knew that was for Camu and Ona.

They've told me they'll go and visit you. I hope they go in camouflage, or else they'll wreak havoc when the other horses and ponies see them.

Trotter neighed and shook his head up and down.

Thank you for everything, my faithful friend, Lasgol hugged him once again and then he left, unable to hold his tears back.

At midmorning, the door to the Panthers' room slammed open and Nilsa came in like a tornado. She went to Lasgol's bed where he was practicing magic, as he did whenever he had free time. Viggo was practicing with his throwing dagger at the far end of the room. Gerd was fast asleep in his bed. The rest of the Panthers were out seeing what the Queen wanted for her protection.

"I know where Eicewald's burial is going to be!"

Lasgol lost his concentration and opened his eyes.

"You do?"

"I told you I'd find out. The Ice Magi aren't at all discrete about some things. Worldly things I mean. When it comes to their magic they are indeed very private and good at keeping secrets."

"You know a lot about the Ice Magi," Viggo said. "I wonder why?" He put his head to one side and eyed her with interest.

"Why would I be? Because I'm a Mage Hunter, and everything that has to do with magic interests me. The nearest magi I can easily study are the Ice Magi; that's why they interest me."

"Well you'd better make sure the Magi of the Tower don't find out your interest in them…" Viggo made a sign that it would not bode well for her.

"I only study them. I'm not doing anything wrong."

"Well, you study them in order to kill them better. I think they would see that as pretty wrong," Viggo smiled ironically.

"Hmmmm…. That's true… if you look at it that way…"

"And the funeral?" Lasgol asked.

"Oh yes. It's tomorrow morning."

"At the Temple of the Ice Gods?" Gerd asked, just waking up from his nap.

"Look here! The great snorer of the north has finally woken up," Viggo said with his hands in the air.

"I don't snore that loud," Gerd waved his arm at Viggo as if saying he exaggerated, and his friend replied with another of disbelief.

"Unheard of!" Viggo stated, turning his back on Gerd as if he were addressing the Ice Gods.

To be honest, the snores the giant gave were so loud they made the furniture shake. Lasgol used them as a concentration exercise. Being able to use his magic in the midst of Gerd's thunderous breathing was quite the feat. Lasgol used everything he had at hand to improve his skills and concentration, and Gerd's snores were especially useful.

Nilsa shook her head.

"They're not going to the Temple. The Ice Magi aren't very religious. It's funny, I figured they would be, but it turns out they're not. It seems they only believe in their magic, in their power. They're not interested in religion," Nilsa made a face that said she did not understand why.

"Then, where's it going to be?" Lasgol asked, intrigued.

"At the Albus Forest, north of the city. It's not far, half a league on horseback," Nilsa replied.

"Why does that name ring a bell?" Viggo wondered out loud, frowning as he struggled to remember.

"It's a bewitched forest. No one sets foot there. People vanish inside it, never to be seen again," said Gerd, opening his eyes wide. "Bad place to go to, really bad."

"It can't be that bad..." Viggo waved his hand in disbelief.

"I'm telling you, it really is a haunted forest. All the trees are entirely white, from their roots to the leaves. There's no vegetation, only a white mist they say is created by the sorcerers who live in it and make whoever goes into their domain disappear."

"Hah! Maybe they're cannibals and eat trespassers."

"Viggo, there are no cannibals in Norghana! And it's not bewitched either, Gerd!" Nilsa yelled at them.

"Then why's it called the Albus Forest?" Lasgol wanted to know. It rang a bell, but he could not figure out why.

"Because it's true that everything in it is white, but it's because of the variety of trees that grow there. They're snow-white oaks, a unique species originating in Norghana. When Egil comes he can tell you all about it, since he's the expert on these things."

"It's always been said that the place was haunted," Gerd insisted. "It's good to heed what stories say... they save lives..."

"That's farmers' superstition," Nilsa retorted. "It's not a bewitched forest, otherwise the Ice Magi wouldn't go there."

"Perhaps they can fight the spells, being magi…" Gerd replied adamantly.

"Bewitched or not, I'm going to the funeral. I owe it to Eicewald," Lasgol said.

Right then Ingrid and Astrid came into the room.

"We're not going to be able to come," said Ingrid.

"Raner has set up Royal Ranger training every day for a season. We're starting tomorrow," said Astrid.

"It seems he doesn't want to make Thoran angry," Viggo said with a smile full of malice as he threw the dagger, which embedded itself in the windowpane.

"Does that surprise you? The oven's too hot to add more wood," Ingrid said.

"Every day for a whole season? Isn't that too much?" Gerd asked.

Ingrid shook her head.

"Apparently not. According to what the First Ranger has told us, the training usually lasts three full seasons. In our case he's going to compress it into one single season."

"That's because he knows we're a thousand times better prepared than the specialists they usually choose for Royal Ranger posts," Viggo said, brushing imaginary dust off his shoulders.

"They spend the whole day on watch duty! What do we need more training for? What are they going to teach us, how to watch? I don't understand it," Gerd said, annoyed.

"They do more than that," Astrid said. "They have to protect the King wherever he goes."

"Even so, it seems like too much training to me," Gerd said.

"We're going to have a great time. Instead of killing someone, they're going to teach us how to stop someone from being killed," Viggo said with a grimace of horror.

"It'll be good for you. You only think about finishing off people instead of saving them," Ingrid told him.

"I'm an Assassin, what else do you want me to think about?" Viggo replied, making an innocent face.

"You must admit he's right," Astrid told Ingrid. "We've been trained to kill, not protect."

"Then this new training will be very good for both of you," Ingrid said smugly. "I, for one, am happy to receive the training."

Viggo stopped throwing his knife and looked at her with narrowed eyes.

"That's because you want to be a Royal Ranger."

Nilsa turned to Ingrid.

"Do you want to become a Royal Ranger?" she asked her, sounding surprised.

Lasgol was also surprised and waited for Ingrid's reply.

"Yes and no…"

"That says it all," Viggo said, joking.

"Let her explain herself," Nilsa snapped, wanting to know what her friend thought.

"Becoming a Royal Ranger is a step on the path I'm after to reach my goal."

"Which is to be the first woman to become First Ranger," Viggo added, finishing Ingrid's sentence.

"That's right," she confirmed.

"Then everything makes sense," Nilsa said, moving over to Ingrid and laying her hand on her friend's shoulder. "You show them, girl."

"I will," Ingrid said firmly. "I'll be Royal Ranger and later on First Ranger."

"The only setback in your plan—which, by the way, I share and fully support," said Viggo, smiling broadly, "—is that Raner has to die. I like him better now. I don't wish him an early death."

"He could leave the post for some other reason," Nilsa intervened.

"He's not the kind to shirk his responsibility. And he's had the post for a short time, so he won't want to leave so soon," Astrid said.

"A thousand things might happen. The thing is that I'll be ready for when the day comes and they look for a new First Ranger," Ingrid said.

"Don't worry. I'll go with Camu and Ona. We'll be all right. Besides, it's a funeral, nothing's going to happen."

"Even so, be careful," Astrid told him, looking worried.

"I will be, don't worry."

"Say goodbye to good old Eicewald for us," Nilsa said, looking sad.

"Yes, please do," Gerd added.

Lasgol nodded. "I will."

Chapter 7

Lasgol reached the first trees of the forest and stopped. He touched the trunk of one of the rare snow-white oaks with his gloved hand. The bark, the roots, the branches, the leaves—everything seemed to indicate it was a regular oak tree and in good health—everything but for a small detail. The oak was white in its entirety, from its roots to the leaves. He looked at it with great interest, wondering how such a thing was possible. He raised his gaze and saw that the rest of the trees in that place had the same characteristics as the oak that had caught his eye.

He remembered studying Albus Forest in one of the tomes of Nature at the Shelter, albeit in passing. He sifted through his memory, searching for what the tome said about this strange variety of oak. It was a unique species and indigenous of Norghana. For some reason the scholars could not fathom, this variety of oak was pure white and gave the impression of being covered in snow that had frozen on the tree.

He took off his right glove and felt the roots and then the trunk and branches with his hand. He studied it, expecting it to be all white or at least slightly frozen. But that was not the case. His hand felt the same as usual. He thought of taking his knife out and cutting a twig off to see what it was like inside, but he dismissed the idea. Many scholars had studied these trees and had concluded they were oaks of a unique variety but natural. It made no sense to stop to investigate, although a yearning to understand what had caused them to be pure white impelled him to.

Much pretty trees, Camu messaged him.

Lasgol turned, but he could not see him since he was camouflaged with Ona. He knew they were right behind him, however.

They are. And it's 'very' pretty. Learn to speak properly once and for all.

I speak much well.

Yes, exactly, Lasgol snorted, looking up at the overcast sky. It was a gray day and the sky was cloudy. It felt like it was going to rain at any moment. They were having a wonderful spring, so this day seemed intent on reminding him they were in Norghana and not to get used to the good weather. Just thinking about it, he knew the Ice Gods would punish him with a spring storm, the kind that unloaded a whole sea of rain on top of you.

Ona growled in warning.

Already come.

Lasgol turned and saw the retinue coming along the path heading for the forest. He quickly leaped away and went further into the Albus Forest. He heard Camu's and Ona's footsteps behind him. Lasgol had left the new mount he had been given tethered in a ravine a little to the south. He had not tried to communicate with the horse since it was most likely a temporary one. Once he returned it, he would be given another one the next time. He was sad to think he would not be able to ride Trotter again. Life in Norghana was hard, and even the bravest and purest of heart suffered and fell.

They no can see us? Camu messaged him, along with a feeling of doubt.

No, and it's better that they can't. The Ice Magi are very reserved and don't like others interfering in their business.

But be funeral of Eicewald, Camu messaged, along with a feeling of annoyance.

Lasgol stopped and bent over.

I know, but they don't want anyone to attend. They told Nilsa it was going to be an Ice Mage funeral here in this forest. Private and discrete. Apparently the dead Ice Magi rest in this forest.

Eicewald great mage. Good. Deserve funeral with honors.

Ona moaned once. She agreed.

King Thoran has ordered a discrete burial. That's why it's going to be here and in private.

King Thoran no like.

You're not the only one, believe me.

Eicewald rest here?

Lasgol snorted.

That's a good question… I don't know. I hope so. At least he'll be in the company of the other Ice Magi who rest here.

You believe souls of magi dead still here?

Ona moaned.

That's a complicated question to answer. There are people who believe the souls of the dead persist on the earth, at least for some time. Then they travel to

60

the realm of the Ice Gods to rest forever.

I not believe that.

You don't? Then what do you believe?

I Drakonian. Not like human.

Yes, we know that. What do you mean by that?

I different soul. Go to different place.

Oh, I see. Well, that might be the case. It depends who you ask and what their religion is. Since we don't know what the Drakonian religion consists of for now, you can believe what you like.

Okay. I immortal soul.

Lasgol snorted again.

There's no need to exaggerate…

I believe that soul immortal. I Drakonian, Camu proclaimed, and he messaged it along with a feeling that he considered the matter closed.

Lasgol sighed and said nothing. Camu was not going to change his mind, not for now anyway. That was how stubborn he was.

They waited in hiding for the Ice Magi to reach the forest. Lasgol used his *Hawk's Eye* skill and was able to see the retinue formed by six Ice Magi, all riding on white mares. Behind them came a narrow cart with the coffin, drawn by a Percheron horse whose reins were handled by the young apprentice.

At the head of the retinue came Maldreck, his chin high and back straight with his Ice Mage staff fastened to the back of his riding saddle. He carried it like a weapon, in case of danger he could reach for it.

Behind Maldreck rode two Ice Magi in their mid-forties. Since they all wore their white hair long and the same Ice Magi clothes, it was hard to tell them apart. Still, Lasgol was able to do so, not just because of his ability to see them well from a distance, but because Eicewald had told him about them on more than one occasion. The last of the Ice Magi was younger, about Lasgol's and his friends' own age, and he was the last Ice Mage who had been trained recently. Eicewald was proud of finding and training him to be an Ice Mage. That was not always the case. From what Eicewald had told Lasgol, many failed and never became Ice Magi. The training and the tests they had to go through in order to become members of the order of magic were strenuous and difficult, similar to those the Rangers had to pass only obviously more focused on magic.

Leading the cart with Eicewald's coffin was a boy. He was the last novice they had found and brought to the Tower to train. Eicewald had had hopes of turning him into an Ice Mage. Lasgol only saw a kid who looked scared and confused about what was going on around him. Lasgol hoped he would be well trained and become a good Ice Mage, since that was Eicewald's wish.

Every time he thought about the Ice Magi or he came across them, especially the youngest, he wondered what it would be like to be trained to become one of them. He wondered whether he could do it. Eicewald had told Lasgol he would undoubtedly succeed but that he did not recommend it, since the type of magic Lasgol was aligned to was not Elemental or specifically Water-based which is what Ice Magi specialized in, but Nature. Even so, Lasgol could not help but wonder what would happen if he were to enter the Tower for training.

Now that was impossible. Those thoughts had been feasible when Eicewald was the leader. With Maldreck in command, it would be suicide to try and become an Ice Mage. Lasgol thought Maldreck knew they had been the ones who had stolen the Star of Sea and Life from him and thrown him in the river, which caused him to fall out of Orten's good will. Or at least Lasgol thought he suspected. In any case, Maldreck was a dangerous character, and it was best to stay away from him, even more so now that he had the King's backing.

The funeral retinue reached the forest and entered through an area where the trees allowed for the passage of the cart.

Ice Magi powerful. Feel magic, Camu messaged.

I can't detect their power. You're getting better and better at sensing magic, because they're quite far away, Lasgol congratulated him.

I more powerful every time, practice much.

I've also been practicing my magic, but I think you're ahead of me.

You no worry. Keep practice. You reach me one day, Camu messaged, along with a feeling of optimism.

Lasgol put a hand up to muffle the guffaw that had been about to escape his lips.

Thank you, my friend. I'm touched by your consideration.

You welcome.

Lasgol shook his head.

Be irony?

Of course it's irony.

Ahhh, I not understand irony well yet.

62

That makes me happy.

You happy I not understand irony?

Don't worry about it. Your head will burst.

My head no can... oh, I understand.

I'm glad, Lasgol smiled and went on into the forest.

He found it strange to follow a funeral retinue through a forest that looked haunted, the former was weird already, but the latter made it even worse. As they went into the forest toward the center, Lasgol could see that there was barely any underbrush. In its place, a low mist seemed to have been deposited on the ground and remained there, imperturbable.

Lasgol dropped to one knee and the mist covered him completely. It was most picturesque. There could be people living in this forest and no one would ever find them. They simply had to crouch or lie down on the ground to vanish in the midst of this dense, white mist.

This place is fascinating. Do you know if the mist is natural? Or caused by magic? I can't pick it up, Lasgol transmitted to Camu as he tried to touch the mist with his hand and watched it slip through his fingers.

I try pick up.

Ona growled once to indicate it must be magic.

Lasgol took off his glove and tried to feel the vaporous substance with his hand. It was not cold or moist, which is what he had expected to feel. It was more like smoke, but it did not affect his lungs. He could breathe it, even when he was immersed in it.

Not natural, pick up magic.

Well, dangerous?

Not know. Not know magic.

It's not any type of magic you've ever felt before?

Not be.

Ona growled twice.

Interesting, at least it's not Drakonian magic.

Drakonian not be.

Good. Be alert in case we find whatever's making this low fog.

Ice Magi not worried, Camu messaged, along with a feeling of doubt.

Lasgol was thoughtful.

You're right. They must notice it too or be aware that there's magic in the forest. Yet they don't seem to fear it.

They continued following the retinue, which was maneuvering

63

through the trees toward the center of the forest. The cart had difficulty passing, but because it was narrow it just managed. The kid driving it was doing a good job at the reins. The Ice Magi walked slowly and kept throwing glances behind them to make sure the cart managed to get through.

Lasgol was worried they might see him. Well, not see him, but perceive him. It was practically impossible to see with the mist, and he remained crouched quite a distance from the cart. The Magi had the ability to sense others gifted with the Talent. Eicewald had explained that if the source of power was very strong, even the least sensitive magi could pick it up at a short distance. As a rule, beyond two hundred paces they were unable to pick up the power of others. Besides, only a few powerful magi with a great capacity to feel magic could do so easily.

He shook his head, dismissing his fears of being discovered. The Ice Magi were powerful but not perceptive. Their specialization was in attacking, offensive magic. Not perception or feeling. They would not discover them even if Camu and he were radiating power. He also did not think the power emanating from the two of them was so great that they would be found out, even from ten paces away. But just in case he decided not to get close.

We stay beyond two hundred paces, he transmitted to Camu.

They not feel us, Camu messaged back.

Yeah, I think you're right, but just in case.

Ona growled once.

I don't want magical surprises in this forest. We're here to say goodbye to Eicewald, not for arcane encounters.

Fun encounters.

Ona growled twice.

I agree with her, Lasgol transmitted to Camu. He did not want any trouble in this place. Unfortunately, many times they found it without meaning to.

Chapter 8

They followed the Magi for a while longer until they arrived at the center of the forest and stopped. The place was unmistakable since there was a tall block of ice—a long square, a frozen monolith. It was surrounded by the mist. For some strange reason the mist did not cover it but seemed to emanate from it, falling off its frozen body and then dispersing around it.

Funny, that block of ice is very peculiar.

Magic come from block.

That's even more interesting. Then it's no sorcerer, mage, or anyone similar who's causing the mist.

Live in forest.

That sounds very complicated to me.

Complicated, yes. Possible, yes.

Hmmm, it might be, indeed. We've already had one similar experience.

Yes. Dragon Orb in ice.

Lasgol nodded.

But that's not Drakonian magic, is it?

Not be.

Well, that puts me at ease. The last thing we need is another dragon orb.

Ona growled twice.

The retinue stopped beside the monolith made of ice. They dismounted and tethered the horses to the nearby trees. Then Maldreck ordered the coffin to be unloaded. The Magi took it down from the cart. Lasgol thought they were going to carry it on their shoulders to the monolith. But that was not quite the case. Maldreck started casting a spell, moving his white staff with an ice jewel at its tip, and under the coffin there appeared a small frozen wave that lifted it to a height above the magi's heads.

The six Magi stood around the coffin, three on each side. Then the six started conjuring, waving their staves and uttering arcane spells. The sky above the forest filled with dark clouds. It started to snow over the whole area around them, large, crystallized snowflakes that disintegrated like snow dust the moment they touched something solid, whether a branch, leaves, the ground, the magi, or the coffin.

For a moment Lasgol thought the stars themselves were falling, frozen, from the sky. It was an awesome spectacle.

Much pretty, Camu messaged him.

It is. Impressive.

On Maldreck's order, the frozen wave holding the coffin began to move toward the monolith slowly. The Ice Magi moved at the same pace, escorting the coffin. The kid who was not a mage yet was watching everything with eyes opened wide.

The Ice Magi conjured again and freezing winds began to fly above them at fifteen feet high, swirling the snowflakes in every direction as a deep chanting, distant and eternal, began to be heard. It was a chant in the arcane language of the Ice Magi, but it was not them who were uttering it. It was the winds of the frozen storm that did. The Magi walked, looking ahead solemnly while the snowflakes fell and the winds sang a farewell to one of their own.

They approached the ice monolith. Maldreck raised his staff above his head and they stopped. He conjured again in the midst of the storm and the solemn chanting. Above the monolith, at a great height, a cloud formed, dark as night. A moment later it began to thunder, as if following the verses the winds recited. A tremendous blast of lightning hit the ground by the monolith. This was followed by more thunder and lightning, which also hit the ground with force.

Lasgol, Camu, and Ona were watching the thunder and lightning falling around the monolith without touching the Magi, only hitting the base of the ice structure. While this farewell show was taking place in honor of the deceased Mage, Lasgol could not help but feel moved remembering the good times shared with Eicewald. They came to his mind, from the journey to the lost world of the Turquoise Queen, to the time they met again in the Kingdom of Irinel and the escape through the sacred Druid Forest. So many good moments when they had shared not only adventures but a good time, so many conversations, some important and others trivial, but all pleasant. If anything kept coming back to Lasgol's mind, it was how careful and well-intentioned Eicewald had been.

He heaved a deep sigh, and upon letting the air out of his lungs, his eyes began to moisten. Memories of the time they had spent in the Forest of the Green Ogre assaulted him now. They had spent so much time there: Eicewald teaching them magic with limitless patience; Camu and him learning, trying to acquire all the knowledge they could. He had taught them about magic and had done so in an entertaining manner, with infinite patience. He remembered the countless little failures both he and Camu had suffered, especially in the beginning, and how Eicewald had never been annoyed. He had always helped them with optimism, confident that they would make it, even if they did not.

The memories formed a lump in his throat that would not let him swallow and caused his eyes to become moister.

Sad? Camu asked him beside him. He had become visible and was hiding behind one of the thick white oaks, close to him.

Yes, sad. We've lost a friend and mentor.

Ona rubbed her head against Lasgol's leg as he remained with his knee on the ground, half hidden in the ever-present mist. The good panther flattened herself on the ground and was entirely covered, except when she raised her head,.

Master good, Camu messaged, along with a feeling of great sorrow which joined what Lasgol was already feeling, and a tear slid down his cheek.

He taught us so much… and he did so always with such kindness, without losing his patience when we did badly.

Much patient. Much knowledge.

Indeed. It's a real tragedy that all his knowledge is lost now.

Part pass to us, part to them, Camu messaged, looking at the Ice Magi.

Lasgol watched them as they continued the strange ritual. Maldreck waved his staff and cast a spell and the wave carried the coffin until it was right in front of the monolith. The Ice Magi stood in a half-moon behind it. They all raised their staves and conjured all together in a strange litany. As they cast their spell, the frozen wave became an iceberg that grew palm by palm. It was as if each Mage were adding to its height, and the coffin rose up to twelve feet. They continued with their strange chants and the coffin, which now appeared to rest on a great pedestal made of ice, started to disintegrate, the wood melting as if it were ice and thawing out.

Yes, I guess not everything is lost. Part is in us and part in them. True. But I doubt his knowledge has passed onto someone like Maldreck. No, I don't believe he has half the magic knowledge Eicewald had.

He not. Other maybe.

Let's hope so. Perhaps the seeds of knowledge he's planted in them and also in us will germinate. Perhaps they will grow in our hearts and minds and some of us will make him proud someday.

I make proud, Camu said, nodding hard.

We certainly should, Lasgol joined him.

Do for him.

Yes, for his memory, in his name. We have to do it, even if it means sacrifice.

Sacrifice? Why?

It requires a lot of studying. You don't acquire knowledge just because. Remember the tomes Eicewald used to bring us.

I remember.

And those were just a few for those of us who weren't savvy in Magic. There are countless tomes filled with knowledge which we must study and learn. Since we're always immersed in complicated missions, it's going to require sacrifice to find the time to study them.

Oh… I understand now.

It's going to be difficult.

We kill Dergha-Sho-Blaska and then find time to study, the message reached Lasgol loaded with a feeling of anger which he felt clearly, overwhelmingly.

Lasgol turned to Camu, who stared at him without blinking.

Killing Dergha-Sho-Blaska is going to be extremely difficult, he transmitted. *I don't even know whether we can do it.*

We kill him. Sure. Honor Eicewald this way, Camu messaged back, and again the feeling accompanying the message was of anger. Great anger.

I don't think Eicewald would want us to face the Immortal Dragon after what happened.

Ona moaned twice.

We owe to Eicewald. Have to kill Dergha-Sho-Blaska. Honor master. Get time to study.

I understand and share in what you mean, Camu, but it's going to be very risky. The dragon is very strong in every way, both physically and magically. The danger is enormous.

Eicewald brave. Fight with honor. Die for us. We fight for him.

Lasgol nodded. He knew Camu was right in what he felt. Eicewald had not hesitated for an instant to face up to the great Immortal Dragon. He had likely been aware during the fight that he would not be able to defeat the Dragon, and yet he had continued fighting, protecting them. He had died like the brave, good, and devoted man he was. He had died like a hero who faced a monster so terrifying he knew he was going to perish but kept fighting nevertheless to protect his people.

He was a hero without a doubt.

We avenge him, Camu messaged with a feeling of almost fury which Lasgol received like a punch. He wondered whether those feelings Camu was sending him could cause him physical harm at some point. Sometimes, like right then, he felt it might. They would have to investigate the matter before they had an accident.

Revenge is a bad goal to pursue. It leads to death or something even worse. You speak like this because you're furious over losing Eicewald.

Worse than death? Camu messaged back, ignoring Lasgol's second comment.

You might lose your soul on the way. It might blacken with the acts you might have to commit, and in the end it might rot or incinerate.

Then make justice, Camu reasoned, which left Lasgol impressed. His capacity to understand complex concepts was growing with time.

I agree with that. We'll do justice—for Eicewald, because we owe it to him, for everything he gave us of his own good will.

For Eicewald. Justice, Camu messaged determinedly.

The coffin finished disintegrating and Eicewald's body was left uncovered on the pedestal.

There he is. I'm so sorry, Master, Lasgol transmitted.

I feel much sorry, Master, Camu joined him.

We'll always remember you and your teachings.

I remember. I justice. You see, Camu messaged, and the accompanying feeling was of great sorrow, the same Lasgol was feeling.

At an order from Maldreck, all the Ice Magi pointed their staves at Eicewald's body. An instant later a crystal-white beam issued forth from each staff, directed at Eicewald's body. The Ice Magi conjured together and the body of their Mage friend became foggy with a winter mist, freezing with crystallized snowflakes on it. The mist headed to the top of the ice monolith and the block seemed to absorb the mist and once again issued from the bottom, joining the mist around the trees.

"May the soul of the Ice Mage rest forever here," Maldreck said suddenly in Norghanian so they were able to understand.

"May his soul forever rest within the white mist," the rest of the Magi repeated.

"May his soul forever accompany those who already dwell in this place," Maldreck said.

"For the souls of all the Magi of Ice," the other Magi replied.

There was a moment of silence. The sky turned clear and the center of the forest was once again like they had found it, unaltered, covered by the mist in which Eicewald's soul now rested.

Chapter 9

Lasgol and Egil were waiting for Nilsa by the barracks, watching the soldiers training. Today, both the soldiers and the training were different, which had caught the attention of the two friends. Instead of the castle soldiers training, as usual, it was the Invincible of the Ice who were practicing, and that was something worth watching.

In the middle of the bailey, about a hundred Invincibles were exercising with sword and shield. They were wearing their usual gear: white winged helmets, cloaks, bedrolls, and shields. What drew the most attention though was how they wielded the sword. The Invincibles did not use war axes like most of the Norghanian infantry, but broad swords, short and doubled edged. They were similar to those used by the Erenal Army but slightly broader. The exercises of attacking, blocking, and counterattacking they were practicing had everyone spellbound.

"They move with perfect precision," Lasgol commented, watching with interest.

"The sword, unlike the axe, requires precision and looseness, not strength. It's said, and not without reason, that any brute can use an axe, but not so a sword."

"I can imagine, seeing how they use it. Those movements are well practiced."

"Where you see a stroke to the heart, a lateral blockage, or a slice to the neck, there's really an art that's been developed through centuries, mainly by sword masters who taught nobles."

"Were you taught?" Lasgol was interested to know.

"Indeed, but I didn't learn much. My arm didn't have the necessary strength to master the art of the sword. Or so I was told repeatedly by my dear father."

"Sorry…"

"Don't be. Besides, there's always time to learn. That's what's good about this life, it's never too late to learn something new. I've learned to use the bow, the knife, and the short axe. Now my arm is strong enough. I'll be able to learn to use a sword properly," Egil said as he watched closely how the Invincibles were training and the

71

moves they were practicing.

"No idea when you're going to make the time for it, but I'm glad you have that in mind," Lasgol said, smiling.

Egil smiled back.

"You're right. I might have trouble finding the time to become a sword master, but the thought and the wish are already planted in my heart. They'll come to fruition someday. It may be far into the future, but they will."

Lasgol nodded and continued watching the Invincibles attack and defend themselves with their swords. Most of the exercises were only with a sword, so the Invincibles had slung their round shields onto their backs. It was as if they wanted to improve the sword wielding to the best of their ability. The use of the shield, much simpler, also required a certain amount of practice, but by now they must have it down to pure instinct.

Among those watching the training they saw Duke Orten and several nobles. They were talking animatedly and mimicking the defensive and offensive movements with their arms. With all certainty, those court nobles had been trained in sword wielding. It also seemed by their gestures that they knew more than the Invincibles. Lasgol doubted this though. Perhaps Orten, but the others looked little inclined toward the sword and more so to their riches and well-being.

"I'd also like to wield the sword as well as they do," Lasgol admitted to his friend, and his tone gave away the envy he felt. "Well, maybe not as well, but at least know how to wield it properly. If I were given a sword today, I wouldn't know what to do with it."

Egil nodded.

"I understand you. But we've chosen the Path of the Ranger, and on our path there's no place for a sword. Consider that a long bow and a short axe and knife are more efficient than the sword when it comes to killing an enemy."

"Is that what you really think?"

"I do. For an Invincible of the Ice to pierce you with his sword, he first has to reach you. You can kill him from a distance, but he can't. It is true, though, that at a short distance his sword has an advantage over our axe and knife."

"That's what I thought."

"Long story short: don't let them get close," Egil joked.

"I won't," Lasgol replied, chuckling.

Suddenly they saw something that caught their attention. Maldreck came out of the Tower of the Ice Magi, followed by another Mage and the young apprentice. The three passed by the Invincibles without glancing at them. They seemed totally uninterested in the warriors.

"You see them?" Lasgol said to Egil.

"I see them. They draw attention leagues away. They shine as bright as if they were made of snow and the sun fell on them directly."

"Well, it looks like they're coming toward us…"

"I doubt it. Maldreck has no business with us," Egil said.

Lasgol and Egil stopped talking and watched how the two Magi and the apprentice were indeed heading to where the two were standing, watching the training. To their utter surprise, they stopped before them.

"I'm looking for Ranger Lasgol Eklund," Maldreck informed them, studying them from head to toe with narrowed eyes.

Lasgol tried to hide his surprise.

"That's me. How can I help the Ice Magi?" he asked, puzzled. Then he thought that Maldreck must have known who they were, each and every one of them. He was sure Maldreck suspected it had been the Panthers who had stolen the Star of Sea and Life from him and made him fall in the river.

"With nothing," Maldreck replied coldly.

"Oh… then?" Lasgol could not think why he had asked for him.

"I'm here to deliver a posthumous wish," Maldreck told him. "It's not something I want to do, but it is the tradition among the Magi to carry out posthumous wishes of those of us who depart, and I being the leader, it's my duty to do so."

"A posthumous wish from Eicewald?" Egil asked, raising an eyebrow.

"That's right. Eicewald was a great leader of the Ice Magi, and his posthumous wishes must be respected," he said firmly, and the Ice Mage behind Maldreck nodded emphatically.

"What posthumous wish is that?" Lasgol asked, eager to know what Eicewald might have left him.

"Apprentice," the Mage called without even glancing at the youth behind him.

The apprentice stepped up to his leader and handed him a leather bag. Maldreck took the bag and offered it to Lasgol.

"Thank you," Lasgol said, a little embarrassed.

"It was found among his belongings," Maldreck explained. "It's for you."

Lasgol opened the bag, and inside he found two objects. A small rolled parchment, sealed with a white ribbon. And what looked like an ice diamond. If he had been puzzled before, he was now mystified. He took out the scroll and saw that there was nothing written on the outside.

"Are you sure it's for me? I don't see my name on it."

Maldreck smiled with superiority.

"It is, I can assure you."

"He's read what's inside," Egil told Lasgol.

"The seal isn't broken…"

"We Ice Magi don't need to break seals to read a message form one of our own. Neither do we expect those who aren't of our people to understand," Maldreck said in a condescending tone.

"We understand, it's written with Ice magic and that's why he could read it," Lasgol explained to Egil.

"That makes sense…"

"Of course it does."

"Then you've read a letter that was addressed to me. That's not very ethical," Lasgol protested.

"I didn't say that. I said that we can read a message from one of our own. I only read who it was addressed to so I knew who to give it to," Maldreck said, lifting his chin in a dignified way.

Lasgol and Egil exchanged a look that said "sure you did." They both knew Maldreck had read every last word of the message, no matter how much he denied it. The fact that they knew Maldreck was a treacherous snake did not serve the mage well.

"And the ice jewel?" Lasgol asked.

Maldreck shrugged.

"It has no value. It's made with Water magic. We Ice Magi use it as gifts for the young ones we train when they climb a level. I don't know why he's left it to you."

"Oh, thank you for bringing us this posthumous present," Lasgol said gratefully, trying not to show his double meaning.

"As I said, it's my duty as the leader of the Ice Magi to fulfill the last wills of our departed," Maldreck said, and with a haughty glance and pose, he left, followed by the other Ice Mage and the young apprentice.

Once they were far enough, Egil and Lasgol looked at the scroll with great interest and spoke their minds.

"This is unexpected," said Lasgol.

"And very interesting," Egil added, eyes widening.

"Let's go back to our room, we'll be able to open it in peace there," Lasgol said.

"I was thinking the same thing," Egil replied.

The two friends left the training of the Invincibles and at a quick pace, although trying to appear nonchalant, they headed to the Tower of the Rangers. Lasgol could not stop wondering whether this posthumous message from Eicewald might be something important, one last piece of information that might help them. From his friend's eagerness to be back in their room, he guessed Egil was thinking the same thing.

Once inside the room, which happened to be empty, they sat on Lasgol's bed and took out both objects: the scroll and the ice jewel. They stared at them. The jewel had a dull gleam, and it was obvious that it was not a real diamond.

"He must've left it to you as a souvenir," Egil told Lasgol.

"Yes, it's thoughtful." He picked it up in his hand and noticed it did not weigh anything at all. He felt it had some magic. The hair on the back of his neck rose. He felt the Element of Water—yes, it was Water magic, "It has some magic," he told Egil.

"Interesting. Maybe it has to do with the scroll."

"That's what I was thinking too."

They focused on the rolled parchment with the seal and the white ribbon.

"Look, the ribbon ties the parchment and the seal is placed right on top of the knot, so if you want to open it you definitely have to break the seal," Egil commented. He looked intrigued and excited at the same time.

"The seal isn't broken and the knot and the ribbon are intact. It hasn't been opened," Lasgol said.

"It hasn't even been manipulated, which is more important still," Egil added. He had picked up a magnifying glass and was peering at the scroll through it.

"But Maldreck has read it… and if he's given it to us, it's because it doesn't contain anything revealing," Lasgol commented.

"Let's not get ahead of ourselves, my friend. Remember that Eicewald wasn't only a great Mage."

Lasgol looked at his friend blankly.

"What else was he?"

"Very wise and intelligent, much more than Maldreck will ever be," Egil replied smiling.

"That's true," Lasgol nodded suddenly, cheering up. Egil was right. The fact that Maldreck had read the letter did not mean that he would have understood or deciphered its true contents. Perhaps the letter did indeed have something revealing which Maldreck simply had not been able to find.

"I think we should open it," Egil said.

"Okay, let's do it."

Egil motioned Lasgol to open it. Lasgol nodded and very carefully began to pull on the white ribbon. As he had expected, when he pulled on the ribbon it became undone and the blue seal broke.

Lasgol and Egil waited to see if anything happened once the seal was broken.

Nothing did.

Lasgol unrolled the scroll.

"It's a letter," he told Egil.

"What does it say?"

"Let me read it to you:"

This letter is addressed to the Ranger Specialist Lasgol Eklund.
I have informed my fellow magi that this letter exists and must be delivered at my death.

My dear Lasgol,
If you are reading this letter, it means I am dead. Do not feel bad for me. I have lived a full life, filled with knowledge, adventures, and magic. I have known love, on more than one occasion. I have become a leader among the Ice Magi. I have traveled through half the continent on my journeys and adventures and I have met exceptional people, as well as fascinating ones. Not only people, also creatures. I want you to be happy for me for all I accomplished and enjoyed in my life. I wish you, Camu, and the Panthers all the best, from the bottom of my heart.

Grave dangers are in wait for our beloved Norghana and her good people. One thing you must remember. No matter how great the danger is, no matter how invincible the enemy seems that is threatening to destroy us, there is always a way to defeat it. Always. What is difficult is finding and executing it.

Do not lose hope. Fight, stand firm, do not become dispirited. Lean on your comrades, you will find strength in them when yours falters. Search for the way to defeat the great enemy that threatens the kingdom and the continent. If there is one thing I have learned, it is that love moves mountains and magic can do so too.

Let me give you one last piece of advice, from a grateful master to his excellent pupil:

Never stop learning and never stop practicing your magic.

With all my love, I wish you and the Panthers a prosperous life filled with health, love, and happiness. You deserve it.

Eicewald.

P.S. Take good care of Camu, he is an exceptional creature, a unique jewel. Give a hug to Ona from me.

"That's a nice letter from a good man with a good heart," Egil commented.

Lasgol heaved a long deep sigh.

"It's pierced my soul."

"It is profound. If you stop to think about what it says, it's natural for it to get to you. Take a moment to process it."

"Thank you, my friend." Lasgol did as Egil had advised him and proceeded to read the letter several times, absorbing the meaning of every sentence, every paragraph. The more he read it, the more he missed Eicewald and the more he felt the loss of his master and friend. In the time they had spent together, Lasgol had come to admire and love the leader of the Ice Magi: a wise, intelligent, kind man, who had generously taught so much to him and Camu. He was going to miss him very much. His lessons and advice were more valuable than gold in Lasgol's eyes. What an irreparable loss. How much he could have taught them of the magical world... and now he never would.

Egil let Lasgol process the letter and what it meant, but after a while he spoke.

"Something's missing."

Lasgol looked at him blankly.

"What do you mean something's missing?"

"Yes. The letter of farewell is deep and beautiful, but there's something missing. Eicewald wouldn't have left you a letter of farewell as a posthumous wish. Not knowing him and everything we have on our hands."

"You think? Perhaps he only wanted to say goodbye and show his love."

"*Never stop learning and never stop practicing your magic.* There's something else here."

"I don't follow."

"The letter… it's enchanted I bet," Egil said confidently.

They both looked at the ice jewel.

"The jewel's magic will show us for sure," Lasgol said.

"Try it then."

Lasgol held the jewel in one hand and the scroll in the other. Slowly, he passed the jewel all along the scroll to see what happened, line by line.

Egil watched, fascinated.

"Nothing's happening."

Lasgol finished passing the jewel over the entire letter.

"I'll try again."

He made another pass, both on the front and on the back of the parchment, hoping the ice jewel would reveal some secret message.

To both friends' disappointment, it was not so. Lasgol left the jewel on the bed and focused on the parchment.

"I can try to pick up the magic of the parchment, although I'm not very good at that."

"Do it. You'll see I'm right. I think that, from the message in the letter, Eicewald is asking you to use your magic."

Lasgol nodded. With one hand he held the parchment, and he put the other on the text, palm open. He closed his eyes and concentrated. He searched in the middle of his chest for the pool of power where his magic energy dwelt. He called upon his *Arcane Communication* skill which allowed him to interact with magical objects or with power.

There was a green flash.

But he could not pick up much. The hair at his nape stood on end, so he knew for sure the letter contained magic. Magic had been used on it somehow.

He tried again, and what he felt this time was that as his magic passed over the text it showed bright white, indicating that indeed the text had not been written with ink, but that it had been written using magic, Ice magic. That was why Maldreck had been able to read it.

"Eicewald has used the magic of the Ice Magi to write this letter," he told Egil without opening his eyes, without losing his concentration.

"Magic of the Water element?"

"Yes. Maldreck could read it without any problem."

"But, if he had wanted to hide something from Maldreck… he'd have used another type of magic, not one an Ice Mage might find…"

"What do you think he's done?" Lasgol asked as he kept focusing on the letter and picking up the magic used on it."

"He wanted you to read it… so he might have hidden something in the letter that only you can read."

"If that had been the case, he would've used Magic of Nature, which is the one I use. I'll see whether there are traces of that type of magic."

"Go ahead, try it," Egil encouraged him in a voice that betrayed how excited he was.

Lasgol directed his inner energy at the letter, intending to find magic similar to his own in it. There was a green flash that ran through the whole letter, beginning at the edges and then spreading along it. It passed over the whole text without revealing anything odd. Then he turned the letter over and repeated the same exercise. He ran over the whole yellowish-white surface of the letter with his magic.

He found nothing.

This left him puzzling. He was practically sure Egil was right. Eicewald had left him a hidden message, that he knew for sure, but he was unable to find it. He was going to try sending more energy into the letter again to see whether it was a matter of magical power when he had an idea.

The ribbon.

He opened his eyes and saw it on the bed. He picked it up with both hands and focused on it. He called on his *Arcane Communication* skill again and sent power running over the ribbon from right to left, on one side first and then the other. All of a sudden, green letters began to appear along the ribbon.

"There's something!" Egil warned him very excitedly.

Lasgol stopped sending energy and opened his eyes. He saw there was writing on the ribbon. He read.

The twelve pearls are hidden in the Island of Weeping. Protect them. They are important. The Immortal Dragon wants them.

"We know where they are!" Egil cried out in triumph.

"Eicewald's message tells us where he hid the silver pearls," said Lasgol.

"And only to us, or rather only to you. Maldreck hasn't been able to read it, first because he hasn't looked at the ribbon but the parchment, and secondly because it's not written with Water Magic."

"I don't know how Eicewald did it, but he wrote it with Magic of Nature."

"A great Mage with surprising secrets and knowledge."

"To the very end," Lasgol added.

"Very true, to the end."

"What are we going to do now that we know where they are?" Lasgol asked.

"We have to make sure they're really there. That the Immortal Dragon hasn't already found them, or his followers."

"Or Maldreck."

"I don't think Maldreck has deciphered the message. He's a powerful mage, indeed but he's not wise. Yet he is a snake so we'd better make sure."

"Yeah, that's what I think."

"I thought it was strange that he delivered it to us, but the beginning of the letter makes it clear that the other Ice Magi knew of its existence," Lasgol commented.

"Maldreck wants to look good before the other Magi, like a straightforward and responsible leader who fulfills his duties and the group's traditions," said Egil.

"Yeah, and surely the other Magi reminded him to deliver it."

"Yeah, I think so too, otherwise he would've destroyed it. He wouldn't even have bothered to speak to us."

"Yeah, that's what I think."

"You'll have to go and check," Egil told him.

"Yup, I'm the only one who can do so now."

"Find the pearls and don't lose them," Egil told him. "For some reason they are important to Dergha-Sho-Blaska."

"I'll find them, my friend," Lasgol said, putting his hand on Egil's shoulder,

"I expect no less," Egil smiled at him and, like his friend, put his own hand on Lasgol's shoulder.

Lasgol picked up the diamond from the bed and studied it on the palm of his hand. Perhaps for the Ice Magi that object did not mean much, since it had no economic value, but for Lasgol it was a souvenir from Eicewald, and it meant a lot to him. For what the Mage meant to him. He would keep it, and every time he looked at it he would remember Eicewald and thank him.

"Thank you for everything, master. I won't fail you," he murmured.

Chapter 10

Lasgol was saying goodbye to his comrades at the Tower of the Rangers with a broken heart. He knew he had to continue the search for Dergha-Sho-Blaska, that it was imperative to destroy the great Immortal Dragon before he attacked and demolished Norghana. But he felt bad having to leave his friends, especially Astrid, the woman he loved so much. It was going to be difficult, but the life of a Ranger was hard and required sacrifice. They all knew that and accepted it.

He had been away from his friends on several occasions now, and he was used to it. But this time, he had the strange feeling that he was not going to see them for a long time. He did not know why he felt this way, but he did. He was only going to follow a lead and see where it took him. But he had the feeling that the journey would be long and difficult, and thinking about it made his stomach turn, and that was never a good sign.

He shook his arms, trying to get rid of that feeling. Nothing was going to happen. He would find the twelve Silver Pearls and make sure they were where Eicewald had hidden them and were safe. It was a simple mission, there was no reason to expect complications. He calmed down a little. He locked his trunk, slung his satchel with everything he needed in it on his shoulder, and turned toward his friends for the final goodbye.

"Well, this time at least, if the weirdo gets into trouble he won't drag us into it too," Viggo said with his usual sarcasm.

"Don't be daft," Ingrid chided him. "We support one another in everything, and Lasgol has never dragged us into anything."

"Whoa, hold your horses, I support him too, I'm only glad that for once I'll be far away when he gets into the next mess," he smiled with irony.

"Don't listen to him," Nilsa told Lasgol. Everything'll be all right. You're simply going to make sure the Pearls are well hidden."

"That's the plan," Lasgol nodded.

"If by any chance Dergha-Sho-Blaska appears, run away, don't fight him. Listen to me and get away from him as fast as you can," Gerd told him.

"Don't worry, big guy, I had enough last time. I'm not going to face the Immortal Dragon until I'm sure I can defeat him, at least not without an army of soldiers and Magi to back me up."

"Hmmmm, then you can grow old waiting," Viggo said. "For either."

"We'll find a way. Eicewald was sure there is a way to kill him, and we'll find it," Lasgol said.

"Of course we will," Ingrid joined in. "I feel awful for not being able to come with you, but the training with Raner is mandatory, and he wouldn't give us permission to accompany you, King's orders, you know…"

"I know. Never mind. You keep training. I'll find out as much as I can and let you know."

"Be very careful," Astrid said. She came up to him, put her arms around his neck, and gave him a gentle farewell kiss.

Lasgol savored the sweetness and love of his beautiful, fierce-looking brunette's lips.

"Hey, if there's going to be that kind of kisses, I'm coming with you," Viggo said, looking at Ingrid and blinking hard.

"You're staying here with us, and don't spoil other people's sweet moments," Ingrid snapped at him.

"How can you be so envious," Nilsa teased.

Viggo smiled from ear to ear.

"What would you do without these moments I provide you with?"

"Enjoy life?" Nilsa said.

"He makes me laugh so much," Gerd said supportively.

"Thanks, big guy. You're one of my favorites. Nilsa isn't."

"I thank the ice gods for that," Nilsa replied, raising her arms.

"Send word when you've found the pearls," Egil told Lasgol. "Don't change their hiding place unless it's necessary. Eicewald chose that location for a reason, there might be something we don't know about."

"I'll do that," Lasgol replied. "Don't worry. I'll be back in the blink of an eye."

"You'd better be," Astrid said, kissing him again. "Don't be too confident and be careful. We've no idea what that dragon's up to. He might surprise you."

Lasgol nodded.

"I'll watch out. Besides, I have Camu and Ona with me. Everything'll be all right."

"Give our love to the bug and the kitten," Viggo said.

"I will, you know they both love you," Lasgol replied with sarcasm.

"Of course, how couldn't they?" Viggo said, looking like he believed himself the center of the universe.

Gerd laughed while shaking his head.

Ingrid rolled her eyes and snorted.

Lasgol said goodbye with his hand on the door of the room. The scene, so typical of the Panthers, touched his soul. He left, saving it in his memory for the moments of nostalgia that were sure to come.

It was not long before he met with Camu and Ona outside the city. They still had not found another safe place to hide, but they could no longer use the Forest of the Green Ogre since Dergha-Sho-Blaska knew it, which posed a risk. For now they had been hiding in the thickest forests around the capital and moved from one to another whenever humans approached.

They both ran out to greet him the moment they saw him arrive at the forest. For this journey Lasgol had been given a white horse with black spots from the Royal Stables. He was a beautiful animal the Rangers often used on their missions, so he was very well trained. Lasgol thought of Trotter and how much he would have liked his pony to come with him, but he remembered that his friend was now enjoying a very good and easy life. Better that he enjoyed his well-deserved retirement.

Lasgol dismounted and petted Ona.

How's the best of the snow panthers this morning? he transmitted to her.

Ona growled once. She enjoyed Lasgol's petting and rubbed her forehead against Lasgol's.

Wow, you're getting stronger and stronger, he transmitted, feeling her weight as she rubbed against him.

We travel? Camu messaged.

Yeah, we're going to find the twelve silver pearls.

Know where?

Yes. Eicewald left me a letter with a secret message. We found out where he hid them.

Eicewald clever.

Yes, he was.

I happy go on adventure, he messaged, along with a feeling of joy that mirrored how Lasgol felt.

I thought so, he smiled.

Ona chirped once and swung her thick tail from side to side. She was also happy to go on an adventure.

Where go?

To the Island of Weeping.

Camu blinked twice, hard.

Not like name.

Yeah, it's a little peculiar for an island.

What sea? Camu wanted to know.

The island isn't in a sea, it's in a river, Lasgol explained.

River? Weird.

Yeah, it's not very common to have islands in rivers, but this island is in one. We have to get to the river Utla.

Great river?

Yes, indeed, on the border with the Masig territories.

Ona growled twice.

Ona not like river.

I know. But we'll have to cross it. The place where we're going is on the other side of the river.

Okay.

Ona relaxed and swayed her tail again.

Ready?

I very ready.

Sure... Lasgol smiled, and they started their journey.

The beginning of the journey went without incident. The three companions traveled alongside roads to avoid people. When a trader's cart or some rider appeared, Camu used his *Extended Invisibility Camouflage* and hid Ona. It was always safer to hide her, since people usually had a very adverse reaction when they came face to face with a snow panther. Lasgol could not blame them.

They reached the green plains of the southwest of the realm. Lasgol always found it shocking how most of the kingdom was so mountainous and rugged and yet so flat in the south. It was as if the Ice Gods had forgotten to put mountains in that area.

They headed to the river Utla. Lasgol knew where there were a couple of jetties, so he went to the one closest to the island. Suddenly, they saw about a dozen riders to the south.

Camu, hide.

Okay.

Lasgol hoped they had not seen them. Being on flat land was going to be a problem, if they got distracted, someone might see Ona and Camu. There was nowhere to hide, only some hollows and a few scattered trees. Camu could not sustain his invisibility all the time either, since it used a lot of his energy. Lasgol had already foreseen this possibility, and in order to prevent trouble he was using his *Hawk's Eye* skill and had detected the presence of the strangers in the distance.

The riders were approaching at full gallop. They were coming to intercept him, but he kept calm. It was a patrol of light cavalry of the Norghanian army. They must be patrolling the southwestern plains. They soon reached him. There were about a dozen soldiers wearing light-scale armor, high leather riding boots, a metal helmet with a rearing horse, and they were armed with light spears and round wooden shields reinforced with metal in the middle which they carried slung across their backs. They looked tense and troubled. That was not a good sign.

They arrived and stopped before Lasgol. Their horses looked as if they had been traveling for a long time without much rest.

"Who goes there?" the officer in the group asked Lasgol. He was a sergeant with a thick blond beard.

"Ranger Specialist Lasgol Eklund," Lasgol replied.

The riders relaxed visibly when they heard.

"On a mission, Ranger?" the Sergeant asked him.

"Yes, tracking the area," Lasgol lied, not wanting to give any explanations.

"I'm glad they're sending Rangers to this side. Most are on the other," the Sergeant replied, pointing his finger to the east.

Lasgol followed his finger to where he was indicating.

"The border with Zangria," he nodded. "That's where the danger is now."

"Our brilliant generals forget that the Zangrians can slip in through this side too."

Lasgol nodded.

"For that they would have to come over the southern plains. I doubt they'd be able to do that without being seen."

"Those Zangrian pigs are capable of going into the Usik forests on the north side to then appear here and surprise us."

"I doubt they'd be so brave."

"Crazy, you mean."

"That's right. No one goes into the Usik forests, not even with a whole army. It wouldn't be the first army to go in and never come out again," Lasgol said.

"Yeah, everyone says that. I only know that you can't trust the Zangrians. They're as clever as they are ugly."

"They could border the Usik forests, heading south along their eastern side and then come up from the west, without going into them."

"That would take them months, but I wouldn't dismiss it."

"How many patrols on this side?" Lasgol asked him.

"Not enough, if you ask me. Half a dozen on horseback, then the Utla is covered by groups of war ships that patrol it in case the Zangrians sail upriver."

"That would be complicated."

"Like I said, I don't trust those furry swine."

"I'll see if I find any sign of them."

"Very well, good luck!"

"The same to you."

The officer motioned his men to continue and they left toward the east.

Better if you stay camouflaged, Lasgol transmitted to Camu.

I stay.

I have a feeling that we're going to encounter more patrols, things being as they are.

War?

Yes, it's very close.

I guess. Much soldier.

Exactly.

They went on, and that evening they stopped to rest in a hollow with a stream running through it. Ona watched the upper rim, doing the rounds as if she were an experienced watch, while Lasgol and Camu rested beside a small campfire. Lasgol had started it using the *Fire Creating* skill they had learned with Eicewald. They now used their skills as often as they could, both him and Camu, because they were aware that this was the best way to improve their magical level.

Lasgol was carrying Aodh's Bow with him. He never parted with the beautiful gold weapon. It was now his main weapon. He was cleaning it and waxing it, although he wondered whether it was really necessary since the bow did not seem to suffer the passing of time or the effect of the elements. It was always shiny, with a special magical glow. When he released with it the shots were always amazing, as if the weapon were incredibly well calibrated, its special string, which looked like a gold thread, perfectly tensed. It seemed unable to miss, as if the magic of the weapon prevented it from doing so, and always sent the arrow at the intended target.

He passed the cloth over the runes engraved on the body of the exquisite weapon and wondered whether it was really capable of killing dragons. Watching it shine gold when touched by the light of the campfire made him believe it was. Besides, he had managed to wound the great Immortal Dragon, even if it had been a shallow, superficial wound. It was enough to create hope in Lasgol's heart. He wanted to believe this bow would help him defeat Dergha-Sho-Blaska. He only had to manage to make the shots more powerful and deadly to penetrate the dragon scales, hard as diamonds, through flesh and bones, to reach some vital organ and kill him.

He snorted. The more he thought of it, the more difficult he found the whole dilemma. But, he was not going to get discouraged and give up. Never that. He would fight with his whole being to the end.

I practice. Like Eicewald teach.

Are you doing exercises to improve your power?

Yes. I exercises.

That's good. In fact, I'll join you.

Much perfect. Both exercises.

Lasgol shut his eyes and started practicing with his magic. He began by going over his Table of Skills' Progression by calling upon all his skills, one after the other, and executing each several times. He always started with the easiest ones, which he repeated only twice, like *Animal Communication*, which he used on Ona so as not to make Camu lose his concentration. The good panther was used to it and did not mind. Then, after seeking his inner energy, he continued with those that were slightly more difficult, which he repeated three times, like *Cat-Like Reflexes*.

He finished his exercises with *Woodland Protection* and *Arcane Communication*, which he still found harder than the others. These he repeated up to seven times, drawing on his inner energy. The green flashes his body emitted indicated to him that he was being successful.

Camu was doing the same. They were practicing all their skills to improve them and try to make, through continued use, their magical level increase. Lasgol could see the silver flashes of Camu's magic, so he knew his friend was also having success.

Once he had finished with the whole Table successfully, he felt much better. The power of calling upon his skills repeatedly and without failure gave him a feeling of safety and calm. It was like when they practiced physical exercises. Once they were done and sat down to rest, they felt good. It awoke something within their bodies that made them feel better, and something similar happened with magic.

Once they finished with their Tables, they focused on the Principle of Magic Creation, the one they liked best, and they both tried to develop a new skill. This took them forever and exhausted them, most of the times without anything to show for their efforts. Even so, they both did their best, since obtaining a new skill provided them with joy and a sense of victory like no other.

That evening they did not manage to create any new skills. They both went to sleep exhausted but happy even if they had not achieved their goal, feeling joy simply for the work they had done and for not giving up. They knew the road was long and arduous. They also knew that the reward would come sooner or later. They simply had to keep working hard and they would come. They both knew this, so they never gave up or become frustrated or upset.

They rested while Ona kept watch and looked after them.

With the coming of dawn, they would resume their journey to the Utla.

Chapter 11

The Panthers were talking to a Specialist in front of the Tower of the Rangers. They had stepped aside so no one could hear what they were saying. They were in a small, enclosed circle with their backs to the surrounding world.

"I don't agree with this at all," Viggo was shaking his head and folding his arms over his chest.

"Yes, you do. It's what's best for the Royal Eagles," Ingrid replied.

"Don't be silly. We have to report before the Queen at once. We don't have time for your jealousy," Nilsa snapped at Viggo.

"I'm not jealous of Captain Fantastic. The thing is, we don't need him at all. I don't understand why you're asking him to join us again."

"If there's no consensus in the group, I'd rather not join you. I don't want to be a nuisance. I'm sure you'll find another Specialist who'll be pleased to help you," Molak protested with a wave of his hand.

"There is consensus. We all agree except for the numbskull," Nilsa said. "We need you."

"We need a substitute for Lasgol, and fast. It's the King's order…" Astrid told him with a shrug.

"You did well the last time," Gerd told him with a slap on his shoulder.

"Finding another Ranger with such a small window of time, whom we trust and who understands us, isn't that simple, I'm telling you," Egil said with a wink.

"I appreciate the trust. I'm well aware that being a part of this group is a distinction, but if there's no consensus I'm not accepting," Molak stood his ground.

"Viggo's not going to be a problem. He'll behave as he should for the good of the group," Ingrid promised, glaring at Viggo.

"I…" Viggo started to protest.

"You nothing. You'll be delighted to have such a good, trustworthy Specialist substituting Lasgol. Because we need him and because I'm asking you," Ingrid told him with a frown.

"Well… if you ask me so sweetly… how could I refuse, my quarrelsome Blondie?" Viggo replied, blinking hard.

"Agreed, Molak?" Ingrid turned to the Specialist.

Molak nodded.

"It would be an honor to help the Royal Eagles in any way I can."

"Good. Then that's that," Nilsa said with a snort. "Now let's hurry, we have to report to the Queen."

"What does she want?" Astrid asked.

"No idea, but I doubt it'll be good for us," Nilsa replied. "In any case, we have to go at once. You know what she's like and how she gets when she doesn't get her will…"

"She's all charm and kindness. I like her," Viggo said with a broad smile.

"Yeah, yeah, all love and sweetness," Astrid replied.

"As soon as I see Valeria, I'll try to find out what the Queen's planning," Nilsa said.

"That's a good idea," Egil told her. "The Queen's a very interesting character…" he added, looking thoughtful.

"Interesting character?" Ingrid made a face. "It must be because she wants to skin us alive and hates us, right? Couldn't be for any other reason…"

"True, but she's also going to play a role in the future of our beloved Norghana," Egil said, rubbing his chin, still thoughtful.

"You think? I've found her quite subjected to Thoran," Gerd commented. "I don't see her as having much to say about the future of the Kingdom."

"I agree with Gerd on that," Nilsa joined in. "The King speaks and she doesn't confront him, or at least she tries to avoid antagonizing him."

"Because she's an intelligent woman," Egil said. "It's not good policy to antagonize Thoran and Orten all the time. That only leads to the dungeons or hanging from the battlements."

"Those two are practical. Yellers and bad-tempered, but practical. They eliminate their enemies and boom, problem solved. I also belong to that school of thought," Viggo said.

"School of thought?" Ingrid glared at him, waving away the "school of thought" idea. "Do you really want to be like them in any way?"

Viggo frowned.

91

"On second thought, better not. Maybe even their rage is infectious."

"I'd bet it is," Astrid said, winking at him.

"We'd better go before the Queen starts yelling for us," said Nilsa.

A moment later, they entered the main building of the castle. With light steps and looking straight ahead, the Royal Eagles went along corridors, stairways, anterooms, and more corridors and stairways until they reached the area of the castle reserved for the Queen. It was a large area with a dozen rooms. Half were used by the Queen for her own needs, which were many and diverse. She had one spacious room for only her spring and summer clothes and jewels.

The guards posted along their way—which were many, since King Thoran had tripled the watch since the murder attempts—greeted them on passing. They practically all knew the Panthers by now, but not all.

Two guards stopped them.

"You cannot enter the rooms reserved for the Queen."

"We're King Thoran's Royal Eagles and we're assigned to the Queen's protection," Nilsa explained in a firm tone.

The two guards looked at each other.

"Wait a moment," the taller one said and vanished around the corner.

Almost at once the soldier reappeared with an officer of the guard.

"Here they are," the guard said.

The officer looked at Nilsa and recognized her at once, then he looked at the others.

"Nilsa, Royal Eagles," the officer greeted them with a slight nod.

"Captain Mansen," Nilsa greeted him back.

"I've been assigned to this area for some time," the Captain explained.

"It's an honor and a responsibility," Nilsa replied courteously.

"Yes, much better than being stationed at the Royal Gate or the battlements. Less cold," the officer smiled. "Although it has other drawbacks," he commented, looking over his shoulder toward the inner area.

"No post is to the liking of a soldier," Ingrid said, since she knew the saying.

"That's right. You'll never know a soldier happy with his post or task. If you do, don't trust him," he advised.

"I won't," Ingrid said, grateful for the advice.

"I see you have a new member in the Eagles, is that right?" Mansen asked, not recognizing Molak.

"That's right. This is Molak—he's substituting for Lasgol, the King requested it," Nilsa explained.

"Understood." The officer turned to the two guards, who were awaiting his orders with their backs to the wall. "They are who they claim to be. They have unlimited access to the Queen's area and most of the castle," he told them.

"Yes, sir," one of the guards said, the shorter of the two, who was still very tall, and he squared up.

"You'd better remember our pretty faces. We're going to be around a lot," Viggo said.

"What I'm going to do is ask for these two to be exchanged for two veteran guards. That way you'll have less trouble and so will I," he told the two soldiers, who nodded slightly and unobtrusively.

"Go ahead. Don't keep the Queen waiting. I don't have a headache today and I'd like to end the day like that. When she starts yelling…" Mansen made a small grimace of horror.

"Yeah… we know…" Nilsa said, commiserating with them.

They continued down the corridor, and after turning left once and another right, they arrived at the anteroom that accessed the Queen's chambers.

"We're here," Nilsa told her comrades.

"Thank goodness, the soles of my feet hurt from so much walking along stone corridors," Viggo protested, and when they all looked at him he shook his head and smiled. "You really will believe anything. Haven't I told you not to trust others? But you don't listen."

They found the anteroom under intense watch, as was to be expected. But they were surprised to find half a dozen Irinel soldiers on duty. There was no doubt they were from the allied kingdom, because they wore green and white uniforms and were armed with the tear-shaped shield and javelin. On their back they carried several more javelins. Apart from that, they all had red hair.

They stopped before the Irinel soldiers and looked at them. There should be soldiers of the Royal Guard on duty, not of Irinel, which they found odd to say the least.

"Why are the soldiers of Irinel still here?" Nilsa asked Ingrid in a whisper.

"I was wondering the same thing. They should've all left with King Kendryk and his retinue after the wedding."

"It's not surprising that a new Queen would want to keep assistants, ladies in waiting, and even bodyguards and some soldiers with her when she has married into a distant kingdom," Egil commented in a low voice.

The soldiers watched them, undaunted. Nilsa was about to address them when the door opened and an Irinel officer appeared.

"Welcome," he greeted them. "I'm Patrick, chamber officer of Queen Heulyn. I'm in charge of helping her with whatever she needs."

"We're the Royal Eagles, the Queen has called for us," Nilsa told him.

"The famous Royal Eagles… it's an honor to meet you."

"Thank you," Nilsa replied, glancing at the comrades.

"Your reputation precedes you. The Queen has informed me that you'd been called. Follow me, please, she's waiting."

The group followed the officer into the Queen's chambers. They crossed a large room that served as a drawing room. It was solid, with elegant furniture of carved oak, upholstered armchairs, and cushions in green and white. The carpets were not Norghanian, they were green, thick and lush. Several paintings were hanging on the walls and there were murals which showed what, without a doubt, had to be landscapes of Irinel. The green fields, the rain, and the bright white-and-green splendor were perfectly portrayed. On two tables were tomes with titles in Irinelian.

"The Queen has made her own little corner of Irinel here," Nilsa whispered to Ingrid.

"She's the Queen, she has a right to feel comfortable in her personal chambers," Ingrid replied, gesturing unobtrusively to the four Irinel soldiers guarding the wide hall.

Nilsa nodded at her friend.

"I see them."

They followed a long corridor and arrived at a wide lobby, also decorated with souvenirs of Irinel. Four velvet armchairs, one in each corner, invited those waiting to sit down. The floor was covered by a huge, plush carpet. There were wildflowers decorating vases and flowerpots on expensive-looking furniture. The Panthers noticed that the Queen had appropriated all these rooms in her area of command and had transformed them into her home away from home. In fact, they could not tell they were in Norghana, seeing the decoration and ornaments that covered rooms, corridors, and halls.

At last, the captain stopped in front of an elaborate door. He knocked with his fist twice and then called out, "The Royal Eagles are here."

For a moment nothing happened. They waited in silence.

The door opened, and the person who appeared eyed them with great interest.

It was Valeria.

"Her Majesty will see them now," she told the officer and waved him off. Then she gave the Panthers one of her smiles. "Come in, the Queen is waiting for you."

"Thank you, Valeria," Nilsa replied with another smile.

They went into the room. It was relatively big, a study with a large oak desk and an armchair where Queen Heulyn was sitting. On the desk she had a brown-covered tome she had just closed when the group entered. To her left, beside some shelves with ancient-looking books, quite worn out with use, were Aidan and two other Druids. The Panthers recognized them; they were the ones who had come with Aidan for the wedding, and apparently they had remained.

"Come in, Royal Eagles," the Queen said without ceremony and waved them to stand in the middle of the room.

"Your Majesty, you called for us?" Ingrid asked courteously.

"Yes, I called. There are a couple of issues I want to discuss with you."

"Always at the Queen's service," Ingrid replied.

"Valeria tells me you're exceptional fighters, very skilled, the kind who know how to hold their own in complicated situations," the Queen said, looking at Valeria, who nodded. "She tells me you'll look after me well, which is why my beloved husband has assigned you for my protection."

"They are, Your Majesty. I trained with them and knew them. They're not Royal Eagles by chance or luck. They are exceptional with weapons and also with their heads."

The Panthers were rather surprised by Valeria's words. They had assumed she would have things to say against them, not in their favor, after everything that had gone on between them.

"We'll protect Your Majesty with all our skills, abilities, intelligence, and experience, like the King's Rangers we are," Ingrid promised.

"Very well. My opinion of you isn't as high as Valeria's, but I trust her and her good judgment. I'll make an effort to tolerate you, something that isn't easy for me after what went down in Irinel, but I hope I can bear with it."

"We'll try our best not to upset the Queen."

Heulyn looked at them one by one with narrowed eyes.

"What I want to make sure of is whether you're here to protect me, spy on me, or let me be murdered."

Ingrid jerked her head back slightly. The comment had caught her completely by surprise.

"Your Majesty… I swear we're here to protect you…"

"At the Temple they were able to eliminate the Assassin before he could deliver the fatal blow," Valeria told her.

"You would've saved me if they hadn't been there."

"Indeed, Your Majesty, but it was they who killed the Assassin. They saw him before I did."

"Which was quite inconvenient."

Ingrid was taken aback again.

"Inconvenient? We protected you, Your Majesty."

"Yes, but you killed the Assassin, and now we have quite a messy situation on our hands with those despicable Zangrians. My husband the King has informed me that war is practically inevitable. They claim they didn't send the Assassin and had nothing to do with the attempt on my life, and least of all with the attempt on the King's life. Thoran doesn't believe them. He's convinced, and so is his brother the Duke, that it was them."

"It is a delicate situation indeed, Your Majesty."

"Is this the leader, the one who always speaks?" Heulyn asked Valeria.

"Yes, Your Majesty, she acts as the leader and face of the group, although there is no designated leader as such."

"She looks like a good warrior," Heulyn said, looking at Ingrid from head to toe with renewed interest. Ingrid noticed and did not like it.

"She is, of the best kind. Her Specialty is the bow, at short distance."

"The one who looks like she's from our land, what does she do in the group?"

Nilsa realized the Queen meant her and became nervous.

"I have no real function…" she started to say, but the Queen raised a finger to shut her up.

"She's the group's diplomat. Very kind and pleasant. She knows everyone in the castle. She's a Mage Hunter."

"Well, Aidan, you and your people had better be careful with her," the Queen said, looking at the Druid.

"I know Nilsa, I don't fear for my life," he said to the Queen, and then he smiled at Nilsa.

"The brunette?" the Queen continued.

"I'm an Assassin. Very good with poisons," Astrid said without waiting for Valeria   to introduce her.

"She's also a spy and a sniper."

"Very dangerous then. I'm not sure I'm happy having her at my back," the Queen commented.

"I'm even more dangerous. In fact, I'm the most dangerous of all. Natural Assassin, brilliant delivering death to whoever and wherever. Perhaps you've already heard about me. Bards and troubadours already sing my deeds," Viggo introduced himself with a small bow.

The Queen's eyes opened wide.

"Is that true?" she asked Valeria.

"Quite true indeed."

"What I remember of you is that you're impertinent, with a very loose tongue. In my service you'll make sure to keep that tongue of yours still, or I'll have it cut off."

"But…"

"You don't need it to kill, do you?"

"The truth is I don't," Viggo had to admit.

"Well, then, enough said." The Queen put her finger to her lips and gave Viggo a look that meant she would take no nonsense from him.

"The tall and handsome one is Molak, an exceptional sniper and a good Ranger at practically everything. He's not from the original group, he's substituting for Lasgol, my favorite, whom the King has withdrawn."

"Ah yes, the one who was involved in the fable of an Immortal Dragon..." the Queen recalled in a lazy tone. "Aidan, what do you think about all this dragon mess? Do you believe that a dragon has truly been reborn and is now among us?"

The Druid meditated on his reply.

"Well, Your Majesty, if others had had this encounter, I would have to think it was false. But, considering that the encounter was with Lasgol and Eicewald, whom I know and respect, and considering that Eicewald died, I have certain doubts."

"Doubts?" the Queen gave him a questioning look.

"The dragon is a son of Mother Nature. He's in Irinel's folklore and also in the tomes of knowledge of our people, the Druids. We believe they did exist. And also that one day they might return. The fact that Eicewald, a mage so powerful and an Erudite in many matters, should die confronting a dragon, is plausible, albeit unlikely."

"Because the Mage was powerful?"

"Because of that, and because he was a scholar. If anyone could find a dragon in Tremia, Eicewald would be one of very few."

"Until I see it with my own eyes, I won't believe it, whatever and whoever says it. I don't care. I won't believe it."

"That's understandable, Your Majesty." Aidan did not push the matter and remained silent.

"Continue, Valeria, I want to know them all. If they're going to spend time protecting me, it's better I know who they are, although enduring their presence is becoming insufferable," the Queen said.

The Panthers looked at one another and said nothing. Ingrid squeezed Viggo's arm hard, who was already about to utter one of his brilliant comments.

"Of course, Your Majesty. The largest is Gerd," Valeria went on explaining.

"That mountain of a young man must be the muscle of the group, I guess."

Valeria looked at Gerd, who made a horrified face. He had not liked the expression "mountain of a young man" at all.

"He's very strong, indeed, and when necessary they use his strength. But, in spite of his size and strong looks, he has a good heart."

"I don't like people with a good heart. They tend to let

98

themselves be taken in or die for some stupid reason," the Queen made a face.

"I'm not that good…" Gerd corrected her. "I have no intention of letting myself be fooled or dying for anyone."

"That's better. Keep it up. The truth is that someone with your size and strength will be good for me. I want you always at my back," the Queen told him.

"Me? Always?" Gerd looked at his friends for help.

"Always. That way no treacherous knife stab or arrow will ever strike me through the back."

"Yes, Your Majesty," Gerd had to accept and bowed his head.

"And there's only the weakling left. He looks like a scribe."

"This is Egil, the brains of the group. I can attest to his privileged mind, in all senses. Very good for plans and strategy, excellent with anything that has to do with using his head."

"That pleases me. He might be useful. I don't have people with good heads at my side." The Queen noticed that the Druids and Valeria were staring at her. "Don't get me wrong. You are all intelligent, otherwise you wouldn't be with me, but your minds aren't privileged."

"We understand, our Lady," Aidan said with a small bow.

"Tell me, Aidan, I understand you know them too. Do you agree with Valeria's description of each of them?"

Aidan eyed the group.

"I don't know them as well as Valeria does, I haven't spent as much time with them. But, from what I've witnessed and the little I know of them, I believe her evaluation is accurate. I will add that they are a close group; they respect and love one another. Even more, every one of them would give their life to save their comrades. That's something exceptional which is rarely seen."

"If that's true, and I find it hard to believe, it's remarkable," the Queen agreed.

The Panthers exchanged glances as they realized that, although they never talked about it, and did not even think about it, what the Druid had said was true, and in their hearts they already knew.

Heulyn studied them from head to toe once again, and then looked at Aidan and his Druids.

"Very well. The reason for this little gathering, apart from knowing you better, which has made my stomach turn so I won't be able to eat today, is that I have orders for you."

"Your Majesty? What are these orders?" Ingrid asked. She did not like to beat around the bush.

"We're going to leave the castle. We're going to a nearby forest," the Queen said, looking at her Druids. "You'll accompany me as my escort."

The Panthers were surprised, and their faces showed it.

"Your Majesty… it's not advisable to leave the castle… we're on the verge of war… the assassins," Ingrid tried to tell the Queen, but Heulyn cut her short, raising her hand.

"I know all of this. We're going to the forest. It's decided. And one more thing. Not a word of this to the King, or I'll cut your tongues out," she threatened, pointing her finger at each Panther.

The Panthers froze. Not only did they have to go out in the open with the Queen, but they had to do so behind the King's back. This was not going to end well. They would lose their tongues or heads. Or both.

Chapter 12

Lasgol sat with his face to the morning breeze and started working on repairing his inner bridge, as he did every morning he could. He always felt better when he was able to follow an evening of magical training with a morning of bridge repair. It gave him a feeling of well-being, of doing what he should, and that with work he would earn the reward someday. When because of external reasons he could not do one or even both practices, he felt bad. He knew it was the law of life, the life of the Path of the Ranger, but even so, he felt he was not doing what he should.

Camu and Ona were watching the surroundings of the hollow. They were both aware of what Lasgol was doing, and they let him be so he could concentrate and work in peace. Since Lasgol had to concentrate hard, with his eyes shut, he was very vulnerable to possible attacks, so the two of them looked after him. There was nothing worse than being taken by surprise or attacked from the back in that state.

Lasgol started calling upon his *Aura Presence* skill on himself, as he always did. It was the quickest way he had to identify his own mind's aura, that of his body, of his power, and concentrate thus on the first one. Going through his mind and finding the tiny white spot where the bridge began had been a long and frustrating process for a long time; but not anymore, since now he identified it almost at once, which made him calm and happy.

He visualized the bridge in his mind. He remembered how at first it was all white. Now it was practically green in its entirety, although there was still a small final part not fully finished. He focused on doing that. He realized he had only a couple of steps left to finish repairing the whole bridge, he almost could not believe it. It seemed to have taken him an eternity to reach this point. At last he was there, about to finish the process.

He called upon his *Ranger Healing* skill, which had become a lot more efficient and powerful with the passing of time. His continuous use and the nightly exercises which had helped develop his magic had led to a productive effect. Transforming one step of the white frozen bridge of Izotza into a green one of Lasgol's magic had taken him an eternity at first, and that was the case for quite some time. But now it was much easier to transform a step, and it also took a lot less time.

He looked again at the whole bridge and marveled at the fact that it was no longer the icy white of Izotza's magic but a strong green resulting from his magic. He put the feeling of joy aside and focused on the bridge. He kept applying his energy and working on repairing it. He could see the end was very close. It was within his hand's reach. This encouraged him. Would it be today that he finally managed to finish repairing the bridge? Just thinking about it made him tremendously nervous. Better to put aside that idea and keep working as he always did.

As he worked, he thought that striving so rigorously every morning, whenever he could, had led him to this point, and he considered it a real achievement. Commitment and effort for its recuperation every day was the only way to do it, he was well aware of that. The fruits of his efforts were clearer every time, or in this case, greener, the color of his own magic. If he reached out an imaginary hand he could touch the end of the bridge, something he had been dreaming about for a long time.

He was happy, because he was well aware that he could not let that fragile link break. This was always in his subconscious, and it reminded him of it every single day, whether he wanted it to or not. Whenever he could not work on it because of Rangers' duty or the trouble he and his comrades got involved in by themselves, he realized he had to work on his bridge at the first opportunity. And so he always did.

He worked, concentrated and calmly without rushing, maintaining his concentration and moving slowly. He did not know how long he spent on it, he never knew. Most of the time it was an external factor that brought him back to reality. But that was not the case this morning. He was able to keep working until he realized he had transformed the very last step. He sent out more energy to finish the end of the bridge. A moment later he verified that the whole bridge, from one end to the other, was now the green of Nature.

He remained with his eyes shut, staring at his great achievement with his mind. Had he repaired the whole bridge at last? Had he done it? He took another look and   had the impression that it was done. He was surprised and did not know how to react. He saw the whole bridge entirely green, the color of his own power. It joined his mind at one end with his pool of inner energy at the other. He had done it, at last. After so much work and frustration, he could barely believe it. There it was, all the white turned into the shade of green he knew so well. He wanted to yell with joy, tell Camu and Ona, but first he had to make sure that he had really done it.

Suddenly, the bridge began to flash in green. It gave off bright, strong flashes, and in so doing it appeared to begin to vanish. Lasgol was concerned. Was the bridge breaking apart after all the headaches and sweat it had cost him to transform? With each flash, the bridge faded until it finally vanished completely. Lasgol thought something was terribly wrong. If the link between his mind and his inner pool of energy broke, he could lose access to his power. He might not be able to use his magic.

He looked again, and what he glimpsed made him change his mind. He discovered that the bridge had faded but it was really still there. He made an effort to check whether he could see it. It was indeed there, although barely perceptible. The link between his mind and pool of energy was fully repaired. It was now a part of himself.

He had done it. At last! He could not believe it.

He concentrated and watched his inner pool of energy. He was in for another surprise. He could now see it in its entirety, as if a veil that had prevented him from seeing the bottom had vanished. He saw that his pool had changed; it was deeper, a lot deeper. And he realized what this meant: he had a lot more energy available.

He was dumbfounded.

He reacted after a moment. It could not be. And yet it was. He could see his pool had a lot more depth, and therefore a lot more energy. He found it strange that repairing the bridge gave him more energy. That was not the goal. He thought again. Perhaps what had happened was that the depth had always been there and he had not been able to see it. What repairing the bridge had achieved was that his mind could perceive the true depth of his source of power.

Another thought came to mind. Edwina had told him a long time ago at the Camp that his inner pool of energy was growing. Eicewald had corroborated that possibility and had told him that it rarely happened in those born with the Gift but that it did happen sometimes. This meant that perhaps while he had been trying to repair the bridge, his pool had continued growing and so now it seemed a lot bigger.

He snorted. He did not know whether it was one or the other. In fact, it might be both. It might be that now he could perceive more depth, now that he had repaired the bridge, and that also his pool had been growing this whole time. He liked this idea and decided it must be the right one, both things were the case, or so Lasgol hoped this was what he was experiencing. Since he had no way of knowing for ·sure, he stopped thinking about it. It was very good news in any case, and he was going to enjoy it.

He was impressed and excited. All that energy at his disposal. He could use his skills a lot longer and more often without fearing they would run out and he would have to stop and sleep to recuperate his energy. He could maximize the skills he already had, using large amounts of energy to do so. He could develop skills that used up a lot of energy that he had not been able to use so far, since he would no longer be limited by the size of his pool. He could do so many more things. It would bring him closer to being a mage once and for all. This was going to change his life.

"This is awesome!" he cried, raising his arms to the sky.

Ona and Camu turned to him and looked at him in surprise.

What awesome? Camu asked him, looking at him with his bulging eyes wide open.

I've repaired the bridge!

Bridge mind-pool?

Yes, at last!

Great news. I happy.

Ona chirped once.

Ona happy too.

It's amazing. I feel so good I could yell to the sky!

Can yell, no one near.

"It's wonderful! I feel great!" Lasgol shouted as loud as his voice and lungs allowed.

Happy dance, Camu messaged, and he started to dance, flexing his four legs and wagging his long tail from side to side.

Ona joined the celebration, imitating Camu: she flexed her legs and hopped in place while she lashed her big, long tail too.

Lasgol was so happy with what he had achieved that he danced with them, only not having a tail he had to wiggle his butt.

The spectacle they made was worth watching. Luckily for them, there was no one for leagues around who could see them.

After the happy celebration they continued their way toward the river Utla. The journey was pleasant and quiet and now, on top of it, they were very happy, which made the journey more entertaining. Lasgol could not stop smiling, and every now and then he gave a cry of joy to the sky. And of course, Ona and Camu joined him. They did not miss a single chance to express their joy.

Just as Lasgol had predicted, they crossed by two more patrols on horseback that stopped him. Once he had told them who he was they let him pass without any problem. He took the chance to speak with the officers and see what the situation was like. The summary was a tense calm—the calm that precedes the storm.

They reached the jetty they were heading for at last. It was not a military post, since he did not want to give more explanations than absolutely necessary to any more soldiers, and these would certainly ask why he wanted a barge. It was better to go unnoticed. He also did not want it known that he was heading to the Island of Weeping, since he did not want to raise any suspicions. For this he had chosen a tiny, lonely jetty without a good reputation, where they would not ask a lot of questions. This had been Egil's idea, since Lasgol did not know the place, which looked pretty run-down.

Stay here and wait for my signal, he transmitted to Camu and Ona, who remained in camouflage.

We wait,

Lasgol went to the wooden hut in front of the jetty with two barges big enough to get to the other side of the river with half a dozen people and some cargo. Both the hut and the jetty looked appalling. Lasgol wondered how it was possible that the boats were still afloat. He stole a glance and one was taking in some water. The other one did not seem to.

"Looking for a boat to cross the river?" a raspy voice asked him.

Lasgol turned toward the voice and saw a man coming out of the hut. He was over fifty and looked awful; he was dirty and his hair and beard were shaggy.

"Yeah, I need to cross," Lasgol lied, not wanting to give any explanation.

"You've come to the right place. My establishment is the most reputable in the Utla regarding barges."

Lasgol had to hide what he was really thinking. Neither the man's appearance, his establishment, or his boats gave that impression.

"One of the barges is taking on water…"

"True," the man said, looking askance. "I'll get to it in a minute. The other one is in perfect condition, good as new."

"As new?" Lasgol raise an eyebrow.

"As in newly repaired. It won't sink."

"I hope so…" he said, trying to sound unconvinced.

"It'll hold, it's trustworthy," the man assured Lasgol with a twisted grin.

Lasgol had no other option, so he had to accept.

"All right."

"The horse can't go. My barges can't carry him."

Lasgol nodded.

"Will you look after him until I come back?"

"Of course," the bargeman said, showing dentures with pieces missing.

"I'll pay you for the barge and for looking after the horse."

"Fine then."

It took them a while, but in the end Lasgol and the man agreed on a price. Lasgol paid him half, with the promise of paying the rest upon his return. The amount was high and he did not trust the man, but he also did not want anything to happen to his horse. Reluctantly, the bargeman accepted. These were bad times, and he had not many customers, especially with the soldiers patrolling and stopping everyone.

Lasgol had the feeling that this jetty was used by smugglers. He had seen traces of carts hidden behind the hut. Surely they had been used to carry illegal goods such as weapons or alcohol. He wondered whether the smuggling was into or out of Norghana; most likely it was in both directions. Thinking about it again, it made sense. If it was Egil who had recommended he use it, it was likely that his agents would use this jetty for their secret business of exchanging goods and information.

Lasgol waited until the man had gone back into his hut and got into the boat that was not taking on water.

Come now, he transmitted to his two friends.

Carefully, Camu and Ona entered the barge, which seemed to be shaken by a wave twice and still kept swaying from side to side. Lasgol had to hold on tight, but he managed not to fall overboard. Camu took up almost all the space, starting at the bow down to where Lasgol and Ona were squeezed together at the stern. Lasgol managed to grab the two oars and began to row as best he could. Gradually, they got away from the jetty and headed to the center of the river.

As they entered the current, Lasgol had the feeling they were heading for something they should not.

Chapter 13

Lasgol started panting. Rowing in these conditions was turning out to be quite difficult. No matter how hard he tried to maintain his course and a steady rhythm, he was not managing very well. He tried harder and used more strength, but the results did not improve much. They were going forward, yes, but the barge was zigzagging as if it were captained by a drunken sailor.

River big, Camu messaged.

Yeah, I'm also impressed by how strong the Utla's currents are.

Ona growled twice. She was not at all happy to be there.

The barge gave a sudden lurch and Lasgol almost lost an oar. He was able to keep a hold on it, but he had been close to losing it. If he lost an oar, things would get really complicated.

Don't move. I'm having trouble rowing in the direction we need to go.

Not move, Camu messaged.

Ona, stiff and with her tail puffed up, was not moving at all.

Could you shrink yourself a little, Camu?

Shrink? I not understand.

Make yourself smaller. You're taking up too much space.

No can.

Perhaps you should develop a skill to make you smaller.

I not want be more small.

Okay, a skill to reduce your size temporarily, so you can fit in places better, like this barge.

Camu did not answer right away. He was thinking about it.

Not be bad idea, he admitted at last, *perhaps I try.*

You should. If you keep growing, it's going to be difficult to take you with me to certain places.

I go fly.

Not until you manage to fly in a camouflaged state. That's just what we need, people seeing you fly. They'd throw stones, sticks, spears, arrows, everything...

People brutes.

Yes, very. Don't let them see you flying. Things would end badly.

I not fly in front people.

That's right.

Some day manage fly camouflage. Then go places.
That would be wonderful.
I work, I manage.
That's the spirit.

Ona chirped once, encouraging Camu.

Ona, get behind me, and you, Camu, try to make yourself smaller at the bow.
I'll get between you and Ona and see if I can manage to navigate like that.

They did this, and with the new placement Lasgol managed to steer the boat somewhat better, which raised his hopes of making it to their destination. They continued navigating the great river, which luckily was pretty calm. In that season of the year, almost summer, the weather was excellent and the wind was gentle. The current was barely noticeable in the barge, and Lasgol gave thanks to the Ice Gods for it.

He looked around as he rowed. The Utla was like a great sea. He could not see the other shore when he was in the middle. It was a pleasure for the eye. He waited until they could not see the jetty, then he changed course and headed for the island. He was carrying a map Egil had lent him where the position of the jetty, the island, and the army posts were marked. It also had a couple of routes followed by the Norghanian assault ships that patrolled the wide river up and down. Counting on the information that Egil always managed to put together for any mission was an advantage many would like to have but could not. Luckily, they did.

Lasgol was rowing as best as he knew and was able to. They were advancing and not drifting, but it was not an ideal navigation. It reminded him of the first trip he had made upriver when he was going to the Camp for the first time. Those were the times, the years that had gone by and the things they had lived and experienced. There had been good things and bad things. He hoped this little adventure would be one of the good ones.

It took him longer than expected to glimpse the island in the middle of the great river. At least they had not encountered any war ships. The island became larger as they approached it. They could see lots of vegetation. A high mountain in the center with two waterfalls stood out on the island. There were other rocky areas, but none as high and prominent as the one in the middle with the two fresh waterfalls.

After a few attempts to moor the boat, which were not very

precise, they reached the island. They landed in a corner of the island on the south side, facing the waterfalls.

No sooner had Lasgol set foot on the island and secured the barge that he understood why it was called the Island of Weeping: it was the waterfalls. The sound of both waterfalls plunging onto the rocks in a beautiful pool of green water sounded like a person weeping. It was most peculiar.

Waterfalls weep, Camu messaged.

Yeah, it's most peculiar. Lasgol was listening to the sound, and although he could guess that no one was weeping, that it was only a weird auditory effect, if he shut his eyes, it was true that it sounded like deep, distant weeping. Not only that, but the sound was also quite powerful. Most likely the weeping could be heard from anywhere on the island. The rocks behind the waterfalls must be hollow, which likely caused that weird sound effect, or so Lasgol imagined, since he could not find any other explanation. If Egil were here with them, he would surely beg to explore the waterfalls to understand the phenomenon. Lasgol smiled at the thought. The three of them were not so curious as to investigate, even if it was awesome.

Much interesting, Camu messaged as he watched the waterfalls with eyes open wide.

I'd never seen anything like it, Lasgol had to admit, still riveted.

Hear not see, Camu messaged, correcting him.

Yes, that, wise guy.

I much wise.

Yeah, yeah, and it's very, not much. Let's see if you learn once and for all, I've already corrected you thousands of times.

I learn everything.

I guess in your own sweet time.

Sarcasm?

Exactly.

See? I much wise.

Yeah, I see and I hear, Lasgol transmitted, making a funny face.

You face funny.

Lasgol realized that Camu had not understood his gesture. He shook his head.

Let's go find the pearls. This place makes me a little nervous with that incessant weeping.

Weeping sad, Camu messaged.

Ona chirped once in agreement.

They headed into the island, which without being big was quite widespread. The first thing they noticed was that it was rocky and also lush. It gave the impression of being a piece of mountain that had fallen from a high ridge to the river and made the island. The mountain with the waterfalls was in the center, and around it there was thick underbrush.

Lasgol made his way through bushes and climbed along the base of the mountain, from whose top the two waterfalls plunged into the pool. Ona and Camu followed him, un-camouflaged. They climbed up to the pool where the waterfalls crashed. It was a pool of greenish water, filled with many rocks of different sizes and shapes.

Where pearls? Camu asked suddenly as he looked around with his bulging eyes wide open.

Lasgol stopped and scratched his temple.

Eicewald didn't specify that.

Search all island? Take much time.

Camu was right. It would take them days to search the whole island. Lasgol started to think. If he were Eicewald, where would he have hidden the pearls? He stopped to think about it. Ona was pacing around Lasgol, sniffing, alert. After a while of turning the problem around in his mind, Lasgol answered Camu.

I doubt it'll be necessary. I believe our good friend hid the pearls the same as he did in the Forest of the Green Ogre.

Bottom of pool.

That's what I think, and I'm going to find out.

Okay.

Lasgol left his satchel, bow, and other weapons by a fallen tree and undressed. The day was hotter than they were used to in Norghana, so he was not cold. He stretched his arms and then dived headlong into the pool. The water was warmer than he had expected, which did not bother him. On the contrary, it felt good. So much rowing had made him hot, and the water was refreshing. He swam to the bottom with his eyes open, although he could not see very much. The water was too murky and the vegetation at the bottom was thick.

He had to resurface in order to breathe.

Find?

Lasgol shook off the water from his hair and face.

I can't see very much. There are lots of weeds and other vegetation down there.

The water is all stirred up.

You find, Camu said encouragingly from the shore where he was watching Lasgol's efforts alongside Ona.

I'll go down again. He swam toward the exact center of the pool. He had a hunch. He swam through the murky water and touched the bottom. He glimpsed rocks and more underwater vegetation. He began to think he had been mistaken. Would Eicewald have hidden the pearls somewhere else on the island? Doubt entered his mind. If that was the case, he was going to be searching for a long time.

He had to surface to breathe. The moment his head came out, he received Camu's message.

No?

Lasgol shook his head.

I'm going to look again around the bottom. There are many rocks, and maybe he put them among them and that's why I'm not seeing them.

Okay.

Lasgol dived again and swam along the bottom of the pool for a good while. He came out to breathe and went back down, but he was not having any luck. Doubt began to turn into certainty. The box was not there. He began to lose heart. He kept trying for another while with Camu and Ona cheering him from the shore.

After another dozen dives, he had to give up. The pearls were not at the bottom of the pool as he had thought. He came out of the water and sat on the edge with his feet still in the water. He rested a little.

Why not be?

That's a good question, I don't know.

Have be in water.

That's what I thought, but…

While they were thinking, Ona moved away from them and went around the pool to where the two waterfalls broke the surface at the far end. She growled once.

Lasgol and Camu looked at one another.

What is it, Ona? Lasgol transmitted to the panther.

Ona growled again.

Ona feel something in waterfall, Camu messaged.

Lasgol got to his feet and went to where Ona was. She was staring fixedly toward the waterfalls, or rather through them.

Do you sense something, Ona?

The panther growled again without taking her eyes off the waterfalls.

Very well, I'll see what I can find.

Lasgol approached the first waterfall. It crashed down hard, and the sound of deep weeping made him hesitate. It seemed to tell him that if he tried to cross it he would regret it. His instincts told him the same thing. The force of the falling water could harm him and, since there were rocks everywhere, if he fell on his back he could break his spine or head.

But he had to investigate those two waterfalls. He had the urge to do so. He made the decision. He called on his *Improved Agility* and *Cat-Like Reflexes* skills, gathered himself, and jumped from one of the rocks to the side of the left-hand waterfall. For an instant he felt the force of the water pounding on his head and shoulders, pushing him down. But with the momentum he had gathered, he managed to cross it. He was left sitting in the middle of a puddle behind the waterfall.

You well? Camu's message reached him, along with a feeling of concern.

Yes, don't worry, I'm fine.

Lasgol looked up and saw he was in a cavern, just as he had guessed. The weeping here was loud, and he had to cover his ears to protect them. He searched around in the cave, and at the far end he found a second smaller pool. Without thinking twice, he dived into the water. Once he was underwater, he stopped hearing the weeping and the torture went away.

Suddenly, a reflection caught his eye. He swam toward it, and in between several rocks in a small depression he glimpsed what could be a box. He got closer and saw what was indeed a box, one that had magical engravings. It was Eicewald's box. He was about to take it when he ran out of air.

Find? Camu messaged from the other side of the waterfall.

Lasgol took a breath and shook the water off his face.

Yes... I think so.

Take out. What you wait?

To catch my breath? Lasgol could not believe that Camu was urging him.

Breathe already. Go back.

Going, Lasgol transmitted before he dived in again. He swam back to the spot where the box was and picked it up. It was not too heavy, so he had no trouble bringing it out of the pool. He set it on the shore and climbed out of the water. He wiped the water out of his eyes and focused on the box. It did not transmit anything to him, but it had to be the one.

Lasgol grasped it tightly and went to the waterfall. He calculated the leap the same way he had come in. Since his skills were still activated, he gathered himself and jumped. Again he felt the pressure on his shoulders and head, but he got out and managed to land on a flat rock without falling on his butt.

Camu and Ona came over to look at the box which Lasgol placed on the shore of the outer pool.

Do you pick up anything? he transmitted to Camu.

Camu was still for a moment, facing the box with his huge eyes shut for better concentration. Then he said, *Not feel anything. Not pick Drakonian magic.*

I think it might be because the box contains it. That's the box's function.

Special box?

Yeah, I think so. I remember Eicewald telling us he had put them in a special box, with the ability of masking magic-radiating sources.

Open and see.

We have no choice if we want to make sure, Lasgol had to agree.

He got dressed first while he wondered whether it was a good idea to open the box or not. He had doubts, but he had found it, which was the important thing. He could leave it at the bottom of the pool where he had found it and go back. But if he did, he would not know whether the pearls were safely in the box or not. On the other hand, opening it was a risk, one he was not sure he wanted to take: Dergha-Sho-Blaska or one of his lieutenants might sense the pearls' magic and come for them. This idea troubled him, he was not sure it was worth taking the risk. On the other hand, they were on an uninhabited island in the middle of the Utla river. Picking up on the pearls' power from wherever the dragon was hiding seemed unlikely, but even so Lasgol could not make the decision.

He bent over to inspect the box. He saw some runes which he identified as Water Magic of the Ice specialization. They were Eicewald's. He did not know their function, but he guessed they held some kind of concealing power to prevent the pearls' magic from being felt. The Water Magic was alien to him, but after spending time

114

with Eicewald he was able to recognize some symbols and runes from the tomes the Ice Mage had let them borrow to study, even if he did not understand them. It saddened him that he could not decipher them, even more so now that he had lost his master. He could never learn to decipher those runes.

He sighed. He was well aware that even if Eicewald were alive and taught him to interpret Water Magical Runes, it would take him a long time to learn. On the other hand, it had never been his intention to learn that type of magic but to learn more about his own. He was seeking to understand his magic, get to know it and thus be able to use it and improve every day, not only in its knowledge but in what he might do with it. He realized that Eicewald could no longer help him. He and Camu were alone now and would have to manage as best they could. With effort and tenacity they would become knowledgeable of their magic and skills, things which they would be capable of developing and which would amaze everyone. This was his wish and hope. He looked at Camu, who was watching him with his huge bulging eyes. Yes, they would do it indeed.

He made his decision. He could not remain ignorant to the pearls' fate and wondering whether they were in the box or not, so he was going to open it. It had no lock, so he tried to unscrew it with one hand on top and the other on the bottom. For a moment, nothing happened. The amount of strength he was using did not seem enough to open it. He exerted more strength but was unable to open it.

I can't open it, he transmitted to Ona and Camu.

Box shut with magic.

That must be it.

Open with magic.

Why did not I think of that, I'll try, Lasgol said, realizing Camu was right.

He put the box on the ground, placed his right hand on the top over the runes, and called on his *Arcane Communication* skill, sending his inner energy to the box. There was a green flash, and suddenly the runes on the box began to light up, shining a bright white.

Runes active, Camu warned Lasgol.

Ona growled once. She could also feel the magic.

Lasgol waited until all the runes of the box lit up. A moment later there was a click, as if an invisible lock had opened, and the top of the box lifted slowly. Lasgol took his hand off the cover.

Lasgol, Camu, and Ona watched the box open and inside, covered in white velvet, were the twelve Silver Pearls. They shone with an unmistakable silver gleam.

Here they are. We found them, Lasgol said, making a fist. He felt joyful and triumphant.

I feel power. Much power. Drakonian.

Then they're the real ones.

Yes, be.

Very well. Let's shut the box. I don't want their power to be detected. Dergha-Sho-Blaska was able to find the great pearl, even with it being protected like these. I don't want to tempt fate.

Better shut box, yes, Camu messaged to him.

Lasgol tried to shut the box and something odd happened. No matter how much force he exerted, the box did not close.

Shut with magic.

Lasgol nodded. He placed his hands on the box, and without pressing down he called on his *Arcane Communication* skill. There was a green flash, and a moment later the runes shone white again and the box shut.

It worked. Lasgol felt thrilled for having been able to open and close the box by using his own magic. He knew that Eicewald had placed the runes, foreseeing that he would try to open the box with his own magic. Once the box was shut, Lasgol felt much more at ease.

Hide again.

Yes, I'll leave it where I found it. We'll avoid problems that way, at least until we know what they're for or how to use them.

Suddenly, Ona growled in warning.

Something's happening, Lasgol transmitted to Camu.

"Well, well, so that's where the twisted mage hid the box," an unpleasant voice said.

Lasgol spun round to find a figure dressed entirely in white and holding a staff of the same color in his right hand.

"Maldreck!" Lasgol cried, unable to believe his eyes.

Chapter 14

Raner was waiting for the Panthers in front of the Tower of the Rangers. Four Royal Rangers were with him. One of them was Kol, whom Nilsa recognized at once and nodded at unobtrusively, smiling, while the Panthers formed a line before the First Ranger. Kol returned the nod, also unobtrusively, and smiled at her, which made Nilsa blush. Kol was the handsome Mage Hunter who tried to court her every time he had a chance. All of a sudden the training did not seem so bad—perhaps it was even becoming interesting. She bowed her head slightly and eyed Kol, who caught her glance and returned it with a playful smile.

Most of the Royal Castle's inhabitants were sleeping, with the exception of the soldiers on duty at the towers, battlements, corridors, and doors. Those on night watch had not been relieved yet. The rest of the soldiers, servants, nobles, and the Royal Family had not opened their eyes yet but would do so presently. The day promised to be radiant. Activity would take over the castle and turn it into a beehive at the Queen's orders.

The Panthers were formed before Raner and his men and were waiting for orders, which did not take long to come.

"I know you haven't asked for the honor of becoming Royal Rangers, but the King's orders can't be ignored. Therefore, I'm going to train you in order to become the elite of the Rangers," Raner said, indicating the four strong Royal Rangers with him.

"I don't wish to contradict the First Ranger, but the Rangers elite are in this line we form," Viggo replied with his usual cheekiness.

Raner glared at him.

"Very well, let's see how good you are."

"Wonderful," Viggo replied, puffing himself up, ready for the fray.

Ingrid threw him a look of incredulity.

"First Ranger, it's not necessary..." she started to say, but Raner waved her off.

"Yes, it is. You might think you're better than them," he said, indicating the men he had brought with him. "You believe that because of all the Specialties you possess, your experience and skill. Because you're Royal Eagles you think you're above them, that you're better than they are. But there's one thing you're not, and that is Royal Rangers. Let me remind you that they are far above you in rank. And that is because they are the best among the Rangers, chosen for a very specific function: protecting the King and the Royal Family. To be like them, you need specific training and to change your way of thinking at the time of action. They defend, they don't attack. They have a great responsibility—they must protect Royal lives. That's a great difference you'll have to learn."

"Yes, First Ranger," Ingrid said.

"You're going to help me teach a lesson to our exceptional Assassin," Raner told Ingrid. "Come to me."

"Ingrid walked up to Raner and looked at Viggo out of the corner of her eye.

"Assassin, prepare your weapons," Raner ordered.

Viggo nodded and drew his two knives with a swift move.

They were all watching the scene expectantly. They had no idea what was going to happen, but it did not look good. Raner was First Ranger and an exceptional Assassin. He was supposed to be the best of all Rangers. Viggo, on the other hand, believed he was better than Raner. If they were going to fight, it would be an epic duel. But why was Ingrid at the center of the dispute?

Raner provided a swift answer to the Panthers. With a quick movement of his hand, he grabbed Ingrid by the waist and pulled her around. With his other hand he drew a knife and put it to Ingrid's throat while he stood behind her, very close, holding her tightly so she could not move.

Viggo started and made to leap forward, but he held back. The rest of the Panthers had a similar reaction. They did not know what was happening, but they did not like seeing Ingrid in danger at all.

"Now, Assassin, how are you going to free the hostage?" Raner asked Viggo, speaking from behind Ingrid.

Viggo made another movement as if he were going to attack, but seeing Raner pulling Ingrid against his own body, he hesitated. He did not attack.

"I see there are doubts," Raner told him, showing Viggo his knife and putting it back to Ingrid's neck, who remained in a fast grip.

"Don't attack…" Ingrid begged Viggo as a warning.

"If you attack in this kind of situation, nine out of every ten times, the hostage dies. Do you want to take that risk?" the First Ranger asked.

"If anything happens to her, you'll die," Viggo threatened icily and with a lethal gleam in his eyes.

"Perhaps, although I doubt you would defeat me. In any case, that doesn't solve the situation we have at hand. How are you going to save the hostage, Assassin?" Raner asked in a serious tone, albeit calmly. He did not seem to fear Viggo, and he did know how the situation could be solved.

Viggo narrowed his eyes and they gleamed. He seemed about to make some kind of attack. Raner slid the knife along Ingrid's throat. This stopped Viggo, who looked at Ingrid's eyes and stood still.

"You'll find yourself in this situation," Raner said, speaking to all now. "The hostage will be the person you're protecting. It might be the King if an Assassin gets to him, or the Queen. For you, your comrade Ingrid is dearer, so you understand what's at stake if this should happen. Do you understand now the importance of what a Royal Ranger does? Because they know what they must do in this case," he said, pointing at the four Royal Rangers with his knife, "and you don't."

"They do?" Viggo said in a daring tone.

"They'll show you. Kol, do the honors," Raner said, motioning for him to stand where Viggo was.

"Yes, sir," Kol said, standing beside Viggo. "Do I have a bow or knife or axe?" he asked.

"Since you're very good with the bow, we'll make it more difficult. You have a knife and axe."

"Very well, sir." Kol removed the bow he carried on his back and left it on the floor. He drew his knife and axe.

"Whenever you're ready," Raner told him.

Kol nodded, and without waiting an instant, he threw the knife at Raner's face with a tremendous whiplash of his left hand. The knife flew straight, and Raner had to duck his face behind Ingrid's head, who felt the knife fly two fingers from her left cheek.

The Panthers cried out in fear. The Royal Rangers did not even flinch.

Kol continued the attack by rolling on the floor toward Ingrid at great speed. He did so following the throwing movement. Raner's head reappeared above Ingrid's left shoulder and saw Kol approaching, so he made to cut her throat.

The Royal Ranger reached Ingrid like lightning. Still at a crouch, he raised his axe. He delivered a downward blow that hooked Raner's forearm and pulled him down hard. Raner's knife left Ingrid's throat from the axe action and Raner's arm was waved aside.

"Run!" Kol told Ingrid.

Ingrid leapt forward and escaped Raner's range.

Kol jumped to his feet, and with axe in hand he stood in a defensive pose, covering Ingrid's escape.

Raner bowed his head to Kol.

"Very well executed."

"Thank you, sir," Kol replied. "Is the arm okay?"

Raner looked down. The vambrance of reinforced leather had a slit.

"I'll have to get myself another vambrance, but there's no wound."

"I'm glad, sir."

Raner looked at the Panthers.

"In this dangerous situation, the first thing to do is distract the attacker. We have to stop him from carrying out his threat. Throwing a knife at the attacker's face is very effective, because if it does reach the attacker it will give us the necessary time to get to him. If it doesn't reach him, the attacker will be forced to take cover. No one stays still when there's a knife coming toward their face. And when they move, it gives us time for a faster approach to the attacker. That's what Kol did. Finally, and this is very important, you don't attack the assailant. We don't do this, because if we did we'd be giving him the choice of killing the hostage. What we need to do is get the weapon and neutralize it, understood?"

"Yes, sir," Ingrid said, looking at Kol with appreciation.

"There's a similar technique performed with the bow. I'll teach you it later on, although the goal is the same: to disarm the attacker and free the hostage unscathed."

"We're going to enjoy that one," Nilsa said.

"Assassin, what do you think now of the Royal Rangers?"

Viggo wrinkled his nose, shook his head from side to side, and finally spoke.

"I admit I underestimated them. I hadn't thought that all this defending and protecting the Royal Family could get so complicated."

"So you admit you have a lot to learn?"

"I do, sir. I may be vain, but I'm not blind. If I see I've made a mistake, I'll admit it. It will be good for us to learn what they know. That combination of attacking and disarming was brilliant."

Raner nodded in agreement.

"I'm glad you can appreciate what they're capable of doing and what this training can do for you all."

"We do, sir," Ingrid said gravely.

"Good. Kol, return to your position."

Kol nodded and went back to stand beside the other Royal Rangers, but he could not help himself and grinned at Nilsa, who was staring at him in awe.

Raner addressed the Panthers.

"As for the training, we'll do it in two groups. This way while one group practices, the other will be protecting the Queen. We can't forget that our main priority is her safety and well-being. The fact that we have to train you in such a speedy manner is a great drawback that we'll have to alleviate. In the morning Ingrid, Astrid, and Molak will train. The afternoons will be when Gerd, Egil, Nilsa, and Viggo practice."

"We understand and are aware," Egil said. "We'll do whatever we can so that everything goes well and no unwonted situation arises. The sooner we train, the sooner we'll be able to devote ourselves fully to the Queen's protection, which is the most important thing."

Gerd glanced at Egil out of the corner of his eye with surprise at his friend's words.

"I'd rather be in the morning group," said Viggo.

"I can imagine. That's why I've put you on the afternoon group."

"Well, that's nice."

"That's what happens when you're so vain," Raner said, shrugging. "Maybe this will bring you down a notch."

"Maybe not," Viggo replied, not at all happy with the arrangement.

"What will happen if the Queen requires full protection? From all of us I mean," Ingrid asked.

Raner looked at her and nodded.

"That might be the case, and if it is, training will be suspended.

First and most important is the Queen's protection, at all times."

"Understood, sir," Ingrid replied.

"On the days when the Queen remains in her chambers, with no visitors, or in any other safe areas of the castle and without company, that's when you'll be training."

"That will be most of the time, sir," said Nilsa.

"Let's hope that's the case, the political situation being what it is at the moment," Raner said.

"Regarding physical training, that will also be part of your preparation," Raner added.

"Oh no…" Viggo moaned.

"Is that necessary?" Gerd asked, looking unhappy.

"We're in very good shape, that's something we never neglect," Nilsa said.

"I see that, and therefore I'm sure it won't be too hard. In any case, it's part of the training and you have to do it. The Royal Rangers have physical training every other day, and you'll join them," Raner said, indicating his men. "There's a group in the morning and another in the afternoon."

"It won't be a problem," said Ingrid, "Besides, it will be good to stretch our muscles a little."

Viggo and Gerd did not agree, judging by their faces.

"You can thank his Majesty the King for that. Remember, this isn't my idea," Raner told them.

"Yeah… I'll go and thank him right away," Viggo snapped.

"Well, I won't go with you," Gerd shook his head.

"Good. And now, without further ado, we'll begin the first practice session," Raner said. "Ingrid, Astrid, and Molak, stay and get in line. The rest of you, go back to the Queen and protect her."

"I'm staying to see what it's like…" Viggo started to say, but Raner cut him short.

"You'll do as you're told," Raner said, pointing his finger to the entrance of the main building of the Royal Castle.

Viggo left, muttering under his breath. He turned.

"I'm watching you," he told Molak, looking at him threateningly as he pointed a finger at him.

"I know, and I don't care," Molak replied, undaunted, looking him in the eye.

"Is there a problem between you two?" Raner asked Molak.

"No, sir, none at all," Molak replied confidently.

"Good. We can't allow for any rivalries or discrepancies when we're protecting the King or the Royal Family. One distraction, one brawl, and the unthinkable might happen. We must always be alert and avoid distractions. The lives of the King, Queen, and the future of Norghana depend on us, their protectors, not making a single mistake."

"There won't be any distractions or problems, sir," Molak promised.

"We won't make any fatal mistakes," Ingrid added.

"We aren't the kind of people who make life-threatening mistakes," Astrid said firmly.

"Good." Raner seemed pleased with the replies. "What you must always remember whenever you're serving as Royal Rangers is that your only job is to protect their Majesties. You must always keep that in mind. An infinite number of things might happen in the course of one day of service, but none can distract you. You're here to protect, and when you draw a weapon it must be to protect, not attack."

"We understand, sir," Ingrid assured him.

"The first thing I'm going to show you is how to position yourselves around the King or Queen at all times and in any situation. Also how to move at a specific pace, retreat, ride, and even navigate."

"We position ourselves around and as close as possible, right?" Astrid said, simplifying. "Well, that's what makes more sense so that a possible attacker doesn't get to them."

"That's a good tactic, but one which the Queen wouldn't appreciate since she's not used to having people so close to her, nor would she allow you to stay at her heels when she's walking. You'd end up stepping on one another's boots."

"Yeah… I guess so…" Astrid said.

"Besides, you must consider two types of situations. The first one is whether you must protect someone like the Queen on your own or with the assistance of the Royal Guard. In most cases, the Royal Guard will be present if it's the King or someone from the Royal Family who has to be protected. In that case, they will be the ones surrounding the person to protect them and will form a ring of safety around them. They'll be the closest to the person being protected. In that case, the Royal Rangers will form a second and wider ring with bows ready."

"That sounds right," said Ingrid. "The Royal Guard watches the inner perimeter and we watch the outer one."

"That's right," Raner confirmed. "But, it might also be the case that the Royal Guard isn't present. This should be very seldom, but it might happen. In that case, you'll form the inner line of defense and there won't be an outer one."

"Then, in that situation it's better to use close-combat weapons," Astrid said, drawing her knives.

"Yes, that's the right procedure," Raner confirmed. "But every situation is a world in and of itself, so you'll have to pay close attention and adapt to any situation that might come up."

"That sounds like improvisation," Molak commented, not looking pleased.

"If you're well trained, you'll be capable of improvising and adapting without thinking about it. It'll be instinctive," Raner assured him.

"Survival instinct," said Ingrid.

"Exactly. The survival of the person you're protecting, not your own," Raner specified. "You'll always have to put the King's life or that of his family first. Yours is inconsequential. If you must sacrifice yourselves to save their life, you will, without hesitation. With honor."

Molak nodded, "Yes, sir,"

Ingrid agreed, but in her tone there was a bit of doubt.

Astrid said nothing.

"Good. We're going to start the training. The situation will be a mission to protect the Queen without the support of the Royal Guard."

"We're starting the hard way," said Astrid.

"As it should be," Ingrid said, smiling.

"Kol you stand in the middle. You'll be the Queen," Raner told the Royal Ranger.

Kol nodded and stood where Raner was pointing.

"Two of you must always position yourselves at the back of the person you're protecting. Here and here," Raner indicated. Then he signaled to two of his Rangers to stand where he had marked. There was a pace and a half of separation from Kol's back. "The space between the two protectors must be minimal. Your shoulders must brush and your arms must touch at all times, to prevent not only a person from passing through but also an arrow."

"Wouldn't it be better if only one person covered the Queen's whole back?" Molak asked.

"No, since in most attacks, there's usually more than one assassin. Therefore, they could overcome one person between two or three of them, or they might surprise the protectors from behind if distracted. With two protectors, it's more difficult for this to happen," Raner explained.

"Understood," said Ingrid, who missed nothing. She was fascinated about everything she had to learn from Raner in order to become a Royal Ranger. She was feeling very well, even happy. For her this was a reason for joy, not a punishment.

"Good. Astrid and Ingrid, take your positions. Molak, you'll be in front of the Queen. The distance is the same. One and a half paces ahead of the Queen. The guarding position is also the same: shoulder to shoulder and arm against arm. No one must assault you and reach the Queen."

Molak nodded and stood in front of Kol.

"Now, we'll practice moving forward and turning. You must always keep on eye on the person you're protecting and the other on the possible dangers around you," Raner told them.

"A little complicated if the person I need to protect is at my back," said Molak.

"And you must walk looking straight ahead, not looking back constantly at the person you have to protect. You'll trip if you do, and besides, the person you're protecting won't be happy with you looking at her or him constantly."

"Yeah, I guess that's true…" Molak said, looking at Ingrid and Astrid behind Kol.

"Whoever goes in the lead has the advantage of seeing what's in front and the disadvantage of having to be very much alert to see what the person they're protecting is doing, but at the same time do so unobtrusively. On the other hand, whoever brings up the rear has the advantage of seeing the person they're protecting but not what's behind them, and that's where the danger will come from in most attacks."

"So, I guess we have to keep looking back unobtrusively," said Ingrid.

"And constantly," Astrid said, looking back over her shoulder.

"That's right, without losing sight of the person you're protecting," Raner confirmed. "We're going to do exercises in walking in all directions and at different paces. Watch out when we go backward. It's not normal, but it might be required if we were to retreat if there's a heavy opposition at the front, and we have to be able to do so without breaking formation."

"Understood," Ingrid said.

At an order from Raner, the exercises began. The First Ranger continued to work with them until he saw they were picking up the basics of what they had to do. He left them practicing with the other Royal Rangers and went to continue the rest of his duties.

Ingrid, Astrid, and Molak exercised with full concentration, listening to all of Raner's explanations. They could not avoid making mistakes and having a lack of coordination at times, but they worked as hard as if they were back at the Camp, because they knew that those exercises would help them, in time, to become elite protectors of the Royal Family.

Astrid was not enjoying the exercise much—being a Royal Ranger was not in her plans. She accepted that she must do it, and so she did. But by the fifth repetition she started seeing it in a different way. She realized she was going to learn things she could later use in her own field as an Assassin. Nothing better than being an expert on how to protect a member of royalty, to later murder him or her using that same knowledge. Indeed, the more she thought about it, the more she liked the idea. This was going to come in very, very handy.

Molak took the training willingly. Like Ingrid, he wanted to become a Royal Ranger, and the chance had been presented to him a lot sooner than he had expected. He had calculated he would still have to serve a few more years as a Specialist before even dreaming about entering the elite corps. As a rule, the Royal Rangers were chosen for being exceptional and experienced. Joining the Panthers to substitute for Lasgol had come with this unexpected bonus, and Molak was pleased with the opportunity it granted him. Being with the Panthers usually meant trouble, danger, and risks. The fact that for once it was something positive, something he wanted so much, was a wonderful change that he accepted more than gladly.

Ingrid, like Molak, was delighted with the chance of becoming a Royal Ranger, and she showed it openly both in what she said and what she did. For her the training was not a nuisance, it was the total opposite. In order to reach her dream of being First Ranger, she first had to become Royal Ranger. It was not an insurmountable requirement, but almost. As far as she knew, all the First Rangers had previously been Royal Rangers. She was going to become one and get closer to achieving her dream, whatever it cost.

The three continued practicing while their thoughts swirled with the goals and aims they hoped to reach.

Chapter 15

Camu and Ona also turned to look at the Mage. Lasgol realized his friends were not camouflaged and that the Ice Magi had seen them.

"Surprised to see me? You and your creatures?" Maldreck said.

"Yes, surprised," Lasgol replied, trying to remain calm while he wondered how the Ice Mage could be there and the possible reason. The fact that Maldreck had discovered Camu worried him so much that he lost the thread of his own thoughts and restlessness settled in his stomach.

"I had guessed as much," Maldreck smiled triumphantly. "It never ceases to amaze me how stupid you are."

"Compared to?"

"Me, of course," the leader of the Ice Magi took a small, vain bow.

"What's the leader of the Ice Magi doing here?" Lasgol was trying to gain time to see how he could get out of this situation. He already guessed what Maldreck was doing there and what he wanted.

"I've come for what my predecessor hid here," he said, pointing at the box beside Lasgol.

"That box is ours," Lasgol said with a wave of his hand.

"Yours? You mean yours and those two beasts? I doubt that very much."

"It's mine. Eicewald left it to me."

"You, Eicewald, and your little games. Regrettable."

"Regrettable? Why is it regrettable?" Lasgol did not like the comment at all.

"Because of your little secret games. Do you really think I didn't know that Eicewald was secretly training you? I knew, and I also knew of the existence of this Creature of the Ice," he said with a nod toward Camu.

"You've been spying on us!" Lasgol accused him, pointing his finger at the mage.

"Of course I've been spying on you!"

"There was no need, we're not enemies."

Maldreck laughed with loud guffaws.

"An intelligent mage knows all of his rivals' movements. Eicewald was my rival, and I had him watched."

"Eicewald is dead. He's no longer a rival to you."

"True. In the end, only the best and most intelligent endure," he said, and his eyes shone with vain authority.

"The end hasn't arrived yet."

"It'll be the same, whether you like it or not, Ranger. I'll get my way in the end."

"There's no need for us to be enemies, not for this," Lasgol said, trying to calm things down.

"It's too late for that. You thought you could fool me. Simply pathetic. I'm much more brilliant than you."

"Even if you are, things might surprise you," Lasgol warned him.

"I doubt it very much. I want the contents of that box, now," he demanded, pointing at it.

"Why do you care what Eicewald has left me?"

"Oh, I do care. I saw that box in our Tower. I know it's a box that contains something issuing power inside it. Therefore, I'm sure that inside that box there's a worthy Object of Power. Otherwise Eicewald wouldn't have used that box, and he wouldn't have kept its contents secret."

"It's a personal gift, and it doesn't concern you."

"Everything that has to do with the Ice Magi concerns me. Everything that has to do with Objects of Power concerns me especially."

"How did you follow us here? I didn't see you doing it," Lasgol asked, puzzled. He could not understand how Maldreck could have done it without him realizing. He should have detected the ice.

Maldreck's face lit up with satisfaction for having fooled them.

"The great Ranger can't explain how I could have avoided his surveillance," he said, laughing heartily.

Lasgol felt awful. He could not figure out how Maldreck had done it.

"No, I don't know how."

"I'll tell you so you learn that you can't measure yourself against one who is way superior to you. Remember Eicewald's scroll?"

Lasgol had it in his satchel, inside the bag Maldreck had given to him.

"Did you bewitch the scroll?"

Maldreck laughed again with superiority.

"Not the scroll."

Lasgol understood then.

"The ice jewel…"

"Finally! I almost had to spell it out for you. The ice jewel isn't a gift from Eicewald, it's mine. It's enchanted with a locating spell. It gives out pulses of ice magic which I can feel from several leagues away, giving me its location."

"That's why I never saw you."

"I've always been out of range of your sight or your magic, at least two leagues away."

Lasgol bowed his head. Maldreck had thoroughly fooled them.

"I see…"

"As I said. Your attempts are regrettable. I'm much more powerful and intelligent."

"The game's not over yet," Lasgol replied, enraged. He was furious for having been fooled so easily.

"It has for you. Give me that box and we'll avoid bloodshed."

Ready to attack, Camu messaged.

Ona growled once and prepared to jump for Maldreck's throat.

The Mage raised his left hand. From among the bushes there appeared a dozen Norghanian soldiers led by an officer. They stood behind the mage. The Officer stood beside Maldreck.

Wait, we're not attacking.

No? want to take pearls.

If we attack, the soldiers will jump on us and we'll have to fight against them as well.

We can get soldiers.

Yes, but attacking Norghanian soldiers is considered treason, more so in times of war. We'd get into real trouble.

Not kill, only knock out.

Even so… it would be treason. No, we can't attack them.

"Captain Jakobson, Ranger Eklund refuses to give me that box which contains a magical Object of Power. If you'd be so kind as to explain that he has to do it…" Maldreck said and waved his left arm toward Lasgol.

The Officer, who was staring at Camu with wide eyes of surprise, focused on Lasgol.

"Why do you refuse, Ranger?"

"It's a gift of the late Leader of the Ice Magi. It's mine, there's no reason for me to give it away."

"That's not the point. It contains a magical object. By law, as the new leader of the Ice Magi, I have the right to take possession of any magical object found in the realm," Maldreck said in a harsh tone.

"We're not in Norghana," Lasgol pointed out, trying to find a way out.

"We're in the Utla, and we Norghanians consider it part of our territory," Jakobson said. "A Ranger should know that."

"The Norghanians have taken the Utla and we control it with our war ships. But it's not a Norghanian territory as such," Lasgol told him.

"That distinction is still irrelevant. I claim the magical object as Ice Mage. No one can stop me, least of all one of the King's Rangers."

"Maldreck is right, Ranger. Give him the magical object," Jakobson ordered.

"And if I refuse?" Lasgol defied the Officer calmly.

"In that case, me and my men will take it by force. It's not something I recommend."

I freeze officer.

No, take it easy. Don't attack.

The soldiers were tense, Lasgol could feel it. They were armed with axes and shields and were staring at Ona and Camu with distrust and fear in their eyes. More than Ona, who was a great cat and inspired fear, they were puzzled by Camu, since they had no clue as to what kind of creature he was.

"That won't be necessary, we'll hand the box over," Lasgol said so he would not have to attack his fellow countrymen. After all, they were only doing their duty.

"That's much better," Maldreck said, motioning Lasgol to hand it over to him.

Lasgol took the box and gave it to him.

"Don't open it, it's dangerous," he cautioned.

Maldreck glared at him with disdain.

"Please, don't insult my intelligence."

"You have no idea who you're messing with," Lasgol warned him.

"Oh, but I do know. I know the story of the Immortal Dragon that landed Gondabar in the Royal Dungeons. I was present when he told the King."

"Then you understand the seriousness of the matter. That dragon wants what's in this box."

"What I understand is that you've lost your mind, which interests me. If it's because of what's in this box, I want to have it and master it. It could become a powerful weapon. I'm thinking of a spell of Illusion Magic of great power and duration. That would explain why several people believe they've seen a dragon and will swear over and over, and will continue swearing despite the King's punishment."

"There's no Illusion Magic spell. We've seen it with our own eyes. The dragon is real. It killed Eicewald, and it will kill you if you don't tread carefully."

"If you think you're going to scare me with a mythological tale, I can assure you you'll fail," Maldreck laughed. "I don't know how Eicewald died, and I'm not interested either. Now that I'm the Leader of the Ice Magi, everything that was his is mine now."

"He died fighting against a dragon, whether you like it or not," Lasgol told him.

Captain Jakobson and his soldiers were beginning to feel uncomfortable with the conversation about magic and dragons.

"Are we going back to the ship?" Jakobson asked Maldreck.

"Yes, we are. I already have what I wanted."

Maldreck, Jakobson, and the soldiers turned around and started walking away. Lasgol did not want to lose the pearls.

"Can we come with you? Our barge is taking in water, and we'd most likely sink in the middle of the Utla," he told them.

Maldreck and Jakobson stopped and looked at each other.

"It's your war ship. I have no say in the matter, and I don't care," Maldreck said, lifting his chin. He knew he had won the game and really could not care less. He continued walking toward the ship that was anchored on the east side of the island.

"A Norghanian never leaves another adrift at sea, least of all a man of the King," Jakobson said. "You may join us."

"What about them?" Lasgol said with a wave to Ona and Camu.

"They're beasts. There's no place in my ship for beasts."

Lasgol was about to insist but decided it was better not to.

Wait for my return.

Why go?

We can't lose the pearls.

Ona growled twice.

I'll come back for you. I promise.

I believe.

Ona moaned once.

I won't be long, Lasgol promised, although he was not sure that would be the case.

"I come, they stay," he informed the Captain.

"Fine then, come along, Ranger," the Captain accepted.

Lasgol picked up his satchel and Aodh's Bow and then followed the soldiers. He gave one last glance of goodbye to Ona and Camu.

Good luck, Camu messaged.

Thanks, friend.

Ona moaned.

Chapter 16

Lasgol was sitting at the bow of the Norghanian assault vessel. They were heading north. Lasgol heard Captain Jakobson scolding some of his sailors. The mariner was at the helm in the stern and shouted orders to his soldiers every time he saw something he did not like. Lasgol realized those soldiers were sailors used to sailing on that ship. He guessed it was one of the war ships that regularly patrolled the Utla.

He had no idea how Maldreck had secured the services of Captain Jakobson and his ship, but he guessed that being the leader of the Ice Magi, he could request war ships if he needed them. A Ranger could not do it by himself, he needed authorization from Gondabar or the King. He remembered the painful fate of the leader of the Rangers at the hands of the King and felt a deep sorrow. He wished Gondabar could return to his Tower soon, although nothing would erase from his heart the punishment and dishonor he had suffered.

Maldreck was sitting in the center of the ship, beside the mast. He had Eicewald's box open and had been examining the twelve Silver Pearls all day. Lasgol had urged him not to do so again, but Maldreck had dismissed him rudely, threatening to turn him into a block of ice which the soldiers would then throw in the great river.

Lasgol had sighed. He knew the Mage was being serious. If he taunted Maldreck, the mage would attack him without mercy. Maldreck was dangerous. He was a viper who wanted to climb high. He would not hesitate for one moment in getting rid of anyone who might get in the way of his aspirations. In fact, he had not brought any of his fellow Magi. Lasgol could guess the reason. He did not want them to know about his finding. He wanted no rivals who later on might take his new treasure away from him, especially if it was as powerful as the pearls seemed to be.

Lasgol thought about Camu and Ona. He had had to leave them on the island. This gave him a feeling of restlessness, although he was sure they would handle themselves well. There was no danger there, but he hated being away from them. He could never be at ease when it came to them, and Lasgol wanted to be present just in case. Unfortunately, he had had no other choice but to go with the ship. He needed to see what Maldreck was going to do with the pearls.

He noticed the gleam of greed that appeared in the Ice Mage's eyes. For Maldreck, the pearls represented more power, and he was not going to give them to anyone by any means. That was going to be a problem, since Lasgol had to steal them somehow. Besides, it had to be before they reached the capital, since once he took them to the Tower of the Magi, they would be lost to Lasgol for good. Not even Viggo would be capable of getting into the Tower to steal them. Astrid had already told him, more than once, that the Tower was rigged with traps and protections of Ice Magic. Only a mage and if possible one of Ice, could enter the building and steal something from there that was well protected.

The breeze was warm and ruffled Lasgol's blond hair. The summer was already starting and it was his favorite season, together with the spring they were already leaving behind. He looked at the box. Somehow, he could feel the power the pearls emitted. He found it strange that he could pick it up, like this, without calling upon any of his skills. It was as if their power were so strong that it bathed him entirely and permeated into him. What he was feeling must have to do with his new magical state from having managed to repair his bridge. If it were not so, he would have felt the pearls in the past, and he had not. That had to be it—Magi were capable of sensing the power of objects without needing to use magic, simply because they were akin to magic itself. He seemed to be beginning to experience the benefits of having his mind and his energy source linked at last.

"You shouldn't manipulate them," Lasgol warned the Ice Mage as he saw him casting a spell on one of the pearls he had in his hand. He knew Maldreck would not listen, but he could not help himself.

Maldreck opened his eyes and gave Lasgol a glare of hatred.

"I told you not to interrupt me when I'm working."

"Those pearls emanate a power you don't want detected," Lasgol warned him.

"Yeah, by an Immortal Dragon no less. I know the tale to scare children you are spreading," the Mage replied in a mocking tone.

"Even if you won't believe me, you should know it's not a good idea to amplify the power those spheres emanate. Other beings, even magi, might pick it up."

"Oh, now it turns out that a couple of lessons from Eicewald have suddenly turned you into an expert mage," Maldreck replied in a disdainful tone.

"I'm no expert mage…"

"You can say that again," Maldreck interrupted him. "You're nothing but a Ranger who was born with the Gift. That's rare, I must admit, but it doesn't make you anything special and least of all a mage, although the illustrious Eicewald gave you a couple of lessons in magic. Remember that we find people with the Talent every now and then. Right now we're looking for new adepts to instruct. So don't think of yourself as special. And don't try to become a mage, you're too old for that."

"I'm not trying…"

"Don't even think about it," Maldreck interrupted him again. "Enjoy the small advantage that possessing the Talent offers you in the way of skills you might use with your bow and your forest traps and leave mage business to the Magi. Never forget that Magi are your betters, ones you must look up to with devotion, respect as superiors, and obey their orders without a word."

"That…"

"Shhh! Didn't you hear what I just said? Be quiet and obey those who are superior to you. Don't make me give you a lesson. I'd be delighted, and it would be one you wouldn't survive."

After Maldreck's death threat, and with the certainty that he was very capable of seeing it through, Lasgol had to keep quiet. He sighed. People like the mage who thought they knew everything and believed themselves superior to others were the most irritating. Lasgol reached into his satchel for a little cheese to eat and felt the bag with the scroll. He took it out and placed the ice jewel on his hand.

It was the jewel Maldreck had located them with. He started fiddling with it, trying to feel the magic it emitted and which Maldreck was somehow able to pick up from leagues away.

After handling it for a while, something interesting happened. He felt the hair at his nape rising. That meant there was magic very close. It must have been the one Maldreck had followed until he found them. How come he had not felt it before? He remembered he had not been touching the ice jewel. It had traveled with him inside his satchel in its own bag. That must have been the reason why he had not felt anything before and now could. Finding this out made him very curious. He might not be able to pick up all the magic of Maldreck's spell, but he could try.

The Mage saw the object in Lasgol's hand.

"You won't be able to detect it, no matter how hard you try. It only responds to my magic," Maldreck told him.

"In that case, it doesn't matter that I try."

Maldreck gave a disdainful guffaw.

"Try whatever you want, you insignificant Ranger."

Lasgol could not care less for his disdain. That Maldreck made fun of him left him indifferent. It was best to ignore certain people. But his words were true. The jewel had a spell so that only Maldreck could feel its magic. That was why neither Camu nor himself had been able to detect it.

He concentrated and began to study the jewel. Now, after repairing his bridge, he would likely be more sensitive to all types of magic, or at least he expected that to be the case. Since he was not detecting the magic, he guessed it meant that most likely Maldreck had not only put a locating spell on the ice jewel, but also one to hide it from other magical eyes. That was why he said that only he was able to detect it.

Taking into account his new power, Lasgol decided he would lose nothing for investigating this spell and the locating one. He might be able to learn something. Maldreck was still very concentrated casting spells on the pearls, so the mage would not bother him. He concentrated and called on his *Arcane Communication* skill, using it on the object. At once, something new happened. He saw two auras around the object. He had not been expecting that at all, so without meaning to his head jerked back and he hit the wooden board of the ship.

That was strange. Every time he used the skill, he found it almost impossible to distinguish some magic to interact with. The fact that all of a sudden two different auras had appeared was a significant achievement. The first aura was whitish, barely perceptible, but Lasgol was picking it up, not with his eyes but with his whole mind. This had to be the hiding spell. He focused on the aura and tried to communicate with it, to interact. At first, he felt a force reject his attempt. His mind immediately felt pain, a sharp sting.

Again, this caught him by surprise, and in a reflex act, he jerked his head back and hit it a second time. Now the front and the back of his head ached. Whoever said that most magic was painless had not experimented enough with it. It was clear that Maldreck's hiding spell also had an element of protection so it would not be accessed and manipulated by strangers. The truth was, it did not surprise him in the least, considering the kind of person the Mage was.

He snorted. The thing was to see whether he could deactivate that protection or not. Perhaps he should not have poked his nose where he should not, or in this case his mind, but he wanted to see whether he was able to neutralize it or not. He considered it almost a matter of pride. If he managed to do it, he would have obtained a tiny victory over the Ice Mage, but a victory after all. On the contrary, if he failed, he would feel disappointed, he also knew that, and disappointments with magic were constant. This he had engraved with fire in his heart.

Despite everything, he decided to try. He concentrated, closed his eyes, and let his mind, drawing on his pool of power, feed the skill and interact with the whitish aura. He prepared to bear the pain. A new sharp pang burst in his mind. This time his head did not jerk back, but he could not avoid the pain, and this made him stop the interaction. Things were not going well, which was not really surprising. The protection was there precisely so no one would tamper with it.

Knowing he would feel more pain, Lasgol prepared himself before trying again. He concentrated on shielding his mind to the attack of the spell. Since he only had one purely defensive skill, that of *Woodland Protection*, he focused on trying to create a similar one for his mind, something that would shield it from attacks. He spent a while thinking about what it might be. He did not need a big spell, just one that would shield his own mind's aura. He tried different approaches, but none worked.

He took a deep breath and concentrated harder. He already had the skill *Ranger Healing*, which had allowed him in the past to heal his mind from evil spells. He tried that. He focused on his skill and had it ready to be called upon when he interacted with the hiding spell again. The sharp pain returned. Lasgol tried to call upon his skill in the midst of the pain, but he could not. This was not going to work—it was very difficult to call on a skill when he was in such pain. Too difficult.

He had to shield himself before the pain hit him so he could defend himself. He thought for a moment, and then it occurred to him to combine *Woodland Protection* and *Ranger Healing*, but applied to his mind instead of his body. It was quite a desperate attempt, since Lasgol had not had much success combining already developed skills. If creating one was difficult, developing one that combined others was even more so.

Difficulties had always hung around him, and this was nothing but another one. He could do it. He simply had to put intelligence, will power, and a bit of luck in the act. Viggo would say it was easy as pie. Lasgol was not so optimistic. The difficulty was great, but he set himself to it. *Whoever risks nothing, gains nothing* was how the saying went, and it was very true, especially in magic.

He concentrated and started calling upon his *Ranger Healing* skill on his own mind's aura. As he was doing this he also called upon his *Woodland Protection* skill. The two skills seemed to mingle, and over Lasgol's mind aura a brown protective layer began to form. For an instant it surrounded Lasgol's whole mind. It was going to work. But suddenly it destabilized and, with a flash of failure, vanished.

"Almost…" he muttered under his breath. He looked at Maldreck, but he was still immersed in casting spells on the pearls. He did not seem to have noticed what Lasgol was doing. Besides, he most likely was not even interested.

Failure did not discourage him. He had been close to succeeding, and he tried again. For a long while he tried different ways of calling and amounts of energy in order to create the protecting skill he was after. He was about to give up when suddenly it happened. A protective greenish-brown layer surrounded his aura. Lasgol almost cried out in joy, but he managed to hold back, although he made a tight fist around the ice jewel.

Now, all that was left was to try his new skill, which he called *Mental Protection*. He called again on his *Arcane Communication* skill and interacted with the jewel. There was the reaction he already expected. The defense spell of the jewel attacked Lasgol's mind, but this time he met the attack. Lasgol readied himself for the pain, but this time there was none. His mind's protection weakened and started losing color, as if it were coming undone.

He knew he had little time. He sent a good amount of energy from his pool to interact with the protection skill. He concentrated on destroying it. To do so he used his *Ranger Healing* skill, as if the object's aura were a poison or toxic substance. The protection resisted. Lasgol did not stop and sent even more energy. Before he had not been able to send such great amounts, but he could now. The defense vanished, as if an antidote had finished with the toxin. The whitish layer vanished and underneath there was a bluish one: the locating one.

He had it. It seemed an incredible achievement. He had just overcome the defense spell Maldreck had created, and of which most certainty he felt very proud. It could be no other way. Thinking about it again, Lasgol figured it must be a strong spell. Maldreck did not dabble in small things, especially for something this important, which gave Lasgol an important feeling of pride.

Encouraged, he decided to try and manipulate the locating spell, which he now distinguished with a bluish aura. He wanted to see whether he could modify it so he could detect it and Maldreck could not. It was a most daring attempt, since it required interacting with the spell of another mage and, on top of that, modifying it. He thought it was too much to ask, but those who don't ask for much, never get anything at all in life. So he set to work on it.

He focused on the bluish aura, and with his *Ranger Healing* skill he began to manipulate it. He knew it was not the ideal skill, but he had no other way of interacting with it. The first attempts did not go well. He could not manage to exert any effect on that aura. The skill he was using sought to heal, and that was not the case now. What he needed was a skill to manipulate an existing spell.

He sent more energy to the aura and tried to modify it. He had the feeling that this situation was similar to one he was familiar with. That of repairing his bridge, changing the magic of Izotza into his own. Indeed, it was very similar. Sure of this similarity, he tried to do the same thing he had done with the steps on the bridge, only this time it was a locating spell. Calmly and without letting himself be frustrated, he tried to modify the blue of Maldreck's spell for his own green one. He set to work on it as he had worked on the bridge.

To his great surprise, there was a green flash, which informed him that he had created a new skill. The aura began to turn green from the original blue, slowly and gradually. Lasgol sent more energy from his inner pool and finished the transformation process. The aura was now green, a green he knew very well, that of his own magic. Once again, he felt great joy and was forced to open his eyes and check that Maldreck had not realized what was going on. The Ice Mage was still absorbed in the study of the Silver Pearls. He had his eyes shut and seemed to be somewhere else.

Now that Lasgol had transformed the spell, it should work for him. There was only one way to know. He manipulated it again and, injecting it with his energy, he sought to cause a green flash only he could feel. For a long while nothing happened, and Lasgol began to think it was not going well, but then suddenly there was the flash he was hoping for. And not only that—besides detecting the unequivocal flash, he knew where the object was. The locating spell was still working. That was amazing, since Lasgol did not know how to create that kind of spell, but he had managed to modify the one Maldreck had created and it now worked for him. More so, seeing the green color it now emitted, Lasgol knew that Maldreck could no longer detect it, since it emitted his own magic and not the Ice Mage's.

Driven by the excitement of his success, he tried to modify the rhythm to see whether he could make it emit faster locating pulses. He guessed it would take him a while and so it was, but he did it. The pulses, like green flashes, started coming at shorter intervals. Seeing that he had managed it, he changed his strategy and slowed them down so they came a lot slower. He also managed that after a good while trying.

It worked. That was wonderful. He wanted to cry out in triumph, but he held back. He decided to call his new skill *Magic Manipulation*, since it had allowed him to manipulate anther mage's spell. Giving names to his skills was not his strong point, he was aware of that. One day he would have to sit down and rename them all, something more striking and arcane. Indeed, he definitely needed to do that. Luckily there was no hurry, he could do it whenever he had a moment. Surely Egil would have good suggestions. And surely those of Camu would be odd.

Lasgol sighed. He was exhausted. Magic experimentation always left him feeling drained. Looking up at the sky, he noticed it was getting dark. He put the ice jewel in one of the many pockets in his Ranger's belt, intending to keep experimenting later. He noticed that Maldreck was still casting spells on the pearls. That mage was tireless. He reminded him of a bulldog, who once he had bit down he would not let go.

All of a sudden the ship swayed form port to starboard, as if it had hit a large sandbar. Lasgol jumped to his feet. They were in the middle of the river. They could not have hit anything. Or had they?

Chapter 17

Nilsa, Egil, Gerd, and Viggo were practicing with Raner and half a dozen Royal Rangers behind the Tower. It was a quiet place where no one would bother them. They were practicing basic positioning, which they had to learn first of all. Raner was explaining to them how they had to position themselves around the person they were supposed to protect. He insisted they had to be well positioned at all times and how important this was to be able to protect someone efficiently from an attack or ambush.

"Gerd, you're too far away, and you, Egil, are too close," he told them.

"Yes, sir," they said and corrected their positions.

"To make things easier we'll call the person you're supposed to protect 'the protectee'," Raner told them. "In most of the exercises I'll take on that role, but not always. Understood?"

"Yes, sir," Nilsa replied for the group.

"Very well. I'll now explain the difference between the defensive positioning regarding whether we act alone or not."

The four listened carefully to everything Raner said. First he explained how having the Royal Guard with them would affect their positioning. The Guard always covered the perimeter closest to the protectee, so the Rangers had to cover a wider outer area. To illustrate this, Raner took the place of the protectee and the Rangers acted as the Royal Guard. Raner told them where to stand and the distances to maintain with the protectee and the Royal Guard.

To make it more realistic, Raner started to move. His Rangers followed his movements as if they were the Guard and the Panthers did so too, but not as quickly or skillfully.

"Maintain the right distance, one eye on me and the other on the Royal Guard," he told them.

Raner moved in all four directions, walking slowly but with long strides.

"You have to keep up with me and not lose sight of the surroundings. Danger will most likely come from there."

"That's a lot to keep track of," Viggo commented. "We only have two eyes."

"Use them all the time."

"I feel like I have two left feet," Nilsa admitted, finding it hard to follow all the directions.

They continued the exercise, moving as a group in the four directions. At a signal from Raner, they changed course but had to keep moving in that direction, remaining as compact a group as they could, in unison and without tripping or missing a step.

After changing directions several times, Raner stopped giving the change signal. Now he swerved without warning. The Royal Rangers followed Raner as if they sensed which direction he was going to turn and when he was going to do so. They seemed to read his mind, they were so perfectly coordinated. Raner gave no indication and simply swerved at will and his men followed him without any trouble. It was obvious they had practiced a lot and had a great rapport.

That was not the case with the four Panthers, who were unable to sense the change of direction or when to make it, so they were in trouble. Once the change was made it was hard for them to adjust their pace and keep the required distances.

"Position, rhythm, distance," Raner kept saying and calling them out when they had difficulties.

They were trying their best to perform as well as possible. On paper it was not a difficult exercise—they only had to follow Raner and do what he did, maintaining their position and distance with the others. It was almost like a group dance, but the reality was very different. Gerd stumbled several times and lost his balance twice. He was having serious trouble maintaining the position because of the problems he was still experiencing from his injury which he had not fully recovered from. He had not told Raner because he did not want any special treatment. He was sure the First Ranger was aware of his situation, but he did not treat Gerd any differently. Gerd's greatest problem was with the abrupt changes in direction, which required him to turn quickly; this was hard for him and caused him to often lose his balance.

Gerd was not the only one having trouble, Nilsa was finding things hard too. She became nervous thinking about which new direction they would have to turn in and had tripped over her own feet three times already. This had made her lose her balance, and she had almost fallen on two of the Royal Guards. She was doing her best to relax and take it easy, since that was the only way to overcome her innate nervousness. And little by little she was succeeding, although she was certain her nervousness would not completely disappear.

Egil was doing pretty well and was not having too many difficulties. He was not turning fast enough, but he recovered well and was quickly following everyone's pace at the specific distance. Egil was enjoying the exercise. He understood the purpose and found it sensible. He saw it as surrounding the protectee with two defense layers to prevent anyone from reaching him or her. Once they learned how to move in unison with the protectee, they would be like two layers of armor protecting him or her and making it practically impossible to bring down the target. As he thought about it, he turned the matter around in his head and started to think of ways to do the opposite: reach the protectee in spite of the two layers of armor protecting them.

Viggo was having the most success. For him following the changes of direction instantly was easy, like a children's game. Keeping the position and the right distance was a bit more difficult because he found it unnatural. He was used to moving with total freedom, doing what he wanted when and how he wanted to. He lived off his reflexes and agility. Being restricted in what he could do did not suit him and he did not like it, so he did it reluctantly.

They continued exercising. They all gave the training their all, because they knew that what was at stake was nothing less than the lives of the King and Queen of Norghana. Finally, and after a few abrupt changes in course, Raner decided they had practiced enough.

"Pretty good," he told them after correcting their position several times in the final stage.

"Thank goodness," Gerd snorted. His forehead was covered in perspiration.

Raner addressed all four of them.

"Now we'll practice without the Royal Guard present. You'll be covering the protectee's immediate perimeter."

"Good, that's going to be even easier," Viggo commented.

Egil looked at him with a raised eyebrow, already picturing it in his mind. "I doubt it,"

Raner gave the order and they started the exercise. The Royal Rangers stood to one side. The First Ranger kept giving them indications in a calm but stern tone. He did not let anyone make a mistake, and these were now more evident since the four were surrounding Raner.

"It's fundamental to maintain the position around the protectee at all times," he insisted, correcting whoever made a mistake.

Contrary to what Viggo had thought and just as Egil had anticipated, this variation was more complicated, not just because they could not count on the help of the Royal Guard, who with their large bodies covered the protectee amply, but because it forced them to be more alert.

"What weapons must we use?" Nilsa asked.

"It will depend on the situation. As a rule, first the bow in case the attack comes from a distance. If they charge, you'll have to switch to your knife and axe. You must do so fast and without hesitation."

Egil nodded, thinking it made sense. They could not depend solely on their bows at close-combat distance. This was great for Viggo, because he could use his Assassin's knives and his light throwing dagger, but for the rest of the team it was not ideal, since they managed better with their bows.

After a series of decently well-executed exercises, Raner gave the order to stop.

"Very well. Now we're going to do a new exercise. Get into position," he ordered.

They all nodded and stood as they had been practicing: Gerd and Nilsa at the back of the Royal Ranger standing in as the protectee and Viggo in front with Egil.

"Off we go. Let's go around the Tower at a light trot," Raner ordered.

The group started and, following the pace set by the First Ranger, they went around the building, concentrating on not going too fast that they tripped on the protectee or too slow that he might bump into the Rangers in front.

They went around the Tower, careful not to lose formation. Suddenly, from behind a tree, Kol sped out and attacked the group's rear. Nilsa saw him approaching at full speed out of the corner of her eye.

"We're under attack!" she cried. "From behind!"

Gerd turned his head just in time to see Kol coming at them. They needed a defensive maneuver. Gerd and Nilsa started to turn

146

and drew their knives and axes as they did so. It was too late. They never finished the move. Kol leapt over them with great momentum, using all the inertia from his run. He elbowed both of them in the stomach and pushed them over. Nilsa was thrown to one side and Gerd bent over, winded from the blow.

Kol got to his feet like lightning.

Viggo and Egil had turned at the front and drawn their weapons.

At that moment, Haines, an unattractive but experienced Royal Ranger Nilsa also knew, appeared from one side of the Tower and lunged at Viggo and Egil, much like Kol had done.

They did not even see him. They were paying attention to the attack at the back and focused on defending the protectee, so they saw him too late.

Haines, who was as strong as he was ugly, ran over Egil. Viggo was almost able to dodge him, but as a consequence he was left badly positioned to counter the attack. He tried to turn to go for the attacker.

At the back, Gerd had recovered and managed to get some air in his lungs. He turned to try and stop Kol.

But Kol and Haines ignored the Panthers. Without even glancing at them, they lunged at Raner, who remained in the center, imperturbable. They "killed" him fictitiously, using their mock weapons without edges or points.

"End of the exercise. You've failed," Raner told the Panthers in a disgusted tone, shaking his head.

"It was all so… so fast… everything…" Gerd said, panting, trying to fill his lungs again.

"We weren't expecting an attack, we thought it was just an exercise to maintain pace and position. That was a dirty ambush," Viggo protested.

"You must always be alert. I've already told you that, and I repeat it every day. I'm not going to warn you when you're going to be attacked, just like an assassin won't   when the day comes and the attack is real."

"Yes, sir," Nilsa said, getting back on her feet.

"Two men defeated four," Egil said. "Very interesting."

Kol and Haines were watching them from the side. They looked sorry for the Panthers.

"I hope you've learned the lesson, because it will be repeated.

And I trust the result will be different next time."

"It will," Viggo promised angrily. He hated that they had done so badly so easily.

"Good. As a reward for how badly you've done, you'll be doing a double session tomorrow," Raner told them.

"Oh no…" Gerd said, looking horrified.

"I don't see why we have to go running around, we're in perfect physical shape," Viggo protested.

"That's not what it looked like to me. You were brought down or knocked off balance easily," Raner told them.

"Because you caught us by surprise, not for any other reason," Viggo snapped defensively.

"Besides, those two knew what they were doing," Gerd said, indicating Kol and Haines. The two Royal Rangers were now looking at Nilsa with apologetic grins. Nilsa could not help smiling back.

"Double run, and double strength session. When they hit you, they must encounter a wall of solid muscle rejecting them."

"The big guy is the mountain of muscles," said Viggo, "I'm wiry." Gerd blushed.

"We have muscle, though not in large quantities," Nilsa said.

"Well, it's time to improve that," Raner replied.

"It'll be good for us to do some exercise. It's good for the body and also for the mind," Egil said, smiling.

Gerd looked at him, uncomprehending. Why was Egil saying that? By nighttime they were going to be absolutely worn out.

"We'll repeat the basic exercises once again. I want you all moving in perfect unison," Raner told them.

They formed up again and continued practicing. It was tedious when there were not any surprise attacks, but little by little, the four Panthers felt like they were improving.

Gerd was not enjoying the training and practice. He had no specific wish to become a Royal Ranger, at least not the kind who spent their time guarding the King, or for that matter, the new Queen. He knew there were Royal Rangers who went on missions abroad for the King which did not involve body guarding, although those were rare assignments. Besides, being a Royal Ranger was not within his personal goals. He was not interested. He was already happy with all he had learned and achieved at the Shelter with the Specializations. Since he had no intention of becoming First Ranger or protecting the King or Queen, becoming a Royal Ranger did not make much sense to him. In his opinion, the best thing about being a Ranger was the opportunity to wander the forests and mountains and spend time among the wildlife. Being shut in the castle was no fun for Gerd. He missed being out in the Norghanian landscapes and enjoying nature in all her splendor. He just wanted to finish the training quickly and be able to leave the city.

Nilsa, on the other hand, was happier every day with their training to become Royal Rangers. At first she had found it pretty difficult, but the more she practiced, the more she enjoyed it and the happier she was. The fact that among the Royal Rangers there were a number of handsome men who all tried to win her favors was an added bonus. If she managed to become a Royal Ranger, she would become part of this elite group and would be one of them, which was even better. Besides, she would be working with the Royal Guard, where there were also strong, tall, and strikingly handsome young men, which was another point in favor of the whole thing. When it came to anything else, being a Royal Ranger did not interest her that much. It was not what she wanted to be, and she did not have Ingrid's ambition of becoming First Ranger. She wanted to be the best Mage Hunter in Tremia. That was her wish. The rest, position and rank, did not interest her much. Yes, it was nice to go up the Rangers' ladder, but it was not something Nilsa wanted that much. But anyway, since she had no choice other than to train, she was going to. She only hoped she would not be assigned to protect Thoran or his brother. That was something she would not like at all.

Viggo, just like Astrid had done already, was beginning to understand that becoming a Royal Ranger might be very good for him. He was going to learn the ways to protect Royalty, which would allow him to find the weak points and exploit them: no one better than an expert at something to then turn the situation around. If he was already exceptional in the art of delivering death to enemies, this new training was going to provide him with the means to be even more deadly. This pleased him and made him feel good. Now, not even kings would be out of the reach of his lethal knives, not the Norghanian rulers nor those of other kingdoms, since their protection systems would be similar. Indeed, the more he thought about it, the more he saw the benefits of this training. One day he would have to kill a king, and when that day arrived, Viggo would be ready for the mission. He would not fail. He would become a regicide, and bards and troubadours would fatten his legend with new epic odes to his name. Yes, the future was looking bright for Viggo, or at least so he saw it. He stopped complaining at practice and focused on learning and learning well. That instruction was worth its weight in gold, this was clear to him.

Egil was another Panther who was not enjoying the training much. Just like Gerd, he did not want to be a bodyguard for the King or the Royal Family and the practice was a pain, especially the physical part. But he also appreciated the advantages of knowing the workings of a King's guard, like Viggo and Astrid were already realizing. The knowledge they were acquiring would be very useful in the future, so he saw it as a positive thing. He did not miss a single detail of what Raner or the other Royal Rangers explained to them about the different protection systems, variations, shifts, rotations, etc. He memorized everything and wrote it down in one of his notebooks afterward. He had the feeling that all the information he was gathering was going to come in handy later on.

Raner finished the training session and let them go. The four friends were left in front of the Tower, chatting a little about everything they had learned that day. They still had a lot of learning ahead of them, but they were progressing, and that cheered them all up. Kol and Haines joined them, along with two other Royal Rangers.

"You're doing very well," Kol said encouragingly.

"Raner doesn't think so," Viggo replied.

"Raner's like that. Tough but honest," Haines said.

"You have a lot of experience," Nilsa said. "You have years of advantage on us."

"Knowing you, with all the qualities you have, it will take you no time to reach our level," Kol said with a seductive smile.

Haines did not want to be left behind and also praised Nilsa.

"And we don't have your sympathy and beauty. Those are sharp weapons as well."

Nilsa blushed.

"Ahhh, don't exaggerate," she said, waving it aside, though it was obvious she enjoyed the praise they were giving her.

"I have those traits too," Viggo interrupted, passing a hand through his dark hair.

"Absolutely, you're the nicest person in Norghana," Gerd said with a guffaw.

"And the handsomest, don't you forget."

"Without a doubt!" Egil said, laughing too.

In a good spirit of camaraderie, the Royal Rangers and the four Panthers went on talking. The following day they were going to have a double exercise session, but that would be the following day, and it was not worth thinking about right then. They let the good atmosphere and easy conversation continue. One day, if everything went well, although that was not often the case with the Panthers, they would be part of the Royal Rangers. Kol and Haines and their comrades knew this and were supportive, since they were aware of the talents the Royal Eagles possessed and were grateful for the reinforcement to their corps after the murder attempts. Perhaps with the Panthers' aid any future attempts would fail or would not even take place. They would have to wait and see what happened.

Chapter 18

A second blow which almost knocked Lasgol down onto the deck made it clear they had hit something. Something big and solid, since the war ship was very stable. He was puzzled. All around there was only water, and it must be considerably deep.

"Watch out! We've hit something!" Captain Jakobson warned.

Hit what?" Maldreck asked while he put away the pearls in Eicewald's box and then stood up.

The sailor-soldiers were looking over port and starboard and were wondering the same thing as Lasgol. What could they have bumped into if they were in the deepest part of the river which was well laden with water?

The answer was not long in coming. A shadow, longer than the ship itself, appeared underneath it, moving with it. They all stared at it with fear in their eyes, for its size and what it might mean. They could see it from any point of the ship.

Suddenly, beside the bow, the shadow came out of the water and rose above the ship. Lasgol grabbed Aodh's Bow and leapt backward while he nocked an arrow in a reflexive movement. He raised his gaze and what he saw froze him. The head of a huge sea serpent appeared higher than the ship's mast. Its mouth was open wide, revealing enormous fangs. It was hissing threateningly, and the sound was as terrifying as the beast's size.

"Monster at the bow!" Jakobson shouted in warning.

The soldiers ran to get their weapons. They kept looking at the nightmare creature that hovered above them showing its deep maw, and deep-yellow reptilian eyes above the mouth. The scales covering the body of the beast were a copper green and larger than the shields of the Norghanian soldiers.

Maldreck grabbed his Ice Mage staff and cast a spell on himself without wasting an instant.

The head of the great sea serpent came down on the deck and took three soldiers in one sweep before returning to the depth of the great river.

"It's attacking us! Defend the ship!" Jakobson ordered as he shouted hither and thither.

Lasgol was aiming in every direction, but the serpent did not resurface and he could not release. The soldiers armed themselves with bows and spears instead of their axes, since there were not enough for all. Lasgol began to call upon all his skills, both the defensive ones like *Woodland Protection* and those of improvement like *Cat-Like Reflexes*. Multiple green flashes issued from his body one after the other. It did not take him long to call upon all of them, the daily practice going over his list allowed him to activate them a lot faster now.

"It will attack again! Get ready!" Maldreck warned as he went on conjuring.

The ship suffered another blow and half the soldiers fell down while the other half grabbed the board, ropes, or anything else they could find. Two were not so lucky and fell into the river amid cries of help, unable to hold on to anything.

"By all the deep seas! That beast's going to make us capsize!" cried Jakobson.

Then, on the starboard side, the huge sea serpent surfaced and rose again above the ship's deck. Its deadly mouth was gaping, revealing stinky fangs dripping with some dark-colored venom.

Lasgol released. The bow flashed with golden light and the arrow headed straight to the open maw. It buried itself inside and the sea serpent felt it, because it shook its enormous head and hissed with rage.

An ice missile in the shape of a trident hit the serpent in the neck, just below the mouth. Again the beast shook itself furiously. Maldreck's attack had hurt it. The Mage had two protective spheres around him, the first one for anti-magic, although the monster did not appear to have magic, or had not made use of it so far. The second one was a solid sphere of ice to protect the Mage from physical attacks.

"Attack!" the Captain shouted to his soldiers.

Several arrows sought the beast's body, but upon reaching it they bounced off. They could not pierce through the scales.

Lasgol saw what was happening and immediately called upon his *Multiple Shot* skill. There was another green flash that ran through Lasgol's arms. The bow flashed too, but gold, and from it there flew three arrows at lightning speed which plunged into the beast's neck where Maldreck had hit it with his magic. Unlike the arrows of the Norghanian soldiers, which were not able to penetrate the scaled skin of the monster, Lasgol's did and went in deep. Lasgol realized this was because of Aodh's Bow.

The serpent attacked furiously. The head came down fast and sprayed the deck with a dark substance that poured out of its fangs. It had to be venom. Lasgol used his improved reflexes to move away and was not hit. Several soldiers were unable to escape and the venom fell on them. It turned out it was not only toxic but also acidic. The soldiers fell amid cries of terror, the acid penetrating their armor and the toxin ravaging their faces. Those who were not hit tried to wound the monster with their spears and axes. The tips of their spears were deflected as if they were hitting metal and the axe blows bounced off without leaving a single scratch on the body of the huge reptile.

Maldreck sent a dozen missiles of ice, which hit the serpent in the head. It hissed again fiercely. The Ice Magic was wounding it. Lasgol was able to glimpse some kind of viscous yellow blood. He used his *True Shot* skill, amplifying the power, and his arrow sunk deep inside its mouth. The monster dived again to avoid Lasgol's arrows and the magic of the Ice Mage.

"We tack to starboard!" the Captain cried as he began the escape maneuver with the few soldiers left standing.

"We must get to shore!" Maldreck yelled at him. His ice shield had been affected by the corrosive venom, and he was trying to regenerate it with his magic.

A new thrust almost capsized the ship completely. Another soldier fell in the water, unable to hold on to something in time. Lasgol prepared himself. The serpent was going to come out again to attack. He stepped back to where the Captain was at the helm while Maldreck stayed by the mast, concentrating on improving his defenses.

The beast came out of the water on the port side, and instead of attacking the crew, it went for the mast, which it broke with a tremendous blow. Lasgol released and wounded the mouth and neck of the sea monster. Maldreck had to move so the mast did not fall on him. He conjured a frost beam, which he threw at the colossal reptile's head. The beast did not like the attacks, and it went underwater once again.

"Blasted freshwater monster! To the oars, everyone, to the oars!" cried the Captain desperately.

As if it were answering the Captain, the great serpent surfaced again suddenly and devoured three more soldiers as they tried to fit the oars. It dived in again when it saw Lasgol and Maldreck ready to attack it.

The problem now was that they had no sails or crew. There were only a couple of soldiers and Captain Jakobson left. The serpent gave them no quarter and attacked again at the bow, only this time, instead of rising above the ship it coiled around it, embracing the whole ship with its extremely long and thick scaly body. It seemed like it wanted to strangle the ship. Lasgol realized that the serpent was almost twice as long as the ship itself. He was dumbfounded by its size and girth.

While Lasgol and Maldreck were attacking the head of the serpent, it began to squeeze the ship. The crunching noise of the wood as it was squashed by the strength of the tremendous body of the beast was chilling.

"It's going to destroy the ship!" Captain Jakobson cried from the helm.

The beast was too large. Lasgol released arrow after arrow but realized that he would need to put about a hundred arrows in its body in order to affect it significantly. The beast squeezed harder as it slid over the captured ship, advancing toward Lasgol and the Captain.

There was another terrible crunch.

The ship was breaking under the terrible pressure the monster was exerting. More crunches followed the first while the ship fell to pieces under the pressure.

Maldreck considered the situation lost and grabbed the box with the pearls in an attempt to escape the ship.

The serpent attacked Lasgol and Jakobson. Lasgol managed to dodge it with a prodigious leap. But Jakobson was devoured in one gulp.

The ship was finally completely destroyed within the coils of the great serpent's body, which with a sudden swerve attacked Maldreck.

The Mage saw the mouth heading toward his head and, leaving the box on the deck, attacked with another frost beam. The serpent ignored it, and instead of attacking the Mage, it closed its mouth on the box with the pearls. A huge viper's tongue appeared and grabbed it, and with an upward movement swallowed it.

"No!" Maldreck cried as he tried to react. But the deck under his feet vanished in a multitude of pieces of broken wood. The Mage fell into the river with a muffled scream.

The serpent opened its mouth to hiss in triumph.

Lasgol also realized he was losing his footing and falling into the water. As he started to fall, he had a fleeting idea. He reached into his Ranger's belt, and with the last hold of his right foot for support, he threw the ice jewel straight into the mouth of the beast. It went down its maw as the big mouth closed. A moment later, Lasgol entered the water surrounded by the thousands of pieces of wood that had been a Norghanian war ship.

He entered the water still holding the bow in his left hand. He did not want to lose it. The river was deep and had a strong current. If he let go of it, he would have a very hard time recovering it. While he swam through the remains around him, he glimpsed the body of the great serpent as it veered and headed south, zigzagging and gaining depth. Lasgol slung the bow across his back while he held his breath underwater and watched the monster leave.

He felt the lack of air and, kicking hard, he broke the surface and breathed to fill his lungs again. He looked around. He saw a couple of dead soldiers' bodies floating by. To his left he saw Maldreck holding on to a large piece of floating wood, a part of the bow from the looks of it, he was letting himself drift downstream.

Lasgol tried to see whether there was any other survivor for him to help. He searched among the floating remains of the ship, but he could not find a single soldier. The only ones who had managed to survive the attack had been him and Maldreck. He swam among the remains a little longer to make sure that was the case while he called upon his skills again so he could see and move better amid all that wreckage.

Before stopping, he dived underwater again to see whether he could see anyone. But he did not find anyone to save, so he resurfaced to breathe. Then he let himself be carried by the current, holding on to a large piece of wood from the stern. He let the river take him while he rested a little and recovered his strength. He saw he was losing sight of Maldreck, who was drifting to the opposite shore carried by the current. The truth was, he was glad to lose sight of the mage.

While he let the current take him to the other shore, he thought about the attack. He had never seen a creature like that. It was too colossal to be a simple river serpent. It was a monster, and as such it had something to do with Dergha-Sho-Blaska. The activities of great reptilian creatures had increased since the appearance of the Immortal Dragon. Lasgol wondered where it might have come from. The bottom of some sea abyss? He had to dismiss the idea since it had appeared in the Utla, which meant it was a freshwater monster. Where it had been hiding until now was another great mystery.

What he did know for sure was that Dergha-Sho-Blaska had sent it, since it had gone for the Silver Pearls. That could have only been done on orders from the Immortal Dragon. This monster must be one of its servants. Instead of coming himself to do the dirty work of taking the pearls, he had sent the great sea serpent. Maldreck had been manipulating the pearls ever since he got them, which had no doubt drawn the attention of either Dergha-Sho-Blaska or the serpent, which must have already been on the lookout for them.

Lasgol favored the second option. The serpent must have been already looking for them and was closer than Dergha-Sho-Blaska. Perhaps the dragon was not in the area, or even in Norghana. Who could tell? Lasgol would certainly like to know. He held on to the wooden piece that helped him float. It was already night, and the stars were beginning to shine in the sky.

Suddenly, he felt a pulse of green light shining in the distance. He did not know how, but he knew it was the ice jewel with the locating spell. More than that, he could tell it was to the east, about half a league away. It was not exactly that he could see it, he sensed it, as if he felt it. It was strange—his idea was working. The great serpent had swallowed the Silver Pearls but also his locating ice jewel so he could follow the monster.

He realized he had done it so as not lose the Pearls, but now there was another factor to take into consideration: it was more than likely that the serpent would meet with Dergha-Sho-Blaska somewhere to deliver the cargo. If that were true and Lasgol managed to follow the serpent, he would encounter the Immortal Dragon. That was going to be dangerous and troublesome. He might lose his life. Dergha-Sho-Blaska would have no mercy.

While he let the water carry him away, he looked around. The destruction of the war ship had been a tragedy. Norghanian lives had been lost, good soldiers' lives. Nothing could compensate the loss of lives, no matter how noble or altruistic the goal was. The only consolation he had left was that perhaps, with a bit of luck, their deaths would not be in vain. Their death in the battle against the serpent was going to lead him to Dergha-Sho-Blaska. Surviving that encounter would be something else altogether.

Chapter 19

Lasgol left the remains of the war ship and swam toward dry land. He could see the tall grass and some trees in the distance, so he swam hard to get closer. It took him a long swim to reach the shore; it was farther than it looked. Distances in the water were always tricky and hard to calculate. Thank goodness he was a good swimmer and was in god shape. The life of a Ranger prepared one for situations like this.

With a nimble push, he stood on a grass-covered mound on the shore and shook the water off his body while he tried to decide where he was. He needed to know approximately where in the river he was in order to go back to the island to fetch Ona and Camu. Now he was glad they had not come with him, they would not have liked the dip at all, and Camu was not a very good swimmer.

The problem was that it was now dark and finding out where he was with only the help of the stars and constellations was never easy. He crouched down and called on his *Guiding Light* skill. A white light appeared floating in front of his head. He brought out Egil's map and calculated how far from the island the ship had come in the time he had been on board. Then he looked up at the stars and refined the calculation. He managed to piece together a pretty exact idea of where he was.

He thought he should follow the sea serpent before losing it entirely. The good news was that the serpent was heading south, to where the Weeping Island was. There was no time to waste. He adjusted his bow on his back and began to run, following the course of the river to the south. The evening was warm and the sky was clear, so there was good visibility. The land was flat and soft from the grass, so he made good time.

He ran all night, making small stops to rest. One of the things a Ranger was well trained in was to save their strength, since once it ran out and they no longer had any energy they were useless. So, Lasgol always knew when to stop and recuperate his strength.

He had lost his satchel in the fight with the serpent, so he had no food supplies. This was a problem, because it might force him to stop and find something to eat. Water would not be an issue—he had plenty running alongside him. On the other hand, he was used to going without eating for a few days; he had done it before. He would recover his energy afterward with a good meal.

He continued running and reached a small Norghanian Army post by the river. It was marked on his map. He decided to ask for a horse and not give too many explanations. Being a Ranger, they should provide him with one, even if they found it odd. Or at least he hoped so. The fort, half stone and half wood, rose on a hilltop almost touching the river. It had a tall watchtower built of wood on one side used to control who went up or down the great river.

He presented himself at the entrance and they let him through. The fort was a small, rudimentary one, but good enough for surveillance missions. It would also withstand a couple sieges if necessary.

"A horse?" the Officer at the top of the battlement asked, surprised.

"Yes, mine had an accident," Lasgol said. He had climbed up to speak to him. It was not the whole truth, but it was not a complete lie either.

"This is the first time I've seen a Ranger lose his mount."

"There's always a first for everything," Lasgol replied with a shrug.

"Yeah, that's true. Good, we'll give you the horse, it's a Masig Pinto," the Officer said, indicating the pen behind the small fort. There were about a dozen pinto horses.

"Trouble with the Masig?" Lasgol asked, wondering where they had come from. The Norghanians were good wild horse trainers. They must have gotten them from one of the tribes of the steppes on the other side of the river.

"Those filthy savages of the steppes are always making trouble," the Officer said with hatred in his tone. "We met with one of their many tribes and took them from them."

Lasgol knew this had not been done without violence. The Masig would never relinquish their horses willingly. They had to have fought and lost. So many rivalries and ancestral hatred among the different realms and tribes of Tremia were most discouraging and frustrating. Lasgol could not understand why they could not reach agreements to work together and that way all could prosper, instead of getting involved in endless, pointless fighting which made the people suffer.

"If you don't mind, I would like to be on my way. I have an important mission," was Lasgol's reply, so as not to let himself be dragged into that conversation.

"Are you heading south?" the Officer asked.

"Yes, south." Lasgol was not going to give more information.

"Good luck then. I hope you come back."

"So do I," Lasgol nodded and headed down from the battlement toward the pen.

One of the soldiers looking after the horses handed him one with a Norghanian saddle. The moment he got on, Lasgol realized the horse did not like the saddle at all. The Masig as a rule never used them. It took horse and rider a while to get used to the new situation, but in the end they managed.

Lasgol rode swiftly, following the river toward the island. He went as fast as the beautiful Pinto could go, which was very fast. Suddenly he felt a green flash in his mind—it was the ice jewel. This meant that he was once again within range of the jewel. This was good news. The serpent had not escaped him, at least for now. He urged his horse to gain on the serpent. He did not know yet how fast that monster could swim, but it could not go faster than a Masig horse at full gallop.

It did not take him long to reach the jetty where he had hired the barge to go to the island. He dismounted and hastened to knock on the ruinous hut's door. The boatman did not open the door. He did not appear to be at home or else he was sleeping. Lasgol opened the door and walked in. He found the boatman sleeping it off. The smell of alcohol was noticeable throughout the hut. He approached the man, who was sleeping on his stomach and snoring loudly, and shook him hard to wake him up.

"What the….!"

Wake up, I need another barge."

"Huh…?" The boatman eyed him for a moment, and the next he fell asleep again.

Lasgol shook him a couple of times more but could not wake him up. He was too drunk. In that state, he could be quartered alive with an axe and he would not even notice. Lasgol felt sorry for the man, even if he suspected he was not a good person. The fact that he drank did not excuse him.

He went to the jetty and the barge that was taking in water. He inspected it closely, if he took it he risked sinking soon after beginning to cross the river but if he did not he had no other means of getting to the island where Camu and Ona were waiting for him. He had to try and communicate with Camu but the island was too far away for any mental message to reach his friend. Still, he had to try. He concentrated and tried to call upon his *Animal Communication* skill, using a large amount of energy to amplify its range.

Camu, can you pick up my thought? Lasgol transmitted and waited with closed eyes and open mind for an answer. A moment went by and the answer did not come. Lasgol considered he had failed.

He tried again, sending a greater amount of energy to his skill, not only to increase the range but also the power of the thought. Not being able to see the aura of the receiver he was sending the thought blindly and Camu picking it up was going to turn out difficult. Luckily, Camu and Ona were used to sending messages in all kinds of situations and environments. As a rule they were able to communicate even if they did not pick up their mind auras. Lasgol was hoping that on this occasion such a communication would also take place.

I'm at the jetty, he transmitted. He felt a large amount of his energy consumed so he knew the thought had gone out. Now it was only a matter of Camu picking it up. He waited another moment, nothing, there was no answer.

He decided to try one last time sending more energy to the skill, as if he were maximizing it.

I'm coming for you, he transmitted. The energy was consumed, so he knew that the thought had gone out, He waited a moment but there was no answer, he had to admit defeat. Either his thoughts were not reaching the island —most likely- or else they did but Camu was unable to pick them up. In any case this was not working.

He would have to go for them without warning. The thing was he did not know how he was going to do that. He would have to improvise to repair the leaking barge. He looked at the derelict hut, he could get wood and nails from there and use his axe as a hammer. He could even use his knife for sawing.

He got down to it with determination. He pulled the barge out of the water with the help of the two horses he now had: the Pinto and the one he had first brought with him which was tethered to a tree behind the hut. He turned the barge over, also with the help of the horses, and studied the problem. There were two large cracks in the hull through which the water was coming in. He would have to seal them.

He went over to the hut and looked for two boards he could use. He found them and pulled them off with the help of his knife. He also looked for nails and rivets and pulled them off as well. He carried it all back to the barge and set to work. He knew the repair would not hold for long, but if it served to get to the island and back it would be more than enough.

Despite the noise of the work the boatman never woke up, he must have had a whole crock of the strong firewater of the north. Lasgol worked hard to seal the cracks on both sides. In other circumstances he would have made a kind of glue from resin to completely seal the cracks, but he had no time to search for resin and prepare the compound. The snake was traveling south along the river and they had to follow it.

A temporary repair would have to suffice. He pushed the vessel into the water and checked how much it took in. Very little, it would do. He got in, grabbed the oars and started to row. As he moved away from the jetty and the water started coming in, he realized that this had not been his best decision. He rowed with all his might going as fast as he could to minimize the amount of water seeping in.

He rowed and rowed, and every now and then, he looked for the island. It was nowhere to be seen. The river Utla was really a large river. He went on rowing while the water was beginning to rise in the bottom of the barge. It was already covering his feet and would soon reach above his ankles. Things were not looking good.

All of a sudden, coming from the opposite direction, he saw a barge. He looked at it blankly. It was coming from the island which he could begin to glimpse in the distance. Lasgol strained his neck and called upon his *Hawk's Eye* skill. What he saw struck him numb. At the bow of the barge was Ona like she was the figurehead of the vessel. Camu was at the stern and he had his long tail in the water. He was flashing blue which meant he was using his magic. It took Lasgol a moment to realize what he was seeing. Camu was using his *Tail Whiplash* skill to propel the barge with his tail.

"I can't believe this …" he muttered in astonishment.

163

In some way which Lasgol was unable to understand, Camu was managing to make the barge sail with his magic and his tail. Not only that but it was traveling pretty straight, with slight deviations to port and starboard which Camu corrected with each whiplash of his tail.

Lasgol! he received Camu's message along with a feeling of joy and surprise.

Camu! Ona! Lasgol greeted them with one of his oars.

We sail.

I can't believe it.

Sail much good.

"*I see,* Lasgol transmitted seeing how they were approaching his own barge.

I much sailor.

I see it and cannot believe it, Lasgol was stunned.

Ona and Camu's barge reached Lasgol's.

You sink, Camu messaged in warning.

Yeah, I know.

You no good sailor like me, Camu messaged proudly.

The worst thing was that Camu was not joking, he was serious. He believed himself a better sailor.

We'll talk about that later. Whose idea was it?

Ona. She moved her big tail in barge.

Lasgol sighed deeply. What a pair those two.

Impressive.

You come to our barge. If not you sink.

Lasgol had to admit they were right. He stepped into their barge and sat at the bow with Ona who licked his face and hair.

To the jetty, please, he said to Camu who used his skill and his tail propelled the barge forward.

Lasgol was quiet the rest of the way. He was speechless. When he told the others about this they were not going to believe him. Vigo certainly was not.

Chapter 20

Raner sent one of his Royal Rangers to the Tower to tell Astrid, Ingrid, and Molak to join him in the anteroom of the Throne Hall. Ingrid and Astrid were already ready, and Molak joined them downstairs at the Tower door, since he shared lodgings with other Specialists on the second floor. Nilsa had suggested they let Molak use Lasgol's bed, but Viggo had flatly refused. He had even insinuated there might be an accident and Molak might end up with his throat cut. As it would have happened with Viggo in a sleep-walking state, they would not be able to blame him. With such threats, they decided not to take any risks. Molak would not share lodgings with them.

The three went to meet Raner at once, along with the Royal Ranger who had come to fetch them.

When they arrived, they found Raner and three veteran Royal Rangers. They knew one of them; it was Mostassen. They had met him during the war mission against Darthor during their fourth year at the Camp.

"Sir, you summoned us?" Ingrid asked formally.

"Yes, indeed. I'm pleased you came so quickly."

"Mostassen, it's been a long time," Astrid greeted the old veteran.

"Astrid, Ingrid, Molak," Mostassen returned the greeting with a slight nod.

"You know Mostassen?" Raner was surprised. "He's not usually found at the castle."

"We know the Tireless Tracker from the war against Darthor and his allies of the Frozen Continent," Ingrid explained.

"We served under him while we were still training at the Camp," Astrid added.

"I've been on a couple of missions under him," Molak said.

Mostassen nodded and smiled in acknowledgement.

"Well, Tremia is small indeed," Raner commented.

"Time hasn't passed by him," Astrid commented, "he's exactly as we remember him." It was true, he had not aged one little bit. He was still the vivid image of a Norghanian warrior: strong of shoulder and

165

arms, tall, with long blond hair. His light green eyes seemed to see it all, and his square Norghanian jaw could take any hook or punch.

Mostassen shook his head but said nothing. Astrid remembered that, contrary to the typical barking, brute Norghanian soldier, Mostassen was very quiet. He hardly spoke. He used to give his orders by gesturing. She wondered if he would be more talkative now, but she doubted it. That was a personal trait that did not change with time. She also remembered something that worried her. Mostassen knew a little about Egil's past and that of the Panthers, which might put them all at grave risk. She would have to make sure they were still safe.

"May we ask what he's doing here, sir? It wouldn't be because of us, would it?" Ingrid asked. She must have been thinking the same as Astrid. That Mostassen was there could be a coincidence, or a serious problem which might explode in their faces at any moment.

"Mostassen is recovering from a wound in his leg," Raner told them. "As soon as he's fully recovered, he'll go back to tracking. The King needs good trackers at the border with Zangria."

"Well, we're happy to see you," Astrid said.

The others nodded, smiling.

"As you see, the Royal Rangers, and the Veterans in particular, can perform many functions. Today, Mostassen will act as your instructor. That's what comes from being experienced."

"Yes, sir," Ingrid replied.

"Good. Now let's focus on the training. Today it will be on how to protect their Majesties in enclosed spaces, like the Throne Hall," Raner explained. "It's one of the main functions of the Royal Rangers, since monarchs don't tend to spend time in open fields, except on rare occasions like visits, hunting parties, parades, or tournaments. As a rule, they spend most of their time safely within their castles or fortresses. Therefore, it's necessary to be clear on how to proceed at all times when they are inside."

"Understood, sir," said Astrid, who was aware that most of the time the Royal Rangers stood against walls or next to columns, watching the hall where the King was.

"Good, follow me to the Throne Hall," ordered Raner as he pushed open the great double doors and led the way.

The others followed after him. Astrid always felt something weird in the pit of her stomach when she entered that hall. She saw the long corridor where several soldiers of the Royal Guard were posted and knew it was because this was where King Thoran and his brother Orten usually were. Now, of course, Queen Heulyn would be there as well on many occasions, and with her would be the Panthers, so they were going to have to be in the hall often. That was not good. What tended to happen in that Throne Hall was almost never good.

"At this early hour you'll only find the Royal Guard here in the Hall," Raner told them.

"And the Royal Rangers, sir?" Ingrid asked.

"They're only on duty when the King is present. Given the increasingly complicated political situation and the imminent risk, I've ordered them to cover parts of the castle," Raner said and pointed to the far end, to the thrones, behind which four Royal Rangers stood on guard.

Ingrid nodded.

"Our main goal is to protect the King and accompany him at all times, together with his Royal Guard. Or we will go on missions when the King commands."

They passed by the Royal Guard posted in the corridor and reached the thrones of the King and Queen. Raner stopped there. Calmly, he explained the details of where the Panthers needed to stand if they had a shift in the Throne Hall. He indicated the positions to take in the hall, one by one.

"In each shift, like now," he said, indicating the four Royal Rangers behind the thrones, "the most veteran Ranger will be who establishes everyone's position. But you must all know the positions by heart, not only those of the Throne Hall, but those of the other important areas of the castle where you might have to stand guard."

"The castle is very big, sir…" Molak said, implying there were infinite places where they might be posted.

"It is, but we only take positions at specific places, those we've concluded are the best for protecting the King. Consider that his Majesty doesn't wander throughout the whole castle. He only walks along certain places, either for his pleasure or because of his position."

"Is there a map that pinpoints the places we must position ourselves at?" Molak asked.

"No, there isn't, and the reason for that should be obvious." Raner turned to them and studied them with narrowed eyes.

Astrid, Ingrid, and Molak thought about it.

"Because, if there were... it could be stolen or copied... and the enemy would have a map of the castle's interior," Ingrid guessed.

"And they would know where the King is inside, since the watch posts indicate it, and that's even worse..." Astrid added.

"If it were to fall in the hands of the Zangrians, they might attempt an attack..." Molak said. "That would be a problem indeed."

Raner was looking at them as if he were analyzing them.

"Good guesses, all of them. Some time ago there was a tome that detailed everything, with schematics and maps of the castle and the areas where the King and his family moved about. Using good judgment, our leaders decided to commit it to memory and then destroy it. Now it's passed down orally. The leader of the Rangers passes it down to the First Ranger, and he passes it on to the Royal Rangers."

"That's a brilliant system, sir," Molak said. "That way the secret is kept between a small group of Rangers. Because I understand it's not revealed to the rest of the Rangers, correct?"

"No, it isn't, not even to our other leaders."

"Sigrid and Dolbarar don't know it?" Astrid asked, surprised.

Raner shook his head.

"Only those I've mentioned."

"A strict and interesting system," Ingrid said. "I like it."

"We'll have to memorize a lot—*everything* in fact," Molak said, frowning.

"Indeed, you'll have to. Everything I tell you. You are not to discuss it with anyone who isn't one of your comrades, and in any case always with discretion."

The three exchanged doubtful glances.

"As you can appreciate, in order to become a Royal Ranger, besides having good physical skills, you must have an almost equally good head. You'll memorize everything I tell you, and I'll test you on it as we go along in our training and practice sessions. Everything will be oral. No writing down anything anywhere. I hope this one works properly," he said, tapping his own head with his finger.

"I guess we'll soon see," said Astrid.

"I'm sure we're up to it, sir," Ingrid said, standing even straighter.

Molak said nothing and looked around, as if he were already memorizing what Raner had told them.

"Good. Now for a little terminology of our own," Raner said. We call the kind of indoor watch duty like our four comrades here are doing behind the thrones 'S.W.', or Static Watch."

Astrid, Ingrid, and Molak watched them for a moment.

"Understood," Ingrid said.

"It's not always static inside, is it, sir?? Molak asked.

"That's right. Remember, there is always a group assigned to the King's protection, and they go wherever he goes. They consist of six of ours. They wait at the entrance to the Royal Chambers, and when his Majesty leaves his chambers, they go with him. You might also be called to form part of that group. We call it 'R.E.'"

"Royal Escort?" Molak guessed.

"Exactly," Raner confirmed. "Only the most veteran can be a part of the R.E. and accompany the King wherever he goes. For now you don't need to worry about being a part of the R.E., although you'll be trained for it."

They all nodded.

"And the Royal Guard?" Ingrid asked. "How do they work?"

"They have a different system. They use different groups for different tasks. They're more militarized, more hierarchical than our corps. There are officers designated to the different groups, and they give the orders and assign the tasks to be done. They also have sub-officers. Ellingsen makes sure everything runs properly. I have to say that they perform their duty very well. We are a good complement for them and they know it, both Ellingsen and his soldiers."

"Are there no rivalries?" Ingrid asked.

"I wouldn't go so far as to say that. There's always some rivalry, but it's a healthy amount, to determine who the best is. What there can't be and what isn't accepted or tolerated are taunting and quarrels. They have a job to do, and so do we."

"A Royal Guard is very good in close combat with their axe or sword and shield. But not good at all with a bow," said Molak.

"That is correct," Raner replied. "That is why they are in charge of defending the King from short-distance attacks."

"Understood," the Panthers said.

"But that is inside, because a Royal Guard wouldn't know what to do in the middle of a forest or a mountain," Astrid commented in a low voice so the Guards present would not hear her.

"You can swear to that," Mostassen commented back.

The other Royal Rangers smiled but held back and said nothing.

Raner's mouth twisted slightly and changed the subject.

"One of the most important things you must learn and which we'll rehearse next is how to get the King out of a dangerous situation and take him to a safe place. I'll stand before the Throne," he said as he did so, "and act as the protectee. Take your guard position beside that column, Molak, Ingrid in that corner, and Astrid in the other corner further down."

The three did as they had been told and stood, ready to act.

"You three will not do anything in this exercise, I just want you to watch and learn."

The three nodded from their positions, "Yes, sir!"

"Good. Royal Rangers, take your places," Raner said.

Mostassen and the others took up positions around the hall.

"At my signal," said Raner. He waited a moment and then raised his hand. "To the protectee!"

At once, all the Royal Rangers in the hall ran to stand around Raner with a speed and efficiency that were truly impressive. In an instant they were all perfectly placed, covering Raner from all directions, bows raised and arrows nocked. They were forming a half moon since the thrones prevented them from standing behind Raner. They were each facing one direction of the huge hall. It was as if Raner were surrounded by a shell of sharp spikes.

Mostassen stood in front of Raner.

"I'll guide you," he said in a calm voice. "Put your hand on my shoulder."

Raner did as he was told.

"Three steps forward!" Mostassen ordered.

The whole group moved and freed up the area around the thrones. The Rangers swiftly completed their protective line around Raner and Mostassen without the obstacle of the thrones.

Astrid, Ingrid, and Molak watched the position each Ranger had taken carefully, studying how they were protecting Raner with their backs toward him and their bows to the front. Wherever the threat came from, it would receive an arrow. If, on the other hand, it was a deadly arrow that sought to kill the protectee, it would be blocked by the body of one of the protectors, since there was no space left for an arrow to pass through.

"We're taking him out!" Raner ordered.

They all moved in unison toward a back door behind the thrones, going around them just enough to free them. It was a real spectacle to see how they did this. They were all moving at once, like in a choreographed dance. Raner was trying to go faster than the group, as if he was eager to escape, driven by fear or nerves. Mostassen did not let him; he made Raner remain calm and follow the pace marked by the group, which was airtight and did not let him out in any direction. They all moved in synchronicity, and it was a pleasure to watch them. The whole group reached the door, keeping the same formation they had adopted around Raner. One of the Rangers closest to the door who was aiming his bow at the entrance opened it. He went out into the corridor.

"Clear!" he cried.

The group went through the door one by one without breaking the formation at any moment. Astrid, Ingrid, and Molak could see, through the open door, how they maintained the formation in the corridor as they headed east.

A moment later they came back in. Raner stood before the thrones once again.

"Those of you on S.W. go back to your posts," he ordered.

The four Royal Rangers nodded and returned to their positions.

"Astrid, Ingrid, and Molak, come over."

"That was awesome," Ingrid could not help saying, looking very impressed.

"It takes time and practice to do it this well," Raner said.

"Lots of practice, I imagine," Molak said, also looking impressed.

"Yes, you'll have to practice a lot."

"And what if the protectee doesn't cooperate?" Astrid asked. "What would Mostassen have had to do?"

Raner looked at Mostassen and nodded for him to answer.

"The life of the protectee is what matters. If he or she doesn't cooperate, we'll have to force them," the Veteran replied.

"That could be tricky. Royalty doesn't like to be forced to do anything," said Astrid.

"And even less if you lay hands on them," added Ingrid.

"We'll do what's necessary," Mostassen insisted.

"That might lead to hanging from the end of a rope by the neck," Molak said.

"It might, indeed. It depends on how badly the King or Queen takes it. It's a risk we have to take," Raner told them. "It's our duty. That's why we're Royal Rangers."

"It's one thing to die defending the King, and a very different thing if the King has you killed for defending him," said Astrid.

"You forget that here your life doesn't matter. Only the King's does," Raner said shortly. "We'll do what's necessary and accept the consequences. The King must live, at any cost."

"We understand," Molak said firmly.

"We accept it," Ingrid said, although not as firmly.

Astrid said nothing.

"Good. Now I'll leave you with Mostassen. He'll explain all the technical aspects of what you've just witnessed, as well as the S.W. positions, which you must memorize here and in the adjacent areas."

"Yes, sir," the three said at once.

Raner left and took the rest of the Royal Rangers with him.

Mostassen came over to them.

"First of all, let me tell you how glad I am to see you here."

"And so are we," Ingrid said.

"I mean training to become Royal Rangers."

"Oh, that. Thank you," Ingrid said.

"How's the wound?" Molak asked, pointing at the leg Mostassen was limping on.

"It's nothing but a scratch," Mostassen waved it aside.

"Well, for a scratch you're limping quite a bit," Astrid said, raising an eyebrow and cocking her head to one side.

"It's a pretty deep scratch," Mostassen had to admit. "Since I can't go on missions, they've brought me to serve at the Royal Castle."

"You won't need to run much here," Molak said, grinning.

"I'm mostly on watch duty here in the Throne Hall."

"Oh, then you won't be bored, what with our beloved monarch and his 'bouts of wrath,'" Astrid told him.

"The truth is, I have no time to be bored. Things have been heated since the wedding."

Ingrid, Astrid, and Molak exchanged looks.

"Bad atmosphere?" Ingrid asked.

"Let's say things are aflame."

"Understood," said Molak.

"You're a Veteran with a lot of experience in this post and also on missions. Do you think we're cut out for this?" Astrid asked him. "Please be honest."

Mostassen rubbed his chin with the back of his hand, thoughtfully.

"I think you'll do well. We need fresh blood with good instincts, and you have them. I realized that when I first met you."

"Thank you, that's an honor coming from you," said Molak.

"Being a Royal Ranger isn't only rising in category, it's an honor and a privilege. Remember that."

"We will," Ingrid promised.

"Many Rangers want to get this far but never do," Mostassen said. "You have to be skilled and resilient."

"We are quite resilient," Astrid said with a mischievous smile.

"It's not an easy job and it's underappreciated," Mostassen warned them. Nothing ever happens, and no one will ever thank you for your loyal service. But if anything happens, as in the last two attempts… then it will be your fault. And the punishments will be extreme."

"Have there been any?" Astrid asked, surprised.

Mostassen heaved a deep sigh.

"There have been, indeed, mainly in the Royal Guard. A number of Ellingsen's guards have been sent to the dungeons. We've had our share too… three of our own have been arrested."

"But they didn't do anything wrong!" Ingrid cried in shocked disbelief.

"That doesn't matter. They weren't up to the challenge, and the King doesn't tolerate mistakes. Ellingsen and Raner have been very close to ending up in the dungeons as well. If it hadn't been because we're going to war and they're necessary, they'd already be in prison."

"I don't think that's fair," Astrid complained.

"Do you believe we'll enter into war?" Molak asked, worried.

"It's practically a fact. The King hasn't liberated the Zangrian delegation. King Caron won't forgive it. He can't. He's currently seeking support for the campaign, and that's why war hasn't started yet. Once he has the support, he'll attack."

"That's bad news," Astrid said.

"I could be wrong, but that's what my nose tells me," Mostassen said, tapping his nose with his finger.

"We always seem to be leaving one war and entering another,"

Molak said.

"Well, that's something we can't prevent," Mostassen shrugged.

"By the way, did you recover your memory after the incident at the bay of the Killer Whales?" Astrid asked him, risking the answer to be yes.

Ingrid flashed a warning look at Astrid. Asrael had bewitched Mostassen so he would never be able to remember certain important events: Egil's treason and that of his brothers in joining Darthor and the Peoples of the Frozen Continent.

Mostassen shook his head and wrinkled his nose.

"Nope, and I think I never will."

"Not important, I only asked to see how you felt," Astrid said, pretending.

Ingrid snorted under her breath.

"I'm fine. It's nothing but another battle wound."

"That's a good way to see it," Astrid nodded.

"We'd better get to work, you still have a lot to learn," Mostassen told them.

"You have all our attention," Astrid said.

"Well, let's get started then," Mostassen replied.

Chapter 21

Ona, Lasgol, and Camu reached the jetty. There was no trace of the boatman, who must still be sleeping it off. They got out of the barge, not without some difficulties, and once they had all landed, Lasgol told them what had happened on the war ship with the sea serpent.

Monster, servant dragon, Camu said, certain.

Yeah, that's what I thought too.

Much clever throw jewel.

Thanks, I didn't even stop to think, it was pure instinct.

Serpent take pearls to dragon, sure.

Dergha-Sho-Blaska must have sent the creature to intercept them.

Can follow sea serpent?

I think so. The locating spell is working. I guess I have to be close enough to feel it.

Follow river.

That's my plan too.

I have two horses I can switch between. I'll ride as fast as they can go and follow the serpent south.

You better go alone, more fast.

And what about you two?

We follow, more slow. No can run like horses.

Ona moaned twice.

I don't like the idea of leaving you again, now that we were just reunited.

We okay. You go, not lose serpent.

Lasgol wondered whether this was the right decision. He did not want to leave his friends—it had been hard enough to find them, and concern for their well-being was always on his mind. He was also aware that he either followed the serpent now without wasting more time, or it was going to slip away, and with it they would lose the last chance they had of finding the Immortal Dragon.

Camu made the decision for him.

No think more. You go.

Ona supported him with a growl.

Lasgol took a deep breath and went to fetch his horse. A moment

175

later, he got on the horse he had originally brought and, grasping the reins of the Pinto, he galloped away.

You find serpent. We find you, Camu messaged him.

Follow the river, on this side. We'll meet again further ahead.

Okay.

The terrain invited a good gallop: tall grass, flat land, with few obstacles. He rode close to the shore of the great river, as fast as his horse would go while making sure the Pinto was at his side. He had no idea how fast the serpent could swim, but he doubted it would be as fast as his horse was going right then, since he seemed to be flying over the green plain.

As he rode he was scanning the horizon and the river and was alert to the pulsing feeling of the jewel's locating spell. He had lost quite a bit of time repairing the barge and finding Camu and Ona. He feared he might have lost the serpent, that it might be too late already. A feeling of failure began to haunt him, but he dismissed it. The serpent had to be in the great river. Where else could such a monster go? It could only be a huge river like this one and perhaps the sea if it could live in salty water, which might not be the case.

The speed he was riding at and the summer breeze on his face blowing his hair around his head made him feel free and happy as he followed the river at full gallop. The serpent was somewhere to the south and he would soon catch up with it. He simply had to keep riding like he was and he would find it. It was just a matter of time, this he knew.

His mount began to lose energy after a while, exhausted by the tremendous pace Lasgol had demanded of it and the weight of the rider, which although light was an added burden. He stopped and let the horse rest. He would have to leave it there. It could go no further, but there was plenty of grass and water and not a soul around for leagues. It would be all right.

He got on the Pinto, which although it had been running alongside them had not carried any weight and was still quite fresh. They were soon galloping at great speed again. Lasgol was enjoying the chase: nothing better than riding a beautiful animal at full tilt following the river Utla to its source.

In fact, he was enjoying himself so much that when the expected pulse reached him, it took him by surprise. He felt the green flash in his mind and knew it was a league south and a little to the west.

"We have it!" he told his horse.

He did not force the pace anymore. Now that he had found the signal, the last thing he needed was to lose his mount by overexerting it. He could not risk an injury or a stroke, they were such loyal animals that they would keep going until they died. Of course, Lasgol would always avoid such a scenario at any cost—a Ranger always took good care of his horse, so said the Path.

When the second pulse reached him, Lasgol went slower, giving his horse a chance to get his breath back. He did not stop, but he went much slower. They were close and the serpent did not seem to be gaining on him, so there was no need to exhaust his horse. He strained his neck toward the river and tried to see, with his improved vision, the shadow of the huge monster under the surface of the river's blue water.

He wondered where it would be heading to. The Utla was getting smaller, and a little to the south it divided into several branches, which came down from mountains and lakes higher up. Whatever the monster was planning, Lasgol had no choice but to follow it and see where it led him. He stopped and dismounted. He left a clear trail on the ground with both hands so Ona and Camu could follow him. He rode again and looked to the north. There was still no trace of them, which did not surprise him—he had gained a great advantage.

He continued following the trail until the Utla subdivided. Then he had to wait for another pulse to know which of the river branches the sea serpent had taken. While he waited and let his mount rest, Lasgol took in the beautiful landscape. To the west he could see the large rocky ranges that surrounded the kingdom of Rogdon. The Fortress of the Half Moon had to be very near, as well as the pass it protected. It was the entrance to the lands of the blue and silver lancers from the west. He wondered where they would be heading next.

He shook his head. He could not imagine the serpent crossing to the west. The Utla ended there, or rather it started where they now were. In any case, he highly doubted the serpent would leave the water to continue by land. Although he had seen stranger things in his short life. Perhaps there was an underground sea in that area and no one knew about it.

The pulse reached him: to the south and the longest river branch. Once again, he left a trail for Ona and Camu to follow, then got on his horse and stroked its neck.

"Come on, handsome, let's keep going, quietly," he said and started following the river branch. The serpent was close, so Lasgol did not want to be hasty but rather wanted to travel warily.

They went up a slope for a good while and saw at the top that they had come to a lake. Looking at it, Lasgol noticed that several smaller streams came down from even higher terrain. These were not mountains as such, but rises on the land with low peaks. It was all covered with tall grass that was beginning to dry with the coming of summer.

He stopped his horse and dismounted to check the surroundings. The lake was wide and it could probably hide the serpent inside, so he decided to be careful. He went down a little to a shoulder in the land so that his horse would not be visible from the lake and left it grazing while he went up to check the lake. He got down behind some loose rocks big enough to hide his body.

A new pulse told him that the serpent was right in front of him and just to his side. As he had expected, the serpent was hiding in the lake. This made him nervous while also giving him a small sense of satisfaction. He had not lost it. The problem was what to do now. That would depend on what the monster did, if it did anything.

Without meaning to, Lasgol looked up at the clear sky where the sun was shining bright. This area was one of the hottest in Norghana. What he feared was that Dergha-Sho-Blaska would come down from the sky as he had done in the Forest of the Green Ogre. Just thinking about it, he felt as if a great invisible claw squeezed his chest. If the Immortal Dragon appeared to retrieve the pearls himself, Lasgol would have a huge and deadly problem on his hands.

Besides, depending on when the dragon made his appearance, it could coincide with the arrival of Camu and Ona, although this meant Dergha-Sho-Blaska would still take a while, since Lasgol's two friends would not catch up to him for a long time. Lasgol knew that Ona was capable of following the trail he had left without any trouble. Camu was no good as a tracker, his sense of smell was terrible, but Ona was amazing.

He waited anxiously, looking up at the sky every now and then. He had the feeling that suddenly the huge claws of the dragon would appear above his head to come down and tear his body in shreds. A chill ran down his back. He had to make an effort to calm down. So far there was no trace of the dragon. Thinking about the worst outcome was not going to help him at all. He was better off being focused and alert.

All of a sudden, a shadow appeared in the lake. It was long, and it blackened the blue water of the surface. The shadow moved, getting closer to the eastern side of the lake. The huge head of the serpent broke the water and its reptilian eyes scanned the surroundings. Seeing it again, Lasgol was struck dumb at the size of it. It looked like a mythological creature, taken from a legend of Nordic gods and warriors, warriors which in all certainty would have died in the confrontation with the monster of the gods.

It poked its viper's tongue out of its mouth and gave out several long, strong hisses, which it repeated a number of times in all four directions,

Lasgol realized what the monster was doing: it was calling out to something or someone. With great care, he brought Aodh's Bow forward from his back and left it at hand. He felt he was going to need it soon. A moment later he was calling on all the skills he always used for fighting. They formed one of his practice lists, the kind Lasgol called his Pre-Combat Table. He finished summoning these skills and felt somewhat calmer as he watched how things developed.

He began to hear the sound of pounding steps. He could almost feel the earth tremble. He bent down and placed his hand on the ground. It was indeed trembling as if something colossal were treading heavily. As the steps thundered closer, the earth shook more. Something heavy was approaching. Would it be Dergha-Sho-Blaska? Lasgol strained his neck to better take in the surroundings.

Then he saw it, or rather he glimpsed it, because his eyes were unable to fully see it.

A monster over sixty feet long, looking reptilian, rather like a giant crocodile, was coming to the lake with long heavy steps on four huge legs. In width it must be at least fifteen feet long, and the head and snout were very similar to those of an alligator. The snout was very long, longer than a croc's. He glimpsed a huge line of teeth, which froze him on the spot. The scaled skin looked tough, and it also had bone protuberances which seemed to make a thick armor hard to penetrate. It looked protected enough to stand up to Dergha-Sho-Blaska himself.

But there was something in the monster that left Lasgol

wondering. As it walked its skin changed color and blended in with the surroundings, that was why he had not been able to see it properly the moment it had appeared. Lasgol rubbed his eyes to make sure he was not seeing things. He was not, his *Hawk's Eye* skill was activated and did not fail him. This ancient-looking monster had a skill similar to Camu's, which left him wondering. Until now Lasgol had always thought that Camu's skill must come from his origins in the Frozen Continent. But this giant, monstrous crocodile or alligator was not from the Frozen Continent. Neither was it from the central part of Tremia. Lasgol thought it must be from a drier area, possibly from the south of Tremia.

"Life always surprises us…" he murmured as he watched the great reptile approaching the lake's shore.

He continued watching the colossal crocodile as it reached the shore and emitted a strange sound, like a very deep growl. It sounded like an answer to the hisses the serpent was uttering, with its head and part of its body raised several feet above the water. For a while the two giant monsters seemed to be having a conversation with an exchange of growls and hisses. Lasgol had no idea of what they might be talking about, but he did not miss a detail. The fact that those monstrous reptiles could communicate was terrifying.

Suddenly the conversation ended. Both monsters stared at each other with their huge reptilian eyes. The serpent seemed to retch while the crocodile opened its long snout filled with teeth. With a movement that left no doubt as to what it was, the serpent vomited part of the contents of its stomach into the mouth of the great crocodile.

Lasgol should have felt disgusted, but he did not because he knew what was happening. The serpent was passing its precious merchandise to the crocodile, which swallowed it in turn.

The serpent hissed and vanished into the lake and did not reappear. The crocodile shut its snout and with a grunt seemed to say goodbye. It turned south slowly and began to move away on its powerful legs.

Lasgol had witnessed an exchange between two monsters that he would remember for the rest of his life. He watched the great beast moving away with slow, heavy movements, but being so large, its steps covered quite a bit of land. What kept Lasgol wondering was that with every step the monster changed colors, imitating those of the environment, mimicking it. If he stopped looking, he lost sight of it and it took him a while to find it again. That monster was something terrible and fascinating. Camu was surely going to love it.

Thinking about his friend, he remembered he needed to leave a trail. He left two clear marks so they would know he had been there. Now the decision to make was whether to kill the monster and recover the Silver Pearls, or not to attack it and follow it to Dergha-Sho-Blaska, which is where Lasgol guessed it was going. An interesting decision—if he killed it and managed to recover the pearls he denied them from Dergha-Sho-Blaska. This was the safest option, but in doing this he would lose the chance to find the Immortal Dragon and learn what he was planning.

Lasgol snorted, both options were good. The first one was safer and the second   one was riskier, since if they followed the monster and it delivered the pearls to Dergha-Sho-Blaska, they would not be able to recover them no matter if they knew where to find the dragon or not. He pondered: knowing where the dragon was hiding might help them find out why he was behaving the way he was. Lasgol felt that if the dragon was not already razing nations, it was not for lack of wanting to. There had to be something that prevented him, or some reason why he was waiting. Lasgol felt that being able to find out what that reason was might be very important. He felt it as a premonition.

He watched the monster walk away and suddenly he felt the pulse. It was coming from the great crocodile.

"Well, that's interesting…" he told his Pinto horse.

The monster had not only swallowed the box with the pearls, he had also swallowed the ice jewel. That was stroke of good luck he had not been expecting. Now he could follow it as he had done with the serpent, although he did not think the great alligator- crocodile-monster was going to shake him off, not with his skills. The footprints it left due to its great weight were too obvious for Lasgol not to find and follow. It was one thing to trick the eye and a very different one not to leave any trace, or disguise it so it could not be found. The monster had the first skill but not the second.

He decided he would follow the monster for now until Camu and Ona caught up with him, but would not confront it. He decided this because he really did not know what to do, so he postponed the decision. He always liked to have clear ideas, but there were times when this was not so easy. Prudence ruled in this type of situation. For now he would be cautious. Later on they would see what to do, perhaps risk everything.

He got on his horse and began the chase, this time slowly. There was no need to run, and he did not want the monster to notice he was following after it. He tracked the great reptile for half a day as it carried ahead south in a straight line, as if it had a fixed route in his mind. In the distance toward the east, Lasgol could see the beginning of the unfathomable forests of the Usik. He remembered the adventure they had lived in there and was glad that the monster was not heading to the territory of the green-skinned savages with faces painted red or black.

He looked toward the west and in the horizon saw the high ridges of the range of mountains that surrounded the kingdom of Rogdon. He tried to remember what Egil had told him about the tribes that lived in the southern area, between the ranges of the Rogdonian mountains and the forests of the Usik. From what he remembered, nomad tribes lived there who hunted and fished for a living, related to the Masig tribes of the north but from a different race and independent of them. In fact, they did not get along well with their northern cousins. The name came to him: the Inon. Their race was characterized by deep red skin, almost as dark as Nocean wine and darker than the copper red of the Masig.

If he came across them he would have to avoid them, just as it was wise to avoid the Masig. They were not tribes that tended to be aggressive but they did not like to find foreigners crossing their lands, especially groups of warriors on patrol. He would have to travel with eyes open wide and avoid them. The problem was that their land was very flat and you could see a rider for a long distance.

Seeing the pace of the great reptile was steady and he could follow it easily, Lasgol decided to go even slower so that Ona and Camu could reach him. When night came the monster stopped to rest, and Lasgol did the same at a prudent distance. He did not light any fire; he really did not need it, the temperature was excellent and the further south they went, the hotter it was.

With the first light the reptilian beast set off again. Lasgol took his time. He wanted to measure the reach of the ice jewel, now that he did not run the risk of losing his quarry. In fact, it was marking its location more than two leagues away. He forced the distance to see whether he received the pulse from three leagues and, to his surprise, it turned out he did. He thought this was impressive. He tried to see whether he could reach four leagues, but that was too far. He had to follow the tracks to make up the lost terrain. The limit seemed to be three leagues. Now that he knew, he would be able to use the jewel better.

Two days later, just before sunrise, Lasgol heard someone approaching from behind. In a reflex move, he fell on one knee and nocked an arrow to his golden bow. If it were the Inon, he might be forced to fight. He raised his bow and aimed toward the sound.

Chapter 22

Lasgol prepared to release. A sense of danger clutched at his stomach. He did not want to fight the Inon, but if he was forced to, he would.

Be us, Camu's message reached him.

Lasgol lowered his bow. He snorted and smiled.

Camu and Ona appeared in front of him and he welcomed them with a hug.

I'm so glad you caught up with me.

We come fast.

Yeah, faster than I had expected, Lasgol smiled.

Ona moaned and rubbed her head against Lasgol's forehead to show her love. Lasgol appreciated the panther's caress with all his heart. She was charming, good, obedient, and lovable, and also deadly when she needed to be.

What happen with great sea serpent? Camu wanted to know.

I'll tell you. It's quite funny.

Surprise?

Yeah, something like that.

I like surprises.

We'll see if you like this one.

Lasgol told them what had happened with the serpent and the monster-crocodile and the situation they were in now. And also about the curious fact that it had a camouflage skill similar to Camu's.

Surprise good.

You say that now. Just wait until you see the size and the mouth of the monster.

Much strong?

Yeah, it's a monster that leaves you breathless.

Have magic?

I don't know. I didn't feel it use magic, but its skill to camouflage might be magical.

Have to know.

Yeah, it's something important we must keep in mind.

What do?

That's the thing, I'm not sure. We could try and take the pearls away from it and put them somewhere safe, or we can follow it and see if it takes us to Dergha-Sho-Blaska.

Much decision.

Yeah, that's the problem. The first option is the safest, but we lose the opportunity of finding Dergha-Sho-Blaska.

I want find. Then kill.

I know, and let me remind you that we can't confront him. Not without powerful allies and one or two armies at least.

Dergha-Sho-Blaska pay for kill Eicewald, Camu messaged, along with a feeling of rage and anger.

We can't let our feelings drive us to make a terrible mistake.

Camu was thoughtful, and after a moment he responded.

We no kill. Only follow monster crocodile.

I assumed you'd choose that option, because it's the one that brings us close to the dragon.

Ona moaned once. She agreed with Camu.

If the pearls are important to Dergha-Sho-Blaska, which they seem to be, and we're giving them to him by not retrieving them now, then what?

We follow pearls to Dergha-Sho-Blaska. Know where hide. Then take pearls.

That sounds complicated and too risky. Lasgol was not at all sure of the plan.

Complicated and risky our specialty.

Lasgol had to smile at Camu's witticism.

Ona chirped once.

You sound like Viggo, which isn't so good.

Viggo funny.

Yeah, sure. But now it's only the three of us. We have to solve this.

We can, Camu messaged confidently.

Lasgol was not as optimistic, nor was he very sure. He snorted hard.

Fine. We'll follow the great crocodile. But we can't let it hand over the pearls to its master.

We take pearls later, Camu messaged.

Lasgol sighed. The plan seemed too risky, especially with only the three of them. If the Immortal Dragon should appear… he did not even want to think what might happen. The last time they had lost Eicewald—this time it would be one of them, or all. The dragon

185

would not forgive them. He had already given them the chance to join him and they had refused. This time he would kill them. Whoever said that freeing the world of evil was an easy task was very wrong. Lasgol resigned himself and accepted that they had to keep going.

With the decision made and dawn arriving, they set off. They followed the great crocodile toward the south.

The first day of traveling was uneventful. Everything was clear and quiet. For a while Lasgol enjoyed the beautiful landscape and put aside the bad omens. Following the great reptile was easy, even though it used its camouflage, so they were not concerned. They maintained a prudent distance, always within range of the ice jewel.

The quiet lasted one more day's journey. Then halfway through the morning of the third day, things changed.

They saw a large group of riders in the distance. Lasgol was able to see them with his *Hawk's Eye* skill and had no doubts: they were Inon warriors. Their skin was deep red, like the color of dark wine. They had dark eyes and wore their hair cut in a way Lasgol had never seen before. They had the sides of their heads shorn and wore a strip of hair in the middle, a handspan tall, from forehead to nape. Lasgol guessed that in order to maintain the hair standing on end they must use animal grease or something similar. Their faces were painted, the upper half in black and the lower half in white.

Their torsos and backs were protected by armor made of tanned leather in several layers, as if they had sewn several pieces together, one on top of the other, without sleeves. The arms were uncovered, revealing the deep red of their skin. Their legs were also bare, since they wore leather pants that only came to their knees. On their feet they wore moccasins. They were all armed with short bows, and Lasgol had the feeling they were warriors who fought on horseback, shooting arrows at their enemies as they rode.

They were all riding Pinto horses like those of the Masig. Lasgol remembered that part of the enmity between the two races was precisely because of the Pinto horses. They both believed this race of horses belonged to them, and the disputes between the north and south over the herds of wild horses were constant. There was really nothing better than having Egil as a friend—the amount of information and knowledge he so generously shared was amazing. Much of it became useful sooner or later, as was the currently the case. Lasgol could not be more grateful to his friend for all he learned from him.

Suddenly, something most curious happened. The great reptile stopped and flattened itself among the tall grass. It must have detected the presence of the Inon warriors. In an instant it was perfectly camouflaged. It had vanished completely. All that could be seen was a green plain with some mounds or ravines covered in green. The great reptile had become one of those mounds.

Camouflage good, Camu messaged, along with a feeling of surprise.

Indeed it is. Can it be magical?

I think yes. Is far to pick up.

Ona growled once. She thought so too.

Then it might also have some other skill. We'll need to be careful, Lasgol transmitted in warning.

I pick up magic if close.

We'll get closer. Easy, but with caution. That monster is enormous.

They watched what happened. The patrol of Inon warriors went down to a plain near where the great reptile was hiding. They did not seem to see it, or else they were more interested in a herd of bison that was grazing a little more to the east, beyond the spot where the monster was hiding. Two of the warriors rode off like lightning to the north. Lasgol guessed they were going to report the herd to their hunters. Here they had meat for the whole summer.

Lasgol, Ona, and Camu waited to see what happened, hiding in a ravine. The Inon warriors headed to the herd of bison and did not see the great reptile, although they passed close by it. The Inon were the lords and masters of the southern steppes—all the territory from the mountains of Rogdon to the forests of the Usik was theirs. Unlike the Masig, who were dispersed in hundreds of tribes throughout the steppes to the north, the Inon only had three large tribes, which moved along the pastures like great nomadic realms.

Lasgol and his companions continued watching, intrigued. Once there were no warriors left in sight, the giant crocodile started heading south again. It moved always in the same direction, in a straight line, its four powerful legs taking great strides. Nothing seemed to worry or bother it, which was no surprise, given its colossal size.

One of the riders remained behind above a small hill. He turned on his mount and looked toward where the great reptile was marching on south. In spite of its camouflage, maybe because it was moving, the rider seemed to see it. He opened his eyes wide and stared in disbelief. He did not seem convinced that what he was seeing was real. He urged his mount forward and approached the reptile from behind. It looked as if the rider had seen the monster's enormous tail. Frightened, he sounded the alarm, shouting in the Inon's tribal language.

The other riders heard his shouts and looked back. They stopped following the herd of bison and rode to where the rider was signaling. The reptile realized it had been discovered and stopped. It lay down and once again vanished from sight, becoming a   grass-covered mound.

The rider was pointing toward the monster and shouting in his own language, obviously upset. Some of the other riders dismounted and searched for the trail. They found it, great reptilian footprints, unmistakable. Then, several of the Inon began to release against what apparently was a mound. The arrows flew from their bows and pierced the monster's back, and something surprising happened. When the arrows hit the monster's scales, they became visible.

The warriors could see that something weird was happening, since the arrows hit a target, and it was not a grass-covered mound. One warrior, who appeared to be the chief of the party, his hair dyed multiple colors, ordered the others to attack the great reptile. The warriors urged their mounts and released at the monster-mound, passing by it at lightning speed.

The giant reptile stood on its feet and roared, opening its huge maw. Lasgol thought the Inon warriors would be scared or at least puzzled at such a monster, but that was not so. They began to shout with shrill yells while they surrounded the monster and attacked it as if it were a gigantic bison they wanted to hunt.

These Inon much crazy, Camu messaged.

I don't know about crazy, but they have to be quite brutish to confront that monster like that.

Ona moaned once.

The warriors were surrounding the giant reptile at full gallop, so it was unable to trap them in its huge mouth since they were riding by so fast. Lasgol noticed that the Inon were remarkable riders, and as they passed the monster at lightning speed they nocked arrows on their short bows and shot at the reptile.

One thing Lasgol noticed at once was that these warriors were skilled archers. All their arrows hit the target. They plunged into the creature's tough, scaly skin and bony ridges. The problem was that the arrows barely pierced the outer layer of the monster's skin. They were only scratching it superficially.

Camu noticed this.

Inon warriors no kill monster. Arrows no go through protective layer.

I noticed that, its skin must be very tough. Unless they hit the eyes or the mouth when it opens it, they aren't going to be able to seriously wound it.

The Inon warriors had completely surrounded the monster-crocodile, which had stopped to defend itself. They were riding around the monster, forming a circle and shooting at it. As they rode they uttered war cries and shrill yells to frighten their quarry with all the power of their lungs and throats.

The colossal crocodile, seeing that it could not catch them with its jaws since their swift horses dodged it, suddenly released a tremendous whiplash with its thick tail. This attack caught the riders by surprise, and half a dozen were hit. They were thrown back, horses and all, and hit the ground several paces away. Most did not get back up. There were dead and wounded among men and horses.

Wow... that was a tremendous blow...

I better whiplash, with magic.

It didn't need magic. That tail whiplash could knock down a building.

Ona growled once.

The warriors continued their attack, enraged by their casualties. They were not managing to seriously wound the monster, and this seemed to make them more furious. The cries of war were shrill and getting louder.

Eventually, the crocodile seemed to tire of the pest bothering it and started heading south again, ignoring the Inon. The riders adjusted their attacks to move on him. They continued releasing arrow after arrow, but they did not manage to hurt it. The monster went on firmly toward wherever it was heading.

Lasgol brought out his map and calculated the trajectory. If it continued moving south without deviating, as it had been doing so far, it was going to reach the Central Sea. This was not good news, Lasgol realized, since they could lose the great crocodile in the open water, and if they did, things would become very complicated once again.

I think it's heading to the Central Sea.
No good, in sea no can follow.
That's what I was thinking.
Inon warriors no let.
I'm not so sure about that. I don't think they'll be able to stop it.
No good.
Exactly.

Suddenly a group of about fifty Inon warriors appeared on a hill to the west. They saw what was going on, their comrades attacking the great monster as it was fleeing. A moment later war cries were heard, and the Inon who had just appeared joined those attacking the monster.

This is getting interesting.
More warriors.
Let's see whether they can stop the creature.

The warriors attacked the huge crocodile similarly to how the rest of the Inon were fighting, by shooting at the monster's sides with their short bows. The skin on its sides was less tough than on the back, and the beast seemed to feel the stings more intensely there. It stopped again and attacked with its tail and jaws. It managed to hit half a dozen warriors, who died from the tail's terrible blows or in the monster's jaws.

The warriors continued attacking despite their casualties. Several Inon managed to jump onto the body of the huge reptile. They started climbing its tail while the monster shook itself, trying to get rid of them amid deep roars. The warriors who had managed to climb onto its back were crawling toward the crested head.

Inon warriors much crazy. Very funny, Camu messaged again, appearing pleasantly surprised.

I can't deny that. Lasgol was surprised at the agility and ferocity of the fighting Inon. They were not only excellent riders and mounted archers, but the courage and skill they exhibited fighting against such a monster was impressive.

Remind of Viggo. Much funny.
I don't agree with that.

The monster was shaking itself hard amid roars of rage. One of the warriors climbing along its back fell to the ground. The crocodile was so gigantic that the fall from such a considerable height broke his back. The others reached the beast's head and started plunging their knives in it.

They won't be able to wound its head, that's where its protection appears strongest.

Monster hard head.

Yeah, like yours. Lasgol was referring to the hard crest that ran along Camu's own head for protection.

Sarcasm?

Not this time, although it could be, yes.

The attack of the Inon warriors continued, but it did not look as if they were going to win. The monster had already killed another dozen riders between its tail and jaws and was trying to get rid of those on its head. One of them reached the beast's right eye and tried to stab it. The monster shut its eye and the knife plunged into the eyelid, which was as tough as a tree trunk.

Enraged, the great crocodile shook its head abruptly, left and right. Another of the warriors on the head fell to the ground. With a grunt and one closed eye, the monster renewed its march south.

It's escaping. We have to follow it, Lasgol transmitted to Ona and Camu.

Okay.

They started after it, maintaining a safe distance, although the warriors were too busy trying to kill the monster to notice them. They did not want to use Camu's *Extended Camouflage* unless it was necessary. They never knew when they would need Camu to make use of all his energy, so it was better not to use it unless they had no choice. They could not forget that Dergha-Sho-Blaska might appear at any moment.

The monster kept going, and every few paces it tried to shake off the few warriors clinging to it or else used its jaws and tail to attack those riding around it and shooting arrows at it.

Lasgol was convinced the warriors would not be able to kill the monster or even stop it, rather the opposite. If they were not careful, it was more likely the colossal croc would kill them all. No sooner had he thought this than he saw one of the warriors, who looked like another chief with his multicolored crest of hair, send three riders south at great speed. Lasgol wondered why.

The monster kept going as if that were the only thing on its mind. It had not slowed down but maintained a steady pace and kept going. The warriors had changed their strategy and were trying to wound its legs now. They seemed to be having some success, since blood was running down the creature's four legs where the arrows had penetrated. The legs did not have as much protection as the back or head.

Amid grunts of rage, the monster kept going. Lifting his gaze, Lasgol could already see the blue of the sea in the horizon before them. They were almost to the Central Sea. Would the monster reach it? The warriors were not going to make it easy, but if it reached the sea, they would lose it.

All of a sudden, to the south, just where the crocodile was heading, there appeared a hundred riders on their Pinto horses, forming a long line. At an order from their chief, the warriors stopped attacking the monster and galloped as fast as their horses could go to join their fellow warriors who were gathering to the south in a line.

They're going to try and stop the monster before it reaches the sea.

Not make it.

I'm not so sure.

You see.

The crocodile headed straight to the line of Inon warriors with firm strides. It was not limping, but its legs were bleeding. The warriors started chanting, raising their bows to the sky and shouting at the top of their voices. They shared arrows with those who had spent them all. They were not going to move out of its way, just like the monster was not going to stop. They were going to crash into each other.

The moment did not take long. The giant crocodile reached the line. It looked as if the monster was going to run them over and continue to the sea, which was already close.

That was not what happened, however.

The warriors rode out, splitting into two groups on both sides of the monster, and began to release at the four legs.

Those warriors are smart. They've found a weakness and they're going to exploit it.

Yes, much crazy and clever.

The riders were going around the monster, releasing at its legs while the giant kept heading toward the sea. There was almost nothing between the creature and the shore now. The war cries were thunderous because of the number of warriors attacking the crocodile.

Suddenly, the left hind leg failed the great reptile and it lost its balance for a moment. It managed to recover, but it was limping now. Soon after it was dragging the leg which had hundreds of arrows embedded in it. They had riddled it with arrows, but still the monster kept walking.

The warriors kept releasing. The initial group had run out of arrows despite having been given some more, and it withdrew to give space to the reinforcements, which continued attacking. The right hind leg fell a moment later, so now both hind legs were badly wounded. But it still kept going, dragging both legs with the strength of the front ones. The warriors realized this and attacked more impetuously. The monster was making a colossal effort, having to drag both back legs, the tail, and part of its body. It was quite a weight, and it began to take its toll. It was definitely moving a lot slower.

Lasgol was watching from the distance. He was not sure the monster was going to make it. The sea was close, but at the pace it was moving now and under the constant attack of the riders, it might very well not reach the sea. If the warriors stopped it or managed to kill it, it would be easier to recover the pearls, but it would not lead him to Dergha-Sho-Blaska.

The monster fought with all its strength amid deep grunts, which seemed to give it energy to keep going. The warriors continued attacking without pause, but like their comrades, they ended up spending all their arrows. A number of them tried to finish maiming the front legs with their knives. The monster devoured them, trapping them with its jaws and swallowing them.

After several fruitless attempts in which more warriors died, the chiefs called a retreat and moved away from the monster. They rode west and stood on a hill to watch. It seemed to Lasgol that they were not leaving the hunt yet, they simply did not want to lose more warriors. If the monster fell, they would have won. If the monster reached the sea, they would have lost. In any case, they would have done what they could.

The giant monster continued dragging itself and, to Lasgol's great surprise, it reached the coast. It headed to a high cliff, and with one last deep grunt it plunged into the sea, letting its huge body fall into the water.

See? I right, Camu messaged to Lasgol.

Yeah, this time you were right. Only by a little, but you were right.

I always right.

No way.

Ona growled twice.

Now what do?

Now we follow the monster by sea before we lose it.

Chapter 23

Raner had gathered the group in the afternoon for training, outside the city, westward and on horseback, which told them that the day's practice would have to do with protecting while riding. They had stopped in the middle of the Royal Road before it went through a birch wood. It was a sunny day with few clouds, and it did not look like rain. This cheered everyone, since the last few days it had been raining pretty heavily.

In the distance above a hill there was an army watch tower, and they could see soldiers, which did not surprise them. The kingdom was preparing for war, and the Royal Army soldiers had been activated and were in constant motion. They were taking over towers, forts, ports, and other fortresses of strategic value throughout the realm. Two of the King's main armies, the Snow Army and the Thunder Army, had gone south to the border with Zangria. From the news that arrived from the Rangers on watch missions at the border, the Zangrian army was also mobilizing and the situation was on the brink of escalation.

Raner looked at them and then addressed the group.

"Today we'll practice something I'm sure you'll all enjoy. It's one of the exercises best remembered by everyone."

"I bet it is," Nilsa said with an optimistic smile.

Viggo whispered beside her, "It's a double meaning."

Nilsa grimaced.

"No it's not."

"You wait and see," Viggo insisted.

"I trust this lesson will remain engraved in your minds," Raner told them as he began to give instructions to his Royal Rangers.

"I'm not sure that sounds so good... I think Viggo's right," Gerd told Nilsa in a whisper.

"I'm always right, and don't be a scaredy-cat, big guy," Viggo whispered back.

"I'm not, I just didn't like the way that sounded."

"Bah, nothing's going to happen to us here," Viggo said with a wave of his hand. "We're in the middle of the Royal Road, in an empty field."

"We don't know that for sure," said Egil. "We think that's the case, but it's not written in stone."

"I've tried to find out about the exercises," Nilsa commented. "I asked Kol, Haines, and others, but no one wants to say anything. They keep silent. It's as if it were a secret that's punishable with prison if revealed. They know me. I don't know why they're not telling me. It's very frustrating."

"So, your seductive ways aren't working then?" Viggo asked her, chuckling.

"You'd better worry about Molak's seductive ways and not mine," Nilsa replied, and at once Viggo's face became somber.

"Captain Fantastic had better not try anything, or he'll regret it," he said angrily. "I'll cut off his ears or worse," he threatened.

"Don't get upset. I'm sure Molak is behaving like the gentleman he is. Don't forget he's one of us, one of the good ones," Gerd told him.

"Yeah, you and your goody-two-shoes view of life. Everything isn't just good or bad, there are in-betweens, shady grays," Viggo said with an astute gleam in his eyes.

"I have to agree with Viggo on that," Egil commented. "We'd like everything to be simpler in this life and that things were always good or bad. Unfortunately, it's not that simple. People have different amounts and combinations of this and that, and the results are complex people with good and bad sides to them and different responses to situations according to that combination. Therefore, it's almost impossible to know how a person's going to behave."

"Exactly, what the wise-guy said in such a convoluted manner," Viggo said.

Gerd shrugged.

"It's a pity people aren't more transparent and predictable."

"In many cases they are," Nilsa said quietly.

"Yeah sure, you dangle a good bag of gold in front of their noses and you'll see what happens. Scary," said Viggo.

"Right. Everything's organized," Raner told them, turning his attention back to them. "This is going to be an exercise with marking weapons, non-lethal. Understood? Confirm you do."

"Yes, sir," the four replied, going over their dull knives and axes and hollow-pointed arrows that left a red mark upon impact but didn't do any harm.

"I don't want any accidents, so make sure."

"Everything's in order," Egil said after checking with his comrades.

"Good. Are you ready for the exercise?"

"Ready," Nilsa said for all of them, but there was nervousness in her tone.

"Very well. Get into formation. We're changing positions today: Viggo and Egil behind, Nilsa and Gerd at the front. The exercise is on horseback. I'll play the role of the protectee," Raner said, putting on a white apron that covered his back and front. "Two Royal Rangers will ride on my left and two on my right; that way we'll have the full formation and cover."

"Understood," said Gerd, watching the Rangers taking their positions. After a moment, the four Panthers did so too with Raner in the middle.

"On we go," Raner ordered, and they headed on toward the forest.

"I'll set the pace. You need to follow without losing your position."

A moment later Raner sped up their riding pace.

Viggo and Egil had no trouble following the rhythm since Raner was riding in front of them. Neither did the Royal Rangers on both sides, since they rode beside the First Ranger. Those having a little more trouble were Nilsa and Gerd, since they were riding ahead and had to keep looking back over their shoulders in order to maintain the rhythm without going either too fast or slow.

Raner rode at a slow trot, and they all more or less managed to maintain the position well. They were good riders. They had no problem keeping a consistent pace. The horses' hooves echoed on the road and the warm breeze touched their faces and ruffled their hair. The forest was ahead and they were approaching it.

"This is a piece of cake for us, a stroll," Viggo whispered to Egil, the look on his face saying this was too easy for experts like them.

"Don't be overconfident. The exercise isn't going to be this simple," Egil said, looking at Raner's back.

As if he had heard them, the First Ranger changed the rhythm and began to ride faster, abruptly and without warning, Viggo and Egil spurred their mounts so as not to be left behind. The Royal

Rangers picked up the pace at once, as if Raner had warned them, only he had not. Somehow they had adjusted to the change in pace instantly. But that wasn't Nilsa's and Gerd's case; they were caught unawares, and they could not adapt to the change in time.

The First Ranger rode up to them.

"Watch out. You must never lose your position. If we had been attacked from behind, you would've hindered our escape."

"Sorry, sir," Nilsa apologized as she spurred her horse.

"Are we being attacked from the rear?" Raner asked, looking at Viggo and Egil.

They both looked back just in case. It turned out they were not, but they had not checked before, they had simply followed Raner.

"No, sir," Egil replied.

"A little late to check, don't you think?"

"Yes… sir," Viggo replied, annoyed with himself for not having looked back first.

"You must be alert to any suspicious movement, whether from the group or outside. Seek the origin and react at once," he told them in a firm tone, speaking above the sound of the horses galloping but without raising his voice or shouting.

No one said anything, and they all adjusted to the First Ranger's imposed rhythm. As soon as they did so and had been riding a short while he did it again, abruptly. This time he stopped his mount at once, pulling on the reins without warning. He said nothing and made no gesture. He was clearly trying to catch them unawares to surprise them.

Nilsa and Gerd realized and stopped their horses a moment after Raner. Viggo and Egil, who saw him pulling on the reins, tried to stop their own horses but were not fast enough and nearly crashed into Raner.

The First Ranger shook his head.

"Too slow. You must react much faster," he told them, not happy.

"That was on purpose," Viggo protested.

The First Ranger turned to him.

"Of course it was on purpose, to see your reaction time, and it was too slow. On the other hand, the Royal Rangers reacted at once and stopped at the right moment."

"Because they know all the tricks," Viggo replied.

Raner's eyes opened wide.

"Tricks? There are not tricks here. One must pay attention and react. Only that. Or are you planning on crashing into the Queen's horse when she stops all of a sudden to look at something? I'm sure she won't like that very much."

"Yeah… that's for sure…" Viggo had to admit.

"Stop thinking with a mind focused on offense instead of defense. We're defending here. You have to always think about reacting and protecting, not attacking."

"We are trying," said Nilsa.

"Your first instinct every time there's an unexpected action is to reach for your weapons. I've noticed. It's your natural reaction."

"That's because as a rule we're risking our lives," said Gerd while he adjusted his bow, which he had reached for as Raner had said.

"It is a reflective act," Nilsa said as she too adjusted her quiver.

"I know, and I understand. Every Ranger has it. But here you must stop to think before reaching for your weapons."

"I don't like that very much… I'd rather draw my weapons first and think later."

"That can be counterproductive," said Egil.

"Very counterproductive. You might create a dangerous situation and even lose the person you're protecting," Raner said.

None of the four Panthers said anything. They understood and knew what Raner meant. He was right, and they had to accept it.

Raner gave the order to continue, and when they entered the forest he began to change their pace as abruptly as the recovery from it was. Halfway into the forest, he suddenly changed direction, completely turning around and riding back along the way they had come. This puzzled the Panthers a little, although they were aware the First Ranger was trying to make things as difficult as possible.

He continued making abrupt changes, traveling to the sides now, and the group had serious trouble maintaining their positions. The First Ranger lectured them every time they did something wrong, but he no longer stopped or waited for them to recover, he simply rode on.

They arrived almost at the beginning of the forest and he switched directions again and started galloping at once toward the center of the trees. The group maneuvered as fast as they could and managed, more or less, to follow Raner, maintaining the formation.

"If he stops suddenly, we'll run him over," Viggo told Egil.

"If he turns east or west all of a sudden, I think we'll also have problems," Egil replied. "We're not doing very well…"

"Watch out for the next maneuver so he doesn't surprise us. I'm getting tired of him playing these games on us," Viggo said with a cunning look.

"I am watching out," Egil replied with eyes open wide, "and they're not just games, he's trying to teach us to always maintain the formation, no matter what happens," he explained while he directed his horse with his knees.

"Well I'm getting pretty tired of it…." Viggo frowned and also used his knees to guide his horse.

The First Ranger executed several maneuvers while crossing the forest and the Panthers held up pretty well, at least as far as they were concerned, although Raner did not think they were doing as well as they should and told them so.

"How are you doing?" Gerd asked Nilsa.

"Fine. I can manage the horse pretty well, at least when we turn left and right. But when he starts galloping all of a sudden, I have trouble catching up."

"It's the same with me, and my horse has trouble getting into the rhythm because of my weight…"

"You'll have to ask for a stronger horse. That one's a little too small for you," she smiled at him.

"He won't catch me off guard again," Gerd said, nodding and looking back to see whether there was another abrupt swerve.

They were reaching the end of the forest, and Raner slowed their pace to a light trot. They all adapted and it seemed they all did well, because Raner had no comment for them. This gave them a slight rest they badly needed. Viggo was about to say something to Egil when suddenly, from between the trees, behind and in front of the group, there appeared several attackers, armed with bows, axes, and knives.

They were being ambushed.

"We're under attack!" Nilsa warned as she nocked an arrow at once and shot at the first assailant racing toward them. She hit him in the chest and he fell to the ground.

"Five in front!" Gerd cried, and like Nilsa he nocked an arrow and skillfully shot the second assailant. He also hit the attacker in the chest, and the man fell to one side without reaching them.

Egil was looking at another four attackers coming up fast on the group's rear.

"Four behind!" he called out and, turning in his saddle, he aimed his bow.

An arrow came straight at Egil, who saw it and flattened himself against his horse's neck. The arrow flew by his ear without touching him.

Viggo opted for a different approach. He jumped off his horse without even turning around. By the time he had both feet on the ground he had already drawn his knives. Two assailants were running toward him. Like lightning, he summersaulted while an arrow flew two fingers from his back. He reached the assailants and attacked them. The first one was nocking a new arrow while the second one was coming at him with a knife and axe.

"Fools," he said before lunging at them.

Egil straightened up and released swiftly at the one who had shot him. His opponent saw him and threw himself to one side to dodge the arrow. But the attacker did not quite succeed—the arrow hit him in the leg. He dragged himself on the ground while Egil nocked another arrow to finish him.

At the front, Gerd had dismounted and was facing an attacker with axe and knife. His opponent was similarly armed.

Nilsa, on her horse, was nocking another arrow while looking for her next target with an expert archer's eye. Two attackers with bows were approaching her from her right and front. The one on the right was almost upon her. She did not think twice and, leaning forward on her mount to have a better angle, shot him in the stomach. The other one came at her from the left. Nilsa jumped off her horse to take cover behind it, because if he released at her she would be a sitting duck. The attacker was on the other side of her horse now. Nilsa dropped the bow and drew her knife and axe to finish him.

Gerd took care of the other assailant, and like Nilsa he turned to finish the one between the two of them.

But this attacker did not go for either of them. He slipped between Gerd's and Nilsa's horses at a gallop, leaving them behind.

"No!" cried Nilsa, seeing the attacker releasing at Raner from between the horses.

The arrow flew swiftly and hit Raner in the torso.

A second arrow coming from the rear hit Raner in the back.

"Oh no!" Egil cried when he saw.

Viggo turned. He had finished his two attackers and saw the archer who had slipped between Egil and himself from the back.

"Blast it!" he muttered under his breath, and kicked a rock on the ground in front of him.

Raner was shaking his head, looking disappointed. He took off his white apron: it was marked in the front and back with two large red stains that showed he had been hit.

"A total failure," he said in an unsatisfied tone.

The fallen attackers started getting back on their feet. They were Royal Rangers. They were all marked with red paint where the Panthers' arrows and other weapons had hit them. All except the two archers, who had slipped past the Panthers and finished off the protectee. Since they had all been carrying marking weapons, no one had been hurt.

"What is your main job?" Raner asked the Panthers as they approached with bowed heads.

"Safeguarding the life of the person we're protecting," Nilsa replied.

"And what did you do?"

"We responded to the attack," said Viggo.

"And what happened?"

"We lost the person we were supposed to protect..." Egil said, ashamed.

"Exactly. I have no doubts you would have finished off all the attackers and that you would've even managed to do so without getting severely hurt, because you are indeed skilled fighters. But that wouldn't have saved the protectee. You've reacted like the good fighters you are instead of like the good protectors we need you to be."

"Yes, sir..." said Nilsa, looking ashamed.

"We should've thought about protecting our target first before responding to the attack," Egil guessed.

"It's pure instinct. If we're attacked, we defend ourselves," Viggo said, raising his arms in frustration.

"It's hard not to respond to a direct attack, sir," Gerd added.

"An instinct you must learn to redirect. I'm not saying you shouldn't reject the attack. But you must always do so while first protecting your target. Otherwise, the same thing will happen as with today's exercise."

"We understand. We have to learn to face these situations from another point of view," said Egil. "It'll take us time, but we'll do it," he promised.

"Some habits are difficult to break," Nilsa said, looking at Viggo.

"You'll have to in order to become Royal Rangers. You have to approach the escort missions always as if you carried with you a vulnerable person in danger of being killed at any moment. You are not the target of the attack, and you never will be. You are an obstacle to overcome to reach the target and bring them down," Raner explained to them, tapping his red-stained chest.

"We will, sir, don't worry," Gerd promised.

"That's better. Good. The exercise is finished. We'll return to the castle. Think about what happened today and what I've told you. Process it."

Nilsa, Gerd, and Viggo nodded.

The Royal Rangers brought back the horses they had hidden in the forest, and they all rode for the castle.

As they were riding back, Gerd was thinking that Raner never shouted, not even when they performed badly. He seemed to stay calm at all times, which was something to be grateful for. There was nothing worse than an obnoxious instructor who yelled all the time. What he did do was speak in a tone that transmitted how unhappy and disappointed he was when they did not meet his expectations. That stung a lot more than shouting or punishments, a lot more indeed. Gerd wanted things to go well so that Raner would be happy. He was going to do his best to impress the First Ranger and knew his comrades were too. Viggo was going to find it a little more difficult to adapt than him and Nilsa. It was the Assassin's nature to attack immediately. But even so, he had hopes that they would manage to adapt, and he also hoped it would not take them too long.

While they were entering the city, Gerd thought of Lasgol, Ona, and Camu. What were they up to? He hoped they would be all right. Confident they were doing all right, he cheered himself up and smiled. Then he thought about all the troubles they had gone through before and about the Immortal Dragon and doubt overcame him. He would need to be careful, keep his eyes wide open, and, more than anything else, keep all his senses alert.

Chapter 24

Lasgol, Ona, and Camu arrived at a fishing village on the southern coast. They were in the southernmost part between the kingdom of Rogdon and the forests of the Usik. Ahead of them spread the Central Sea. As far as Lasgol knew, it was a warm, quiet sea. The weather was usually mild, so there were no rough seas and sailing was easy as a rule, but of course with them you could never be sure. For starters, a monstrous crocodile had jumped into the sea.

The Central Sea separated the upper part of Tremia from the lower. The kingdoms of Central Tremia, like Erenal or Zangria, were located in the upper part, and in the lower, beyond the sea, were the territories under the control of the Nocean Empire, with the deserts and the scorching sun, which made it difficult to live in certain areas because of the scarcity of water.

Go village? Camu messaged to Lasgol.

Yeah, I'll go. You follow me camouflaged but at a safe distance. We need a ship.

Dangerous?

Lasgol checked the fishing village from the distance. It looked quiet. He counted about thirty small, simple houses. A rustic jetty which two men were repairing had three fishing boats moored to it. Out at sea he could see about a dozen boats fishing, not too far away, within eyesight. It looked quiet, almost idyllic, but it was an Inon village, so he did not know what he would find. He was hoping they would not be too aggressive toward foreigners.

I don't know, we'll see.

Be careful.

Don't worry, I will be.

Ona moaned once. She wanted to go with Lasgol.

Sorry, but you can't come, you'd scare them. I'm sure they've never seen a snow panther so far south.

We near.

That's right. Stay outside the village but nearby while I try to negotiate something.

Okay.

Lasgol headed toward the village. He had never had any contact with any of the Inon. So far all he knew was that they looked terrifying, were excellent archers and horseback riders, and fought with great courage. He hoped the fishermen of this race were less aggressive.

He entered the only street the village had. He was riding his Pinto horse and going slowly. Aodh's Bow was slung across his back, and the weapons at his waist were concealed by his cloak. He did not want to give the impression that he was looking for trouble. When he had gone about a quarter of the way down the street, he noticed that his presence had drawn the attention of the locals. Several seven- or eight-year-old kids, who to his surprise already wore their hair in that unique style—shorn at the sides and with a crest in the middle—ran off to inform the adults.

He also saw some women sewing fishing nets who ran inside their houses as soon as they saw him coming. Other women were washing clothes beside a river. Lasgol was surprised to see that the women wore their hair parted in two long braids that came down on either side. He also noticed that they wore paint on their faces. He had no idea what the circles and other shapes they wore meant or the reason behind the colors they used. All the women he saw had their faces painted the same way, and he found that singular.

No-one came out to attack or welcome him, so he headed to the jetty slowly. There, the two men he had seen working on it stopped what they were doing and stood up. They both reached for their knives. They were not warriors, but they wore the same hairstyle as the fighters. It must be something tribal, not linked to the function of each one in their society. Their deep-red arms and legs were uncovered.

Lasgol lifted his hands, showing them his spread palms.

"You have nothing to fear from me," he said in Norghanian.

The two men spoke in their own tongue, but Lasgol was unable to understand a word. He had to resort to sign language. First he wanted to let them know that he did not mean them any harm. Out of the corner of his eye he saw three other men approaching with knives in their hands. To make his stance more obvious, he un-slung his bow and, without dismounting, dropped it on the ground. Then he did the same with the quiver, finishing with his Ranger's knife and axe.

The five fishermen were looking at him with distrust in their eyes. They continued asking questions in their own language, but they seemed more at ease now that Lasgol was disarmed and sitting on his horse without attempting anything.

The fruitless conversation continued for a while. Lasgol did not understand anything they were saying to him. He dismounted slowly, keeping his hands raised and palms spread. He went up to one of the boats. It was a small fishing boat, but it was the biggest at the jetty. It had a sail and was quite ample. Lasgol calculated that the three of them would fit in it; it would be tight, but they would manage.

"I need that boat," he said, pointing at it.

The fishermen made negative signs and continued speaking in their language, so Lasgol was unable to understand a word.

"Fishing boat for gold," he told them, and slowly he put his hand in his Ranger's belt until he found his gold pouch. He took out two Norghanian gold coins and showed them to the men.

The fishermen recognized the gold—it was an international currency. Every kingdom or tribe appreciated it, no matter what archaic symbols were engraved on either side, as long as it was gold.

"Two gold ones for the boat," he said and made signs indicating the boat and then the two coins.

Suddenly, one of the fishermen showed him four fingers and started saying things.

"Four?" Lasgol showed the man four fingers.

The man was nodding.

"Four is too much for a fishing boat. I'll give you three," said Lasgol, who knew he was being swindled, but he needed the boat, whatever he had to pay for it.

The other fishermen joined in the conversation and started haggling with Lasgol as well.

After a while of negotiations and haggling with signs, Lasgol managed to obtain the boat for two coins, which in a way he considered a triumph. The fishermen had begun to bid up one another, and in the end this had favored Lasgol.

He paid and exchanged the Pinto horse, which he could not take with him, for food and drink for a week. He picked up his weapons and satchel full of supplies and said goodbye as best he could to the fishermen, who returned to their tasks. Lasgol guessed they had already had some foreign visitors and they were used to negotiating with gold. The locals most likely traded with other kingdoms. Rogdon was near, and the Nocean Empire was on the other side of the sea, which was not that large.

At last, when he was ready, he called Camu and Ona to come aboard. The fishing boat was made to catch fish with one or two people, not to transport cargo, so they were going to have a most uncomfortable sailing. They settled down as best they could. Camu took up most of the space, but Lasgol managed to sit at the stern. Ona had no choice but to get on top of Camu. Since they were both invisible, Lasgol did not know they were like that until they left the fishing village and were out at sea.

Are you all right? he asked while he tried to fix the sail as best he could. They needed wind to sail.

I on side, Ona on top no good.

Ona growled twice.

You'll have to bear it for a while.

No have boat more big? Camu complained.

This was the biggest boat at the jetty. I couldn't wait until a bigger one came back. We can't lose the crocodile.

I no happy.

Ona joined in the unhappiness with two more growls.

It's not that bad, don't protest so much, Lasgol transmitted to them. He felt bad for both of them, but he could do nothing more than give them a little tough love.

Where crocodile?

That's a good question. I haven't received any sign yet. We'll go south, which is the direction he was following on land.

Perhaps south only to get sea.

True. That's what I'm afraid of too. It might have changed course now that it's at sea.

They sailed on and passed some other fishing boats. Camu and Ona camouflaged using Camu's skill, and Lasgol waved at the fishermen, who stared at him with their mouths wide open. They were expecting to see a fellow man with hair in a crest and deep red skin, not a pale blond with strange flat hair.

As soon as they left the fishermen behind, Lasgol felt the jewel's signal. It came from the south about two leagues away.

I have it. It's still heading south.

We pursue and catch.

We'll try. Let's see whether we can get closer.

Lasgol set a southern course, and they were lucky enough to have a favorable wind. The fishing boat was faster than Lasgol expected, considering how much the three of them weighed, especially Camu.

To the east, they saw an island. Lasgol tried to remember its name. The map he carried did not cover the Central Sea. He had not calculated he would need maps of that region. It was the Island of Coporne. It was inhabited by a race, the Coporneans, natives of this island and who, with the passing of centuries, had taken over all the islands of the Central Sea. From them they controlled all maritime trade.

Big ship, Camu messaged in warning.

Lasgol saw a large ship coming from the south. It was a huge trireme. It looked like a Copornean war ship on a patrol mission. He checked the sails and saw the initials "CP" clearly. They were painted in black inside a large circle, also black. It was the emblem of the Coporneans.

Hide yourselves, we don't want any trouble with them.

Them? Who?

The Coporneans. They're from a nearby island. They're maritime traders who use large triremes both for trade and war.

Ship pretty.

Yeah, it is.

The great trireme was spectacular. It must have been carrying a crew of close to a hundred people, most of which were at the oars, judging by the speed they were approaching.

Why war?

The Coporneans hold a great rivalry with the Nocean Empire to the south, and with the Kingdom of Erenal and the Confederation of Free Cities of the East. They all want to control the Central Sea and its trade, but the Coporneans are currently the ones in control.

Gold?

Yeah, gold, silver, iron, silk, food, spices, and any number of other things traded between nations.

Come to us?

Yeah, don't let yourselves be seen. They shouldn't attack us.

The great trireme passed close by the boat. To starboard Lasgol could see several Copornean soldiers. They had white skin, although tanner than that of the Norghanians. Their features were fine and they had brown eyes and long hair and beards, which were also brown. They used bronze-colored armor with matching breastplates, vambrances and greaves. On their heads they wore a plain helmet, also bronze-colored, which left their eyes and nose free while covering the rest of the head. And they were armed with short swords and bows. The soldiers stared at Lasgol from the high ship's rail, and he pretended to be having trouble with the sail. Beside the great trireme, the little fishing boat looked like a toy.

Don't you dare move, they're inspecting us, Lasgol transmitted to Camu and Ona.

At an order of its captain, the trireme went on, leaving Lasgol in peace. He snorted in relief. If they had stopped, things would have become complicated. Especially if they had boarded the little boat to requisition merchandise, something quite common in this sea. Several strong waves caused by the passing of the trireme hit the boat, almost making it capsize. Camu nearly fell in the water, and Ona held on with feline skill.

Almost in water! Camu protested.

We almost capsized, which is even worse. Those war ships are enormous and move a lot of water as they pass by.

You tell they look where go.

Better we don't say anything and not get into trouble.

No better, but agree.

They continued sailing south and Lasgol received a new signal, which worried him. If they kept going in that direction, they would arrive to the north coast of the deserts, which were under control of the Nocean Empire. Was that where the crocodile was headed? And if it was so, where? The chase was starting to become quite dangerous, since they were entering territory of the southern kingdoms, and not exactly the kind that took kindly to foreigners who came to sniff around. Unfortunately, there was nothing else they could do but follow the great reptile and hope that nothing bad would happen.

They sailed for several days, following the pulse that always indicated south. They came across two other Copornean triremes, which ignored them as they went by at high speed, making waves in their wake. Lasgol snorted in relief to see they wanted nothing with them.

Other ship. Different, Camu said suddenly.

Lasgol turned and looked at the ship now passing before them in the distance.

That's a Nocean ship, the hull and sails are different.

No trireme?

No, they're a different type of vessel.

Stronger?

Faster.

The fact that they were already seeing Nocean ships indicated they were very close to the north coast of the south of Tremia. This meant they would soon encounter more Noceans, which was not good news. The Noceans were not keen on finding foreigners in their lands.

Lasgol was not mistaken. They soon spotted dry land on the horizon. A long brown line with a layer the color of sand on top appeared rising from the sea.

Land, he informed Camu and Ona.

High time. Side hurts, Camu protested, but it was true that he was sort of boxed in the boat.

Ona chirped once and turned over to be able to see it.

No move, Ona, tickles.

The poor panther lay down again on top of him, but this time looking toward land.

Soon after, Lasgol received a new signal indicating the position of the crocodile. It was still going south.

The crocodile has reached land and is continuing south.

More slow on land.

Yeah but it's in Nocean territory, in the deserts...

What we do?

Lasgol thought for a long time while he maintained his fixed course. He could not lose the pearls, and they had to find Dergha-Sho-Blaska.

We follow it.

Chapter 25

They reached the Nocean coast of the Central Sea and landed at a small beach with dunes. Lasgol dragged the boat up the beach in case they needed it to go back; he did not want the tide to take it. He looked around. They were alone on a beautiful beach of white sand, with the sea at his back and in front large dunes with some vegetation between them, which foretold what they would likely find beyond.

We keep going south, he transmitted to Camu and Ona.

Okay.

Ona chirped once.

They started up the dunes, soon encountering a landscape that was as beautiful as it was desolate. An enormous desert began beyond the first dunes, which still had some vegetation and spread as far as the eye could see. To the southwest they saw the walls and towers of what looked like a large city, the city of Marucose, one of the northernmost cities of the Nocean Empire.

Very desert.

You can say that again. The worst thing is that the desert spreads for leagues and leagues in every direction.

No water?

There are some cities, villages, and oases, but water is scarce in this part of the world.

No good.

No, it's not.

The sun was shining bright in a sky with barely a couple of flimsy and far-apart clouds in the immense blue. What troubled Lasgol was that it was summer and they were about to enter the Nocean desert. This was never a good idea, but least of all in the summer. They were going to be roasted alive.

Going on is dangerous without a guide… and in this climate…

No can stop now, Camu messaged to him.

Ona chirped once.

Fine, but remember that the desert will kill you if you're not careful.

We careful.

They started into the desert very restlessly. From the beginning, the way was hard. The burning sand and the scorching sun were terrible. They were going to have a hard time. Besides, one step in the desert was twice as tiresome as one on flat land. It was even more difficult than on snow. It might also be that they were so unused to it that they found it difficult and exhausting.

As they walked on, Lasgol tried to cheer his friends despite the adverse conditions.

Imagine we're in the northern territories and that the sand is snow.

Imagine a lot.

Lasgol smiled. *I know, but it's the only thing I can think of to ease the journey.*

Suddenly Lasgol received a pulse, indicating the crocodile's direction. He stopped to make sure he located it properly. Camu and Ona waited beside him in silence under a sun they felt ever more scorching. It was as if it wanted to roast them for some serious offense they had committed against it.

It's turned aside and going southeast. It turned a little to the east, although it's still heading south. It's moving away from Marucose. It's going the opposite way.

Is good?

I don't really know. I've no idea what cities or settlements are in that area.

No map?

Lasgol shook his head.

No, we have no map, and we need one. Going into that desert without one is madness.

Follow crocodile.

And if it leads us to die in the desert?

Then no good.

Ona moaned twice.

Let's go a little further, but if things get ugly, we'll come back to the beach, said Lasgol, jabbing his thumb behind him.

They kept up the pursuit, and Lasgol soon found the trail of the great reptile. It was a huge trail which could be seen for a great distance in the middle of the desert sand. What surprised him was that it was still walking, dragging both its maimed hind legs. It could not get too far this way. Besides, it must be making a considerable effort, dragging itself along the desert in that manner. In the sea it must not have noticed how bad it was, but on land it was a very different matter.

Let's follow the trail. It can't have gone far.
Better. I much hot.

Ona, with her tongue hanging out, did not even make a sound.

Yeah, you and Ona aren't made for this climate. Cold is your thing.

Lasgol felt bad for the two of them. For a Norghanian the desert was a terrible torture, but for creatures of snow and ice like Ona and Camu it was even more so. The sun was scorching, and it punished them with every step they took in the sand. They could barely breathe they felt so hot. They seemed to be slowly roasting on a grill with the sun burning down on them and the sand broiling them from below with every step.

Lasgol was wearing his hood up to protect his head and face from the sun. His hands were also covered with gloves. But it did not take long for him to be soaking in sweat. They walked on the sand slowly, following the clear trail the monster had left on the sand. The monster was likely not suffering the sun's punishment as much as they were. Sea crocodiles were used to high temperatures, at least those that lived in Nocean territory.

The journey soon became an inferno. The scorching sun and the burning sand were merciless. Camu and Ona were walking with their tongues hanging out. Ona had placed herself in the shadow of Camu so the sun would not punish her so much. Lasgol was walking, trying to show fortitude, but the torrid heat he felt was making the journey miserable. He had never thought he would ever wish to be back in the frozen lands, freezing cold.

The first day came to an end and night fell. They stopped to rest where they were. Lasgol looked around, but all he could see was an endless desert without a soul in it. Ona and Camu dropped down on the sand, exhausted by the intense conditions they had suffered. Lasgol gave them water from the supplies he was carrying. When his friends finished drinking, he drank.

Better? he asked them.

Ona moaned once.

Little better.

How are you coping with the heat, Camu? Can you go on?

Heat bad. Hard breathe.

Are your scales burning?

Not burn. Feel roast inside.

Well, that's bad.

No think can walk desert. Bad for me.

Yeah, I was just thinking that. And Ona isn't much better than you with all her winter fur.

The snow panther moaned.

I think the best thing to do is to travel by night. If we keep going during the day under this fearsome sun, something might happen to you.

And crocodile?

With the trail its leaving, it's impossible to lose it.

But perhaps arrive late.

Yeah, that's a risk we'll have to take.

You go ahead, we go after.

Lasgol wrinkled his nose. He understood what Camu was saying, but he did not want to leave them behind again.

You go. We follow trail night. Rest day.

No. No way. I'm not leaving you in the middle of a desert. Forget it. We'll all go together at night.

Ona chirped once.

Rest a little and we'll keep going.

Okay.

A few hours later, the three friends renewed the pursuit. The night was cool and there came a time when it was even cold, which the three appreciated down to their core. They were able to go pretty far before dawn arrived. As soon as the sun began to rise and got strong, they stopped.

We have to improvise some sort of shelter, or we'll roast alive.

How shelter?

I don't know… I didn't bring a tent, Lasgol transmitted ruefully.

He studied their surroundings, but there was not a tree in sight, or a rock. Nothing but an immense sea of sand which would soon burn and consume them in its flaming ardor.

Try magic.

You want to experiment now?

No shelter, we roast alive.

True. But I don't think we can create a skill in these conditions.

Try.

You're right, we don't lose anything by trying. At least while we can.

They both began trying to create some kind of shelter. Lasgol concentrated, shutting his eyes, and sought to create a tent that would protect them from the sun. Not only protect them, but deflect the sunrays that burnt their bodies. But what he feared happened. The terrible heat and the difficulty he had breathing prevented Lasgol from creating the skill. Every time he tried part of his energy was consumed, but the skill did not come. The green flash started to form and then went out an instant later, and Lasgol felt quite frustrated.

Beside him, Camu was trying with the same result. His eyes were shut, and every time he failed he shook his tail in frustration. Ona watched them, sitting between the two, first one and then the other. As the failures occurred, the panther hunched down more.

The attempts went on for half the day, and the sun began to be insufferable. They were being burned alive under its strong rays. There was nowhere to hide. It was as tough as it was unpleasant.

Then suddenly Camu flashed with a strong silver light. Lasgol saw it and his eyes opened wide. That was a skill—he had managed something. Or at least Lasgol hoped so, for the sake of all three of them. An instant later a dome was covering them. It was translucent. Similar to what Camu created to protect himself from external magic. But once formed the dome began to freeze, and a moment later frost appeared, covering it entirely and creating shade inside.

The sun rays tried to penetrate the dome of frost, but they bounced off. Not only that, but inside the dome they began to feel a certain cool caused by the ice the dome was made of.

Ona rubbed against the ice wall to cool off.

You did it, Camu!

I much good.

It's awesome! It protects us and cools us off!

Only a problem.

Lasgol guessed at once.

It's melting.

Much melt. I use more magic.

Well, it's not perfect, but it works. Use magic to strengthen it. But only use what's necessary to maintain the effect, let's see how long you can keep it up.

I try.

To Lasgol's surprise, Camu was able to keep the ice shelter active almost the whole day. This allowed them to be safe from the inclement sun and keep cool. So they continued their way before night came, once the shelter melted away.

Do you have any energy left? Lasgol transmitted to Camu, quite concerned.

Yes, you easy, I save little.

Wonderful. Lasgol was afraid that Camu might exhaust all his inner energy and then faint. They both had to take this into account.

What are you going to call this new skill?

Frozen Shelter.

I like it.

Ona chirped once.

They followed the trail of the great reptile and Lasgol noticed, from the tracks it left, that it was having trouble going on. It was much slower and dragged more of its body. Its strength was beginning to fail. He shared this with Camu and Ona and increased their pace to reach the monster.

Walking at night in that desert, under the stars and a completely clear sky, was not altogether bad, particularly when the temperature went down quite a bit. Camu and Ona were fine and Lasgol felt pretty well, except for the sand that got into his boots, which was going to leave his feet covered in sores. He would have to treat them during their next rest. He definitely preferred the snow-covered mountains of his own land to the desert.

They found the monstrous crocodile at last, and the place and the manner in which they found it left them speechless. It was in the water of a pond in a large oasis in a hollow between two sand dunes.

That be water. How can be?

It's an oasis. Under the sand there has to be a natural deposit of water, Lasgol explained.

Crocodile enjoy.

Lasgol watched the great reptile floating in the water. It occupied almost the whole pond. It was slumbering, or at least its eyes were shut. It seemed to be enjoying the bath and the rest.

This be the place?

I don't know. We'll have to wait and see what happens.

They got down on their stomachs on the dune and watched the great crocodile. What they were not expecting was that it would be there for quite a while. For two whole days the giant crocodile remained soaking and resting. Ona, Camu, and Lasgol had to set up camp a little further back so the monster would not see them. Since the oasis was in a hollow it was not likely, but they could not afford to take risks.

Much envy, Camu messaged to Lasgol.

Yeah, me too.

Ona joined in the feeling with a moan.

Seeing the monster enjoying the water of the oasis was a torture, especially when the sun was hotter and they had to seek refuge in the *Frozen Shelter* Camu created around them.

This shelter is also very good.

Shelter good, oasis better.

Ona moaned once.

Yeah, and besides, it doesn't force you to use magic the whole day.

On the third day, the monster finally moved. With clumsy strides, it came out of the water and began to climb one of the dunes to the east.

It's leaving, Lasgol transmitted in warning.

Now walk better.

Yeah, I think it's been resting, healing its wounds and recuperating its strength.

This no be place.

No, it's going on. We'll have to follow it.

They let the monster go on so they would be out of its range of vision. Then they went down into the oasis. The three friends drank at once, and after they had quenched their thirst, they all got into the water and enjoyed a bath that was worth half the gold of the Norghanian treasury. It was not only fresh, clean water, the oasis was also surrounded by palm trees and other exotic, deep-green plants they did not know. The plant life gladdened the soul in the middle of that arid, yellow world.

Lasgol climbed up to see whether the crocodile had continued its course or doubled back. He did not want it to surprise them there while they were bathing. He saw it was keeping its course without looking back, crossing the desert toward the southeast. He came down again and jumped into the water to splash along with Camu and Ona, who were already having fun chasing each other in the water.

For a long while they forgot their woes, the scorching sun, the desert, the burns, the heat, their noses burnt inside and out, and enjoyed themselves. Afterward, they lay on the shore under the lovely shade of two palm trees to rest before continuing their chase.

Five figures in blue clothes were watching them from the dune behind them.

Lasgol felt something was not right. He turned over on the ground and saw them.

Watch out, behind us!

Chapter 26

The afternoon was warm and the sky was clear, which cheered up everyone before beginning their practice. Nilsa, Egil, Gerd, and Viggo were waiting at the meeting point outside the city toward the south, at the crossing of the Royal Roads. They were beside the wooden sign with the names of the nearest cities. They had left their horses tethered to a pair of ilex oaks east of the road, and they were chatting easily.

"What a lovely day," Nilsa said contentedly, spreading her arms open and turning her face toward the sun for the warm light to bathe her.

"A perfect day to be ruined by a war, an attempted regicide, or something of the sort," Viggo said, chewing on the tip of a blade of grass.

"Don't jinx it," Gerd chided. "We're doing well, let's just enjoy the moment and the beautiful day."

"Raner won't be long. I'm impatient to know what we'll learn today." Egil was rubbing his hands together and had a lively look and smile on his face.

"I bet you the lesson will be about helping the King mount his horse by us getting on all fours like a footstool, or perhaps something even more humiliating."

Nilsa and Gerd laughed out loud.

"I doubt that'll be the case," Egil said, also laughing.

"Then it'll be something as important as cradling his Majesty and singing him lullabies so he can sleep at night," Viggo continued the joke.

"That I'd like to see," Gerd said, still laughing.

"I wouldn't. I don't even want to imagine that," Nilsa said, horrified.

"You're impossible," Egil told Viggo with a slap on his shoulder.

Raner appeared soon with four Royal Rangers, and the moment of relaxation for the Panthers ended. The day was glorious, but Raner wore a worried look which made clear something was happening.

"Sir?" Nilsa greeted him questioningly with her head to one side.

"Ranger Specialists," Raner greeted them.

"Is everything all right, sir?" Egil asked.

Raner snorted.

"The King has ordered all his armies to be on alert. It seems war is imminent. He's also started recruiting the eastern militia. He's sent orders to the Western Nobles to send their soldiers to be a part of the army, or else to join the King's armies personally leading their own troops."

"I'm sure they'll be delighted," Viggo said wryly. "They'll all run in personally to be first in line."

"That's inconsequential. They have to obey. They're the King's orders," Raner's severe tone left no doubt that he was a King's man.

"I'm sure the Western Nobles will answer the King's call," Egil said in a pacifying tone.

"The whole kingdom must unite when a foreign force threatens it," Nilsa commented, looking at Egil out of the corner of her eye. Her friend returned the glance without saying anything.

"I still hope we won't have to fight," Gerd said hopefully. "Maybe they'll find a peaceful solution to this situation."

"I'm afraid things have taken the opposite turn," Raner told him.

"But the King hasn't been able to prove that the murder attempts were ordered by Zangria," Gerd replied.

"That won't stop our King if he's convinced that's the case and that he's within his rights. I'm afraid that's the situation we find ourselves in," said Raner.

"Let's wait and see what happens. It's not good to anticipate events and conclusions. It's usually counterproductive," said Egil.

Raner nodded.

"That's true. Well, let's focus on the training," Raner went on. "Today we'll practice protection in situations where you are on foot but the protectee is on horseback."

"Is that frequent, sir?" Gerd asked, surprised.

Raner wrinkled his nose.

"It's not desirable, since it leaves the protectee in a clearly vulnerable position, but it can happen."

"That's what I was thinking, sir. It's dangerous," said Nilsa.

"It is, very dangerous. That's why we must be prepared. This usually happens in parades, retinues, outings and the like. The protectee—one or several, since there might be more than one—will be riding slowly, which leaves them visible and vulnerable. The Royal Rangers are on foot, surrounding the protectee. It's a complex and dangerous situation."

"Why aren't we on horseback like them, sir?" Gerd asked. "If we surround him, we can cover him much better."

"It's not always possible. There are occasions when the protectee wishes to be the central focus, a visible and radiant figure, the center of attention. On those occasions, he doesn't want anyone to overshadow him," Raner explained.

"Oh, I see…" Gerd was thoughtful.

One of the Royal Rangers commented something to Raner in a low voice and they began to talk in whispers.

Viggo seized the chance and whispered in Gerd's ear.

"Why do you want to surround him? To receive a poisoned arrow in his place?"

Gerd looked at him with disbelief.

"We're his protectors," he whispered back.

"You're a goody-two-shoes and a fool," Viggo said in his ear. "I'll bring flowers to your grave. I have no intention of dying for cretin Thoran or his obnoxious wife."

Gerd looked at him, opening his eyes wide.

"It's our duty…"

"It might be yours, but it certainly isn't mine. Open your eyes, big guy. Don't waste your life on someone who doesn't deserve your loyalty."

Gerd was about to reply, but he stayed quiet and thoughtful. Viggo's words sank in deeply and made him wonder.

"Good. Let's practice. I'll be the protectee and will be riding. Everyone else, take up your positions as if I were on foot."

"Yes, sir," Nilsa said for their group.

The Panthers took their positions on the sides: Nilsa and Gerd to the west, Viggo and Gerd to the east. The Royal Rangers left their horses tethered with the others. Two of them went to the front and two behind so as to have all six members of a protective group, which was the minimum required. They surrounded Raner, following the instructions they already knew by heart.

"Imagine that we're in the middle of the capital. I'm the King and I ride through the masses, waving at the people as we come down the main avenue out of the Royal Castle. It's a clear day. The whole city has come out to watch the parade, to see their King," Raner explained as he went forward on his horse.

"Do we have reinforcements above, sir?" Nilsa asked.

"Not in this exercise. There might be an archer hiding in some high position," Raner informed them.

"That puts us at a disadvantage, sir," said Gerd.

"It's a difficult exercise, but one that happens frequently," Raner said with a shrug.

Viggo did not look satisfied.

"If the exercise puts us at a clear disadvantage, we can't be expected to do it well."

Raner glared at him.

"Are you a real Ranger, or are you someone who balks at the first obstacle?"

Viggo muttered something under his breath along the lines of wishing Raner would get off his horse so he could teach him what a real Ranger was, but he decided it was better not to confront the First Ranger, at least for now. The day would come.

"I'll stop the arrow sent at your heart with my own hand, don't worry, sir," he replied in a tone filled with irony.

"I would expect nothing less of my Royal Rangers," Raner said, and by his tone he meant it.

"Yes, sir, will do, sir," Gerd intervened so there would be no problems.

Raner rode on, and they came to a farm to the left of the road. They could see two wooden buildings, what must be the farmer's house and a shed for the cattle beside it. The buildings were about a hundred paces from the road. Opposite the farm, on the other side of the road, was a small birch wood.

"In this bodyguard situation, you have to be alert to anyone attacking the protectee from a short distance. He's a clear target for an archer, but also for an attacker trying to get to him."

They went on along the road. When they came level with the farm and the forest, they increased their precautions. Raner was riding nonchalantly in his role of careless monarch and was turning right and left, waving and nodding in greeting as if he were really moving through a crowd that had come to see him. Even if all that was there were a few cows grazing by the farm and squirrels and birds in the woods.

"Buildings to the east, possible archers," Raner alerted, pointing at the two buildings.

"Let's cover them," Egil told Viggo as he nocked an arrow.

"I think I see someone on the roof of the shed," Viggo said, also nocking an arrow.

"I don't see him, are you sure?" Egil asked.

"If we could stop for a moment to watch, I'd make sure," Viggo said, looking with narrowed eyes. He turned to Raner. The First Ranger continued his advance on his horse.

"Shed or farmhouse?" Egil asked, aiming his bow at one and the other.

"Shed. I swear I saw a shadow moving on the shed's roof."

They both aimed at the roof of the shed, trying to locate the archer while keeping up with the retinue as it continued moving forward.

All of a sudden, from the trees of the wood to the west, there came five Royal Rangers with spears who lunged at Nilsa and Gerd, who were protecting that side.

"We're being attacked! From the west!" Nilsa cried out in alarm as she nocked an arrow.

"They have spears!" Gerd warned, raising his bow to aim.

"Get rid of them! We keep moving!" Raner ordered, pointing ahead.

The two Royal Rangers in the lead kept advancing, following Raner's orders. The First Ranger went with them, unflinching in the saddle. He did not break into a gallop. Neither did the Royal Rangers who brought the rear.

"We have to help them!" Viggo cried when he saw there were five attackers, all carrying spears.

Egil was watching Raner, trying to think of the best way to proceed in that situation.

"We never stop! We keep moving!" Raner ordered them.

"But…" Viggo said, pointing at Nilsa and Gerd.

"We move on!" Raner insisted.

Nilsa released, and her arrow hit the attacker closest to her, who fell down. Rapidly, she took another arrow from the quiver at her back and nocked it.

Gerd released and brought down another of the attackers, who fell to one side. He started to nock another arrow but realized he would not have time to release. One attacker lunged at him with his spear ready, a spear that covered the distance separating them in a flash. Gerd hit the tip of the spear that was heading to his stomach with his bow and deflected it. It brushed his side. He dropped his bow, and with his two large strong hands he grabbed the attacker by his clothes. He was almost as big as Gerd but not quite. With one strong pull, Gerd lifted him a handspan off the ground and threw him to one side. Before he had time to react, Gerd had drawn his knife and axe and was on him.

Nilsa had time to release again, and she hit the attacker in the shoulder, which made him drop his spear. But the wound was not deadly. The attacker realized this and drew his knife and axe. Nilsa did so too, and they lunged at each other.

Ignoring what was happening, the fifth attacker went straight for Raner. Nilsa and Gerd had left the side unprotected when they got into the fray. The attacker reached Raner. The two rear Rangers raised their bows to bring him down.

Unfortunately, the spear was very long and reached the protectee first.

With a tremendous pull, Viggo dismounted Raner toward him so he fell on his side. Raner nimbly broke his fall by rolling over.

The spear only met air.

Two arrows brought down the attacker.

Nilsa and Gerd finished with the two attackers they were fighting against.

Raner rose slowly without looking at Viggo. He stood up and brushed the dirt off his clothes. The fall would have been hard for a noble, but not for the First Ranger who, like a big cat, had avoided hitting the ground by landing on his feet and arms and then rolling over to minimize the blow. In any case, it had been a drastic solution which Raner would surely disapprove of. He straightened up, and for a moment he said nothing. Then he spoke.

"Failed exercise," he called.

Viggo raised his arms in protest.

"What do you mean by failed? I saved the protectee and all the attackers are dead."

Egil joined his partner.

"The solution was a little forced and extravagant, but it worked."

Raner looked at them with narrowed eyes and frowning.

"That's not the right way to solve the situation."

"Okay, it might be the wrong way, but it worked. That's what counts in the end, isn't it?" Viggo insisted. He could not believe Raner was not congratulating him for saving him from the spear.

"You can never pull the protectee off his horse, and least of all using force," Raner said.

"It was the fastest way," Viggo said defensively.

"Yes, it was, but he could have received a bad fall, injured himself, or even gotten killed if he hit his head on the pavement or a horse had stepped on him."

"Nothing like that happened…" Viggo continued defensively.

Raner stared Viggo in the eye.

"What do you think would happen to you if you pulled Thoran down from his horse by force?"

Viggo imagined and wrinkled his nose.

"He wouldn't take it too well."

"Exactly. Even if you saved him, the punishment for laying a hand on the King is death, and being a Royal Ranger doesn't exempt you from it."

Viggo made a face that practically said "how ungrateful," but he did not say anything out loud.

"How was I supposed to dismount the King?" he asked instead of arguing.

"What you should've done was go under the horse and stand in the way of the threat before it could reach the protectee."

"Well… I didn't think of that at the time…"

"I saw it. That's because it was easier to pull me off the horse. The easiest solution isn't necessarily the best. You must think and then act, taking into account all factors."

"That's a lot of thinking. Besides, there was another threat on the roof of the shed," said Viggo, waving his hand in that direction. "I couldn't stop to think about two threats at the same time."

"The threat on top of the shed was a decoy to fool and distract you," Raner told him, and he pointed to the side of the farm where a Royal Ranger was emerging.

"Huh… that's great…." Viggo folded his arms over his chest and looked grim.

"The attack was elaborate and difficult to solve," Egil said, delighted with all the explanations Raner was giving them.

The rest of the attackers, who were Royal Rangers too, stood up. No one was hurt because they had all been carrying marking weapons, not real ones.

"The protectee and his escort always keep going, whatever the situation might be and the danger around them. Otherwise, if they stop, the protectee will die. This is something you must always keep in mind. During an attack, you have to get out of the situation, or in other words, get the protectee out of danger."

"That sounds like fleeing," Viggo commented. "Wouldn't it be better to repel the attack, problem solved?"

Raner turned to Viggo.

"No, that's the reaction we all have when we're under attack, but it's not the best choice for the protectee to come out alive from the trap. We have to get him away from the ambush quickly. Therefore we can't stop."

"And what if there's a barricade, or a fire, something that prevents us from going on?" Egil asked.

"In that case, we have to find another way to escape but never stand still. This is applied to almost any situation, whether on foot or on horseback."

"Understood, sir." Egil seemed satisfied with the explanation.

"You said *almost* any, sir. When doesn't it apply?" Nilsa wanted to know.

"There's one very specific situation when this rule doesn't apply and we stop. I'll show you later on."

"Very well, sir," Nilsa said.

"One more thing. For forcefully shoving me off my horse, you'll have a double physical exercise session," Raner told them.

"All of us, sir?" Gerd asked.

"All of you. You may thank Viggo."

Viggo was shaking his head, and his face showed disbelief for the punishment.

"But…" Nilsa began to protest.

Raner raised his hand to stop the protests. "If it's any consolation, be aware that with pain and effort, the learning sinks in better."

They left with Viggo muttering curses under his breath.

Chapter 27

Ona and Camu jumped up and turned toward the five figures who were watching them calmly from the dune. They were wearing long black and blue robes, which covered their whole bodies except for the face and hands. On the head they wore a scarf, desert style, and they were armed. At their waists they carried knives and scimitars.

They're desert dwellers, Lasgol transmitted to Ona and Camu as he carefully retrieved his bow and quiver from his side.

Enemies?

I can't tell. Some are friendly and some are not.

No friendly, you see.

Yeah, with our luck that would be the case.

The desert dwellers continued staring at them without making any movement. Lasgol assumed they were not looking for conflict, although it could also mean that they were taking their time. The truth was that Lasgol had barely any knowledge of the peoples of the desert and their habits. He missed Egil terribly in these kinds of situations...

We retreat slowly, he transmitted. It was a defensive maneuver. He wanted to show that he had no intention of owning the place and did not want confrontation.

Okay.

The three moved slowly back, bordering the water to stand directly opposite from where the five dwellers were watching them. The five figures kept watching them without moving while Lasgol and his companions retreated.

What do now?

No idea. If we run away they might let us go, or they might chase after us.

Only five.

Five that we can see, there might be more behind those dunes.

Ona growled once.

Ona say be more.

She must've caught their scent. We'd better not run then. I don't want them to attack us, whether it's only a few or many.

I ready for fight.

Ona growled.

I know you're ready to fight, but it's always better to avoid fighting—if possible of course.

One of the five, the one in the middle, raised his hand. Lasgol did not know what to do, so he raised his hand too and they both stood there with their hands raised. It was a bit comical. The dweller signaled them to stay where they were. This Lasgol understood. Especially when the man pointed to his sword. That was a clear threat— Lasgol wanted to insist on the fact that they had no intention of causing harm, so he raised both hands with palms open. The dweller turned and said something behind his back.

Shortly after, a caravan of camels came down into the hollow. It was made up of about twenty dwellers, mostly men with a couple of women among them. They led the camels to drink and started to fill water-skins and other vessels with the precious water. They were all dressed in blue and had their heads covered. Their faces and hands were tanned and their eyes were dark. The women wore slightly different clothing with brighter colors in their robes and long skirts. Their skin was light brown. They were undoubtedly desert dwellers.

Lasgol guessed it was a trading caravan or part of a desert tribe perhaps, moving to some other place. They did not look dangerous.

I'm going to try and communicate with them.

Good idea?

I don't know, honestly, maybe not, but I'd like to know where we stand. Also where we're going. It makes me uneasy not to know.

We alert.

Ona growled once.

Lasgol made a sign to draw the attention of his interlocutor, who noticed at once. Lasgol indicated through signs that he wanted to speak with the man. The desert dweller did not seem to understand because he did not move. Lasgol tried again with other different signs; it was clear to him what he was trying to imply, but the man did not seem to understand. Suddenly, the man made some signs which Lasgol understood meant he wanted them to speak alone.

Lasgol nodded. The dweller made a sign and pointed at a spot in the oasis to the west. Lasgol nodded in agreement.

I'm going to speak with him, don't move from here.

Sure? Can be trap.

228

No, I don't think so. If they wanted to attack us they would've done so already. They're a large group.

Okay. We alert.

Good. But don't intervene unless I ask you to.

We wait signal.

Ona growled once.

That's the way.

Lasgol started going down the dune toward the designated spot. He was thinking that Camu and Ona most likely would not wait for his signal and would act as soon as they sensed any kind of danger, even though he had told them to wait. They were a blessing and a curse at the same time, but Lasgol could not love them more, although they often disobeyed or made decisions that did not agree much with his wishes.

He arrived at the meeting point and waited. He had Aodh's Bow on his back and his knife and axe at his waist. He hoped he would not need to use them, but just in case he went through the Pre-Combat List of skills quickly. The green flashes came one after the other while his interlocutor approached at a slower pace. Lasgol guessed that this man of the desert was not a mage, so he would not be able to tell Lasgol was calling upon his skills.

"Hello! My name is Lasgol," he greeted the man as soon as they met and mimed the greeting, pointing at himself afterward.

Now that Lasgol was closer to the man, he could see the dweller was older than he had thought. The man had taken off the scarf that covered his mouth and Lasgol could see he had a white beard. The tanned skin around his deep dark eyes was covered with deep lines. He had bushy white eyebrows. He greeted Lasgol, raising a hand.

"Abudbalis," he introduced himself, bowing slightly.

Lasgol nodded, showing he understood.

"Where are we?" he asked, indicating the oasis and then at the four directions.

The man tilted his head and asked something in his own language which Lasgol did not understand.

"Lost," Lasgol said, making a confused face. He waved at the oasis again and the four directions.

Abudbalis smiled and said something in his language.

Lasgol did not understand, but he had the impression that the dweller had understood him.

"Wahalatan," Abudbalis said, pointing toward the oasis.

"Oh, the name of this oasis is Wahalatan," Lasgol said with a wave to the oasis.

Abudbalis nodded.

"Where are we in relation to the city of Alaband?" Lasgol asked, encouraged to see they were making progress.

"Alaband?"

"Yes, where?" Lasgol made signs asking in which direction the city lay. He needed to know how far they were from it.

The man nodded and signed to Lasgol to wait. He turned and slowly went back to the caravan, which was already resting in the shade of the oasis palms.

Lasgol was left somewhat puzzled but did as instructed and waited for the dweller's return. He walked back with the same leisurely pace. He did not seem in a hurry at all, or perhaps it was a technique so the heat would not affect him so much—possibly both.

Abudbalis brought something out from under his long blue robe, and Lasgol was startled because the movement was swifter than he had expected. It was not a weapon. What he took out was a map drawn on the tanned skin of an animal, most likely camel. Abudbalis showed him the map. The drawings were plain, rustic. Dots with names which Lasgol could not read, lines that showed the sea and rivers, and some symbols that must stand for the oasis or similar landmarks. He pointed at a dot on the map with a long, thin, light-brown finger.

"Alaband," he said.

Lasgol understood. He was showing him the location of the city. Abudbalis pointed at another dot southeast of Alaband. It was another city.

"Marucose."

"Oh, okay, and this oasis, Wahalatan?"

The desert man showed him on the map. When he saw it Lasgol's head jerked back; they were a lot farther southeast than he had thought.

"Sure it's here?" Lasgol pointed at the ground with his finger in the leather glove he wore in spite of the heat so that the sun would not scorch his skin.

Abudbalis nodded repeatedly and pointed his finger at the ground between them.

"Trader?" Lasgol asked, pointing at the camels. Then he mimicked exchanging something with Abudbalis.

The desert dweller looked at him blankly but then seemed to understand. He pulled at Lasgol's cloak, shirt, and pants and waved toward his camels and the west.

"Lamura," he said and indicated an oasis on the map to the west.

"Lamura," Lasgol nodded. That was where the caravan was going. "We south," Lasgol pointed in that direction.

As soon as he did that, Abudbalis made a horrified face and shook his head.

"No? Why not?"

Abudbalis pointed at the trail of the giant crocodile. He made signs with his arms of something huge. Then, continuing to keep his arms together, he mimicked a crocodile's mouth opening and closing.

"Yes, we know. Crocodile. Giant," Lasgol repeated Abudbalis' gestures and nodded. He wanted him to realize that they were aware that the monster had gone south. It was likely they had seen it and had been waiting for it to leave the oasis to come down just like himself, Ona, and Camu.

The desert trader gestured negatively. He showed him his index finger and pointed at the trail of the giant croc. Then he showed him two, three, four, five fingers and   pointed again at the croc's trail. Was he telling him there were more crocodiles? That they would find five or more giant crocodiles when they reached the destination of the one they were following?

"Five?" Lasgol showed him the five fingers in one hand.

Abudbalis showed him all ten fingers.

Lasgol was petrified.

"Ten?"

The reply was more affirmative gestures. Then he moved his hands but Lasgol did not fully understand. He thought he caught "snake" and maybe "lizard," or some other desert animal.

This was terrible news. If there were a dozen crocodiles, snakes, or giant lizards wherever they were headed to, the situation changed completely. It was one thing to have a hypothetical confrontation with one monster, and a very different one to fight a dozen of them.

"Where is that?" Lasgol asked in case Abudbalis knew the exact place.

The man showed him the map. He pointed at some mountains

and at the end of them a city, south of where they were now.

"Salansamur," he said.

"Salansamur. City? Like Alaband?" Lasgol pointed at Alaband on the map.

Abudbalis nodded and then shook his head.

"Alaband," the man said. "Salansamur," and jabbed his finger at Lasgol's chest and then wagged it negatively, looking horrified. He was miming, but the horror looked genuine.

"Salansamur, not go? Why?" Lasgol asked, signaling with his hands and face.

The trader tried to explain with words in his own language and with hand signs, but Lasgol could not understand. What he would not give to have Egil there with him so his friend could help him in this situation. He was sure Egil would manage to understand what this man was trying to tell him. It certainly seemed important, and a warning.

Abudbalis took the map and showed Lasgol a course to the south, deviating southeast to avoid Salansamur and reaching the city further south from the center of the deserts and which looked on the Southern Sea, right below where they were on the map.

"Zenut," he said nodding repeatedly.

"Okay, Zenut, yes," Lasgol nodded. "Salansamur, no," and he shook his head.

Abudbalis smiled. He had understood.

The city of Zenut rang a bell. It was an important, large city in the Nocean Empire. By its position on the map, it was clear that this was the biggest city going south and that it looked out on the sea. He was hoping he would not have to go that far, since that would mean he would have crossed all the deserts along the central part of the south of Tremia. He broke into a sweat just thinking about it.

"No one Salansamur?" Lasgol said with a wave to the people in the caravan. He wanted to understand whether he and Camu and Ona should not go there because they were foreigners or if no one should go.

The trader shook his head and his hands.

"Salansamur," he said, and then he took his knife and made as if he were cutting his throat. Then he indicated his caravan and repeated the gesture, pointing at his people.

"I understand. No one goes there. If they go, they die."

Abudbalis indicated Lasgol with the knife.

"Salansamur," he said and brushed the knife against Lasgol's throat.

Lasgol understood. No one went to that city—it was a death sentence. The only problem was that Lasgol knew with absolute certainty he needed to go there. If there was a forbidden city in the middle of the desert, known for killing whoever approached, that was where they had to go.

He looked at Camu and Ona, who were waiting at the top of the dune, and snorted. Things were starting to get ugly.

Chapter 28

Lasgol tried to get some more information out of Abudbalis. The desert caravan chief was kind and seemed like a nice person, the kind who helped someone in a tight spot. Being desert dwellers, they were most likely used to encountering people in need of assistance: those lost, thirsty, and scorched by that incessant, unforgiving sun.

He managed to find out that there was a mountain range beside the forbidden city of Salansamur. It was called Amsaljibal, and from the explanations of the good man, Lasgol understood they were called the Mountains of the Past, or of Yesterday. Abudbalis also told him it was better not to go to those mountains. It seemed that it was better not to go near anything that was close to Salansamur.

He also told him of another oasis south of the Mountains of Yesterday which he called Tanwalha. It was located between the cities of Salansamur and Zenut, west of both. Lasgol was grateful for the information and for the man pointing at everything on the map repeatedly. There was nothing better than knowing where a nearby oasis was when traveling through the desert. The more Abudbalis told him, the more reckless Lasgol felt for having the audacity of entering this immense desert without having any idea of where he was heading and without a map. Never again in his life would he make the same mistake. It was a lot to ask for, he knew that, but at least he would try and be aware of the risks of such folly.

Lasgol said goodbye to the chief of the caravan, thanking him a thousand times by voice and gestures he hoped the good man would understand.

"Receiving your help touches my heart," Lasgol told Abudbalis, putting his hand on his own chest and then pointing at his.

The desert man raised one hand, and with the other he gave Lasgol the map they had been communicating over.

"For me?" Lasgol asked, surprised and grateful.

Abudbalis smiled and said something in his desert language.

"Thank you so much." Lasgol took out two Norghanian gold coins from his Ranger's belt and offered them to Abudbalis.

The trader looked at them and then gestured that there was no need. Lasgol replied with another gesture, insisting that he accept them.

He took them at last. Lasgol said goodbye again, thanking the man as best he could for his help. Judging by Abudbalis' smile and head bowing, Lasgol thought he had understood him.

He climbed the dune where Ona and Camu were waiting. He told them everything the desert dweller had said and emphasized the prohibition to go to the city of Salansamur.

Now know where we go, Camu messaged at once.

Yeah, that's what I thought. If they mention a forbidden city where everyone who enters dies, that's where we have to go.

Ona moaned once.

We'll wait for night and then we'll set out. I don't think they'll mind if we shelter from the sun under the palms on this side of the oasis.

Okay.

Lasgol was right. The members of the caravan did not bother them at all. They kept to their side of the oasis while Lasgol and his friends stayed on theirs. They looked warily at Camu and Ona, but Lasgol had the feeling that this was not the first time they had seen strange creatures in the desert.

Abudbalis sent over a youth with some dates and other exotic fruits they did not know and which they assumed were native to the area. Lasgol gestured gratefully.

At nightfall, the three friends got to their feet. Lasgol waved goodbye to Abudbalis and the man wished them luck. This they did understand.

They set off, following the trail of the giant reptile. They were sorry to leave this dreamlike place to go into the terrible desert once again. But they had no option if they wanted to recover the pearls and they knew this, so they marched on with heaviness in their hearts.

The oasis was soon left behind and vanished in the distance. It was as if the desert had swallowed it. Lasgol knew they had been lucky the reptile had been wounded and had stopped at the oasis, otherwise their journey through the desert would have been a nightmare.

A night sky entirely filled with stars, which seemed to wink at them from above while they walked on the sand below, cheered them a little. Lasgol felt they were heading toward a situation of great danger, and he transmitted as much to Camu and Ona. The three walked, alert to any danger that might come from among the dunes. The crocodile's trail was clear, so they only needed to be alert to the dangers that might appear in their path.

Dawn came and so did the scorching sun. Camu made use of his new skill and created the frozen shelter around them. The sun punished it hard and Camu had to use almost all his energy to maintain it for half a day. Lasgol decided it was more important that he saved part of his energy than protect them from the sun. He had the feeling they were going to need it. So, after half the day they set off again and had to withstand a terrible heat in the middle of that ruthless desert.

When night came, they rested a little so that Camu could recuperate his energy. They slept half the night and moved on for the other half. They went on like this for several days. They were tough days, full of painful marching and few words. The desert was a hostile and sorrowful environment. Lasgol finally received a pulse indicating that the giant reptile was already only two leagues away; it was nearby again. They would not lose it even if it traveled to the center of the desert itself.

They went on for several more days. They used the same strategy of resting half a day and half the night and kept going the other two halves. They all suffered from the dreadful punishment the ardent sun delivered. Lasgol was thinking that the deity that must be the sun in this land had to be terribly angry and that was why it punished anyone who dared travel under its gaze.

One scorching half evening, they glimpsed what had to be the Mountains of the Past, or of Yesterday, and the city of Salansamur. They stopped to check. It was a most curious landscape. Between the sand dunes they could see a long, high mountain range toward the west. At the end of the range, on the eastern side, rose the city of Salansamur. From what they could tell from that distance, it was a beautiful city with tall buildings of white walls and golden domes.

Pretty city, Camu messaged.

Lasgol, who was already using his *Hawk's Eye* skill, noticed something peculiar.

There are no people in that city. The buildings appear intact, but it's a ghost city. There's not a soul in sight.

Cursed city?

Forbidden city, that's for sure, Lasgol nodded as he searched for some trace of life among the buildings. It was a big city, with space for several thousands of people, and it had not suffered the ravages of war or invasion. All the palaces, buildings, fountains, and squares were still standing. Even the gardens and palms that decorated the rich areas of the city were intact.

No detect magic.

You don't? I was thinking that if the city is empty but the buildings intact, it might be because Blood or Curse Magic had affected the inhabitants.

Blood and Curse Magic? Camu messaged with a feeling of doubt.

Yeah, it appears that the Nocean Warlocks practice that type of magic and it's really bad for humans.

Yes, now remember Eicewald tell. Think Nocean warlocks do this?

Lasgol rubbed his chin. He had many doubts.

It could be that, or it might be that Dergha-Sho-Blaska has killed all the residents.

Where bodies?

That's a good question. I don't see any. I don't see any blood stains either or sign of fighting in the streets of the city.

Strange.

Yeah, very. Such a big city wouldn't have surrendered without resistance. It must've had armed men to defend it.

Perhaps all flee.

That might be. But what could make a whole city flee without any resistance?

Dergha-Sho-Blaska.

Yeah, I was thinking just that.

Crocodile arriving.

Lasgol checked the first buildings of the city and saw the great reptile arriving at them.

We'll have to get closer to understand what's going on there.

Much careful.

Ona growled once.

That's the way, Lasgol transmitted, and the three started again at a crouch. The dunes hid them, but not entirely.

Camu, it would be better if you made all three of us disappear. Can you?

Much close.

We'll be right beside you.

Better if touch.

Ona got closer to Camu at once.

Perfect. We need to approach without being detected. If you get to the point where you can no longer maintain the camouflage, let us know.

Okay. I tell when no can.

They approached the city warily in a camouflaged state. The sun continued to burn them, and the three were having a difficult time walking. The camouflage did not hide them from the sunrays, which flattened everything they fell on, visible or not. Lasgol was perspiring so much under his Ranger's clothes that even with the hood protecting his head and face he feared he would leave a trail of sweat so obvious it would be impossible not to detect and they would be discovered. Camu and Ona had their mouths open, tongues hanging on one side, suffering unspeakably from the heat and having serious trouble breathing.

They arrived at the north side of the city and sought protection against one side of a tall building. The city was not walled, so it could not be a border city. From what little Lasgol had been able to see and the beautiful architecture of the tall dome buildings, he guessed it was, or had been, a rich, commercial city. Perhaps there were mines in the mountain range that began almost in the city itself and the people there had lived off the rich trade they provided. Certainly there were no tilled fields or forests for timber.

Let's move south, bordering the city, always keeping to the shade, Lasgol transmitted.

Okay.

The three were moving as one, which was not easy, but they soon mastered it. Ona was a natural at this. Where Camu put a foot she did, almost at the same time and in the same spot. The one who had trouble was Lasgol, since he only had two legs and had to move in the middle of his friends' movements. Camu went in the middle, Ona on his left side and Lasgol on his right. And as Camu had told them, both Ona and Lasgol were touching him.

The city was in complete silence. There were no animals in it either—no dogs, cats, fowl, or goats, nothing. The desert wind ran through the empty streets and raised clouds of sand, and that was all the sound there was. It looked like a ghost city, where its inhabitants had been sent to the beyond by the forces of evil. Lasgol preferred not to think about that.

Something weird was going on there, something bad, but it was best not to get ahead of events. Everything always had an explanation. That was what Egil said. The thing was that the explanation was not always to the liking of whoever was searching for it. Especially when it referred to matters that had to do with death.

They arrived at the southern area of the city and found that the giant reptile was waiting at the entrance in silence, in front of a majestic palace with high walls. The windows and three domes of different heights were all painted a golden color. It looked like the palace of a trader or city noble. Lasgol took a glance inside through one of the windows and saw it was empty, although all the furniture and other objects were still in place. It was as if the owners had been carried away by the desert wind.

They stopped to watch from the corner of the last building furthest to the east. Since they were in a relatively safe position, Lasgol asked Camu to stop using his camouflage and not spend more energy for the time being. They might need it later on.

Okay. I save energy.

Ona, retreat a little so it can't see you.

Ona obeyed at once.

What was the great crocodile waiting for? It could not go into the city—it was too big to pass through the streets. Not even along the main avenue, which was right in front of it. In case it saw them and they had to fight, or if Dergha-Sho-Blaska suddenly appeared, Lasgol went over his Pre-Combat List of skills. Camu noticed.

I ready fight.

That's good, but let's not start anything until we know what's going on here.

The giant reptile opened its huge, long snout and gave out a strange steady grunt. It sounded more like a moan than a growl. Then it remained silent for a moment and afterward repeated its long roar.

I think he's calling someone.

Dergha-Sho-Blaska?

Could be, yes.

Better kill crocodile now. Take pearls.

Lasgol snorted.

I don't know whether it's the best option. What if Dergha-Sho-Blaska doesn't appear and we kill the crocodile? And I'm really not sure we could kill it. And if another monster appears to take them someplace else?

That be too.

Ona growled again.

I'm not too excited about attacking a monster of such size. It can rip all three of us to pieces. We look like baby chicks beside it.

Chick much fighter.

Yes, you are, Lasgol smiled at him.

Suddenly, the sand began to stir around the giant reptile. Six spirals formed where the sand was stirring, coming up to the surface. Something was stirring it from below.

Watch out, something's happening, Lasgol transmitted in warning.

From one of the spirals where the sand was being stirred there suddenly appeared a large pincer in blackish-blue. This was followed by a second one right after. In the other spots where the sand was being stirred, there began to appear similar pincers in blackish green and brown.

Lasgol, Camu, and Ona could not help themselves and watched agape from the corner. The three heads appeared one on top of the other while their bodies were flattened against the wall and could not be seen, at least from where the crocodile was standing.

They had no idea what was going on, but those pincers did not forebode anything good. Lasgol wondered what was going to surface from the sand. There was some kind of creature buried under it. The fact that it was by the entrance of the city led him to believe they had to be guardians of some kind.

The first creature appeared before the giant crocodile. The pincers were followed by a head with jaws and a long body covered by a black shell supported by eight legs, four on each side, also covered. But what left no doubt about what kind of creature it was, was the long tail that ended in an enormous stinger that curved above the body.

That's a scorpion.

Much big.

I'd say a king scorpion, but of a size never before seen.

Lasgol tried to calculate its size once it left its hiding place. Compared to the crocodile it was not that big, but for a scorpion if was colossal. It must be the size of the three of them together, which made it gigantic for a scorpion. The other scorpions came out of their holes surrounding the crocodile. They were all the same size. It was as if someone had experimented with scorpions and made them as big as a cargo cart drawn by two Norghanian Percherons.

Can you tell whether they have power?

No detect magic, but can be, normal not be.

That's for sure. The last thing we need is for them to have magic on top of everything else.

Wait and see. If have, no emit much. I no detect anything.

Lasgol sighed. This was a small comfort. The fact that Camu did not detect whether they had power indicated that if they did have it, it could not be too much, which made him feel a little easier. Well, as easy as one could feel before a colossal crocodile and six enormous scorpions. With those stingers, they looked like siege machines capable of getting through the gates of any city. Suddenly the vision of one of those monsters piercing him from side to side with its stinger came to his mind. He quickly rid himself of the idea, since it was no use having that kind of fear.

The six scorpions that had been buried in the sand were now on the surface and waiting for something. Were they waiting for Dergha-Sho-Blaska to arrive? There was no doubt this was a meeting point and that those creatures served the great dragon. It could not be otherwise. Where these creatures had come from was something Lasgol would love to know.

The body of the giant croc suddenly shook. It suffered a convulsion. This was followed by a second and a third one. It opened its mouth and vomited. The box with the Silver Pearls came out. And the ice jewel too which emitted a location pulse which Lasgol was able to feel. He saw the jewel on the ground beside the box.

It's delivering the cargo.

To scorpion?

It looks that way. Let's see what happens.

Lasgol felt some relief to learn they would not have to kill the colossal crocodile to retrieve the pearls. That might have ended up in disaster.

Two of the scorpions approached the box and they seemed to sniff at it, or feel it somehow. One of them picked it up between its pincers and lifted it off the ground. The second scorpion closed its pincer on something and lifted it too. Lasgol, who was watching closely from the corner with half his face out, saw what it was and had to muffle a cry.

It had picked up the jewel!

He put his head back in to avoid being seen. He did not like what he had just witnessed. That they had found the jewel led him to think that it had either shone brightly from the reflection of the sun and that the creature had seen it, or it had felt it and so those scorpions had some type of magic. He leaned toward the second explanation. If there were two options, it was always wiser to think that the worst one was the right one. It was almost always the case.

The scorpions seemed to gather together and have some kind of conversation in front of the giant crocodile. After a while they went into the city along the main avenue, heading north.

What do? Camu messaged.

There's only one thing we can do.

Follow pearls?

Lasgol nodded hard. *Follow the pearls.*

Chapter 29

Astrid, Ingrid, and Molak were waiting for Raner on their horses east of the capital, according to his orders. They were half a league from the Royal Road and were to wait for the First Ranger to join them. Not very far away they could glimpse Beaver Hill, so called because of a rock at the summit that looked very much like the animal.

"What do you think the First Ranger has in store for us today?" Molak asked his comrades.

"So far, everything he's had prepared for us has been enlightening and interesting," Ingrid said in a satisfied tone. "So I hope that whatever he has for us today will be so too."

Astrid stroked her horse's neck.

"I feel the same way. The truth is that training to become Royal Rangers has pleasantly surprised me."

"You weren't expecting it to be interesting?" Molak asked, surprised.

"To be honest, I wasn't expecting it to be useful and so I thought I'd be bored. But it's turning out to be the opposite. I think that in the Assassin Specialty at the Shelter, they should study part of what we're learning here."

"From the point of view of the attacker, you mean," Ingrid said.

"Exactly. I think I'll tell Engla when I see her next. It's valuable knowledge."

"Perhaps they already know and don't teach it for a reason," Malik said thoughtfully, stroking his horse's neck too.

"What do you mean?" Ingrid asked blankly.

"He means that they're not teaching this for a specific reason, not out of neglect or because they haven't realized how valuable it can be for the Assassins they train," Astrid said, catching on to Molak's meaning.

"And what reason would that be?" Ingrid asked.

"That they don't want us to know how to kill our beloved King," Astrid replied.

"Exactly," Molak nodded.

"Is that what you think?" Ingrid looked incredulous. "It can't be that."

"Well, if you think of it, it makes sense," Astrid argued. "The only Rangers who would be able to kill the King would be the Royal Rangers, and among them those who'd find it easier would be the ones with Assassin's Specializations."

"Raner has it all," Molak commented with a gesture that meant it was worth considering.

Ingrid shook her head emphatically.

"You're forgetting that this idea would require there being traitors among the Royal Rangers, and that I refuse to believe."

"Let's hope you're right," Astrid said, raising her eyebrows.

"I'm sure she is," Molak said confidently. "I don't think there are traitors among our comrades," he added.

"Thank you, Molak. Sometimes I feel like I'm the only one who trusts the integrity of the Royal Corps and the Norghanian Army."

"You're welcome. You know we think similarly about many things, and this is one of them," Molak said, smiling at her.

"Thanks. It's so frustrating when speaking with certain people about this. It's as if we've completely lost the honor that must always be present and guide any military corps."

"We, the new generation, have the obligation of maintaining the corps' honor and the principles that guide it," Molak said supportively.

"I wish you two good luck with all that. I'm sure our monarchy and its nobles will appreciate it," Astrid said in a tone dripping with irony. "We only have to see where our leader has ended up, such an honorable and faithful servant to the realm."

Ingrid was about to reply, but she saw a group of riders coming toward them along the Royal Road.

"I think they're coming."

"Before they arrive, I wanted to thank you," Molak said, surprising them.

"Why's that?" Ingrid asked.

"For letting me be a part of the Royal Eagles. Because of it I'm going to become a Royal Ranger, and it's an honor and a privilege I hadn't thought I could reach. That's why I want to thank you from the bottom of my heart."

"You're welcome, Molak. You're doing us a big favor by

substituting Lasgol. It's us who should be thanking you," Astrid told him.

"I feel the same," Ingrid said. "Besides, you were going to become a Royal Ranger by your own merits anyway, of that I have no doubt. You're an excellent Specialist with a great background. The only thing we've done is speed up the process a little."

Molak bowed his head, moved.

"Thank you anyway. Especially you, Ingrid."

"Me? Why?"

"For not opposing it. You know… because of our past…" Molak lowered his eyes. "I thought you might have misgivings."

Ingrid looked at Molak and her expression softened.

"What's past is past. It's a little awkward for both of us, I'll give you that. But it's all in the past. I've always thought you were an exceptional Ranger, one of the best, with a brilliant future. Let's look forward. I hope to see you competing with me to be First Ranger someday."

Molak smiled and nodded.

"You can count on it," he said.

Raner rode up to them, accompanied by five Royal Rangers.

"Good day, Rangers," he greeted, stopping beside them.

"Good day, sir," they replied.

"Today we have a complex exercise. I've brought Veterans with me," Raner said, jabbing his thumb behind him.

"We recognize Mostassen," said Molak, greeting him with a nod which the veteran returned.

"Also Nikessen," said Ingrid. "It's been a while," she said, nodding at him.

"You don't say. I'm glad to see you're keeping well and progressing," the Green Cartographer replied. They had met him during the war between Uthar and Darthor, just like Mostassen.

"Astrid, you must remember me as well, don't you?" a third one said.

"Ulsen, it's been a long time," Astrid acknowledged with a smile.

"That's right," Ulsen replied, smiling back. "Since the war with Darthor."

"We had a surveillance mission, Ulsen was leader," Astrid explained to the rest. "Wow, time flies!"

"You're telling us veterans!" Ulsen smiled.

"It seems that all the Veteran Rangers are back," Ingrid commented with surprise. "Seeing them here makes me feel like we're back to the time of the war against Darthor and the Peoples of the Frozen Continent. That's not a good omen."

"Most are back. We've summoned them. War is upon us, and we must prepare for it. They're here to receive their orders and new war missions. Meanwhile, they're going to help with your training," Raner told them.

"It will be an honor to be taught by veterans with so much experience," Molak said gratefully.

"There's no doubt that we'll learn a lot and well," Ingrid joined him. "It's a privilege."

"Very well, let's begin today's exercise," said Raner. "The placement will be like this: Mostassen and Nikessen at the front, Ingrid and Molak on my right, Astrid and Ulsen on my left, Maltron behind with Lowel."

"At your command."

They all maneuvered their horses to take their positions according to the First Ranger's indications. Once in position, they checked their weapons.

"One more thing: today we'll all be wearing white aprons," Raner told them, reaching into his saddlebag and bringing out a bunch of them. He handed them to everyone.

Ingrid and Molak exchanged blank looks. As a rule, it was Raner who wore the white apron. This was odd. Astrid gave them a look from the other side, one of suspicion.

At a signal from Raner, they started riding along the Royal Road at a peaceful trot. Astrid, Ingrid, and Molak were looking in all directions, not trusting what the First Ranger might have prepared.

He did not take long in changing the pace, which they all adapted to quickly, the veterans almost instinctively and the three newbies as fast as they could. All three of them were good riders, and after all the practice they had been doing, they were getting better at adapting to Raner's maneuvers, who always attempted to surprise them somehow.

A large forest of ilex oaks appeared under Beaver Hill in a wide depression in the land before them. The road divided the forest in two. The section right under the Hill was smaller, leafier and steeper. The other side spread down to a big river, and it had plenty of ilex oaks and some linden trees more to the east.

Upon seeing it, the three Panthers exchanged warning glances. It was more than likely that an ambush was waiting for them in the forest. Since they were all wearing white aprons, they assumed the attack would be carried out by a large force. Subconsciously, they all reached for their bows.

As they were entering the forest, Raner set a more leisurely pace. It was clear he did not want to cross the forest at a gallop, which strengthened their suspicion that they were going to be attacked at any moment from both sides of the road. Since they were expecting the attack, Ingrid unobtrusively grasped her bow and got ready. Molak did the same, and an instant later Astrid did too.

The three were sweeping the forest with their eyes, searching for suspicious movement to release at. But to their surprise, the attack did not come. The forest was quiet, on both sides of the road. They could hear birds singing and even caught a glimpse of a small deer. This puzzled them. If there were attackers hiding among the linden trees, the birds and deer would have most likely vanished. They would neither hear nor see the animals.

Astrid glanced at Ingrid, who caught her meaning of "something's odd." Ingrid made a sign that meant she was thinking the same thing. Ingrid looked at Molak and saw something in his eyes.

"They won't attack in the forest," he told Ingrid in a tone that meant he had figured out what was going on.

They heard a deadly whistling sound they all identified. It was the sound of an arrow cutting the air. Mostassen received the impact in the middle of his chest. It was a dull impact, and the veteran fell off his horse to one side.

"We're under attack!" Nikessen cried out.

"Grab your weapons!" called Ulsen.

In an instant all the Rangers had their bows in their hands, an arrow nocked and aiming at the trees. They were looking for an enemy to release against. Unfortunately, they did not see one. No one came from the forest to attack them—the road in front of and behind the retinue was clear. There was no enemy there.

Raner was still riding calmly, not saying a word.

The deadly whistling came again, and this time it was Molak who called out, "Sniper!"

The arrow caught Nikessen full in the torso and dismounted him.

"Where?" Ulsen asked.

Molak pointed to the top of the hill.

"At the Beaver!"

"Defend the protectee! Release!" Ulsen ordered.

They all released against a silhouette they could barely see hiding behind the beaver-looking rock. The arrows flew accurately, but none reached him.

"He's over four hundred and fifty paces away!" Ingrid cried.

"We're carrying composite bows, we'll never bring him down at this distance!" cried Ulsen.

"We need long bows," said Ingrid, checking their saddlebags for the long-distance weapon, although she was sure they only had the composite bows.

"The Sniper has a Sniper's bow," Molak said, indicating one of the arrows that were longer than usual.

"We could go for the Sniper," Astrid suggested, looking at the summit.

Ulsen looked at her and shook his head.

"We don't leave the protectee."

A third whistle warned them that another arrow was heading toward them.

"Sir, take cover!" Ulsen told Raner and placed himself in front of him to protect him since the two leading riders had fallen.

The arrow caught Ulsen on the side and he fell off.

Raner seemed to react and began to gallop away.

The others joined the escape.

Maltron was riding in the rear, and he spurred his horse to get in front of Raner to protect his escape and control the protectee's horse with his own so it would not bolt.

They were passing right below Beaver's Hill when there was another whistle.

Astrid saw the arrow coming at her torso and leaned on the opposite side of her horse. She almost fell off because of how fast she was going, but she managed to hold on and the arrow did not hit her.

"We have to get out of his range!" Molak cried.

"Come on, ride faster!" Ingrid joined him.

A new arrow brought Lowel down at the rear.

"We're not going to make it!" Astrid yelled as she sat in the saddle again.

They were going as fast as their horses could gallop, and Raner gave them no clue as to what they should do. He continued riding in silence.

An arrow came from the heights and hit Maltron full in the back. A moment later he fell off his horse.

"He's bringing us down one by one!" Molak said, looking up at the top of the hill.

"How far until we're out of range?" Astrid asked.

"Thirty more paces!" Ingrid replied, taking the lead to force Raner's horse to go faster.

The whistle was heard again, that lethal sound they all feared.

This time the arrow hit Raner squarely in the back.

"Oh no!" cried Astrid, clenching her teeth.

Raner pulled on his horse's reins and let it stop gradually. Astrid, Ingrid, and Molak stopped with Raner.

"Failed exercise," he told them.

"Yeah… we're sorry, sir," Ingrid apologized.

"You should be, because you've done horribly."

"Horribly? We almost managed to escape. Ten more paces and we would've been out of his range," Ingrid replied.

"Let's go back to the others and talk about it," Raner said, motioning for them to turn their horses around.

They all gathered halfway back. The veterans were rubbing the areas where they had received the impacts of the marking arrows. They did not kill but were quite painful nevertheless. They would have nasty bruises. Sniper arrows were longer, and they hit harder from the gathered momentum.

"Everyone okay?" Raner asked, checking for wounds.

"Everything's all right, sir," Mostassen confirmed.

"Good shots, clean and precise," said Nikessen.

"Good archer," Ulsen said appreciatively.

They waited until the archer came down from the hill. As they had guessed, he was carrying a Sniper's bow.

"This is Royal Ranger Eyegreson. As you must have guessed, his Specialty is Forest Sniper."

"Indeed, I had already guessed when I saw a shadow by the Beaver," Molak said with a wave at the summit.

"Your call was good, Molak. Good eye and good guess," Raner

congratulated him.

"What did we do wrong?" Astrid asked him.

Raner turned to Eyegreson.

"If I hadn't asked you to shoot at the veterans first, how many shots would you have needed from that advantageous position to finish me?"

"One, two at the most. The position was very advantageous."

"Even at full gallop?" Ingrid asked.

"Let your comrades answer that, they're Snipers as well," Raner replied.

Astrid sighed.

"He's right. From up there, the protectee would've been dead in two shots."

"You can even do it in one, as Eyegreson said, the first one," Molak admitted.

"Then how do we defend him?" Ingrid asked.

"The beginning was good. Molak guessed the danger. At that moment he should've prevented the protectee from being an easy target," Raner explained.

"Galloping away?" said Ingrid.

"How well have you been doing with that?" Raner replied.

"Not very well," Ingrid had to admit.

"Think about it, Astrid, Molak. From up there, would you have missed my back even if I had galloped off?"

Astrid shook her head.

"We would've taken you down, sir," said Molak.

"Then? I don't understand… what should we have done?" Ingrid asked, annoyed.

"I believe your Snipers can tell you," Raner said with a wave at Astrid and Molak.

"Seek cover at once," Astrid said.

"Hide from the Sniper," Molak added.

"Both correct," Raner confirmed. "You should've dismounted and sought cover in the forest. Not gallop away. This is that special occasion I mentioned to you in which you shouldn't move forward with the protectee. When dealing with a Sniper, you must always dismount at once and seek cover. Never keep going."

"Oh… now I see," Ingrid nodded.

Astrid and Molak looked at one another.

"I don't know why we didn't think of that," Astrid said regretfully.

"Because we're used to the opposite. We shoot and expect others to gallop away from us," said Molak. "That's why we assumed that was the best option, because that's what those being attacked usually do."

"Because of that, and because you're still thinking like an attacker instead of a defender," Raner told them.

"Yeah, I see," Astrid nodded, realizing the mistake they had made and why.

"The Sniper who's already in position and waiting from above has an advantage that's practically impossible to escape. That's why they're the greatest danger the protectee will ever encounter."

"And it's the one occasion when we shouldn't run away with the protectee but hide from the Sniper."

"Exactly. Once the protectee is under cover and safe, you go and neutralize the threat, not before."

"We'll keep that in mind," Astrid promised.

"I hope so, or else the protectee will die and we can't afford that," Raner said, staring them in the eyes.

The three nodded.

"It won't happen, sir," Ingrid promised.

"Very well. We'll leave it at this for today. We must go back to the capital."

Raner and the Veteran Rangers galloped away a moment later, leaving the three comrades talking about what had happened and what they should have done instead.

"One thing… after what we've witnessed and learned today, it's no longer the Royal Rangers with an Assassin Specialty who can more easily kill a king. A Forest Sniper can do the job more easily in my opinion," Molak mused.

"I think you're right…" Ingrid agreed thoughtfully.

"I agree too, and besides, this makes it a little more amusing," Astrid said with a wise grin.

"Amusing? How?" Ingrid asked her.

"Because Molak and I are Snipers. And if everything goes well, we're going to be Royal Rangers,"

"You can't be suggesting…" Molak tilted his head and stared at Astrid.

"I'm not suggesting anything," she raised her hands in the air. "I'm only saying it's an interesting situation. Two of us out of the Royal Eagles could kill the King relatively easily, or at least we'd know how to do it."

"That's an idea we'd better keep to ourselves," Ingrid said.

"That includes Egil…" Astrid commented.

"Egil will realize like us the moment he does this exercise, if he hasn't already," Ingrid said, nodding.

"And why do you mention Egil?" Molak asked. "We'll all figure it out."

Astrid and Ingrid exchanged glances.

"It's nothing, don't worry about it," they answered at the same time.

Chapter 30

Lasgol waited a moment and wondered whether his plan might work or if they would be discovered and end up having to confront those monstrous desert creatures. He was not at all sure it was a good idea to follow the scorpions, least of all through the forbidden city. But when there were no other options, it was best to be determined.

Watch out. We're going to follow the scorpions. I don't think they can see us under Camu's camouflage, but we must be very careful.

Camouflage good. They no see, Camu messaged confidently.

There's more than one way of seeing. They might detect us by sound or by the trail we leave, for instance.

Ona moaned once.

Oh I understand. I no can help that.

That's why I'm saying we must take extreme precautions.

We always careful.

Yeah, always... Lasgol was watching with one eye from the corner of the wall. *They've entered the city. Following them through the streets will be dangerous.*

City empty, no dangerous.

The entrance was also empty and the scorpions appeared.

Camu had to admit Lasgol was right and nodded with his big head.

Ona, you go left, I'll go right. Camu, keep always to the middle of the streets.

Okay.

They went into the ghost city of the desert along the main avenue

It was wide, with space for at least five of the enormous scorpions side to side. The buildings that lined the great avenue were of a beauty which Lasgol could not but admire. In Norghana everything was square, made of rock, and a gray-black color. Sturdy, but not pretty. These buildings were painted in bright colors, white, gold, and silver. There were also lilacs and blues in the decorations of some balconies and windows. The architecture was very different from the Norghanian. Here all the buildings had domes and domed shapes, with arches on entrances, balconies, patios, and the like.

Nothing was square or rectangular like in Norghana.

They went along the street without losing sight of the scorpions ahead of them. They kept a prudent distance in case those creatures could hear or detect them somehow. Lasgol walked with all his senses alert, prepared for any possibility. He peeked into the buildings, palaces, and residential homes which must have been filled with people and riches back in the day. In more than one place he could glimpse objects of value, from silver cutlery to rich tapestries and exquisite carpets. He was sure that in the inner quarters there were still trunks and chests with jewels.

It was strange to walk along the avenue, following those monsters with enormous stingers. They came to a crossing of streets shaped like a plaza with a fountain in the middle. The scorpions bordered the plaza and continued north of the city. When they arrived, they looked east and west. There were two great avenues, one in each direction with well-preserved buildings on either side. It gave the impression that everyone had vanished recently. They must have left in haste, because they had not taken anything with them. Lasgol was sure of this now that he could see inside the buildings. He only hoped they had been able to escape alive, but since he had not found any trace of blood   he was optimistic. They must have made it out safely.

What happened here was recent and took the city by surprise, he transmitted to Camu and Ona.

No look fight.

Yeah, that's the strangest thing of all.

See scorpions and flee?

Might be, but they would've fought, one way or another.

Mystery.

Yeah, and of the bad kind I think.

They continued following the scorpions, which passed by two other squares and then turned to the east. The desert wind blew through the streets of the ghost city with a whistling that made the hair on Lasgol's nape rise. It blew first from the east and then the west as if it wanted to hit them in both directions.

Suddenly, four of the scorpions they were following turned around. They started down the street where Lasgol, Camu, and Ona were.

Stay still and be quiet, Lasgol transmitted.

Discover?

I don't think so. Perhaps they've only finished their escorting mission and they're going back to the city's entrance .

The scorpions came to within fifteen paces from them and stopped. Lasgol found this strange. He looked back toward the plaza they had just passed.

He froze.

Six Royal Cobras of unthinkable size, nine feet tall at least, had entered the plaza. They were raised on their vertebrate bodies, as wide as a Norghanian, six feet off the ground and showing their fangs. Their forked tongues went in and out swiftly. The hood those nightmarish cobras had on the side of their heads left no doubt. Their scales were olive green, with stomach patches of yellow. The scales on their heads were black and fearsome.

Ambush! Lasgol transmitted in warning to his friends.

They no can see us! Camu could not understand it.

They might not see us, but they know we're here!

How?

I don't know!

Lasgol checked the trail they had left in passing. Perhaps the cobras had found it and followed it all the way here. The enormous snakes had their tongues out.

Lasgol realized then what had happened.

It was not that they had seen them or their trail. They had smelled them! He remembered his lessons about snakes—they had an acute sense of smell. They put their tongue out, and with it they picked up surrounding smells and then transported them to their palate. They breathed through their nostrils, but they smelled through their tongues. When they put out their forked tongue they were really picking up chemical scents from the air.

They can smell us through their tongues, Lasgol transmitted.

With tongues? I no can.

They do, believe me. They pick up smells all too well.

He readied his bow and nocked an arrow fast. He called on his *Woodland Protection* skill, looked to his left, and saw there was the wall of a small palace about nine or ten feet high. He looked right and saw three tall houses close together. The doors were   closed and likely locked. They had no clear escape on either side.

Beware, we'll have to make a way out.

Scorpions or cobras? Camu messaged.

255

Lasgol looked at the enormous scorpions and their black shells, then at the cobras and their scaled bodies. He decided on the snakes. He thought it would be easier to kill them than the scorpions. It was only a guess, but this is what he thought at that critical moment.

Cobras.

Okay.

I'll deal with the cobras. Ona, you help me. Camu, make sure the scorpions don't catch us from behind before we can clear the way .

I make sure.

Lasgol aimed his bow at the cobra in the middle and prepared to attack.

We can.

I hope so. I don't like these monsters one bit. Don't make the first move, I think they aren't sure exactly where we are.

Suddenly three of the snakes hurried forward, and when they were a few paces from them they spit venom from their fangs, a jet of some venomous substance that fell on all three of them on different parts of the body.

It's venom! Don't let it get into your eyes, nose, or mouth!

Hit my legs! Camu messaged.

Lasgol looked down at his own body and saw that he had been hit around the stomach. He looked at Ona and saw the venomous substance on what had to be the panther's rump, since she was a little more forward. He adjusted his Ranger's scarf, covering his nose and mouth. Only his eyes were not covered. Then he realized something that was not good at all. If he could see the venom spots on himself and on Ona and Camu, so could the cobras and scorpions!

The six cobras lunged in to attack. They had marked them with their venom, and although the snakes could not see their entire bodies because they were camouflaged by Camu's skill, they were not fully covered since the venom that stayed on their bodes was visible. Now the cobras could smell and partially see them, well enough to kill them with their fangs or venom.

Lasgol did not waste a moment and called on his *Multiple Shot* skill, aiming at the snake in the center. There was a green flash in his arm and three arrows flew simultaneously. When they left Aodh's Bow, the weapon shone with a faint golden gleam. The three arrows hit the snakes dead center, as they slithered toward them, in their hoods and under the mouth. Lasgol was sure that with that shot he would kill the three.

That was not the case.

The arrows plunged into the bodies of the cobras, but not deep enough. The scales that covered their bodies prevented the arrow tips to penetrate deeper.

The arrows don't penetrate the scales! Lasgol transmitted in warning.

The snakes hissed and showed their maws. The arrows' impact against their bodies caused the cobras to jerk back momentarily, but they were soon erect again and ready to attack. It was a horrific sight. They were as big as they were horrible, and their fangs and venom made Lasgol's stomach turn.

Ona saw a snake was coming at her with the intention of biting her, and without hesitation she counterattacked. The panther's reaction was faster than the snake's, and Ona was extremely fast and precise. The snake lunged forward to bite Ona, who dodged the fangs and in turn bit the cobra in the neck, squeezing the snake between her jaws with all her might. Royal Cobra and Snow Panther fought, rolling on the ground.

Camu turned to the scorpions—two were coming straight at them. He stopped using his Extended Camouflage skill, since they were already marked with the venom and he would rather save his energy. The three became visible the moment Camu opened his mouth and used his Icy Breath skill. A tremendous jet, a mixture of freezing water and steam, came out of his throat and hit the first of the scorpions. The monster received the jet full force on its mouth, pincers, and body. Even so it kept coming, trying to reach Camu to stick its great stinger in him. Camu maintained the frozen jet, but the monster's   shell protected it from the ice too.

Scorpions tough shell. Maybe magic.

Snakes too, Lasgol transmitted to him.

Camu continued blasting the creature with his freezing breath, using more energy for the skill, and the scorpion could not withstand the low temperatures. It stopped two paces from Camu, fully frozen.

Meanwhile, Lasgol was trying to find a way to kill the huge cobras before they fell on him. He changed his tactic and, moving to one side in a blur, he called on his *Elemental Arrows* skill. He aimed at the middle cobra and released, creating a Fire Arrow. The green flash of Lasgol's skill was followed by the golden one from the Bow. The Fire Arrow hit the cobra in the hood under the mouth and it pierced the creature slightly. When it entered there was the burst of fire, and the snake must have felt it because it began to lag behind while it shook its head from side to side in defensive, sinuous movements.

Seeing the Fire Arrow had some effect, Lasgol used his skill again while he moved toward the wall. He wanted the cobras to follow him. This time he used an Earth Arrow which burst on impact, and the cloud of earth and stunning material left the snake half-blinded and dizzy. A third one lunged at Lasgol and tried to bite him in the neck. Lasgol ducked like lightning to avoid the deadly bite, and as he was crouching he called on his *Dirt Throwing* skill and a cloud of dirt and dust went straight into the open eyes and mouth of the cobra, which was left blinded.

Lasgol noticed that his skills were now more powerful and had more range. Instead of releasing again, since he had the snake on top of him, he drew his Ranger's knife and stabbed the snake with a dull blow. To his surprise, the knife did not penetrate the scales. He was certain now that the cobras were using some kind of magic to harden their scales. Since the snake was blinded its mouth was open seeking something to bite, so Lasgol stabbed the inside of its mouth. The knife went in hard and struck the brain.   It died instantly. Lasgol withdrew the knife and the snake fell to the ground.

The scales are tough, but the inside of the mouth isn't, he transmitted to his friends.

Ona had the snake in her jaws by the neck and was squeezing hard since she could not pierce its scales, although she could exert quite a lot of strength with her strong jaws. The cobra tried to coil around Ona's body, but the panther got away nimbly and now with her two powerful front legs had the snake pinned to the ground.

Camu had entirely frozen the second scorpion that had tried to sting him. But the third one attacked fast and dodged Camu's icy breath. It reached him and dropped his stinger toward Camu's back. But just before it touched him, Camu managed to hit the scorpion with his Tail Whiplash skill. Camu's tail sent the scorpion several paces back and the stinger did not reach him. The scorpion attacked again, and when the stinger was coming down toward him Camu received it with his Frozen Claw Slash skill. The tip of its stinger flew through the air—the slash had cut it off cleanly. The scorpion attacked with its pincers, trying to immobilize Camu with one and cut his neck with the other. Camu's answer was swift: two Frozen Claw

Slashes and one Tail Whiplash with his tail left the scorpion belly up, dying.

Lasgol took advantage of the fact that one of the snakes was blinded and stunned by the Earth Arrow and called on his *True Shot* skill. He waited for the snake to open its mouth to poke its tongue out and then he released. There was a green flash, which surprised Lasgol for its swiftness. This skill was one of the hardest for him to invoke, and barely a moment had passed between calling on it and it activating. The arrow struck true, entering the mouth and plunging deep into the palate. The snake died without coming out of its stunned state. Lasgol's skills were working better than ever; they were more powerful and swift and consumed less energy than usual. Lasgol was delighted. The only problem was that he found himself in a complicated situation.

Ona finished suffocating the cobra she had trapped in her powerful bite. Another cobra attacked her by spitting venom in her face. Ona leapt to one side, as if she had been startled from behind, and the venom flew by without touching her. Once she landed, she leaned on her powerful hind legs and took a prodigious leap, knocking the cobra down, using her front legs to keep the cobra from rising. An instant later Ona was biting the snake's mouth and part of the head with all the strength of her jaws. The cobra tried to open its mouth to bite, but Ona's jaws were like a vise—there was no way to escape them.

Camu was having more trouble with the last of the scorpions. It had grabbed his tail with one pincer and with the other his neck, pulling his head backward. He could not use his Tail Whiplash or his Icy Breath skills. He started to desperately unleash Frozen Claw Slashes with all his might, since the stinger was coming down toward his face. An arrow flew swift and hit the stinger. It was followed by another and another, and still more. Lasgol was using his *Fast Shot* skill repeatedly, and the arrows flew at amazing speed. The stinger was riddled with arrows, and when it fell on Camu's body it hit his scales and could not enter. It fell off the scorpion's tail. The Frozen Claw Slashes had destroyed the scorpion's mouth and eyes, and it died a moment later.

Lasgol had turned his back on the cobras to help Camu. He glimpsed a shadow out of the corner of his eye and in a reflex act he leapt, leaning on the wall of the small palace and, gathering speed, took another leap. In midair he turned and called on his *Blind Shot* skill to hit the cobra's right eye as it tried to bury its fangs in him. The moment he landed he jumped again with the help of his *Cat-Like Reflexes* skill and used his *Blind Shot* skill again. He hit the cobra in the left eye, blinding it. The scales were   great armor, but the eyes and mouth were weak and vulnerable.

The last of the cobras attacked Lasgol, spitting its venom first and then trying to bury its fangs in his arm. Instinctively, he slid to one side, avoiding both attacks. His *Cat-Like Reflexes* and *Improved Agility* were working well, and he was wearing his *Woodland Protection*. He wondered whether the fangs would be capable of piercing through it and reach his flesh. Probably not, but it was not a good idea to stop and see. Better if nothing bit him in any part of his body. He called on his *Elemental Arrows* skill again and released another Earth Arrow, which hit the snake full in the mouth and left it stunned and blinded. He waited for it to open its mouth a little more and killed it with a *True Shot*.

Ona finished killing the cobra she had clamped in her jaws.

Lasgol looked around. The cobras and scorpions were all dead or frozen. Lasgol released against one of the scorpions to see whether his arrow could pierce its shell and got proof that it could not.

Those scorpions have a tough shell.

Use Frozen Claw Slash. Be magic attack, shell no can stop.

Good thinking.

I much clever.

Sure, and handsome.

Much, much handsome.

Lasgol rolled his eyes.

Ona, are you all right?

Ona growled once.

You weren't stung, were you?

Ona growled twice.

Thank goodness.

Monsters tough. Have magic in skin.

Yeah, Dergha-Sho-Blaska must be giving them that magic. But where have those monsters come from? They seem to have come from the depths of the desert.

Not know. Not good.

If the Immortal Dragon now has these allies, we're going from bad to worse, that's for sure.

Serve Dergha-Sho-Blaska, that sure.

Yea, that's what I'm afraid of too, Lasgol said, snorting and looking all around. Then he turned to his two friends. *You were amazing, both of you!*

No problem, Camu messaged.

Ona growled once.

What do now?

Now we have to follow the pearls, that's all we can do.

Pearls with scorpions.

Let's see what other surprises the desert has in store for us.

Surprises no good, you see.

Yeah, I can imagine.

But no problem. I much powerful.

Yeah, no problem.

Chapter 31

Ona, Camu, and Lasgol went through the ghost city, following the enormous scorpions that had taken the Silver Pearls. The trail was quite clear since two sets of eight scorpion legs walking on streets partially covered by desert sand were unmistakable. Lasgol was having no trouble following them. Besides, they had carried away the ice jewel so if he lost the trail he could wait for a pulse that would tell him where they were.

Lasgol was thinking how lucky they had been that the crocodile had not joined the fray in the middle of the city, since that would have been an additional problem. On the other hand, the croc would have destroyed half the city if entered it, so to a point it was logical it had not come in. Well, as logical as one giant crocodile at the entrance of a city in the desert with colossal scorpions and cobras as guardians was. When he told the tale in Norghana they were not going to believe him.

They turned left and then right. They were not in camouflage since the venomous substance the cobras had spit on them had marked them. It was a problem for Camu's skill. Although it was a great skill, they were already finding faults in it: the cobras had smelled them, and the trail they left behind could also be seen. Now, on top of that they had to be careful with alien substances which the camouflage could not hide. The world of skills and magic in general was full of surprises and limitations. There was no spell, enchantment, or charm that was infallible.

Suddenly, from one of the buildings with an open garden there came out what looked like two rhinoceros beetles. They were the size of an elephant, only they were covered by a black and brown armor and in the middle of the head they had a horn that looked as if it could knock down a house.

Watch out, trouble! Lasgol transmitted in warning.

Beetle big and ugly.

And dangerous I'm afraid.

The two beetles charged at them as if they were really huge rhinoceros. Lasgol could barely believe it. Those enormous armored beasts were going to pose a serious problem. He had the feeling that the giant beetles' armor would be even tougher than the scorpions'.

Lasgol moved to one side, and the beetle charging at him passed him by and crashed into the building behind them. It knocked down half the wall with the blow. The other beetle attacked Camu and Ona. Ona took a powerful leap that got her out of the course of the assault. Camu released a Tail Whiplash at the beetle as it was charging, since he did not have the agility or speed of his friends to get out of the way.

It was not a good idea.

The whiplash caught the beetle but did not slow it down, and it rammed into Camu.

"Camu!" Lasgol cried, worried to see the blow he had received. Camu was thrown back and hit another building. He was left lying on the ground.

Ouch... he messaged.

Lasgol realized he had to do something against the two armored masses that were going to crush them. The beetles attacked again, trying to get Lasgol and Ona. They both jumped away nimbly. If they were hit by the horn it would skewer them from side to side; they did not have tough scales like Camu. The beetles hit two other buildings, and part of the façades collapsed from the terrible impact. Those creatures had   devastating strength.

Not having a clear understanding of how to stop such monsters, Lasgol nocked an arrow to his bow and released at the beetle attacking him. He used his *Elemental Arrows* skill and released a Fire Arrow to find out whether fire scared these monsters. The arrow hit the head of the beetle and there was a flame. The beetle did not like the fire and shook its horned head up and down and side to side.

Ona did something unthinkable, when the beetle attacked her she jumped onto its head. She started attacking its eyes with her claws, seeking to blind it so it could not go on attacking.

Lasgol knew that in order to penetrate the armor covering the monster's body he was going to need a very powerful shot. He focused on the monster as it maneuvered in the street, turning around to charge again. Lasgol needed a powerful shot to pierce through the armor. He concentrated and sough his inner energy.

The giant beetle charged.

Focusing, Lasgol imagined his shot piercing the beetle's armor to the right of the huge horn. He tried to create the skill as the beetle charged. The green flash almost came, but he failed. The skill was not created. The beetle's horn was coming straight at Lasgol's torso, but at the last instant he managed to skip sideways and the beetle rammed into another wall, bringing it down.

Ona continued delivering claw blows while the beetle she had climbed onto was shaking its head in every direction, trying to knock her off. Ona was holding on as best she could and did not fall off. At one moment she clung to the horn itself in order to stay on.

Camu started to get up slowly. The tremendous blow had left him aching and dizzy. He managed to stand and, stumbling, went to shelter in a patio with a fountain that had no water.

Lasgol tried once again to create the skill for a powerful shot, one with enough   power to pierce armor and shells. If he could develop it, it would come in terribly handy in this environment. The only problem was that this might not be the best time to try and develop a new skill. Or maybe it was. The pressure and critical timing of the moment might be the key to creating a skill. It was risky, but he could not think of anything else he could do against those two monsters, each so enormous and with such   hard shells.

The beetle attacked Lasgol, who concentrated on what he was seeking to achieve. He poured a large amount of energy into creating the skill while he stayed on his feet in the middle of the street, the giant beetle running at him like a rhinoceros. The skill began to form and Lasgol poured more energy into it. He had to achieve the powerful shot, or else those two monsters were going to destroy them.

There was the green flash, followed by the golden one from the Bow. The arrow flew with tremendous force and buried itself in the beetle's forehead deeply, piercing through the tough shell. Lasgol threw himself to the right at the last moment, and although he got out of the way of the horn, he could not avoid the huge body, and the blow caught him in the legs. The impact was so great that Lasgol was thrown in the air, rolling over himself. He fell a few paces back with a terrible pain in both legs.

He did not know whether they were broken.

He grunted in pain and felt both legs carefully to check that they were not broken. It took him a moment to check in the midst of the pain, but they were only very battered. He got to his feet as fast as he was able to.

The rhinoceros beetle was shaking its head, trying to dislodge Lasgol's arrow. Seeing his opportunity, Lasgol called upon the new *Powerful Shot* skill again and let the arrow fly. It hit the beetle in the head again and the arrow went in deep, perforating the shell as if it were brittle, which it was not. The monster made some strange sounds of agony. Lasgol wasted no time and shot three more arrows, one after the other, in the middle of the head. The monster fell forward and was still, dead.

He turned to the other beetle, which had managed to throw Ona off its head but still could not impale her with its horn. The panther was dodging the attacks with great agility, taking tremendous leaps to get out of reach of the giant beetle. Seeing what was going on, Lasgol called on his *Powerful Shot* skill again. He hit one of the legs to maim the monster and give Ona an advantage. The arrow went straight through, since although it had a protective layer, this was not as strong as on its body.

Before the monster turned toward Lasgol, he released three shots in a row and pierced the three legs. The giant beetle went for Lasgol, enraged. It tried to run him over, but it could not with its wounded legs. Lasgol could not move very well either, the blow to his legs had left him more than sore. He released three more shots at the same legs and managed to make the beetle falter and go to one side. It hit the ground hard like a boat running aground in a beach of white sand.

How are you? Lasgol transmitted to Camu as he tried to walk over to his friend. The pain in his own legs prevented him from doing so.

Be sore.

Wounded?

Blow strong, hurt.

Ona went over to Camu, who had sheltered behind the fountain and was lying on the ground, and licked his head lovingly.

Anything broken?

Not broken, sore.

That's good. Don't make any sudden moves. We'll wait a moment to recover.

They waited for the pain to subside a little. Lasgol felt his legs. Although they were not broken, they had taken a fierce beating. From how much they hurt, he was sure   they had been on the point of breaking, and he was very thankful to the Ice Gods that they were okay.

Camu was in a similar situation. He had not broken anything, but he had received a tremendous blow. He had been lucky, this time. The next time he might not.

We have to be more careful. There are powerful monsters here.

Tough and big.

Ona growled once.

You kill with arrows?

It's a new skill, Powerful Shot I think I'll call it. It works very well.

I see. I like.

Lasgol managed to walk at last, although he was limping a lot. He had large bruises on his legs and his right ankle ached   , although not enough to stop him.

Go on? I ready, Camu messaged, along with a feeling of courage.

Let's go, but carefully.

They walked along several streets, and Lasgol looked for the scorpions' trail until he found it. Then they followed it slowly with eyes wide open. Every building they bordered, every crossing, every small palace or plaza, they checked before making a move. The last thing they wanted was to come face to face with another danger. They had overcome the ones they had found so far, but they might encounter something   they could not defeat.

Lasgol had the feeling that this desert ghost city was a big trap to finish off anyone who dared to cross it. What had him worried was the fact that the city was coming to an end and they were still heading in a northwestern direction. Where were the scorpions going? He was beginning to have a bad feeling about this. He tried to calm his nerves and negative thoughts and focused on solving the situation they were in—step by step, difficulty by difficulty. Once they had overcome them all, they would be safe. And with a little luck, the Silver Pearls would be in their hands and not in those of the Immortal Dragon.

They followed the trail and went down a street to the west. A grand palace appeared before them. They stopped. Lasgol saw that the scorpions' trail went inside. They checked the great building before going into it, in case an ambush was waiting for them.

Let's study the place.

I not feel magic.

That's a good sign, but we should be careful anyway.

266

The palace had four round towers with golden domes. A large part of the interior was made up of gardens and open terraces, very elaborate, with marble floors of different colors and several fountains. Since they were not being looked after, the sand was everywhere and the fountains no longer had any water. No doubt in the recent past   that palace must have been a beautiful place.

At the bottom of the gardens there rose a main building, beautifully painted white with oval, gold-and-silver roofs. The large, wooden double doors were open. The scorpions must have gone in through them.

Ona, do you smell anything?

The panther stepped forward a little to inspect and came back quickly.

Two growls were the answer.

There doesn't seem to be anyone.

Lasgol shut his eyes and felt whether his combat skills were still activated. They were.

We're going in. Don't be overconfident. Stay alert.

They entered the gardens. Lasgol had an arrow nocked already and checked every corner and shadow of the beautiful place. Camu was on his left and Ona was on   Camu's left. The three moved at the same slow, wary pace. The palace must have belonged to the lord or ruler of the city, or perhaps a desert prince, since it was not only beautiful but quite large. Or maybe some other influential noble, since there might be a greater palace in the city they still had not seen.

They had come to fifteen paces of the open doors of the main building when two of the giant scorpions appeared at the doors.

Watch out, Lasgol transmitted in warning, and they stopped.

Those were not the scorpions they were after. They must be guards. The ones that were carrying the pearls must have gone into the building and these were stationed to stop them from following.

Only be two. No problem, Camu messaged, along with a feeling of confidence.

Be wary... Lasgol transmitted. He did not trust them in the least.

The scorpions started to tap their pincers on their shells, creating a weird, hollow metallic sound.

What happen?

I have no idea. Lasgol was looking at the scorpions and all around in search of an answer that did not come.

Suddenly, a shadow flew past them above their heads.

Lasgol's heart shrank as if it had been squeezed in the hand of a stone golem. He looked up at the shadow, convinced it was Dergha-Sho-Blaska who had come to finish them off. The flying shadow descended and landed in front of him.

It was not Dergha-Sho-Blaska.

It was some kind of dragon, but smaller than the Immortal Dragon.

Lasgol studied it. It looked like a real dragon, only smaller. It must measure about twenty-seven feet wide with its wings spread and was as long from the head to the tip of the tail. The looks of it though were not those of a youngster or pup dragon, but of a young adult. It might be smaller, but it was undoubtedly a dragon and it looked strong, powerful, and dangerous. It was reddish, with streaks the color of sand that ran down its back and torso. Its reptilian eyes were red, and it had a crestless and hornless head which made it look young. It opened its mouth, showing its fangs, and Lasgol was sure this was a full-fledged dragon in control of its faculties and power.

Drakonian Minor. Dangerous, Camu messaged to Lasgol.

What is a Drakonian Minor? Lasgol asked blankly, surprised that Camu knew what the creature was.

Servant of a Drakonian.

How do you know that?

Drokose tell I one day have Drakonian Minors in my service.

Wow, and it didn't occur to you to tell me?

You not let me have servants.

Lasgol had to admit that Camu was right, he would never let him have servants or slaves. That was wrong—worse than that, it was terrible, whether they were Drakonian or not.

We'll talk about that.

I know …

The minor dragon spread its wings and flapped them, showing their full span and raising sand that blew at the three friends. It raised its head and roared, showing its terrible teeth to its rivals. The roar was powerful and frightening. It stomped its claws on the ground so they would notice how sharp and strong they were. It had the superior attitude of something that believes itself superior to its enemies.

A human, a Superior Drakonian, and a snow panther. Strange company, they received the dragon's message and felt it as if it had hit their mind hard.

The three jerked their heads back, surprised and stunned. That dragon could send mental messages and did so forcefully. Ona shook her head as if trying to get the dragon out of her mind.

Lasgol called on his *Animal Communication* skill and picked up the aura of the minor dragon. It was a strong red. He tried to communicate with it.

Can you communicate?

Of course I can communicate, human. The strange thing is that you can.

My Gift allows me to.

You must be of the blood then.

Of the blood? Lasgol wanted to know what that meant.

Of the Drakonian blood. Only those of the blood can use the power of the mind.

Lasgol was puzzled, although this statement was consistent with similar ones that said that part of his power was of Drakonian origin.

I'm human. I can't be Drakonian.

No, but you can have Drakonian ascendancy.

How's that possible? Lasgol saw the chance to get an answer, and he tried to seize it.

I am not here to teach a human, even if you are of the blood.

Because I'm human?

Humans are weak of body, mind, and power. Drakonians, on the contrary, are strong of body, mind, and power. We are born to rule, you to serve.

Even those of the blood?

Especially those of the blood. Your purpose is to serve us. That is what you were created for.

And those not of the blood?

They can choose between serving on their knees and in pain or death. We prefer the latter.

You don't have much appreciation for humans.

I don't appreciate you at all. Those of my blood only appreciate those of their own blood, because we are superior to animals and humans, between which there is not much difference in our eyes.

Not superior to me, Camu messaged in a defiant tone.

The minor dragon bowed its head. It seemed to analyze Camu as if it were picking up his power.

No, I am not superior to you, but I do not serve you either.

Who do you serve? Lasgol asked.

My lord and master and creator. The king among dragons, Dergha-Sho-Blaska.

Lasgol nodded. *Do you have a name?*

My name is Saki-Erki-Luzen.

What do you want, Saki-Erki-Luzen?

This city is under my surveillance. No one may enter, be it animal, human, or Drakonian. Whoever enters, dies. Those are my master's orders, and those are the orders I will fulfill.

We didn't know. There's no need for any more bloodshed. We'll leave, Lasgol transmitted. He had the feeling that, minor or not, that dragon would be a formidable adversary better left alone .

The dragon laughed and messaged it as a feeling.

Hahaha, humans are so predictable. Begging for their life when there's no salvation possible.

I am Superior Drakonian. Order you let us go, Camu messaged with a feeling of command.

I only serve my lord Dergha-Sho-Blaska. It's time to die.

270

Chapter 32

Nilsa, Viggo, Egil, and Gerd were coming back from doing physical practice with six of the Royal Rangers, among which were Kol and Haines. They were both running at the front with Nilsa and chatting with her. It was painfully obvious that both of them were greatly interested in the friendly redhead. They were not the only ones. Another Royal Ranger joined them on the way down toward the capital, whose lights they could see in the distance. Night was falling and hunger and tiredness were beginning to have their effect, but whoever wants to be in shape must suffer a little. The Royal Rangers knew this better than anyone else. They had to endure whole days on their feet standing by a wall on watch duty. This numbed and softened anyone's muscles. Therefore, it was important they went out to do physical exercise.

Viggo was running in the lead, as fast as lightning. He wanted to arrive as soon as possible and show all the Royal Rangers that he was better than them. Nilsa and Gerd had already told him that was stupid, but as usual, Viggo had a mind of his own and did what got into his head without paying heed to his friends. Two of the Royal Rangers were running beside him, ready to show him he was wrong and that he would not be able to outrun them. The faster they ran, the more Viggo strove to leave them behind. Soon the distance from the rest became noticeable.

Gerd and Egil brought up the rear, making their own group of two, running at their own pace, since this was a maintenance exercise after all, not a competition. Besides, Gerd could not run as fast as he used to before his injury, so Egil preferred to go somewhat slower alongside his friend, for moral support and also to save his energy.

"If he keeps running like that, he's going to hurt himself," Gerd said, referring to Viggo.

"I can't even see them, they've left us so far behind," Egil commented.

"And the ones in front of us are so absorbed in Nilsa that they couldn't care less," Gerd commented with a nod toward the group ahead.

"It's what it is," Egil smiled.

They ran past an oak forest and heard the howling of a wolf, which made Egil and Gerd look in the direction of the sound. They saw nothing but shadows. It was not unusual that some wolves would roam the forests, although this was quite close to the capital, which was not so usual.

Egil stopped suddenly and bent over to hold his ankle.

Gerd stopped beside him.

"Twisted ankle? Are you hurt?" he asked him, concerned.

Egil looked up and saw the two groups before them continue on toward the city.

"I'm not hurt, take it easy."

Gerd looked at him, puzzled.

"Are you faking?"

"Until they no longer see us," Egil said, watching their comrades disappearing in the distance.

"You want to shake them off."

"That's the idea," Egil confirmed.

"The wolf?" Gerd asked, looking toward the forest.

"Irrefutable, my dear friend."

"I figured, I thought there was something odd in that howl."

"As if it were a little human?"

"Oh, I see, yeah, that's it."

Egil smiled.

"Let's go into the forest. I'm expected."

"One of your secret meetings?"

"Those are always the best."

"Well, I'm not so sure about that," Gerd said, looking toward the forest, a hand already on his axe.

"Take it easy, I don't foresee any trouble."

Gerd adjusted the bow on his back and the knife and axe at his waist.

"You may not. I like to be prepared. Your clandestine meetings don't always work out well."

"Very true, my dear bodyguard," Egil admitted and like Gerd adjusted his weapons.

"Let's go," Egil said with a nod.

The two friends went into the forest warily. It was not long before they could make out three figures further in. They were standing beside their horses tethered to a tree. A little further in were three more figures, also beside their tethered horses.

"Are you sure they're friends?" Gerd whispered to Egil.

"Supposedly," Egil replied.

Gerd made a face. His answer had not made him at all easy.

They went toward the figures and stopped five paces from them. Gerd and Egil watched them, trying to guess who they were. They did not make any abrupt movement, which was a good sign, although Gerd did not relax for a moment. At the first suspicious movement he would draw his weapons and take control of the situation.

"Do you respond to the call of the wolf?" a voice Egil recognized replied.

"The western wolf calls and the pack answers," Egil said in the agreed-to greeting.

"Greetings, King of the West," the one in the middle saluted him and bowed in respect. Those with him also bowed.

Egil returned the salute with a slight nod.

"You honor me."

He recognized Count Malason in the middle with Dukes Erikson and Svensen on either side, which surprised him. They were the top ranks of the Western League. Something must be happening for them to be there.

"We're glad to see you well," Count Malason said.

"So am I to see you. I have to say I'm surprised that the three of you have come to this meeting. I only needed one agent. Is there anything important going on that requires my presence?"

"Our lord is very perceptive," Duke Erikson said.

"Is the forest secured?" Egil asked, glancing around, which Gerd did too.

"It is, Sire, we have men posted at the perimeter," Count Malason confirmed.

"We need to agree on what to do now that Thoran and the new Queen Heulyn have survived the Royal Wedding," Svensen replied.

Egil nodded.

"The attempts didn't succeed. It was to be expected. According to my calculations, there was one chance in a hundred of a successful assassination, given the circumstances which weren't in our favor."

"And they failed, as our lord had foreseen," Malason said.

"Which makes us reconsider the future and our next moves,"

Svensen added.

"I understand. The first thing I want to know with certainty is that the second attempt, the one against the Queen, was not our doing," Egil said, looking at the three Western Nobles sternly.

"It was not. We had nothing to do with the attack on the Queen," Erikson said.

"Otherwise we would've warned you," Malason said.

"Are we certain it wasn't the job of someone from the West?" Egil insisted in a harsher tone, and his gaze fell on Duke Svensen.

"It wasn't us," Svensen assured him. "There are divisions in the League, but no one's going to make such a decision without permission and without having planned it to the last detail, as was done with the attempt on Thoran."

"Is our lord losing his trust of us?" Malason asked.

"Losing my trust isn't exactly the term. We have the same final goal, but the time of execution is different. Some of you have more aggressive agendas when it comes to timing and method," Egil replied, still eyeing Svensen.

"That's true. I won't deny it," the Duke replied. "But that doesn't mean we'd act without the knowledge and approval of the leaders of the League and, of course, our lord."

Egil looked at the three people at the back and nodded.

"We agreed, and I helped you with the escape plan, on a strike against Thoran at the dinner. The risk was tremendous, and it did not succeed, as I had foreseen. I said I would help you because I knew you would go ahead with the attempt anyway and the results would've been catastrophic. All of you here would have been hanged from the castle walls, since Thoran would've found out you were behind the attempt. I did it for you and for the Kingdom, and that's why I demand your word of honor that you did not take part in the second attempt."

"You have it, my lord," Malason said with his fist over his heart.

"And mine too," Duke Erikson said as well.

"I swear on my honor. I did not take part in the second attack in any way," Svensen swore.

Egil nodded twice slowly. He was turning the matter around in his head.

"We must assume, therefore, that the attempt against the Queen's life was perpetrated by other interests."

"Everything points at the Zangrians," Erikson said.

"From what we've been able to find out, most of the kingdoms take it for granted that it was the Zangrians," Svensen said.

"That's what we think too, and what Thoran believes," Malason added.

Egil shook his head.

"And yet, I don't think so."

The three nobles reacted with surprise at Egil's words.

"You don't? Why's that, Sire?" Svensen asked.

"Precisely because it fits too perfectly with what everyone wants. Thoran wants it to be the Zangrians in order to go to war with them with the support of Irinel. Erenal's rubbing their hands together and will wait and see how Zangria does in the war. Then Erenal will attack them from behind or directly join Norghana and Irinel and crush Zangria. The Rogdonians or the Noceans, as well as the City States from the East, see the war in Zangria as a positive thing because it weakens other powers. All this, and the fact that King Caron hasn't made his move yet, lead me to think that the attempt is a well-planned and executed gamble for some other reason which has been kept hidden."

"Who or what is this other hidden reason?" Duke Erikson asked.

"That's what we must find out before making any precipitated move, since we really don't know what's going on or what the next move will be from whoever planned all this. It could be counterproductive for us to act without having all the necessary information."

"If the war breaks, and from what we're seeing it will shortly, it might be a good situation for us. Thoran will have to come out in the open," Svensen reasoned.

"In an open field, in the midst of a battle, there'd be possibilities to kill him," Erikson said.

"It is an option, indeed. But is it the best option? In my opinion it isn't," Egil said. "There are better ways for a regicide than trying to kill him when he's surrounded by thousands of soldiers loyal to his cause."

"He'll also be surrounded by thousands who aren't, but who are instead loyal to us," Svensen told him.

Egil smiled lightly.

"Those will be on the front lines of combat. Not near Thoran, he will make sure of that, and so will his nobles of the East."

"Most likely," Count Malason agreed. "He won't let us be close enough."

"Which leads us to another problem we're going to have to face: the war and Thoran calling on us to fight," Erikson said.

"True. If the war breaks out, and everything points to that being the case, the Thoran will call on us to serve him, as he did in the war against Darthor and the forces of the Frozen Continent," Malason said.

"We can't refuse. Not after the Civil War," said Erikson.

"We won't refuse," Egil said in a cold tone.

Once again, the looks on the three nobles showed surprise. They had expected to get a different answer.

"We should," Svensen said.

"But we won't," Egil insisted. "We won't do anything that might give him an excuse or chance to attack the West. Thoran and Orten know who you are and what you're up to. Don't think for a moment that's not the case. You're the most important nobles of the West, and they know you don't accept his rule gracefully. They haven't gone against you because they haven't had a clear opportunity. We can't provide them with the reason they're waiting for to act against us. Your heads are in real danger."

"They've always been in danger and always will be," Svensen said with a dismissive wave of his hand.

"Yes, but before Thoran and the East were in a weaker position. Now they're strong, and with the alliance with Irinel even more so. It's not good for us to confront them now," Egil told them.

"Yes, that's what we thought, and hence the attempt on his life at the banquet," said Erikson.

"What are you proposing?" Svensen asked Egil.

"First, we have to make sure the attempt can't be traced back to us and give Thoran the occasion he's been waiting for to go against us."

"The perpetrators are well hidden. They haven't been found and they won't be," Erikson replied.

"That's not good enough. They must leave Norghana," Egil said.

"We'll make sure of it," Malason said.

"I want the details," Egil demanded.

"You'll have them, of course," Erikson replied.

"Second, we have to find out who attacked the Queen and see how that affects us. It might even turn out to be something positive. Perhaps we have a possible ally in the shadows who, if we find them, might serve our purposes."

"That's going to be more complicated," Erikson commented.

"Our agents haven't managed to gather much information about that," Svensen said in a disappointed tone.

"We haven't searched that deeply either. We took it for granted that it was the Zangrians," Malason commented.

"We need to go back to the beginning and assume it wasn't the Zangrians," Egil told them. "So, if it wasn't the Zangrians, then who was it?" he asked, looking into the eyes of the three nobles.

"Understood. We'll investigate," Erikson said.

"Third, if the war breaks out and Thoran summons the Nobles of the West and their soldiers to fight with him, we'll come. No one will refuse," Egil told them.

"He'll place us on the front line of battle. We'll be cannon fodder for the Zangrians."

"That's better than the three of you hanging for refusing and then sending your forces to the front line anyway," Egil told them.

"We could delay, claiming logistic problems, and join at the end," Malason said.

"That's a good idea. That way he won't be able to send us first," Erikson commented.

"We'd better think of good excuses for the delay. They're not going to like it," said Svensen.

"You can swear to that," Malason agreed.

"Very well then. We agree," Egil said. "Before leaving, I need one of your agents to find out some information for me."

"Absolutely, whatever you need," said Erikson.

"Good. Better if we leave the meeting here. I don't want to delay any longer. I have to go back to the castle. Good luck to everyone," Egil said as he started to leave.

"Good luck to you, King of the West," Malason said in farewell.

"Good luck for the West!" said Erikson.

"For the Throne!" Svensen cried.

Egil made a sign to Gerd and they left the forest as the nobles vanished into it. For a moment they did not speak but went on running at a quick pace so as to recuperate some of the time lost and not raise suspicions."

With the city already near, Gerd spoke.

"Now I see why you wanted the physical training. That way you can speak with your contacts outside the city once we're done."

"Irrefutable, my dear friend," Egil said, smiling at his friend.

"Well, you might find another way, this is a small torture for me."

"Which will be very good for you, and for me it's also a wonderful opportunity to have meetings and conversations in the dark. It's imperative that these conversations are not heard by unfriendly ears."

"I understand…" Gerd sighed. "Be careful. We're still close to the city, and there'll be spies of different sides all around."

"I'm keeping that in mind, indeed. Don't worry about it, my giant friend," Egil promised him in a soft but firm tone.

"That means you're going to continue taking risks."

"It can't be any other way," Egil smiled.

Chapter 33

Saki-Erki-Luzen, the minor dragon, attacked without any warning other than an intimidating roar. It took a step forward, opened its mouth as if it were going to roar again, and issued forth a gust of fire directed at Lasgol, Camu, and Ona.

Lasgol leapt to one side using his reflexes and improved agility. It was an instinctive move at seeing the fire and feeling its scorching heat.

Ona moved to the other side with a powerful leap to get out of range of the flames so they would not touch her. Her feline instincts saved her from ending up torched by the dragon's attack.

Camu opted for a different defense. He could not jump with the agility of his two friends. He opened his mouth and used his Icy Breath skill. The jet of freezing breath he sent crashed against the flames heading toward him. Upon contact both attacks, fire and water, canceled each other. Neither of the two managed to reach the rival.

The scorpions guarding the door, seeing their lord was attacking, also lunged at Ona and Lasgol from the sides. They moved fast for their size on their eight articulate legs. Their stingers were getting ready to drop and inject a large dose of venom in the bodies of their prey.

Lasgol got down on one knee, aimed at the scorpion closest to him, and, using his *True Shot* skill, released. There was the green flash in his arm and another golden one in his Bow. The arrow flew straight at the right eye of the scorpion. It hit it fully and stopped the attack for a moment. The giant scorpion moved its pincers from side to side while it emitted a strange sound that had to be some kind of muffled cry.

Ona avoided the attack of the scorpion's pincers by jumping to one side. The scorpion turned and attacked again, this time with the stinger, which fell swiftly onto the panther's head. With another leap backward, Ona dodged the stinger, which hit the floor of the terrace hard.

Camu and Saki-Erki-Luzen were immersed in their own battle.

The dragon threw a blast of intense and concentrated flames at Camu's body, forming a cone. The flames caught him from the sides of the cone, since the middle was countered by the icy breath Camu was sending. He felt pain, the intense pain of a burn. He did not like it at all and it made him angry. He had to prevent the flames from reaching him. He had to improvise, since his Icy Breath came out of his mouth like a jet and did not spread much. He sent magic into his skill and focused on modifying it. He had to counter the fire attack. His scales were withstanding the fire for now, but the pain he felt, which was growing by the moment, told him they would not hold for much longer. He moved his mouth unawares and the frozen jet began to change shape, opening up. He continued modulating it until he managed to create an icy cone, similar to the fire Saki-Erki-Luzen was using against him. The pain began to fade as he rebuffed the cone of fire the minor dragon was sending to him.

Lasgol threw himself to one side to dodge the pincers of the one-eyed scorpion attacking him. He called on his *True Shot* skill again and hit the scorpion in the other eye above the mouth. The beast stopped its attack again, finding itself wounded once more. He had blinded it. He looked to see how Camu and Ona were faring to help them and saw that Camu was containing the minor dragon's attack. He found it awesome. He called on his *Elemental Arrows* skill and released against the other scorpion which was trying to sting Ona. He hit the mouth with a Fire Arrow and the flame made the scorpion stop.

He was about to release again when the stinger of the scorpion he had blinded came straight down toward his head. Instinctively, he leapt backward. The tip of the stinger, which was the size of a long knife, brushed his nose. His reflexes and improved agility had saved him. The movement had been lightninging fast, and he realized again that this had to be because he had repaired the bridge. Now all his skills seemed to be stronger.

The scorpion attacked again, this time with its pincers, and Lasgol rolled to one side to avoid them. This was not possible—the scorpion was blind. How could it see him? He looked up at the scorpion's head, and then he saw it. It had five more eyes on one side. Lasgol could have kicked himself for not remembering that. Scorpions have several eyes on the sides, besides the main ones above the mouth. He had made a mistake he would have to fix at once.

Ona gave a tremendous leap and fell on the head of the scorpion attacking her. She   started clawing at it and biting, but the shell was too hard for her teeth or claws to penetrate it. The clever panther clawed at one of the front eyes and gauged it out cleanly. Then she went for the other one. The scorpion tried to shake her off with its pincers but could not reach her. It was spinning on itself, trying to make her fall, but the panther kept her balance by leaning on her tail and would not fall. Since it could not get her with its pincers, it tried to sting her, but by then it had no eyes on the top of its head so it could not aim properly. Ona saw the danger and, turning around, attacked the stinger. She bit into it with all her strength just behind the dangerous sac. Her jaws found the hollow between the joint of the two parts of the tail shell and managed to penetrate.

Camu was already countering Saki-Erki-Luzen's fire with his own icy breath, so they remained in stalemate for a long while until at last Camu managed to put out the dragon's fire. The icy breath reached the head of the dragon and Camu knew he had it. He would freeze the dragon whole and win.

I superior. You minor. I win, Camu messaged Saki-Erki-Luzen, along with a feeling of victory.

You are nothing but a Superior Drakonian pup. Do not fool yourself. You cannot defeat me. I might be a Minor Drakonian, but I am fully formed and developed, in my mind, body, and power. You have none of the three, Saki-Erki-Luzen messaged back, along with a feeling of mocking.

Camu was about to reply, but he noticed that his icy breath had found some type of magic defense on the scales when it hit the dragon's body that made them flash silver. The icy breath did not pass through the dragon's magic protection.

I much superior, Camu messaged without hesitating.

You have a lot to learn still, little one. It is a pity you will not be able to. Your days end here, Saki-Erki-Luzen messaged, along with a strong feeling of pain.

Camu suddenly felt the pain in his mind as if he had been attacked physically, only this was a mental attack. It stopped him from keeping up his Icy Breath skill, and he took a step back, hurting. This was different. It was not a physical or elemental attack, it mental.

Lasgol was facing the scorpion, and this time he used his new *Powerful Shot* skill to release at the mouth. There was the green flash, followed by the golden one from the Bow, and the arrow flew straight with tremendous force into the scorpion's mouth. The creature stumbled back from the power of the shot. Lasgol wasted no time and called on the same skill again. A second shot flew from his bow and the arrow went forcefully into the scorpion's mouth, which forced the creature to take another step back.

Ona was hanging from the tail of her scorpion like a dead weight with her jaws buried behind the stinger. The beast was trying to get rid of her, but the panther weighed too much for the scorpion's tail, which could not hold her. Ona touched down with her hind legs, and as soon as she did, with the help of the support she now had, shook her head so hard that she pulled off the end of the scorpion's tail with the stinger. She threw it to one side and growled.

Camu was trying to recover from the mental attack. He decided to counterattack with his Tail Whiplash skill to hit the dragon hard so it could not attack his mind. He called on the skill and there was the silver flash. His tail hit the dragon's body of the dragon with tremendous force. But the attack died out on the dragon's scales without any impact. As Saki-Erki-Luzen received the hit a silver gleam flashed from the dragon's body which protected it from the magic attack.

You will not get through my defenses with your magic. It is pitiful that being the creature you are I have to give you the last lesson of your life, Saki-Erki-Luzen messaged disdainfully and attacked again with another mental blow which Camu received as if he had been hit on the head with a mallet. He was left stunned, a tremendous pain in his mind spreading through his whole body. In a moment everything hurt, from his head to the tip of his tail, through his legs. It was a terrible sharp pain, of the paralyzing kind.

Clenching his jaw to bear the pain, Camu counterattacked, leaping forward and delivering a Frozen Claw Slash. The slash should have hurt the dragon, but its magical defense gleamed once more, preventing the attack from doing any harm. He could not hurt the dragon.

Do you not know that all Drakonians have an innate magical defense? Your magic cannot affect another Drakonian, or to be precise, you must overcome the magical defense your rival has.

I know, Camu messaged, taking a couple of steps back. He had not actually known, but he was not going to admit that.

You know? I do not think so. You also don't know that those of our blood, the Drakonians, can use their mind to attack and dominate the mind of other beings. Besides, we consider that all beings are inferior to us.

I know everything, Camu lied. He needed more time to compose himself.

That is not true. I shall instruct you a little before killing you. With your mind you can kill or dominate inferior beings like humans, half-humans, and beasts. Those two who are with you, for instance.

Be friends.

Friends? Drakonians do not have friends. Not among us, and least of all with inferior beings.

I different.

You are indeed. I feel some pity at having to kill a Superior Drakonian, one of the blood. On the other hand, this will bring me glory, and my lord and master will reward me for it.

Killing pup not glory, Camu messaged with rage.

True. You do not even know how to express yourself properly. Like I said, I am sorry. But my master will reward me when I deliver your heads.

Camu had gained some time with the chat and the pain had subsided a little. He understood what was happening to him and he also understood how the dragon was attacking him with its mind. Now he was going to stop it. He concentrated, and before the next mental attack arrived he called on his skill to cancel magic. He created a defensive dome around him, preventing any magic from happening inside it.

It is time to die, Saki-Erki-Luzen messaged as he sent a strong mental attack.

Camu had just finished raising the protective dome. The attack hit the dome, which gave off a silver flash, and when the attack went through it dissipated.

The dragon's eyes opened wide when it saw Camu did not suffer the attack.

Meanwhile, Lasgol was releasing his fourth *Powerful Shot* against the scorpion which fell to the ground, dead. Then he went to help Ona. The giant scorpion had trapped one of the panther's legs with its right pincer and was trying to grab her neck with the other one while Ona defended herself, clawing at the pincer and deflecting it. Lasgol nocked an arrow and aimed at the pincer holding Ona's leg. He called on his *Elemental Arrows* skill and released. The arrow flew from the bow, and this time he created an Air Arrow. When it hit the pincer there was a small explosion that sounded like thunder and an electrical charge hit the pincer. The scorpion, caught by surprise, opened the pincer and shook it, trying to get rid of the charge.

Ona was free. She took a tremendous leap to get out of range of the great pincer.

Lasgol called on his *Powerful Shot* and an arrow went through the scorpion's mouth. Upon impact the creature went backward. The first *Powerful Shot* was followed by two more and the scorpion fell to the ground, dead.

Saki-Erki-Luzen tilted its head and roared at Camu. It opened and closed its jaws as if it were speaking but no sound reached Camu.

Suddenly, he realized that by canceling the magic with his defensive dome, he was also canceling the dragon's mental messages. He concentrated and tried to filter them so they could pass through the defense while keeping out the rest of the dragon's magic. It was dangerous, and he hoped he could do it right, because he did not want the attack to slip through with the message.

The pup learns fast, Saki-Erki-Luzen messaged in a mocking tone.

I much intelligent.

I have no doubt. You are a Superior Drakonian after all.

Surrender and live, Camu messaged.

Saki-Erki-Luzen laughed, hard. *I shall live. You shall not. You cannot defeat me. I am a dragon. I find it amusing that you believe you have the slightest chance. Let me assure you that is not so.* The minor dragon spread its wings and, gathering momentum with them, it leapt forward to fall on Camu with its four claws spread open as if it were a giant royal eagle hunting prey.

Camu tried to react and move out of the way. He was not fast enough. He received the blow on the right side of his body. The claws hit his scales hard. They did not manage to penetrate though, but Camu felt the force of the impact and was left lying on the ground feeling sore.

Lasgol and Ona saw that their fried was in danger and they both attacked the dragon. Ona ran and with a leap lunged at the dragon's back. Lasgol aimed swiftly and using his *True Shot* skill released at Saki-Erki-Luzen's eye. The arrow flew swiftly to bury itself in the eye. But the dragon saw it coming and, opening its mouth, released a gust of fire that incinerated the arrow, reducing it to ashes. It did not reach its target. Saki-Erki-Luzen's reflexes and the speed at which it spewed fire were astonishing.

Taking advantage of the fact that the minor dragon was distracted defending itself from Lasgol's attack, Ona fell on its back and went straight into burying her fangs in the long neck of the dragon, which was already turning its head to see who or what was attacking it from behind. Ona reached the neck before the dragon finished turning and bit down with all her might. Her fangs pressed on the red and sandy scales but did not manage to pierce through them. Even so, she squeezed with all her strength on the piece of neck she had bitten, pressing down, seeking to penetrate the scales or make it difficult for the creature to breathe.

Stupid inferior beasts and humans! Saki-Erki-Luzen messaged them, and Lasgol and Ona felt the enraged insult like a slap to their minds.

The dragon sent another gust of fire at Lasgol, who was about to release again. He could not follow through on his attack and was forced to throw himself to one side to avoid the fire. Saki-Erki-Luzen whipped its neck and Ona was thrown off to one side, unable to hold on with her teeth. The scales were like metal, and she could not maintain a hold on them.

It is ridiculous that inferior beings think they can fight against someone like me. I will show you how insignificant you are, Saki-Erki-Luzen messaged with rage.

It fixed its reptilian red eyes on Lasgol and launched a mental attack. Lasgol felt a terrible, sharp headache and fell on his back as if he had received a blow to the skull with a Norghanian war axe. He became dizzy while the pain spread throughout his body, rendering it useless.

Saki-Erki-Luzen looked at Ona and launched another mental attack. The panther leapt and twisted in the air violently, then fell to the ground where she lay on her back, convulsing.

I think you are beginning to understand. I shall make your deaths painful for having the audacity to attack me. Ignominies are paid in suffering and pain.

Camu got to his feet. His body hurt terribly, but that was not going to stop him from helping his friends. He had to. The dragon was destroying them, and it was going to kill them all if he did not find a way to stop it.

I finish with you, he messaged the dragon.

You? You do not even know what you are capable of, pup. if you do not want to suffer, you can bow your head before me and I shall give you a quick and

285

painless death.

I prefer you die.

Saki-Erki-Luzen laughed again. *I gave you your chance. When you beg, remember, because I shall not have mercy. Those of the blood do not have it, nor do we have patience.*

Chapter 34

The Panthers were waiting to be received by Queen Heulyn before her chambers. They were waiting in an antechamber decorated as if they were in Irinel. There were shields and javelins from that realm hanging on the wall. Several Irinel soldiers guarded the entrance and would not let them through. They had told them, kindly but firmly, to wait there. Since the Queen had requested their presence, they could do nothing else.

The double doors opened and a familiar face came to greet them.

"Good day, Royal Eagles," Valeria said with a lively spirit and a big smile on her face.

"Good day, Valeria," Nilsa returned the greeting with a light smile.

"The Queen has summoned us," Ingrid said with a hint of interrogation in her tone.

"And it's a little too early for our taste," Viggo complained, yawning ostentatiously. "You might let the Queen know that these are inappropriate hours for morning meetings. Better to have them after a good breakfast, say mid-morning."

Valeria gave a little laugh.

"I don't think I can tell such a thing to the Queen. She doesn't like to have her orders or words questioned."

"Yeah, and that's why I'm telling you," Viggo made a comical face.

"You're so charming, Viggo. But you better tell her your complaints in person. I'm sure she'll be delighted to hear them," Valeria smiled.

"Don't you dare say anything to the Queen," Ingrid said to Viggo forbiddingly. "She already dislikes us enough. There's no need to make things worse."

"If I'm charming, how could I make things worse?" Viggo shrugged and smiled as if he had never in his life said or done anything bad.

"What does the Queen want from the Royal Eagles today for her to call before dawn?" Egil asked, raising an eyebrow, in a certain suspicious tone.

"The Queen wishes her protectors to accompany her this morning," Valeria replied.

Astrid and Molak exchanged suspicious glances.

"In that case, let's not make her wait," Egil said.

They all followed Valeria, who took them inside the Queen's chambers. She led them along a corridor to a small library beside the Queen's bedroom. The room had the walls covered in books on four huge bookshelves that ran from side to side and floor to ceiling. There was a round oak table in the middle of the room and two big armchairs for reading.

"Come in," Valeria told them, and as they did they saw Queen Heulyn and the Druid Aidan at the end of the room. It would not have seemed strange that they were both there, reading or studying tomes, if they had not both been dressed as Rangers, which more than surprised the Panthers.

"You called, Your Majesty?" Ingrid asked, unable to hide her surprise at their clothing.

"Yes. I need you to come with me and protect me."

"Of course, Your Majesty. We're always at your disposal to protect you," Ingrid said.

"I know, and that's what I expect," the Queen replied drily.

"Absolutely, Your Majesty," Ingrid assured.

"You've been training as Royal Rangers, so I expect you to protect me like true experts."

"So it will be," Ingrid said.

"Good. Because today you'll have to protect me outside the capital," she told them without even looking at them.

"Your Majesty... you can't leave the safety of the castle... you're in danger after the murder attempt," Ingrid said.

"Excuse me! How do you dare tell me what I can or can't do? I'm the Druid Queen, and I'll do what I please when I please," the Queen's tone was harsh.

Ingrid kept silent.

"What we mean to say is that the King doesn't want any member of the Royal Family leaving the castle, and least of all the city. That's what we've been told," Egil said to tone down the tension.

"I will do whatever I want, whether my husband likes it or not. No one tells me what I can or cannot do. We're leaving the capital, and no one is going to stop me or tell the King. Have I spoken clearly enough?"

The Panthers exchanged glances. There was doubt in their eyes. They could not disobey the King, but neither could they disobey the Queen. The situation was impossible for them. If they disobeyed the King they would get into deep trouble, but they would also pay the consequences if they disobeyed the Queen. Whatever they did, they would come out the losers. They all saw this clearly.

"Her Majesty has spoken with absolute clarity. Of course we will carry out her orders," Egil said in a soft tone that sought to please her.

"That's better. Let me remind you that you're assigned to protect me. I could go without your protection, but then you wouldn't be fulfilling your duty. If anything   should happen to me, the King would hang you for it. Do you prefer that?"

"Absolutely not," Egil replied. "The safety of our Queen is our primary concern."

"We have to do our duty, and so we will," Ingrid said.

"We'll say no more about the matter. We leave immediately. Is everything ready?" she asked Valeria.

"Everything's been organized," she confirmed with a nod.

"Before starting, I want your word as Rangers that nothing of what you see today will be known to anyone outside this room. This must remain secret, since otherwise my life will be in danger and you will have failed in your duty to protect me."

The Panthers looked at one another. Egil urged the others to accept.

"You have our word," Ingrid promised.

"I want you all to promise, one by one," the Queen demanded.

They all swore on their Ranger's honor, and as they did they realized this was not going well at all. It had every appearance of jumping headlong into a big mess, otherwise the Queen would not bother with so much secrecy and promises.

"Very well. Let's go then," the Queen ordered.

The Panthers turned toward the door and, to their surprise, Valeria closed it. They looked at the Queen blankly.

"It's this way," Heulyn said as she pushed three books in the middle of the second bookshelf at the back of the room and they heard a metallic 'click'. Part of the bookshelf slid back as if the wall gave in and sank. A trapdoor appeared on the floor, which had been hidden by the bookshelf that had been on top of it until then.

"Allow me, my Queen," said Aidan, who bent down to pull the trapdoor up by a ring embedded in the wood. With a shriek, the trapdoor rose, revealing some stone steps that went down to some dark place.

"This is the Queen's Passage," Heulyn said. "It was built for the Queen to escape in case of someone coming to kill her. Since you are my bodyguards, it's only logical that you know of its existence. Also that you keep it secret."

"Absolutely, Your Majesty," said Ingrid, looking at Egil out of the corner of her eye. They had not been expecting that.

"We haven't been informed of the existence of this or any other passages in the castle," Egil apologized. "It would've been of great help to know them in order to better protect you."

"Now you know about this one, and of course, if the Queen has an escape passage…" Heulyn said.

"The King does too," Egil guessed, finishing the Queen's sentence.

"Smart boy," Heulyn said.

Valeria lit an oil lamp on a small auxiliary table and passed it to Aidan. Then she lit a second one which she kept herself.

"I'll lead the way," Aidan offered, and he started down the stairs.

Heulyn was about to follow, but Ingrid stopped her.

"We'd better maintain a protection formation, Your Majesty. We don't know what might be waiting below or further on."

"You're the bodyguards. Tell me how you want us to proceed. I will not oppose to being protected."

"Astrid, Nilsa, Molak, and I will go first. Then Your Majesty, and after her Gerd, Egil, and Viggo. Valeria can bring the rear."

"No, I want Valeria always at my side," the Queen demanded.

"As Your Majesty wishes," Ingrid conceded.

Following Ingrid's indications, they went down the stairs that led to a long corridor was formed like a tunnel but square and built like a passage. It was wide enough for two people and about six feet high. Viggo came last and shut the trapdoor behind him. Aidan maneuvered a lever below, and they heard the sound of chains sliding on the rock. The bookshelf moved back into place, covering the trapdoor above their heads.

The oil lamps they carried gave enough light to walk along the tunnel without any trouble. It smelled damp, dusty, and closed off. The atmosphere was rancid. Not much air circulated, barely any. It did not look like it had been used much either, which made sense, since it was a secret escape passage.

They arrived at some other stone stairs and went down them. They came to a small fork with two doorless exits.

"Down the right," Aidan said and kept going.

They all wondered where the one on the left would lead to, but no one asked. They went on silently down a new passage similar in size to the first one. They went down three more stairs, each one coming to another passage similar to the previous ones. The only thing that varied was that the deeper they went down, the more humidity they noticed around them, as well as a lack of air. It was clear they were going down quite deep.

"This is the last flight of stairs," Aidan told them.

They went down them and entered a new passage. They noticed they must be under the surface level. It smelled of damp earth and the walls were wet. They were not only underground, but there was water near, a river most likely. They were not pleased with this idea. If water came into the tunnel, they could all drown and it would be a horrible death.

The passage felt endless, as if they were walking to the other end of Norghana. Every few paces it turned right or left, which confused them as to the distance they were traveling. Whoever had excavated this underground escape route must surely have taken years to do so. And considering it would have been a job done secretly, it must have taken even longer.

At last, Aidan stopped before a solid stone wall that blocked the passage. On one side of the wall was a metal lever. The Druid pulled it. Once again they heard the sliding of chains on the rock, and the stone wall opened like a door in an angle that only allowed passage for one person.

Aidan went out first. Then the others followed one by one. They were underground in a small hall. Aidan indicated a trapdoor over their heads. He pulled on it and it opened inward. He jumped out of the trapdoor and offered his hand from above. There were no stairs. They all climbed out. The Queen was given a hand: Gerd got on all fours and Heulyn used his back as a step to then climb out with Aidan's help.

Once they were all out, they realized they had appeared inside an old abandoned stone mill. They took positions with their bows in their hands and looked outside.

They heard a noise to the east among some oaks, and the Royal Eagles aimed their bows in that direction.

"Take it easy, they're ours," Aidan informed them.

They saw two Druids with horses for everyone. They must have left the castle beforehand and obtained the mounts.

"We'll continue by horse," Valeria said.

They left the mill, protecting the Queen like Raner had taught them. They realized they were outside the capital. They could see the city to the south; the walls and buildings were unmistakable, about half a league away. That was why it had seemed such a long walk underground. Around them, there was only the old mill, a fast-flowing river, and two forests, one to the north and the other to the west, which hid the mill almost completely. There were no paths or roads leading there.

They went to where the Druids were waiting with the horses and rode off. They arranged themselves, protecting the Queen as they had been practicing with Raner in their training as Royal Rangers, and let the Druids guide the group.

The ride did not last long. The place they headed to was a linden forest northwest of the abandoned mill. They were far enough that no one would suspect they had come from the mill, but close enough to not waste too much time getting there.

"It's here," Aidan announced when they arrived at a small clearing with a pond and a stream.

They dismounted and the Panthers secured the area. Valeria took care of the horses.

Aidan, the two Druids, and Queen Heulyn went over to the pond, ignoring their escort.

"We'll form a circle of protection," Ingrid told her partners.

The group stood, shielding the Queen on all directions and at a distance of two hundred paces so no mage might get close enough to attack her. They all knew what they had to do and the risk it posed having the Queen in a clearing in a forest during the turbulent times running through Tremia.

While they kept surveillance, the Panthers were also watching the Druids and the Queen out of the corner of their eyes. Although they did not understand what they were witnessing, it was clear it had to do with the magic of the Druids and Nature. Aidan and Heulyn were sitting beside the rim of the pond. Aidan had one hand in the water and the other on the grass. He signaled for Heulyn to sit in the same way. Then they closed their eyes and Aidan began to recite strange words, which Heulyn repeated. The other two Druids were both behind the Queen and also intoned phrases in the magical language of the Druids.

Around Heulyn, a small whirlwind began to form, and it made her red hair fly in every direction. The whirlwind was natural, they could all feel that, but what they did not know was whether the two Druids that must be helping the Queen were creating it or not. Suddenly, a pillar of water began to rise from the pond beside Aidan. A moment later another one, a lot smaller and unstable which rose and fell somewhat un-controllably, began to rise by Heulyn's hand.

They all watched the Queen's magical exercises in silence. Valeria did not say anything either. She was watching the proceedings, slightly apart from the group but without interfering. It was better to leave magical business to magi, or in this case, to the Druids.

The exercises went on for a long time until the Queen fainted on the grass. She had not managed to control the pillar of water, and the effort seemed to have been too much for her.

Valeria went over to her and knelt beside her to make sure she was all right. The Queen came to shortly after.

"I'm fine. It was nothing," she told Valeria.

Aidan and the two Druids were watching her silently.

"You fainted, that's not 'nothing'," Valeria told the Queen.

"It's the price you have to pay to learn how to use the power of Nature. I pay it with pleasure. Let's continue," she told Aidan.

"Are you sure you're okay?" Valeria asked in a concerned tone.

"I am, don't worry."

Aidan and the two Druids led the Queen to one of the linden trees. The four placed their hands on the tree trunk and started to recite phrases of druidic power. They did this for a long while. The leaves of the tree began to fall down on them, but they appeared to flutter like butterflies and did not touch the ground.

The Panthers continued watching out of the corner of their eyes and did not understand beyond the fact that the Druids appeared to be communicating with the linden and its leaves, which was most strange. On the other hand, the magic of the Druids was that of Nature, so it was not odd they were interacting with the tree, although the Panthers did not see the purpose behind the exercise.

At last the Queen was exhausted and they had to call it a day.

"Let's go back, that's more than enough for today."

"Yes, let's go back, I need to rest," the Queen said.

Ingrid arranged the guard formation and they all got on their horses. They went back to the abandoned mill. There they parted ways. The two Druids left with the horses and the rest of them entered the mill to retrace their way back to the Royal Castle. They reappeared in the library, which had remained locked from inside.

"Not a word about what's happened today, to no one, or I'll have you skinned alive before killing you," the Queen warned them.

"No one will learn anything from us," Ingrid promised.

"It had better be that way," the Queen said, fixing them with lethal eyes.

They did not need the Queen's threat; they knew very well what they risked if they shared the Queen's secrets with anyone.

"Go now," the Queen dismissed them, looking haggard.

The Panthers left, leaving the Queen with Valeria and Aidan.

When they were back in their room at the Tower of the Rangers, the Panthers started discussing what had happened. None of them could wait to give their opinion about the day.

"It's been refreshing and interesting. I love it when they throw us headlong into secret passages, and then to forests to experiment with Druid magic. You really can't have a better day than that," Viggo said with great sarcasm.

"Shut up, you numbskull, it's the Queen's orders, and you know we can't disobey them," Ingrid snapped.

"I agree with you, Viggo. It's been most interesting," Egil said. But the scholar was serious, unlike the Assassin.

"Interesting? What do you mean interesting?" Ingrid looked at him blankly. "Now we're in a real mess. What are we going to do if the King asks us?"

"It's a very complicated situation for us," Molak joined her. "We could be hanged for this."

"And if we keep silent?" Nilsa suggested, rubbing her hands.

"Not saying anything isn't exactly treason."

"If we speak we'll get into trouble, and if we keep quiet we will too," Gerd said sounding miserable. "The King will consider the fact that we don't tell him as treason."

"Egil said it was interesting because of the Queen's Passage," Astrid explained.

"Irrefutable," Egil smiled. "It's a great find. Now we know the Queen's escape route in case of a serious situation in the castle."

"And the way to get to her from outside and kill her," Astrid added, raising both eyebrows.

"Once again irrefutable, my friend," Egil continued smiling.

"We also know there's another passage for the King's escape, so we can also get to him and cut his throat," Viggo said.

Irr…" Egil started to say.

"We know," Gerd interrupted him with a pat on his shoulder.

Egil smiled.

"Another thing I don't like at all is that they might try to kill her in the forest," Ingrid commented. "Then we would have serious trouble explaining it."

"Taking precautions and watching carefully, we can prevent it," Molak said. "Although I must admit I have a terribly bad feeling in the pit of my stomach. I feel as if I were betraying the King I've sworn to serve faithfully."

"You'll get used to it…" Viggo said. "With us there's no good or evil. We're always walking the thin line in the middle."

"And I am loyal to the King and Norghana. There's no middle line."

"Yeah, I see how well you're walking on the good side," Viggo mocked him.

"The situation is very complicated," Molak said defensively.

"Wait a little and it'll become even more complicated, you'll see."

"And what if they prepare a really elaborate ambush?" Ingrid said, worried, returning the conversation to the matter of the forest and the Queen's Druid training.

"Nothing happened today," Nilsa replied.

"No, not today, but what about the next time?" Gerd asked.

"We'll have to wait and see what happens," Egil said with an odd smile.

The others looked at him, and none of them felt at ease.

Chapter 35

The minor dragon rose, flapping its wings hard, and prepared to drop once again onto Camu to strike it with all the power and weight of its considerable size. In comparison, the dragon was larger than Camu, who recognized the situation and what it meant. Seeing it was going to lunge down at him and knowing he was not exactly nimble, Camu decided to change tactics to avoid the crash.

The dragon lunged at Camu with its four claws outstretched.

Camu called on his Drakonian Wings. There was a powerful silver flash along his body and the wings appeared on his back, glowing in all their splendor. He leapt, flapping them vigorously, and rose up off the ground.

The dragon hit the ground with its four claws hard, breaking the marble slabs of the patio, which flew in shards all over the place. Camu was already nine feet up. He had escaped the attack by a scale's breath.

The dragon looked up.

So, the pup can fly. Then he is not such a pup, it messaged and flapped its wings. It took a powerful leap and went to attack Camu in the air.

Camu saw it and began to soar to avoid being caught. The problem was that if his magic had no effect on the dragon, he would not be able to defeat it. He did not have sharp claws, terrifying jaws, or tremendous strength to attack with, something the dragon did have. For the moment he could dodge it, but that was all he could do. He flew as fast as he could so it would not catch him.

Meanwhile, on the ground, Lasgol was trying to recover. The sharp pain he felt in his head and his whole body prevented him from moving. He could barely think. The dizziness was passing, which was good news, but he needed to be able to think and move, which he was not managing to do. His subconscious, which was the only thing that seemed to work, told him that recovering his mind and shielding it were the first things he needed to do, or else the dragon would kill him with another mental attack.

Ona moaned and Lasgol heard her. If he was feeling so bad, Ona must be the same or worse. He had to help her. He tried to concentrate through the sharp headache. It was as if he had a migraine the size of the Norghanian Royal Castle. It was not going to be easy but he knew that if he did not manage something, it was more than likely that the dragon would kill all three of them. It was a terrifying thought that seized him and made his stomach turn.

He looked up at the sky and suddenly he saw Camu gliding by, followed closely by the dragon which was trying to catch him. It looked like an eagle chasing a hawk to kill it. Camu was in trouble. He guessed that if his friend was fleeing, it had to be because he had not been able to hurt the dragon with his magic. This made him very uneasy: it was the last thing they needed. He had to calm down, focus his mind, concentrate, and recover.

He took a deep breath and held it before letting it out again three times in a row. He reached some kind of relief and used it to concentrate. He called on his *Ranger Healing* skill. He did not think he could call upon it with the acute pain in his head, but maybe he would be lucky. The skill did not activate. Luck was not on his side. But he did not let himself be defeated by pessimism. He breathed in deeply three more times while he watched Camu fly in circles over his head, chased by the dragon throwing flames at him.

More concentrated now, Lasgol tried again. He called on his *Ranger Healing* skill, and this time the skill activated. He immediately applied it to his own mind's aura, which felt very fuzzy, almost nonexistent, as if something had attacked it and nearly destroyed it. He knew at once what he had to do. He had to strengthen it. He sent a large amount of inner energy from the pool to his mind. And with the help of the skill his aura began to shine stronger. At once his headache began to decrease until it vanished after a moment.

He was already feeling better. Now he had to protect his mind in case the dragon attacked him again. He used his *Mental Protection* skill, which he had recently developed and protected his aura. He hoped it would serve against a mental attack, although he was not sure whether it would work. With a clear mind, he tried to stand. The body aching persisted—it was as if his whole body had been attacked, as if he had been stabbed from the throat to feet. He felt it worse along his back and in his heart, which worried him. It was more than possible that the dragon could manage to make his heart explode with one of its deadly mental attacks. He sent energy to strengthen his *Mental Protection*. He did not want to give the dragon a second opportunity to kill him.

He stood up with difficulty from the pain that tortured him with every movement and saw Ona lying not far away. He knew he had to help her. His skills only worked on himself. He felt tremendous pain and rage hearing her moan, asking for help. His eyes moistened. Two shadows flew above his head once again and he saw Camu was in trouble. Lasgol had to do something. He ran first to where Ona was and picked her up in his arms, then ran with her into the main building, checked whether there were any more scorpions on guard, and, seeing the room was empty, put her down gently and left her inside. He did not want the dragon to kill her while she was defenseless.

He came out of the building and looked up for Camu and the dragon. He did not see them at first, and he took the chance to go over his Pre-Combat list of skills. Some of them had become exhausted, and he made sure to strengthen his *Woodland Protection* skill in case the dragon tried to split him in two or shred him to pieces with its claws. It was more than likely it would try.

They suddenly appeared in his field of vision. Lasgol was aware that he could not pierce the dragon scales with a regular shot, so he decided to use his *True Shot* skill. He called on the skill while he aimed his bow, guessing the path Camu and the dragon would trace in the air. It was not an easy shot—if they changed course abruptly he would fail, and because of that he was going to use a *True Shot*. The skill activated with a green flash and Lasgol released. The Bow flashed gold. The arrow went upward and slightly to the right.

It hit the dragon's body, penetrating the scales, although not too deeply.

The dragon stopped chasing Camu and remained suspended in the air, flapping its wings hard. It checked the wound.

How is this possible? it messaged, looking at Lasgol, who was already nocking another arrow.

Come down and I'll show you, Lasgol transmitted. He was hoping to draw the beast's attention to get it away from Camu.

The insignificant human will die in a sea of pain for this, the dragon messaged threateningly and dived toward Lasgol.

As the dragon was coming down at him, Lasgol called on his *Powerful Shot* skill, but this time he maximized the shot. Sending a large amount of energy into the skill, he released an arrow and his powerful shot hit the beast's torso in mid-flight. Once again the arrow buried itself into the dragon, penetrating the scales a little deeper. Unfortunately, it did not go in deep enough. The dragon's scales managed to cushion the impact so Lasgol could not hit any vital organs.

With a roar of rage, the dragon sent a jet of fire at Lasgol at full tilt. Seeing the fire coming at him, Lasgol threw himself to one side to avoid the flames, but they still caught him in the leg. *Woodland Protection* saved him, although it could not entirely prevent him from burning. He felt part of his leg roasting. The fiery breath of the dragon was too powerful, it could incinerate anything. He was left on the ground with a grimace of pain and looked down at his leg. It was burnt, but he would not lose it.

He stood up and aimed his bow again. He needed more power to pierce the scales and get his arrows to go deeper. The problem was that he had already tried to maximize the skill by using all of his energy, and even so it had not been enough. Perhaps the physical protection of dragons was too strong for his magic.

Let us see whether you survive this, you weak human, the dragon said as it flew nearby and launched a deadly attack.

Lasgol felt the attack in his mind. It was as if a huge Wild Man of the Ice had hit him in the middle of the forehead with a double-headed axe. His head jerked back. The attack reached his mind and Lasgol thought he would fall down in a sea of agony. But he did not. His mental protection was able to minimize the harmful effect of the attack. Lasgol felt an acute pain in his mind, which spread throughout his whole body, but it was much less than the first attack. He clenched his jaw hard and bore the pain. He kept on his feet, bent forward with pain but without falling.

How can this be? the dragon asked, unable to believe Lasgol was not writhing on the ground in a sea of pain while it rose over Lasgol, hovering in the air, flapping its huge wings.

Bec.... because... I ... am... also... of the blood, Lasgol replied.

A descendant of the blood cannot have the power to stand before me.

Perhaps... you are wrong.

A dragon is never wrong. I will show you.

Lasgol was sure it was going to send an even stronger mental attack. His *Mental Protection* skill had died out, so he tried to call it back, but with the pain he was suffering he was not able to. The dragon was going to kill him. He tried to raise the bow for one last shot, although since he was unable to use a skill it would be in vain.

The dragon prepared to attack.

Camu landed abruptly with one of his forced landings and took Lasgol away with him in the crash, dragging him about a dozen paces along the ground. They were both left tangled up in a kind of strange embrace.

What do you think you are doing, little pup? That is not going to save your insignificant human.

Camu rose together with Lasgol and created a dome of magic cancellation around them to protect both of them from any magical attack. There was a silver flash and the dome formed. It was translucent but with some silver sparks.

The dragon sent a mental attack against Lasgol, but Camu's protection stopped it. The dome shone with a silver flash, canceling the magic trying to penetrate it.

Not be my human and not be insignificant, Camu replied angrily.

The dragon was watching him but said nothing, which surprised Camu. He realized that the dome prevented him from receiving the dragon's mental messages. He sent energy to the dome and let the messages come through, but only the messages, not any feeling or force along with them.

You deserve to die. You are not worthy of the Drakonians. None of us stoop to helping a human. That behavior is despicable, of someone weak, without the strength of character of a Drakonian, it messaged disdainfully.

I no weak. I honor, you not.

The dragon came down and landed before Camu and Lasgol. It planted its four claws on the ground. It spread its red wings to their full span, stretching its body and tail as long as it was. The sand-colored scales shone with the reflection of the sun on them. It lifted its head and opened its mouth to show its fearsome jaws. It was a powerful, large, beautiful and terrifying monster.

Honor, the ignorant pup says. Of course I have honor. Toward my own. I am a minor dragon, but a full-fledged dragon, nonetheless. You cannot defeat me. Neither you, nor a whole army with its magi and warlocks. Their weapons cannot pierce my scales. Their magic cannot overcome my Drakonian magical defense.

Yes, can.

The time of men is coming to an end. A new era is about to begin. One of dragons. We shall destroy the world and will rule over the new kingdoms that come out of the ruins as the superior beings we are. No one will be able to stop us, whoever submits to their new masters and worships us as gods will survive. The rest shall perish.

That won't happen. We'll stop you, Lasgol transmitted, who had already recovered enough and was aiming at the dragon with his bow.

You will not be able to. It is too late. My lord and master Dergha-Sho-Blaska has everything strategically thought out and prepared. He will carry everything out and the world will go back to belonging to the dragons, its original owners, as it was before. It is already inevitable.

We defeat you, Camu replied without any fear.

Everything can be prevented, Lasgol joined in.

I shall show you. You will die, and in your last instants of life, in the midst of your suffering, you will know everything is useless.

The dragon released a tremendous blast directed at both Lasgol and Camu and maintained it, trying to pass through Camu's protective dome.

Camu sent more of his inner energy to maintain the protection, which was weakening since he also had to cancel the magic of the dragon's attack. The attack was powerful, which meant it could destroy the dome if Camu did not keep it up and strengthened it with his inner energy. The dome withstood the first blow. The problem was that he would not be able to maintain it forever. His energy would consume itself until he lost the defense.

Lasgol knew he had to help Camu. He had to find a way to wound that dragon or Camu's defenses would collapse and they would both die burnt to ashes. It was just a matter of time. Something told him that the rate at which Camu was consuming his inner energy to protect them both was greater than what the dragon used in its attack. In the end, his friend would lose the battle.

An idea came to his mind. If the legends were true, and they very well might be, the bow he had, Aodh's Bow, could kill the dragon. He had to find a way to make it work. He had seen the golden flashes it emitted every time he used it, together with his own skills. It was as if it were telling him that it was also ready to be used and imprinted some of its magic to each shot it released. Because of this he had managed to pierce, albeit shallowly, the dragon's scales, which he could never have done with a regular weapon.

Camu was holding up, but he assumed he was going to exhaust all his energy since he was consuming it at a high rate. He thought of attacking the dragon with his Icy Breath skill, but that would only use more energy and most likely that was what the dragon was expecting and the reason why it had planted itself before them. It could attack them from the sky with mental attacks, but if it stood before them it was to provoke him into using his skills to attack. It was a trap indeed, and he was not going to fall for it. He would defend Lasgol to his last drop of energy.

Lasgol used his *Arcane Communication* skill, this time to interact with Aodh's Bow. After all, this was an Object of Power and was enchanted with some kind of powerful ancestral magic. It was not the magic of the Drakonians; Lasgol knew this because Camu did not feel it as such and he had not been able to interact with the magic of the weapon. It could only be the magic of those who had defeated the dragons and had forced them to leave Tremia. If what he had been told was right, something he did not know for sure, he was a descendant of that lineage as well as that of the dragons themselves and thus should be able to use the weapon. It made sense, since the weapon responded with golden flashes when he used it. It had to be because it recognized his blood, his power, or half that power, at least.

He cheered up a little, although the situation was complicated and they were running out of time. Camu was not going to hold up much longer, and the flames were attempting to reach them and burn them. The skill allowed him to pick up the aura of power of the weapon. He visualized it like a flash of gold all around the bow. He tried to interact with the golden aura. He sent his inner energy, and upon contact of his own energy with the aura of the bow something odd happened: his energy split in two. One part interacted with the bow, and another died out as if the skill had failed. This puzzled him. But half the energy that had managed to interact with the bow made his aura shine more powerfully. This was a good sign. He was increasing the weapon's power, which meant that, perhaps, the shot would be more powerful and more harmful. This discovery encouraged Lasgol very much.

Not much energy left, Camu messaged, along with a feeling of concern.

Hold on, I think I've got something.

Good. Do something fast. We die.

Lasgol called upon his *Powerful Shot* skill as he kept sending energy to Aodh's Bow with his *Arcane Communication* skill.

The dragon saw the flash.

You will do nothing but scratch me slightly. Prepare yourselves to burn alive until you die. I am going to enjoy every scream of suffering that comes out of your tortured throats, the dragon boasted.

The green flash of Lasgol's skill was followed by a powerful golden one from the Bow.

What...? The dragon did not like the golden flash. It suspected some kind of danger.

The arrow flew from the Bow an instant after the golden flash and went straight to the dragon's torso. When it saw the arrow coming at it, it covered itself with its wing to protect itself. The arrow reached the wing and hit the scales. It went through and continued through flesh and bone and to the other side of the wing, and kept going toward its torso. The arrow reached the dragon and went in, penetrating the scales and burying itself up to the fletching.

The dragon roared in pain.

This is impossible! it cried in pain and fury.

Lasgol saw the arrow embedded deep in the dragon's flesh and knew he had succeeded. His own magic plus the Bow's had done the unthinkable: gotten through the innate defenses of the dragon. He did not waste a moment and nocked another arrow to the bow. He lifted it to release and began to repeat the process. He had the chance and had to take it, now or never.

The dragon reacted with rage. It flapped its wings and leapt forward to destroy Lasgol with its powerful claws.

Lasgol realized the danger and threw himself to one side, somersaulting out of the way.

I shall eat your body for this! Piece by piece, while you watch! the dragon threatened as it delivered a blow with its tail that caught Lasgol as he was rolling on the ground and sent him rolling faster still.

The *Woodland Protection* and *Improved Agility* skills protected him from the blow, and rolling a little further, he managed to get out of the dragon's range. He had not suffered any serious harm thanks to his skills.

Watch out! Camu messaged urgently.

Lasgol straightened up and saw that the dragon was about to deliver a blast of fire. He lunged forward and rolled over his head again. The flames nearly scorched his back, but he managed to avoid them by a hair's breadth.

Come to me! Camu messaged. He was still holding up his anti-magic dome.

Lasgol ran as fast as he could, fleeing the flames that pursued him while the dragon was sending them at him like a terrifying igneous jet that charred everything they touched.

With one last effort, Lasgol reached Camu's side. He stopped short, turned around, and called on his *True Shot* skill. Then he sent more energy into Aodh's Bow and realized he could interact with it without needing to call on his *Arcane Communication* skill. This surprised and delighted him. A link had been created between his magic and that of the Bow. Now he could send energy to the weapon almost unconsciously, as he did when he communicated with Camu.

I shall shred you to pieces! The dragon cried with a thundering roar of rage, and it leapt, intent on destroying them with all its might.

There were two flashes, green and golden, as the dragon fell on them. The arrow went in deep through the dragon's right eye.

Lasgol and Camu received the terrible blow of the attack and the claws that tried to rip into them. They were both thrown backward. Camu's scales held, but the impact left him very sore. Lasgol's *Woodland Protection* saved him, but he received a slash in the stomach and another one in the leg. In great pain, he saw that he was bleeding a lot.

The dragon was roaring furiously and seemed to have lost its mind. It was turning over itself, sending flames here and there with spread wings. The arrow had gone in deep, reaching the back of its head. It must have reached its brain and that was the reason for its erratic behavior, as if it had suffered a stroke.

Lasgol wasted no time. Ignoring the pain from his cuts, he nocked a new arrow and lifted it, aiming at the dragon's head. The mad roars and fury of the creature continued, and it sent random blasts of fire everywhere.

Camu came over to Lasgol's side to protect him in case one of the blasts hit him.

Lasgol was wondering which skill to use since the dragon was spinning and shaking its head in unpredictable angles. *True Shot* would not do—perhaps another of his shooting skills might be useful, so he called on Blind *Shot*, aimed at its left eye, and then shut his own eyes. He released. There were two flashes and the arrow sought the left eye, changing direction in mid-flight. The arrow found its target and buried itself in deeply.

The dragon roared in rage and pain. It tried to flee, take off, but it could not. It gave a strange hop and a moment later collapsed on one side.

Camu and Lasgol looked at each other with uncertainty. It might be a ruse. They did see that both arrows were buried in the dragon's eyes to the brain and the third one was sticking out of its torso. It was still breathing, weakly and gasping.

Watch out, it's still alive, Lasgol transmitted to Camu in warning. It might still stir one last time.

No live more.

Lasgol watched the dying creature and nodded. It only had a few moments left.

Camu put his head close to the dying dragon's.

Understand now? Not be human insignificant. I tell. We kill you. You die, us no.

The dragon exhaled a little flame, which died out at the same time as its life.

Chapter 36

The afternoon group was running back from doing their physical exercises around the capital. Viggo was still intent on proving that he was better than the Royal Rangers, so he was flying downhill, five paces ahead of two Royal Rangers, who were trying hard to catch up with him and overtake him.

The howling of a wolf from the forest to the east warned Egil, who was running beside Gerd at the rear of the group, that he was wanted. He looked at the giant, who returned a gaze of complicity. He raised his right hand and turned aside.

"I have to stop!" Gerd warned his comrades.

Nilsa and the Royal Rangers who were running in front stopped to look at him.

"Are you all right, Gerd?" Nilsa asked, concerned.

"Yeah, it's my hip, it's bothering me. Nothing to worry about. It'll soon pass, go ahead."

"Are you sure it's nothing?" Nilsa came over, concerned, while the Rangers she was running with remained a little further.

"Don't worry, it'll pass in a moment," he said without straightening up.

"I'll stay with him. As soon as he recovers we'll keep going," Egil said pleasantly.

"All right. If you need anything, I'll be waiting at the entrance of the city," Nilsa said, still a little worried.

"Thanks, I really don't think it's necessary," Egil told her.

"Go on, Nilsa, it's nothing but my... injury..."

"Oh, okay. I'll keep going then," Nilsa replied and went on. She reached the two Royal Rangers and signaled them to keep going.

Egil and Gerd waited for them to be far enough not to see them and then went into the forest. As soon as they entered, they saw two figures waiting.

Egil recognized them. They were Duke Svensen and Duke Erikson. A little further back there were two more figures.

"We meet again," Egil said in greeting.

"It's always a pleasure to see the King of the West," Erikson greeted him with a slight bow.

"A pleasure and an honor," Svensen added as he also bowed.

"The pleasure and honor are all mine for having such good allies," Egil said with a nod.

"We are faithful servants of the West and of Norghana," Erikson said.

"I see we have a young relative in the group today," Egil said, squinting at one of the two youngsters at the back and in a louder tone so they could hear him from there.

The young man he was referring to stepped forward to reveal himself.

"Greetings, Cousin Egil."

"Hello, Lars. Come closer, please, and let me see you properly. How's the last of the Berge?"

Lars nodded and walked over to where the Dukes were. Egil studied his cousin's features. He still did not see an Olafstone in him, but of course, he was a Berge. The eyes, gray and sad-looking, were like those of his aunt. Egil did pick up the likeness.

"I am healthy and well, thanks for the concern."

"Come, give me a hug," Egil said, opening his arms wide.

"I'm happy to see you," Lars said, and they hugged in the cold, Norghanian style reserved for distant relatives, although they were closely related.

"We're family, the only family we have left. We must worry about one another," Egil said, and in his voice there was a double entente. Egil was acutely aware that his cousin Lars could keep him from the path to the throne and go for the crown himself. In fact, when Egil had refused to help with the murder attempt on Thoran, some Western Nobles had suggested it. He had to watch them, him and those who supported him, since any day young Lars might stab him in the back. Egil was sure of it.

"You honor me," Lars said with a bow. "It gladdens my heart that my cousin worries about my well-being and wants to strengthen family ties."

"They've kept you hidden from me for too long. We must close that distance. I'd like to see you more and establish a sincere friendship between us. Family must endure," Egil told him in a heartfelt tone.

"That's also my wish, Cousin," Lars assured him.

"And ours too," said Svensen. "The more united the West is, the stronger it will stand and the better our chances of victory."

"The whole League agrees on that," said Erikson.

"You have him at your castle, Svensen?" Egil asked with a glance toward Lars.

"Yes, he acts as my adopted son. The rumor is that he's an illegitimate son and I've given him my name."

"It's a good cover-up, and besides, it does you credit," Egil nodded with a smile.

"Thoran and his brother must not know of Lars' existence, or his life will be in danger," Erikson said.

"And so it must be," Egil agreed. He thought that if Lars became an enemy, simply sending an anonymous tip to Thoran with information about the existence of another heir to the throne in the West would solve the problem. He hoped he did not need to go there, but one must always be wary and have ways prepared of defending and counterattacking.

"We've been informed of something that has greatly roused our interest," Erikson said, changing the subject.

"What is that information?"

"That Thoran has assigned you to be part of the Queen's escort," Svensen said.

"That's right. Thoran has ordered his Royal Eagles to protect Queen Heulyn," Egil told them, guessing the interest was not simply informative.

"That represents a great opportunity," said Svensen.

"A great responsibility is what it is," Egil replied.

"Svensen is right. We could try a coup. You'll have all the information about her movements and how to plan the best moment to execute it," Argued Erikson.

"You want to kill the Queen?" Egil asked in a harsh tone.

"That would weaken the alliance with Irinel and would rid us of an enemy in the path to the throne," said Erikson.

"It was attempted once and it did not work," Egil said.

"Not from the inside, and not with firsthand information from someone with direct access to the Queen," Erikson argued.

"Have you come to suggest this murder?"

"It's not the main reason for this meeting..." Erikson had to admit.

"We're here because the two men who made the attempt on Thoran's life have gone missing," Svensen explained in a worried tone.

Egil grew serious. This was horrible news.

"Gone missing? I thought we agreed that you'd take them out of Norghana precisely so they would not be found."

"We did," Erikson confirmed. "We hid them in Rogdon. We've had news that they've vanished."

"That's very serious news. This puts us all in grave danger," said Egil. "If they talk and confess, Thoran will know it was the West that tried to kill him and not the Zangrians as he believes now."

"We don't know whether Thoran's agents or those of his brother have found them, although that's what it looks like," Svensen said.

"That would seem like the most plausible option," Egil said while he looked up at the sky, thinking. This was a serious setback.

"Perhaps they escaped. They weren't happy to be hiding for so long," Erikson suggested.

"Was there bloodshed?" Egil asked.

"They found the two guards we had with them unconscious. We don't know whether it was they who attacked them or whether it was external agents."

"We must put ourselves in the worst-case scenario and assume they're in the hands of Thoran or his brother's agents," Egil said.

"In that case, we're in trouble," Erikson admitted.

"Were they men loyal to the West?" Egil asked.

"They were," Svensen said.

"Even so, they'll talk under torture. Can they point to anyone in the League?"

"Not directly. But they're men of the West, we'll be accused of the murder attempt anyway," Erikson reasoned.

"True. How long ago did this happen?"

"Two days," Svensen informed him.

"Then they're still on their way. Those men can't reach Norghana," said Egil.

"We'll watch the entry routes, by sea and land."

"They won't come to the capital," Egil said.

"They won't? Won't they be brought to King Thoran?" Erikson asked blankly.

"I'd bet all my gold that they'll be taken to the fortress in Skol," said Egil, scratching his chin.

"To Duke Orten's fortress?" Erikson did not look convinced.

"I have the feeling that this has been arranged by Orten. He'll want to interrogate them personally, and he'll do that in his own fortress."

"Then we'll watch the fortress closely," Erikson said, changing his plan.

"We won't let them be taken to Orten," Svensen promised.

"There's a lot at play in this. I warned you of the risks. Your heads might roll if Orten questions them. He'll make them point at you the moment he knows they're from the West. It's a unique excuse to finish off the nobles of the League in one stroke, and don't think he doesn't know that you're still plotting, because he does," Egil told them.

"We've always been very careful. He can't attack us without good reason and sufficient proof," said Svensen.

"He'll have both when the murderers confess," Egil said.

"They won't reach Skol," Erikson said, closing the matter.

Egil nodded. "Did you get the information I asked you for?" he asked, changing the subject.

Erikson and Svensen looked at each other.

"It wasn't at all easy," Erikson replied.

"It has cost us a fortune we can't afford…" Svensen said with a grimace.

"I can assure you that it's a fortune well spent. It will produce numerous results when the day comes."

The two Dukes of the West looked at each other again.

"What the King of the West wants, he will have," Erikson said, and stepping forward, he handed Egil a piece of parchment with a name on it.

"Miroslav," Egil read.

Both Dukes nodded.

Egil turned the piece of parchment over.

"Will I find him here?" he asked.

"Yes, but be careful, he's really dangerous," Erikson warned him.

"Thanks, I will be," Egil said, nodding as he read the location.

"As for the Queen?" Svensen asked.

"I'll tell you the same thing I told you when you suggested killing Thoran. Too risky and it's not the right time."

"But this is a clear opportunity," Svensen insisted.

"It is, but it's an opportunity we'll keep having. Remember that."

"And what if they take you off the guard detail?" asked Erikson.

"I'll still have all the information and the opportunity will still exist. It'll be harder, true, but it will still be a possibility with everything I already know."

"Will you plan it then?

Egil thought for a moment.

Lars, Svensen, and Erikson were staring at him intensely, waiting for his answer.

"I will, but it'll be my decision and mine only to execute the plan."

The three nodded in agreement.

Chapter 37

Lasgol and Camu were staring at the dead dragon on the floor of the patio in front of them, unable to fully believe they had killed it. Camu would never admit he found it hard to believe, since his fighting, stubborn character had made him absolutely sure they could defeat it. Lasgol, on the other hand, thought it was nothing short of miraculous that they had managed to kill it. An unthinkable enterprise, one that had almost cost the three of them their lives.

A moan made them both turn around. Ona was coming toward them from inside the building.

How are you feeling, Ona? Lasgol transmitted to her, bending down to hug her. As he crouched, he grunted with pain from the two cuts he had in the stomach and thigh. He had already realized they were not simple scratches.

The snow panther reached his side, moaned, and licked his face.

Ona, we kill dragon, Camu messaged to her, proudly nodding toward it.

Ona growled once.

And it almost killed us, Lasgol transmitted.

We defeat. Much good. Powerful.

Don't let it go to your head….

I say truth, you know.

Let's go inside the building and treat our wounds. I don't like being out here in the open. Another dragon might appear.

That nothing good.

Exactly. Let's go inside and seek shelter.

Lasgol led the way, holding his wounds. He was bleeding quite a bit, which was not good. Ona was limping and Camu was stumbling as if his hind legs hurt. They were in a bad state, all three of them. Lasgol begged the Ice Gods not to send them any more enemies to fight against just then, if possible not until they had managed to recover from this battle.

They went into the building and Lasgol sat down in a long velvet armchair in front of a large mirror with carved wooden frames. Ona and Camu lay down in front of him on one of the thick, soft carpets that looked very rich. They were certainly expensive, the kind rich nobles used. All the furniture looked good and expensive.

Carefully, Lasgol left the bow beside him on the sofa and took off the quiver and satchel he carried on his back. He left them on the floor beside him. Inside the satchel he had a water-skin, which he took out. He was going to need it.

I have to stitch up these wounds. Shall I help you first? Lasgol transmitted.

You heal first. Then us, Camu messaged, along with a feeling of calm.

Ona chirped once.

I'll do what I can, he transmitted to ease them, though he knew that against strong blows there was little he could do if there was internal damage or bleeding, which was very dangerous and might kill them. Many times, an internal wound you could not see was a lot more dangerous than an external one, like the ones he had at that moment.

He cleaned his wounds with water and a disinfectant soap he carried in his Ranger's belt, one of Annika's specialties. It hurt him more to waste the water than washing and disinfecting the wounds themselves. Then he took a needle and suture thread and got to work. It was unpleasant to see but it did not hurt as much as it looked. He could bear it quite well, at least the Rangers bore it well. He stitched it as best he could, but it would leave a scar. They were pretty deep cuts, so there was no way to avoid it. At least he could boast of being a weathered Ranger when Astrid saw them. He did not think she would mind; in fact, she would probably like them because it made him look more seasoned. Or maybe not. While he was thinking whether Astrid would mind the scars or not, which really was stupid, he finished stitching up both cuts. He was sure Astrid cared more about what was inside than outside. He had to admit he felt the same way about her.

He put the box with the needle and thread in its compartment in his Ranger's belt and then applied an anti-infection ointment all Rangers carried with them. It was a life saver. Badly healed infections killed more people than weapons themselves. For every death by the sword there were five by infected cuts. He applied the ointment all along the cuts in both wounds. He would have to do it again the following day. Well, if they did not find themselves in another tight spot.

When he finished, he put away the ointment and waited a moment to recover his strength a little. Stitching oneself was never a pleasant or easy task. Once he felt a little more like himself he tried to help Ona. He lay down on the carpet beside her.

Tell me where it hurts. I'll press gently to see what's wrong, he transmitted.

The good panther moaned once.

Lasgol began to feel around carefully, starting at the head in case she had a bad blow which could be dangerous if on the head. Ona did not complain, which helped Lasgol breathe in relief. He went on with his physical exam. When he got to the ribs on her right side, Ona moaned loudly. Lasgol stopped. Her right ribs were hurt. He hoped they were not broken, because that could pose a great problem. He continued his examination, and when he got to her right hind leg he met with the same reaction. He began to worry.

Turn on your other side, he transmitted.

The good panther did as she was told, amid moans of pain, and lay on her right side. Lasgol examined her left side and noted that the damage here was to both legs. The poor panther had received a good beating.

Don't worry, I have an ointment for blows that's very good.

Lasgol took it out again and proceeded to apply it on every painful spot that hurt the good panther, and when he finished he left her resting. He felt bad for not being able to do more for her. If Egil were there, with his knowledge as a Healer Guard, he could do more. He wished and prayed she had nothing broken, only thin fissures and some harder blow, nothing more, and especially no internal hemorrhaging.

Now you, Camu.

Okay.

Lasgol checked Camu and found that both hind legs and his ribs were hurt. The truth was that the dragon had given him a tremendous beating. In fact, if it had not been for his scales, Camu would be dead. Just as he had done with Ona, Lasgol applied the ointment for blows. He hoped it would work with Camu. He knew it would work on him and Ona, but on Camu it was a mystery. They would have to wait and see. Camu's body was different, and sometimes it worked in mysterious ways. Lasgol wished he could do some healing, regenerating magic, to help him heal. But it was only a wish, and wishes rarely became true.

Let's rest a little. We'll let our bodies recover.

Lasgol handed out the rations he had left in the satchel and drank from the water-skin. They had survived and that was important, at least for the time being. They fell asleep for a while, which helped them recover not only their strength but also magical energy. It was not a deep rest, since they were alert to any sound and they woke up every now and then, but in spite of the dangers of the place and the situation, exhaustion finally won and they were able to rest.

Bow work, Camu messaged suddenly to Lasgol, who was just waking up.

Yeah, I was able to interact with the magic of the bow, Lasgol transmitted, now fully awake, and proceeded to tell him everything that had happened.

You half magic work.

It looks that way.

Can kill dragons now.

I'm not sure that's entirely true, but at least we can wound them—minor dragons and reptilian creatures I mean. I have my doubts regarding the Immortal Dragon.

Sure you can.

Those are minor creatures, at least regarding their power. Dergha-Sho-Blaska is a dragon thousands of years old, he'll be a hundred times stronger and tougher than these.

Then seek more weapons, be more.

That's a good idea. We'll have to talk it over with the rest of the group when we go back.

What do now?

We can flee, or we can investigate a little more.

Investigate, Camu messaged confidently.

Have you seen the state we're in? We can't even walk.

We can.

You are too optimistic.

I always be right.

Not always. Being stubborn and being right are very different things.

I much always.

Lasgol rolled his eyes and did not continue arguing. It would be in vain and he knew it. Then suddenly he felt the pulse of the ice jewel. It was coming from the northwest, but something did not fit. It seemed to come from above, not the same level they were on at that moment.

Strange pulse …

What be strange?

The ice jewel is moving, toward the northwest and upward.

Upward?

Lasgol indicated the roof of the building.

Second floor?

More like the fourth floor.

Go and see.

I don't know…

Now all better.

Lasgol did not want to give up and hand over the Silver Pearls to Dergha-Sho-Blaska, but they were in no condition to fight. At least, not one as hard, and that was what they would meet if they kept sniffing around.

Ona joined them and growled once for yes.

Two against one, Camu messaged.

Yeah, but I decide here, because you two don't make the best decisions and least of all when there's a lot of danger involved. I know the two of you very well.

Camu was about to retort and Lasgol cut him short. Raising his finger, he thought about it.

We'll continue a little longer. But at the first sign of trouble, we run away.

Much agree.

Lasgol sighed deeply. He hoped he was not making a mistake, because if he was it might very well be his last.

They followed the trail the scorpions had left through the building. It was not difficult, since they already knew where they were heading from the pulse. They crossed several distinguished rooms and an inner courtyard with a fountain that seemed to be made of gold. They arrived at the back of the building and went on. Lasgol was looking for stairs that led to the upper floors. They had passed by two already, but the trail the scorpions had left did not go up them.

They came to the last room in the most northern part of the building and there found what looked like a storage room. It had water in barrels and crates of salted food. Lasgol checked them to see whether they could use them. They seemed to be in good condition, so he put some food in his satchel and filled the water-skin. They all drank from the barrels so as not to consume the water they had stored.

Suddenly Camu noticed something.

Drakonian Magic here.

Lasgol looked around. There were only crates, barrels, and four walls of rock with one door, the one they had come in by. In fact, the trail of the scorpions ended here. He was surprised, not understanding how that could be. He hoped there would not be any hidden dangers they were not seeing.

Camu went over to the back wall. He shut his eyes and remained, feeling the magic for a moment. Lasgol watched him; he was not picking up anything. He passed his hand down his nape where he usually felt active magic, but he felt nothing.

Are you sure you're picking up Drakonian Magic?

Sure, Camu replied as he moved to the left corner where the two walls met. He put his head to the corner and, to Lasgol's great surprise, Camu's head went through the corner.

Ona moaned twice.

What was that? Lasgol could not believe what he was seeing. Camu's head was inside the corner and had vanished while the rest of his body was still in the room.

Be secret passage, he messaged.

Be careful, don't... but Lasgol could not finish his transmission, Camu had already crossed over to the other side, vanishing completely. For Ona and Lasgol, what was in front of them was a corner formed by two walls of solid rock.

Come. No problem, he messaged from the other side.

You are a problem when you dive headfirst into trouble, Lasgol transmitted as he went in through the corner and onto the other side. He looked around the place he had entered. It was a square room and it was empty and dark. Lasgol waited for his eyes to get used to the lack of light. A door on the west wall seemed to be the only way out.

Ona moaned from the other room, she could not get through.

Don't worry, Ona, the corner is fake. It's an illusion, come.

Unfortunately, the walls Ona saw looked very real to her. She could not cross them.

She moaned twice.

I'm going back for her, Lasgol transmitted to Camu and went back into the room.

I watch this side.

Ona, get on my back. Come on, Lasgol transmitted to her as he bent over, offering her his back.

Ona obeyed as she always did and leapt nimbly onto Lasgol's back.

Wow, you weigh as much as an ox, Lasgol complained as he felt his wounds strain with the weight.

Close your eyes, we're going to go through.

Ona chirped once.

Lasgol crossed into the other room, and as soon as he did he told Ona to get down. The panther jumped down and looked around distrustfully.

Lasgol snorted. His wounds were aching.

Camu was already at the exit door, looking out.

No feel anyone.

Let me be in the lead, Lasgol said once he had recovered.

Everything dark. No see anything.

I'll deal with it, Lasgol said as he called on his *Guiding Light* skill. A point of white light appeared before Lasgol, lighting the door and the corridor beyond it.

Follow?

Yes, let's go. Lasgol led the way with Ona following him and Camu bringing the rear. The *Guiding Light* was a great help, since there was no light whatsoever in that corridor. It was wide, abut twelve feet wide and the same in height. Lasgol was looking for the trail of the scorpions, but on the stone surface it was going to be hard to find. In any case, they had to have come this way, and sooner or later he would receive a pulse and know whether they were going in the right direction.

They went down the long passage until they came to another wide hall. The walls and ceiling of this place were no longer human made. They were those of a cave. The three looked around it and realized they were no longer in the building they had come in through but behind it, to the west.

I think we're inside the mountains, Lasgol said.

Yes, look it.

Watch out, I don't like this.

The cavern only had one way out toward the west, so they followed it. They started to go down a natural ramp that wound as it went along. One side was the rock of the mountain, but on the other side there was a dark abyss that appeared to go down many feet toward the darkness. Lasgol stopped and, picking up a loose stone from the wall the size of an apple, dropped it in the abyss. He waited for the sound of it hitting bottom and it took a long time.

It's very deep, be careful.

I can fly.

True. Ona, you and I had better be careful.

The panther growled once.

They continued going down and reached some kind of catwalk over the abyss, the wall that gave them some sense of safety had vanished so they were left only with the abyss on both sides of a bridge. Luckily the way was about fifteen feet wide, so there was not much risk of falling. Lasgol did not like the fact that the bridge was so wide. It meant it was made for quite large creatures.

The *Guiding Light* was a great help since it lit up the surrounding darkness of those caverns, and they could only guess how high up they went. But it left them very exposed in case they came across some watch or guard. Lasgol had his *Owl Hearing* skill activated. They crossed the bridge over the abyss and reached another large cavern with two exits. One continued downward and the other one went up.

What do? Camu was watching both exits, unable to decide which one to take.

We have to go up, according to the signal of the ice jewel. But first let's see where the one that goes down leads.

Okay.

I'll turn out the Guiding Light, in case someone's watching.

Ona growled once. She did not like so much light either. And, on the other hand, the panther could see in the dark better than Lasgol and Camu.

They went out the downward opening and started going down a spiral which Lasgol thought was not natural. No, the spiral was definitely carved out of the rock. He stopped to check the floor and saw marks on it. There was no doubt, it had been chiseled by humans with tools. It was not natural and there was no magic. It was the work of humans. The problem was that they had not seen a single human since they had entered the ghost city. Besides, the spiral was still about twelve feet wide, a width human did not need. This had been made by human hands but for large creatures like the scorpions or snakes they had encountered.

As they went down, following the spiral, Lasgol began to worry. He had no idea where they were going, and the last signal he had received indicated up, not down like they were doing. He was beginning to regret having taken this road, and then suddenly, after going down one more level in the spiral of rock, he heard something and lifted his hand. The three stopped short and let the darkness envelop them.

They stayed still, listening. A tapping began to reach them from the depths. It sounded like a hammer tapping the rock, only in a chaotic manner, without any rhythm or pace. He strained his hearing and continued picking up the sound. He guessed it was not a single hammer but the sound of many, tapping together.

Lasgol snorted and thanked the Ice Gods for having thought of turning out the *Guiding Light*. A few levels below where they were, they could glimpse light and movement. A lot of movement.

Complete stealth now, Lasgol transmitted to Ona and Camu.

Use camouflage?

How's your energy level?

Not much. Need sleep more.

Yeah, I'm the same. Better save your energy. We might need it later on.

Okay. I save.

Not being able to take a long sleep to recuperate their energy was a big problem. But they were not in a place where they could rest, and besides, in order to recuperate all the energy they had consumed, they would need a whole night's sleep and their bodies also needed that. But they could not afford such a luxury where they were right then.

They looked at what was going on below, lying on the floor and poking their heads out a little. At about thirty feet deep they saw a large cavern. It was lit by an infinitude of torches that hung from the walls and large bonfires on the floor. The cavern was colossal, and it was watched by scorpions and cobras in great numbers. There must have been a hundred of both scattered throughout the cave's expanse. But that was not what surprised them. What really struck them numb and left them breathless was finding over a thousand humans working with picks, spades, chisels, hammers, and all kind of tools to work the rock at different levels on the four sides of the enormous cavern.

There they are, Lasgol said, understanding.

Are who?
The inhabitants of the ghost city.

Chapter 38

The Panthers could not decide which was worse—the days they trained with the Royal Rangers or the days in the service of the Queen. The training was beginning to be routine, since they had already learned everything they needed to know and now they simply did increasingly complicated maneuvers, bordering on the impossible. It was as if Raner had decided they were going to fail anyway and had created situations which were practically impossible to solve without the protectee dying. Protecting the Queen was not easy either. They had to endure the queen's shouts throughout the castle all day and part of the night, or cover her in her nocturnal escapades to the forest with the Druids.

It could be said that the Panthers' spirits were low. To make things slightly worse, there was talk that shortly the King's armies would set out toward the border with Zangria, which could only mean that war was close. Because of this, when Raner called them early in the morning, they expected a day that would be between bad and worse. Of course they would not complain, except for Viggo, who complained about everything. They knew it was their duty as Rangers and they accepted it. Whoever wanted a quiet life should not enter the Corps.

"Royal Eagles?" Raner greeted them at the door of the Tower.

"First Ranger," they returned the greeting.

"You'll be coming with me today," he told them.

"At your command," Ingrid replied.

No one asked where they were going or why. If the First Ranger said they had to go with him, they would do so without hesitation. What surprised them all was that he did not take them to practice or assign them to protect the Queen. He led them to the Royal Dungeons, something none of them had expected.

They went down to the underworld that was the King's Dungeons, trying not to stare at what went down there. It was not good for the soul. The less they were contaminated by that environment, the better.

Raner went to the cell where they kept Gondabar, which was

guarded. He knocked on the door.

"First Ranger Raner reporting."

"Come on in, Raner," they heard Gondabar's voice.

Raner stepped in and motioned them to follow. They found Gondabar working at his desk. He did not look well, and it was not only due to the horrible place he was in. He looked weak and wilted, consumed.

Yet he greeted them all with a big smile.

"I'm happy to see my First Ranger accompanied by the Royal Eagles."

"Our leader honors us," Raner said, and the Panthers saluted with respectful nods after standing in line.

"I see you're all very well, it makes me happy. It appears Molak is taking Lasgol's place."

"That's right," Raner confirmed.

"It's an honor to be able to do so," Molak said.

"I'm sure you're doing very well. You're an elite Ranger," Gondabar praised him.

"Thank you, Sir, I try," Molak replied, blushing slightly.

"Any news on the Immortal Dragon?" Gondabar asked the group.

"No, Sir," Ingrid answered. "There's no news of sightings or attacks in Norghana."

"Or in any other kingdom," Raner added.

"How strange," Gondabar said, nodding slowly. "I can't stop thinking that if the dragon isn't making appearances it's because he's planning something."

"Or because he's keeping a secret he doesn't want to reveal yet," Egil added.

"Yes, that might be it too. It might be that the secret is the plan he's going to execute and that he doesn't want us to discover."

"I was thinking the same thing," Egil agreed.

"Such a powerful being could have attacked and already destroyed Norghana. If he has not, it's for a very important reason," Raner added.

"Perhaps he's not fully recovered and is waiting to complete his recovery after being reborn," Astrid suggested.

"That makes sense. They could be both be right," said the leader of the Rangers,

"We're still searching. As soon as he appears, we'll know," Raner said.

"Well, yes, we have to find out his plan and stop him," Gondabar said.

"I brought you the Royal Eagles as you requested," Raner said, seeing that Gondabar was losing himself in his musings.

"Oh, yes, of course," Gondabar returned to reality at once. "Raner has informed me that you've done an excellent job in training as Royal Rangers. I had no doubt that you would excel. You make an excellent group."

They all appreciated his evaluation.

"Thank you, Sir," Ingrid said for all of them.

"I have informed our leader that I consider your training as Royal Rangers concluded. I would have liked to have more time, but I don't think you would have improved a lot more. It's been an accelerated training, but with a group as exceptional and with as much talent as yours, you've assimilated everything at a speed that has pleasantly surprised me. That's why we're here now, to name you Royal Rangers."

The seven Rangers, who had not been expecting this, were taken by surprise.

"We've finished the training?" Nilsa asked.

"That's right. You're more than ready," Raner told them.

"We would've had enough with half the training," Viggo retorted.

"Don't get started. You've had the right amount of training you needed," Raner replied.

"We're happy and honored," Ingrid said gratefully.

"Yes, it's an honor," Molak joined in.

"It has been most interesting," said Astrid.

"And a little exhausting with so much exercise," Gerd added.

"Very well. Let's make it official," Gondabar said, rising from his desk and picking up a leather bag he had beside him. He walked over to Ingrid and looked her in the eye.

"Ingrid Stenberg, for having completed the training successfully and having the approval of the First Ranger, I name you Royal Ranger. Bow your head, please."

Ingrid did as Gondabar requested. The leader of the Rangers took a wooden medallion out of the bag and hung it around Ingrid's neck.

"It's an honor and a privilege," Ingrid said as she contemplated the medallion. There was a crown carved on one side, and on the other a bow over a short axe and a knife, the weapons of the Rangers.

Gondabar smiled at her. He stood before Nilsa and repeated his words. Then he hung the medallion around Nilsa's neck which she accepted with a nervous gesture.

The leader of the Rangers named them all Royal Rangers, and he hung the medallions around their necks. Once he finished, he addressed them in a solemn tone.

"You are now Royal Rangers, the best among the Rangers, those who have as their main responsibility the protection of our King and his family. Do not fail the King, and do not fail Norghana. Do your duty and always act with honor. For the King and for Norghana."

"We will do that," Ingrid promised, and the rest joined her.

"Very well, with this the ceremony is concluded. I would have liked to have it someplace else, but the circumstances are what they are," Gondabar said ruefully.

"Our leader honors us, we couldn't be more grateful," Egil said with a kind smile.

Gondabar appreciated his words.

"Go now and serve Norghana with courage and honor."

Raner led the way and the others followed. They had done it— they were Royal Rangers. It was not anything they had asked for, but now that they had achieved it, deep down they were filled with pride.

Their joy at becoming Royal Rangers did not last long. No sooner had they arrived at the Tower of the Rangers that they met Kol and Haines.

"First we want to congratulate you, you've earned it," Kol told them.

"You don't say. I'd never seen anyone understand and learn the exercises like you. You're quite good for being so young," Haines told them.

"We're the best," Viggo corrected him. "Well, I am at least, and they aren't far behind."

Ingrid elbowed him in the ribs and Viggo doubled up.

"See if you find your humility somewhere, you must've dropped it," she told him sarcastically.

"I'm sorry to rain on your parade, but there's bad news," Kol told them.

"What's going on?" Egil asked.

"The King has ordered the armies to deploy."

"Where's he sending them?" Egil was very interested.

"To the border with Zangria."

"Is only the army going?" Egil asked again.

"So far yes, along with some Rangers."

"Nobles and their armed men?"

"Not yet, but I'm guessing that'll be the next thing he'll do," said Haines.

Egil nodded and remained thoughtful.

"Then we're at war with Zangria?" Nilsa asked, looking horrified.

"We don't know. It hasn't been said openly, but the army is going to the border."

"So that means it will be declared soon," Astrid finished the sentence.

"That's right," Haines said.

"Bad business," Gerd said, shaking his head.

"Wars always are," Egil said ruefully.

Chapter 39

Ona, Camu, and Lasgol watched in disbelief at all those humans working under the surveillance of the scorpions and cobras. The tapping they had been hearing now made all the sense in the world. There were lines of men on great wooden scaffolding set against the four walls of the cavern. The workers seemed to be doing their job by areas and at different levels on the rocky walls. Seeing all the surveillance, Lasgol realized they were not workers but slaves.

What do humans?

I'm not sure… they're carving the walls, but I don't know what for.

Stairs?

No, what they're doing has nothing to do with access tunnels.

Gold? Silver?

That might be it, but I don't see them piling material… I don't know, this is very strange.

Go down and see better?

I'm tempted, but I'm not sure the risk is worth it. There are too many guards down there, and they're the tough kind.

The decision was made for them. A group of six snakes started climbing the spiral.

They're coming up. We're leaving, Lasgol transmitted.

Okay.

The three got to their feet and, careful not to make any sound, started going up the spiral to get away from the cobras. They went up at a crouch, in silence, until they reached the cavern they had started from.

Let's go up, I want to understand what's going on in these mountains and why these people have been enslaved.

They took the way out of the cavern that went up and entered a wide, long tunnel that led them west. As they went on in the dark, they noticed the way was getting steeper. They were going up fast. The tunnel did not seem to have an end and it was not natural, it had been excavated to join the cavern they had started from to the one they had come out in.

They looked around and saw that this one was a smaller cavern.

There were torches hanging on the walls to light up the cave. In one corner they found over a hundred large water barrels. In another area there were piled crates which, from their moldy smell, held salted meat that was a little spoiled.

This is an intermediate storage room to feed and water the workers.

Not workers. Slaves, Camu corrected him.

You're right. Let's keep going, I have a bad feeling about this place.

They left the storage cave and found a large catwalk also twelve feet wide that went up. They crossed it, and as they did so under them they saw another large cavern. It was like the first one and also filled with slaves watched by scorpions and cobras. They lay down to watch. They were once again on some kind of bridge that spanned the huge, deep cavern at whose bottom the slaves were working. In this cave they were all picking at and chiseling the floor, not the walls.

Much slaves.

Yeah, I'm beginning to think they have the whole city here in the depths of these mountains working on something.

Be what?

I don't know, but we're going to find out.

They crossed that bridge and went on through various tunnels, always in a western direction. Lasgol thought they had to be crossing through the mountains and that all those passages, tunnels, and bridges had been created for this end, since they were mostly not natural. He also guessed that whoever had done all that work had to be the slaves they were seeing.

To increase Lasgol's unease, which he was feeling strongly turning in his stomach, they passed two more caves like the ones they had left behind. They found the same situation in them as in the others, over a thousand slaves working at whatever they were doing, some on the walls and some on the floors of the caverns, all watched by the scorpions and cobras. Now they had no doubt the creatures had all the surviving inhabitants of the city working as slaves in the different caverns inside the mountains. It was horrible. Apparently some slavers had taken the mountains to have their riches extracted by thousands of slaves. But the truth was even more horrible, since the slavers were enormous reptiles that should not exist and that served the Immortal Dragon.

For a moment he thought that perhaps all this was nothing more than a mining operation, but he had not seen any carts filled with ore, or any material being transported anywhere, which had him very confused. What were they taking out of the rock if it was not mineral? What else could it be? Precious stones which were so tiny Lasgol could not notice them being moved? No matter how much he thought about it, he could not think what it might be. They would have to keep investigating in order to find out. The problem to reach valid conclusions was that the prisoners were deep in the bottom of the caves and going down to see what they were extracting from the rock was too risky. Lasgol did not want to take such risks. If by any chance they were found out, and it might happen as it had with the Royal Cobras, they would not be able to escape from the depths of those mountains.

They went along another large stone bridge and came out onto a platform that ended in another spiral that went down an even greater cavern than the ones they had found so far. It must be a hundred and fifty feet deep from where they were standing and another sixty to the top of the cave. As to length and width, Lasgol calculated over three hundred feet either way. The walls of this immense cavern were blue with white streaks, which surprised him. In the center of the great cave there was a lake and the water was bubbling, giving off a steam that climbed to the upper part of the cave. Water fell from several points on the walls toward this underground lake and also gave off steam.

Great cave. Lake strange.

Very curious indeed. I believe they must be thermal waters… from the steam they give off.

Thermal? Camu messaged, along with a feeling of confusion.

Hot water.

Be in desert. Everything hot.

Yeah, but this isn't an effect of the desert or the sun. It's because of the temperature under the water. There's no sun or heat here, Lasgol explained, pointing down at the darkness of the cave, which in comparison with the outside temperature was almost cold.

Okay. Hot water. Understand.

Don't touch it. It might be extremely hot, even at boiling point. There's a risk of getting burned.

No like this lake. Water bad. Better water oasis.

No doubt, I'm only telling you what I think it is and to be careful not to touch it. If we fell in we might suffer a painful, horrible death.

I no fall.

Ona hopped backwards to indicate she would not either.

I can't be sure that it's what I've told you, but just in case, be careful.

A pulse told Lasgol that the ice jewel was at the bottom of the cavern.

We've arrived. The jewel is down there.

Much below, Camu messaged as he put his head out at the end of the platform to try and see what awaited them.

They looked at the base of the colossal cavern and noticed many lights but little movement and no tapping, which puzzled them.

Not working.

It looks that way. Something different is going on in this cave.

Go down?

Yes, let's go down, but very, very carefully.

They went down stealthily, crouching, alert to any light and sound. As they went down the more danger they were in, since now the sounds or the light could be coming from below them or above them. They were more exposed, and their escape might be cut off if they were found out.

They managed to reach a level close enough to spy on whatever was happening without risking being seen. There were no slaves working in this cave, neither did it look like a storage for supplies or material. Everything was silent, although they could see several groups of reptiles and even a couple of small groups of humans. Lasgol tried to see who they were. He identified a group of scorpions to one side. One of them was much larger, like three of the giant scorpions, and red-colored. Lasgol did not like it at all. It must be their leader. Another of the groups was formed by the cobras, and just like with the scorpions, they had a leader that was three times larger and red in color.

The large red scorpion and the large red cobra must be the leaders. Watch out.

Be much ugly.

Ona's fur was on end all along her back and tail.

And they must be dangerous.

We can, Camu messaged confidently.

We're injured and we 'can't' anything right now.

Truth, I forget.

They watched closely everything that went on in that cavern.

331

Apart from scorpions and cobras, they saw a giant beetle. And if that was not enough, there were also half a dozen crocodiles. They were at least three times as big as a large crocodile.

There are many reptiles here and they're dangerous. I don't like this place at all.

Better not found out.

That's for sure.

They also saw two groups, one with three and the other with four humans, separated from each other. At first Lasgol thought they were prisoners from the city, like the ones they had seen working in the other caverns. He was greatly surprised when he was able to identify them by the clothes they were wearing. The group of three men was of Defenders of the True Blood and the other one Visionaries.

Have you recognized the humans?

Yes, recognize.

They seem to still be in the service of Dergha-Sho-Blaska.

Strange.

Yeah, I don't understand why the reptiles don't kill them.

Be allies.

Yeah, but seeing those reptiles, I don't think Dergha-Sho-Blaska needs his human servants.

Perhaps yes.

You're right. If they're here and they're still alive, it must be for some reason. They must provide a service the reptiles can't, whatever it is.

From their present position they were able to discover something which they had not been able to see clearly from above and that petrified them. On the right wall from where they were placed, there was a huge fossil of what looked like a great reptile. It was incomplete, but it looked like the skeleton of a dragon.

Drakonian, Camu messaged to Lasgol.

Well, that's not good. Is Dergha-Sho-Blaska trying to bring another dragon to life?

Not complete. Bones missing.

True, there's no back part for that skeleton. It won't be enough to bring it back to life, will it?

Not know.

Look at the left-side wall, Lasgol transmitted to Camu. The wall was filled with fossils. There were more than twenty different animals. By the looks of the fossil skeletons, they were mostly reptiles. Many had to be from ancient times because Lasgol did not recognize them, and the ones he did recognize were too big. They were a lot larger than they were supposed to be.

Many skeletons.

Of reptiles… some enormous…

Lasgol stared at the walls, trying to understand what was going on there. This place looked like an ancient reptilian graveyard. Something must have killed them inside the mountains and now he was looking at their fossils.

I think this place is an ancient graveyard of large reptiles.

Like crocodile.

And like the water serpent…. Lasgol was still turning over in his mind everything they had found out so far, trying to make sense of it.

Scorpions and cobras, Camu messaged.

Lasgol nodded. They continued spying, hiding in the darkness of the spiral which was barely illuminated. They could not be seen, but Lasgol did not feel safe. He was worried they might be detected by smell or the magic that both he and Camu possessed.

Know where pearls?

I know where the jewel is, so I guess the pearls are close to it. There are two scorpions near the end of the cavern, where another cave seems to begin.

Yes, I see now.

Suddenly, from that back cave they had just mentioned there appeared two reptiles, two creatures which Ona, Camu, and Lasgol would rather have not seen.

They were two minor dragons.

One had blue scales and the other one brown. They both were about the same size as the red dragon they had killed, so Lasgol guessed they were about eighteen feet wide with their wings spread. He could also appreciate the fifteen feet from their heads to the tip of their tails. The sight of them made him shiver. They looked like young, strong dragons. They must be powerful, like the red one. They both had red reptilian eyes that made him think that somehow they were not natural reptiles. From their earlier experience he knew they would be dangerous. He also saw that they had sand-colored streaks that ran down their back and torso like the red one had had. This must be significant, although he was not sure why; perhaps they had been born in that desert.

That supposition made him wonder how those dragons might

have been born. Had they been hidden in that cavern for hundreds of years? Had Dergha-Sho-Blaska brought them back like he had done with himself? How was it possible that they existed and no-one had ever seen them before now? The more he thought about it, the less sense it made.

Much trouble, Camu messaged him, along with a feeling of great concern.

I think that doesn't even begin to express what I'm feeling.

Ona was making no sound, but her ears were flattened along her head.

If find out much problem.

You don't say. We won't get out of here alive.

Better not find out.

That's exactly what I think. Don't even breathe.

At the entrance of the two minor dragons, all the reptiles present bowed their heads to touch the floor. It was clear who ruled there. The dragons were the superior reptiles, even if they were only minor dragons.

They watched the minor blue dragon stand before the two scorpions that had the box with the pearls and the jewel.

Servants, present the objects, the mental message of the blue dragon reached them clear and powerfully.

The three friends were surprised to pick up the message.

Why receive message? Camu asked.

Ona shook her head.

It must be that they message without filtering the recipients. They don't need to do so since they're the lords and masters of the place and the creatures that inhabit it.

We understand.

Yes, and that's curious. That message is for the reptiles, it can't be in any human language, and yet we understand it.

Message in Drakonian.

Oh, but then I shouldn't understand it, right?

Perhaps yes.

Whatever the reason, we can understand the mental messages, which might be helpful.

Egil perhaps know.

Yeah, we have to tell him about all this and see what he thinks. Well, if we get out of here alive.

334

Leave the objects on the floor, the blue dragon went on.

As soon as the scorpions received the mental message they put both objects on the floor.

Human servants, open the box, the brown dragon commanded.

Two humans Lasgol recognized by their clothing as Defenders stepped over swiftly in response to the dragon's request. Carefully, they manipulated the box and opened it. As soon as the lid was open, the power of the twelve pearls became manifest.

It is the pearls, we really have them, the blue dragon messaged with great satisfaction.

Our lord and master will be very pleased, the brown dragon messaged.

Lasgol, Camu, and Ona not only received the mental messages but also the feelings that accompanied them, as Camu used to send when he used mental messages too. This worried Lasgol, because if the dragons sent strong feelings they could be hurt, since they did not know how to defend themselves from them.

Dragons have pearls. Not good.

I know… this puts us in a very delicate position.

What do?

Let me think of a way out, Lasgol transmitted.

Think fast.

Lasgol began to think of some plan to get out of there with the pearls. The options were few and risky. He thought about what his friend Egil might do in such a situation, but he did not come up with any brilliant plan because he was not Egil. How he missed him, and more so in this situation! Perhaps there was no solution. They might have enough to worry about with getting out of there alive. Perhaps they would have to give up the pearls in order to save their lives. But he did not want to give up so easily. He wanted to find a solution, try something, even if it were dangerous.

And at that moment there was a clangor. As if part of the dome of the cavern had fallen to the floor. The cavern started to shake. Lasgol, Ona, and Camu looked at one another. They feared something terrible was about to happen.

They were not mistaken.

From the other cavern there appeared Dergha-Sho-Blaska.

Chapter 40

Astrid, Nilsa, Ingrid, Egil, Gerd, and Viggo were watching the road south of the kingdom, sitting on their horses on top of a distant hill.

"Are you sure it'll be here?" Ingrid asked Egil.

"That's what the information I was provided with said."

"Is that a yes?" Viggo asked.

Egil nodded.

"It's an 'it should be yes.'"

"But the information might not be correct," Astrid pointed out.

"Maybe," Egil admitted.

"Your information is usually solid nine out of ten times," Gerd said. "I'm sure this time it'll be too."

"Let's hope so," Egil smiled at him.

"And as for the day?" Nilsa asked.

"The same. It should be today," Egil confirmed.

"Well, let's hope so," Nilsa nodded.

"You still have time to go back and not get involved in this action," Egil offered.

"It's a little late for that. We're with you. We already decided. We'll help you get the crown," Astrid said with conviction.

"And I will have so much fun in the process," Viggo added with a grin.

"Don't joke about it. This is serious. We could be accused of high treason," Ingrid said.

"Only if they catch us, which isn't going to be the case," Viggo said convinced.

"What did Molak say?" Nilsa asked. "He'll have thought it odd that we're all gone."

"I told him it was Panthers' business and that he'd better not be involved," Ingrid said.

"You did well," Egil agreed. "It's better that he stays out of this."

"I'm sure Captain Fantastic loved being left on the side like old times," Viggo commented acidly.

"He did not like it, and it's logical, it shows we don't trust him.

And leave the past in the past."

"We do trust him, but not in this," Astrid corrected. "Besides, it's better for him not to be involved. That way they won't be able to hang him for treason."

"No-one's going to hang us for treason," Gerd said. "We're not going to be caught, and it's not treason if you're helping the rightful king."

"Oh yeah, you tell that to Thoran and Orten, you'll see how well they understand the difference."

"I'm grateful to you for risking your lives for me," Egil said. "I mean it from the bottom of my heart. I'm sorry it has to be this way."

"For you and for Norghana," Ingrid said with a wink.

The road they were watching came from the southwest, from the river Utla, and headed south of Norghana to the fortress of Skol, which controlled the entrance to the kingdom in the south. From where the group was standing they could see the great fortress against the mountains in the distance. It was impressive. It looked impregnable and, according to folklore, it was. That was one of the reasons why Orten had claimed it and made it his home. He was safe there. At least from invading armies. Assassins in the night were another matter, although these might have difficulty because of the high walls and how strongly it was guarded. These were precisely measures to stop anyone from killing Orten. Yet, a special assassin perhaps might manage to succeed. But this was not the reason they were there today. Their purpose was to stop certain people from reaching the fortress. If they made it inside, the Panthers would have failed. The fortress had at least a couple thousand soldiers garrisoned in it.

Egil was watching with his eyes half closed. He was expecting a group to appear heading to the fortress. One they had to stop from reaching Orten, or the West and its leaders would suffer a devastating blow. He did not like the idea of having to intervene this way, but he knew that this operation was too important to leave in the hands of a third party. He had let others carry out a coup they should not have attempted and now they were in this complicated situation. If Thoran and Orten found out that the attempt on the King had been carried out by the Western league, they would be finished.

Suddenly, a group of riders appeared to the west of the road. There were more than Egil had anticipated. At first sight he counted two dozen riders escorting two prisoners in their midst. The prisoners were easy to recognize because they were thinner and shorter that the rest of the riders. No doubt the captors were soldiers of Orten, unmistakable for their huge size and rough looks.

"They're coming," Ingrid warned.

"Is that them?" Nilsa asked.

"They are. Everyone, to your positions. Follow the plan and everything will be all right," Egil guaranteed.

"Very good, let's go," Ingrid gave the order.

They all put their hoods on and covered their mouths and noses with their Ranger's scarves. The group split into three. Astrid got off her horse and positioned herself on the hill. Viggo, Ingrid, and Nilsa headed to a small forest to the east. Egil and Gerd headed to a group of trees to the west. The road passed in front of all of them so they had a good tactical arrangement.

It took the group of soldiers a good while to reach the first position, that of Egil and Gerd. The two had dismounted and tethered their horses to a tree. They had their bows in their hands and each had an arrow nocked. They were watching the road carefully, making sure they were not seen.

The group of riders passed right by them. Egil and Gerd hid behind the trees and were not seen. They let the soldiers go by. Egil checked that he had counted correctly—there were twenty-four soldiers and two prisoners, gagged and with their hands tied. The soldiers were the kind who could split a man in two with their huge axes. Or break a nose and several teeth with a single punch. They rode big horses because they weighed too much for light horses or ponies.

The group continued moving along the road. The soldiers looked in every direction, alert to any possible attack. Luckily for the Panthers, the soldiers were not used to seeing beyond the edge of their axes. They would not see a Ranger hiding in the shrub even if they tripped on him or her by accident. Egil felt sorry for them, but this quickly passed. He knew they were brutal, surly, and ruthless. They were not good people, and it was because of this that Orten had them in his service. They would kill without hesitation, and they did not care who they killed or why.

The riders passed along the cleared area. On the hill, lying on the ground, covered by a camouflage blanket so as not to be seen, lay

Astrid. She had her Sniper's bow on her right and her quiver with long, special arrows on the left. She watched them go by at the slow pace they were keeping and smiled slightly. Those wretches had no idea what they were getting into, but they would soon find out.

The soldiers were approaching the forest where the rest of the Panthers were waiting. Because of the soldiers they were, they did not have scouts, trusting that no one would dare stand up to them. This was a great mistake that they would soon come to realize.

A third of the riders were already passing by the forest. All of a sudden, three arrows flew and fell in the midst of the soldiers. Strangely enough, the three arrows flew in a wide arc and missed the soldiers entirely, hitting the ground. When they did, the sound of glass containers breaking was heard, and from them came a blue gas that rose from the ground, spreading among the riders.

"What's this?" the rough-looking soldier who was in the lead said, looking in every direction without seeing who or what was attacking them.

"Are we under attack?" the next one asked, who looked even more brutal.

Two of the soldiers fell off their horses in the midst of the blue substance that continued spreading among them. Three others fell a moment later.

"We're being attacked!" the lead soldier cried.

"Sound the alarm!" cried a soldier in the middle.

"To arms!" cried another further back.

Three arrows flew straight toward the leading soldiers who were still standing. They were Earth Arrows. They hit the soldiers in the torso, and upon detonation the men were blinded and stunned with the substances prepared for that purpose. A moment later they were reached by the Summer Slumber and fell off their horses, unconscious.

"We're being attacked from the forest!" another soldier cried.

"Charge! Go into the forest and kill them all!" said another.

Six of the soldiers obeyed and entered the forest at full gallop. The first two were hit by two Air Arrows in the torso, and the electrical charges that followed the loud noise knocked them out. They fell off their horses as the other four dismounted and headed into the forest. Two were knocked out by two Earth Arrows, followed by blows from Ingrid and Nilsa. Viggo jumped on the last two soldiers from a tree, and as they fell he hit them with the butts of his knives until they passed out.

The remaining soldiers realized they had lost half their men and opted for a retreat.

"We retreat!"

"Grab the prisoners and retreat!"

Several soldiers took the two prisoners away, who were watching what was going on with eyes wide with fear.

They ran off at full gallop in the opposite direction, away from the forest where the ambush was taking place.

Astrid came out of her camouflage cover and released against the leading man. She hit him in the head with a hard-tipped arrow whose function was that of hitting the victim hard without killing them. It blew the winged helmet off the soldier's head and knocked him off his horse with the power of the shot. The one immediately behind looked toward Astrid and received another arrow in his cheek. It hit him with all the power of a right punch from a Wild One of the Ice. He fell off the horse, unconscious before he hit the ground.

"Attack the shooter!" cried one soldier.

"Charge at the archer!" cried another.

Astrid saw two soldiers coming at her. Calmly, she nocked another arrow in her Sniper's bow. She aimed, took her time, and released. The arrow hit the first rider in the middle of his forehead. The winged helmet flew off and the soldier jerked his head back and fell off his horse. Astrid had no time to release again with her big bow, so she ran to her horse and grabbed her composite one. She nocked an Air Arrow and released against the soldier charging at her. She hit him in the torso. The discharge made him fall off when he was already on top of Astrid, who dropped her bow and drew her Assassin's knife. With two blows to the temple she left him unconscious.

The rest of the soldiers who could still ride were trying to flee to the west with the two prisoners. They reached the trees where Gerd and Egil were waiting and the two released. Their arrows hit the bodies of the first riders. They were arrows tipped with Winter Sleep, which was more potent than Summer Slumber. The blue-violet substance enveloped not only the first riders but the next two. The four passed by the trees where Egil and Gerd were aiming again, and they fell to the ground only a few paces after leaving the trees behind.

"Ambush to the left!" cried one soldier with horror.

"There are archers everywhere!"

"They're decimating us!"

Gerd and Egil released again at the soldiers, who fell shortly after. The last ones, seeing they were being knocked down by arrows, left the prisoners and fled at a full gallop to the west.

A moment later, Egil and Gerd came out of the trees and approached the two prisoners, who sat completely still in their saddles, looking terrified. Nilsa, Ingrid, and Viggo came out of the forest and went over to check that all the soldiers were unconscious. Whoever was not they knocked out with a blow.

Astrid remained on the hilltop. Once again she had her Sniper's bow in her hands in case she needed to take care of any other approaching danger.

"Don't worry, we're not going to do you any harm," Egil told the two prisoners.

They tried to talk, but they were still gagged.

Egil motioned Gerd to take off the gags. The giant did as he was told.

"Please don't kill us!" one pleaded. He was blond with blue eyes.

"We haven't done anything wrong!" said the other, who had brown hair and eyes.

Egil raised his right hand.

"I'll tell you what's going to happen now. You're going to come with me to a safe place and we're going to have a conversation."

"But we're innocent!" the blond one cried.

"I haven't accused you of anything."

"We haven't done anything, we swear!" the other one protested.

"I did not say you had."

"Let us go!" pleaded the blond one.

"I can't do that. You have dangerous information, very dangerous for many people."

"We won't tell anyone!" the other one promised.

"First things first. Let's talk, and you'll tell me what you've done and who you've talked to. You'll also tell me what happened in Rogdon. For your own good, I hope your answers are the ones I expect," Egil said in a tone of distrust.

"We won't tell you anything!"

"I'm afraid you'll tell me everything, and the truth besides. I have a couple of friends, Ginger and Fred, who will make you tell me the whole truth," Egil said with a smile.

They both denied everything and asked to be let go. Egil signaled Gerd to put the gags on them again.

"Is it necessary?" Gerd asked Egil in a worried tone when he had finished gagging them again.

Egil sighed and nodded.

"Unfortunately, it is."

"And if they have betrayed the West?" Gerd asked, turning his back on the two men and whispering so as not to be heard.

Egil gave him a stone-cold look.

"In that case, the West will make sure they pay."

Chapter 41

If the situation was already complicated, now it was impossible. The great Immortal Dragon was coming into the cavern, making it quake with his footsteps. He was so large, strong, and heavy that every step of his body, which was over a hundred fifty feet long, made the whole mountain shake.

Lasgol recognized the yellow reptilian eyes that shone intensely in a crested head with horns, as big as it was terrifying. A ridge went down from his head along his back to the very tip of his long and powerful tail. In the scant light of the cavern Lasgol could see the reddish-black scales that covered his whole body and the huge wings he had folded flat against his body. He walked on his four short, powerful legs that ended in sharp, piercing claws.

Camu, Ona, and Lasgol could only watch in terror the chilling monster and all the power and death he represented.

The two minor dragons, all the reptiles, and the humans bowed their heads before their lord and master. They did so to show homage to their god on earth.

We have recovered the tears of Sher-Mosh-Dara, my lord, the blue dragon messaged to its master.

We hope it pleases our lord and master, the brown dragon messaged.

I feel their power, it calls to me, Dergha-Sho-Blaska messaged back as he walked to stand a few paces from the box with the pearls.

The Immortal Dragon looked at the box, and at a movement of his head, the twelve pearls rose to hover in midair before the towering dragon. Dergha-Sho-Blaska used his magic, and suddenly the twelve pearls began to give off silver flashes at different intervals.

They have Drakonian power no doubt, a lot of power. This pleases me, he messaged.

They have also brought this object, my lord. It was with the pearls, the blue dragon messaged, making the ice jewel levitate.

Dergha-Sho-Blaska looked at the ice jewel. Lasgol's heart skipped a beat. He was going to find them out. Camu looked at him. He was thinking exactly the same thing. The great dragon was going to discover the location spell and would know that someone would have

343

followed it there. He would realize they were here, find them, and kill them.

I perceive Magic of Nature. This object has nothing to do with the tears. It should not be here. He opened his great mouth and a blast of fire issued forth from it, destroying the jewel in an instant.

Lasgol waited to see whether there was any repercussion, ready to run away from there, although he really did not believe they could even reach the upper platform before Dergha-Sho-Blaska incinerated them. His stomach turned. Camu and Ona had worried looks on their faces; right now their lives were hanging from a thread.

Dergha-Sho-Blaska turned his attention to the pearls, forgetting the jewel he had just destroyed.

Are they the real ones, my lord? The brown dragon messaged,

By the power they emit, I believe they are, the blue dragon messaged in turn.

There is only one way to know whether they are the real tears of Sher-Mosh-Dara, Dergha-Sho-Blaska messaged back.

Shall we prepare the ritual, my lord? the brown dragon messaged,

Go ahead. Make everything ready. I want to make sure they are the real tears. I have been looking for them for a very long time. Too long.

As you wish, the brown dragon messaged. Dergha-Sho-Blaska kept the pearls in the air. They were no longer shining. He must not be using them, but he was studying them closely. His yellow eyes shone with the gleam of ancient intelligence and wisdom and at the same time were deadly and ruthless.

Lasgol and Camu looked at each other, and Lasgol signaled to Camu not to say a word. Then again so he would not use his magic. He would not either, not mental messages or magic of any kind. They were too close to the great Immortal Dragon. If they used magic, they risked Dergha-Sho-Blaska detecting it. They knew he was capable of picking up Drakonian magic from a distance of leagues. He had proven this when he located the great Silver Pearl. Camu's magic was Drakonian; it was more than possible he could detect it, being as close as they were. The same went for Lasgol's, which was in part Drakonian. They could not take any risks, not here. Camu seemed to understand what Lasgol was communicating to him with gestures and nodded twice.

The brown dragon went to one of the corners of the cavern where there were a dozen singular ceramic containers. They looked like large amphorae and were filled to the brim with a substance that looked like liquid silver. They bore runes that differentiated them. Lasgol had no idea what the runes meant, but they looked Drakonian. Camu was watching too. Lasgol questioned him by raising his eyebrows. Camu replied with a shake of his head. He did not know what the runes meant.

The dragon flashed silver, which Lasgol interpreted as the dragon using its magic. From three of the amphorae rose some objects. They could not tell what they were until all the liquid silver fell from them. They looked like bones and fossilized parts of animals. Lasgol guessed they were of reptiles from what they had seen in the other cavern, although they had no way of knowing where they were from. The dragon turned around and walked back to its lord while the fossils continued to hover in the air.

Lasgol and Camu looked at each other. This was becoming very strange. Something was going to happen, and Lasgol sensed it was not going to be anything good. When there were dragons and reptilian monsters involved, it never was.

The blue dragon approached the lake and flashed silver. Its magic went to the thermal water. The bubbles on its surface increased suddenly, as if the water were beginning to boil as an effect of the magic.

While the two dragons were using their magic to prepare the ritual, all the reptiles in the cavern started to utter a strange sound. It was like a deep hiss coming from the ones and a deep growl coming from the others. Lasgol had no idea of the meaning of that sound—it was strange and at the same time soothing, as if its function were that of calming the nerves which all of them felt in the presence of the great Immortal Dragon. Then he realized that the only ones with reason to be nervous were the three of them. The reptiles and humans were absolutely devoted to their lord and master. They were not nervous, they worshipped the Immortal Dragon.

He thought again and realized that it really sounded like a prayer, one uttered by monstrous reptiles. Seeing the great dragon and the reptiles with bowed heads hissing and growling the strange prayer to their master whom they idolized, Lasgol realized that what they were witnessing was a god of the reptiles whom his subjects were worshipping. He began to realize the magnitude of the problem they were facing. They were not only before an immortal dragon, but before a deity with devoted reptiles at his service.

The brown dragon presented the fossils to its lord who looked at them for a moment, studying them.

They are acceptable. Continue.

Using its magic, the brown dragon surrounded each fossil with a silver bubble made up of Drakonian energy which gradually entered the fossilized bones. After a moment, the remains of ancient reptiles began to shine with silver flashes.

Meanwhile, the blue dragon made a column of water rise from the center of the lake, several feet tall. The column seemed to be made of boiling blue water, which gave off a steam that rose to the upper part of the cavern.

Dergha-Sho-Blaska watched the preparations while he maintained the twelve pearls in the air as they shone again brightly. He seemed to be interacting with the pearls and perhaps measuring their power.

The essence of our blood has been purified, the brown dragon messaged, presenting the fossils to its lord.

The holy water has been consecrated, the blue dragon messaged, showing the column of boiling water that was boiling and steaming.

Let us begin the ritual of the new life after death, by the grace of and to serve the Immortal Dragon, king among ancestral dragons, the first and most powerful, Dergha-Sho-Blaska messaged.

The reptiles continued with their strange prayer.

Dergha-Sho-Blaska selected one of the pearls and sent it to hover about three feet above the column of water. Then he used his magic to place the three fossils he had been presented with between the pearl and the column of water.

Lasgol was watching the dragons move Objects of Power with the power of their minds and found it impressive and fearsome. They could likely move human beings the same way they moved those objects, he guessed. The thought froze the blood in his veins.

The chanting intensified. It was so odd that all those monstrous reptiles would give themselves to that invocation that Lasgol was struck numb by what he was witnessing. He guessed things were going to become ugly any moment now.

Be witness to the power of life and death by the grace of your lord and master, the blue dragon messaged.

Let the ones once dead revive to serve the Immortal Dragon king, the brown one messaged next.

The Immortal Dragon used his magic. A silver sphere appeared, enveloping the pearl, the tree fossils, and part of the water column. The pearl started to emit part of its energy, which filled the whole sphere. It was like a silver cloud that was expanding until it filled it entirely. At the same time, the water that was also inside the sphere began to expand too, blending with the energy of the pearl. The fossils vanished in the midst of the sphere, enveloped in water and energy.

Lasgol, Camu, and Ona were watching with fascination. They did not miss a detail. The ritual was strange.

Dergha-Sho-Blaska made the sphere emit a strong flash. Then he began to make it come slowly down the column of water while it continued shining a strong silver. When the sphere reached the surface of the lake, the sphere flashed three times, and after the third time it disintegrated. The fossils fell in the water and the silver pearl went back up the column of water to the top, occupying the same place it had at the beginning of the process.

There was a pause while the chanting continued.

Suddenly, from inside the lake of thermal water, there appeared one of the fearsome black scorpions.

Be reborn and serve your lord the Immortal Dragon! the blue dragon messaged triumphantly.

The scorpion was followed by a Royal Cobra, which came out of the water hissing as it returned to life.

Bow before Dergha-Sho-Blaska, your lord and master, the brown dragon messaged, and the snake obeyed.

After the scorpion and the cobra there followed a crocodile of gigantic size.

The servants return to the world of the living to serve the king among dragons, the brown dragon messaged.

Take your place among your own, the blue dragon messaged, and the three newly reborn creatures went to their respective groups.

Dergha-Sho-Blaska brought the pearl back to him.

The ritual has been a success. This confirms it. The tears are the true ones. At last they are in my power. With them I shall be able to continue with my plans. This world will belong again to its legitimate lords and owners, the dragons.

Lasgol felt a shiver. Now he understood what Dergha-Sho-Blaska was planning. He was going to create an army of monstrous reptiles in his service to conquer the world. That was why they had been seeing a growing number of great reptilian monsters in Norghana and other regions. It was just the beginning. He must have created them here or woken them up from their slumber with his magic. Now he was creating scorpions, cobras, crocodiles, rhinoceros beetles, and other reptiles using his magic and the power of the pearls.

Suddenly Lasgol knew what it was that all those slaves were digging out of the caves. It was not gold, or silver, or diamonds. It was reptile fossils. The whole mountain was a graveyard of reptiles, and they were looking for fossils and other remains to create Dergha-Sho-Blaska's army. The idea of an army with thousands of those enormous reptiles in the service of the great dragon made Lasgol's stomach turn. What human army could defeat such a force? More so if it came with minor dragons or the Immortal Dragon himself.

The time of men is coming to an end. It is now the time for a new era of dragons to begin, Dergha-Sho-Blaska messaged.

Our lord will rule as immortal king of the dragons, the blue dragon messaged.

We, his servants, will help him to rule now and always, the brown one joined in.

I am Dergha-Sho-Blaska, Immortal Dragon, king among dragons, reborn in a new body to rule in a new era, came the powerful message.

The Immortal Dragon gave a nod and the Silver Pearls glided to his right, by his head. Compared with the size of it, they looked like cherries. Then he gave another nod, and from the back chamber another silver object came flying in, which placed itself on the left of the Immortal Dragon's head.

It was the great Silver Pearl he had stolen from them. The one Eicewald had died defending.

The image was terrible and discouraging. Dergha-Sho-Blaska had all the pearls with him, and he was going to use their power to further his plans of dominating the world.

It is time to see whether the tears have enough power to create a minor Drakonian servant.

The great tear has it. With it we were created, the brown dragon messaged.

Should the minor tears not have the same power, my lord? the blue dragon messaged.

We shall see now. Bring me a relic of a Drakonian, Dergha-Sho-Blaska messaged back.

The two dragons went to the wall where the huge dragon fossil was. There were three amphorae placed below it. Using its magic, the blue dragon took a fossilized dragon bone. The brown dragon inspected it carefully.

The relic is in good condition. It has been purified in the sacred silver, he messaged.

From what they had witnessed so far, Lasgol guessed that what was in the amphorae was some type of silver they had imbued with magic. It must be part of the process of preparing the fossils, both reptile and dragon. The more he saw, the more impressed he was with all this arcane world of the dragons they had known nothing about. Why was silver so important to them? How did they make these preparations? Why did they treat them as if they were sacred rites over relics which were also considered sacred? No doubt the beliefs and myths of the Drakonians had to be of the most intricate and complicated kind. Perhaps if they gained knowledge of what the dragons believed, worshipped, and respected, they might find a way to create understanding between them and humans and reach some kind of agreement with them.

Bring me the relic. We shall create a powerful servant to serve me and fight at my side against men and their armies. The day when all humans serve me as slaves is near. I shall reign as an immortal god and they will serve me on their knees as the inferior and insignificant beings they are.

Lasgol swallowed. He realized then that, no matter how well they understood the dragons, no matter how much they wanted to reach a peace agreement with them, it was clear this would never happen. The dragons wanted nothing to do with humans. What they wanted was to reign over the whole world and enslave men. They would accept nothing less and would destroy whoever stood up to them.

Another, darker thought came to Lasgol's mind. Dergha-Sho-Blaska was very intelligent. He was not going to take any risks. He was planning all this precisely so as not to take any risks, so that nothing and no one could stop him. One single dragon against all of humanity was one thing. Humanity would have a chance if it joined against him. Dergha-Sho-Blaska knew this and was not going to risk letting that happen, no matter how powerful he was or how minimal the possibility of men defeating him. But he had opted for having an army of monstrous reptiles and minor dragons that would assure him a victory with barely any risk. The chances of humanity were decreasing by the moment, and that was if they joined forces, something that was practically impossible, knowing humans.

The two minor dragons took the purified relic to Dergha-Sho-Blaska. The Immortal Dragon looked at it, studying it.

I am pleased. Let the ritual begin of the new life after death for a Drakonian, one of ours, one who deserves to come back to serve me and rule over the world at my side.

Upon hearing the voice of their lord and master, the reptiles intoned their strange litany again. Lasgol and Camu exchanged worried glances. Things were getting uglier by the moment.

Dergha-Sho-Blaska looked at the Great Pearl for an instant. Then he looked at the twelve Silver Pearls. He selected one of them as he had done before and sent it to the top of the column of water. Then he used his magic to glide the dragon relic until it was placed between the pearl and the column of water. Finally, he created the silver sphere that enveloped the pearl, the dragon relic, and the column of water. The process was repeated inside the sphere, where the energy of the pearl, the water, and the relic blended. The sphere came down the column of water until it was submerged in it. It flashed three times and vanished.

Lasgol was wishing the ritual would be a total failure, that Dergha-Sho-Blaska would not achieve his purpose. The disappointment he suffered when he saw a white minor dragon with sandy streaks coming out of the water was tremendous.

Witness the return to life of a new minor dragon by the grace of my wisdom and power.

The chanting rose louder among the reptiles at the sight of the miracle of life.

Our lord and master is wise beyond millennia, the blue dragon messaged.

Our lord and master is powerful beyond time, the brown dragon messaged too.

Approach, reborn. And bow before me, your lord and master, Dergha-Sho-Blaska messaged to the minor dragon.

The white dragon approached and prostrated itself with spread wings and head, neck, and wings on the floor before his lord.

You come to serve your master. To die for him without hesitation. Your name shall be Zuri-Bada-Zara, and you will submit my enemies in my name.

Zuri-Bada-Zara I shall be, and my lord and master I shall serve to the death, the white dragon messaged as an oath.

The Tears have enough power to create minor Drakonians, as I had anticipated, Dergha-Sho-Blaska messaged, looking at the Silver Pearls hovering beside his head. He brought the one he had just used back with the others. *I shall be able to save the power of the Great Tear for some other more important purpose, one which no one imagines and which will return this world to its ancient splendor and beauty.*

We await our lord's orders eagerly, the blue dragon messaged.

I must make some preparations. A journey awaits me which I must undertake before I start my final plans.

What must we do, lord and master? the brown dragon messaged.

Continue with the plans I have set in motion here. There must be no delay. The sooner we finish our work here, the sooner we will reign over the outer world.

We shall fulfill the wishes of the Immortal Dragon. The plans shall continue without interruption, the blue and brown dragons messaged.

The journey I must undertake is long, and it will take time. Wait for my return. Do not disappoint me, or the consequences shall be paid in blood.

The three dragons bowed deeply to their lord.

The rest of the reptiles in the hall did so too.

I am leaving the Tears here. Let no one use them in my absence. Only I shall use them for the end I consider they are worthy of. The power of the Tears is finite. Once consumed, the Tears are destroyed. No one must use them. Whoever does I shall destroy with my own claws.

No one will dare to touch them, great Immortal Dragon, the minor dragons messaged.

Dergha-Sho-Blaska looked at his dragons and reptiles a moment longer, as if calculating whether his threat had been clear enough, and then turned around. He did this slowly and heavily, since he barely fit in the great cavern. A moment later he vanished in the back cave, taking all the pearls with him.

Lasgol saw the great dragon leave and felt a tremendous despair. Dergha-Sho-Blaska was leaving with the pearls. He knew he could not leave the pearls there with the dragon. What Dergha-Sho-Blaska was doing was much worse than they had suspected. They had witnessed it and still could not believe it. He was creating an army to serve him and conquer Tremia with. Not only that, but he was also creating minor dragons for his own ends. The most unlikely nightmare was coming true. Not only would they have to defeat the Immortal Dragon, but his army too. The more he thought about it,

351

the more terrified and uneasy he felt. That was why no one had seen the Immortal Dragon, because he had been hiding in the depths of these mountains, executing his secret plans of conquest. And where was he going now? What was this secret journey he had to undertake, and which he did not even tell his faithful servants about? After what they had witnessed, it could not be anything good. That was sure.

He tried to calm down. The situation was critical and the future had a terrifying look after what they had found out, but he had to control his nerves and face up to what was coming. The first thing he thought of was that he had to tell the Panthers and Gondabar. Not everything was lost, it could not be. There had to be hope, although at that moment and in that place he found it hard to find.

Chapter 42

The Panthers were looking at the southern wall of the capital, watching King Thoran's armies marching to the border with Zangria on the southeast. Up on the eastern battlement they watched them maneuver in front of them in the great yard, getting into marching position.

Thoran, Orten, and Queen Heulyn were atop the gates of the city on the battlements, and forming at their feet were the Invincibles of the Ice, who did not let anyone near the King and Queen. They were not very large soldiers for all that they were Norghanian, but they did look nimble and weathered. They were known for being expert swordsmen. They were also known for dressing always in white: winged helmet, breastplate, and cloak, even their shields were white. Only the steel of their Norghanian swords was not white.

The Queen did not need the Royal Eagles today—she had the Royal Guard and the Royal Rangers protecting her and the King. By the way the Invincibles of the Ice were guarding the entrance to the city, and by how Thoran and Heulyn were placed, they seemed to be saying goodbye to the armies. It did not look as if they were planning on going with them.

"Do you know whether the King will join the Invincibles and his other armies?" Ingrid wondered.

"I'd say he doesn't have the slightest intention," Astrid replied.

"And it's more prudent if his armies make their way to the border. Later on he'll join them," Egil commented.

"It would seem that way," Gerd joined in.

"If you were thinking that Thoran was going to lead his armies all proud and courageous like an impressive leader, you don't know him well," Viggo boasted.

"Very true," Nilsa agreed.

The first to place themselves in formation to maneuver were the soldiers of the Thunder Army. They were unmistakable, they were so big and strong. True Norghanian assault troops. They wore winged helmets over their blond hair and golden beards. They were rough-looking warriors, tall and tough. They wore full scale armor, carried round wooden shields reinforced with steel, and axes, one at their waist, and many carried another double-headed one on their backs. The breastplate was red with white diagonal streaks on the torso that made them stand out.

"They're impressive. They look like they could tear down that wall," Nilsa commented.

"*They make way and the armies follow*," Ingrid recited, recalling their motto.

"Too brutal for my taste," Astrid said. "They're like furious white bears."

"I'm with you. Someone with our skills could finish them off before they raised their huge axes to hit us," Viggo said, looking at Astrid.

"They're almost twice as big as a Zangrian," said Ingrid.

"You shouldn't underestimate the Zangrians. They're strong, even if they're not tall, but they're good at fighting with their spears and steel shields," Egil told them.

"Apart from the fact that they're hideous," Gerd contributed with a grin.

"Yeah, I'm sure they'll scare our furious northern bears with their looks alone," Viggo said, laughing.

The Snow Army began to position themselves behind the Thunder Army. They were also made up of strong, large soldiers, and they wore pure-white breastplates over their chainmail that covered them down to their thighs, which identified their group. They each carried a sword and an axe at their waist.

"Our heavy infantry," Ingrid commented, seeing them maneuver.

"Good at fighting in formation against other infantries," said Egil.

"The Zangrian will soon fear them," Gerd said.

"I bet they already do," Nilsa said.

The last to march were the soldiers of the Blizzard Army, in light armor with breastplates with horizontal red and white stripes. They had light scouting cavalry, and archers and lancers. They formed a mixed multifunctional group: mounted scouts, long-distance shooting, and anti-enemy-cavalry lancers.

"Shouldn't they go first at the front?" Nilsa asked.

"The light cavalry will set out and do advanced scouting to make the route safe," Egil confirmed.

"The archers and lancers will stay back," added Ingrid.

Once the three armies were formed in three rectangles, one behind the other, King Thoran gave the order to march. Amid horns that announced their departure, they started out toward the border.

"How many soldiers do you calculate in all?" Gerd asked.

"I've calculated eighteen thousand men, by the number of lines I counted in the rectangular formations," Egil replied.

"About six thousand per army then," said Gerd.

"That's right."

"And who leads them? Because Thoran and Orten are here with the Invincibles of the Ice, but they're not marching along with the other armies," Nilsa asked.

Ingrid looked at Egil.

"Do you know?"

Egil nodded smiling. "I do. The Thunder Army is led by General Olagson. The Snow Army is led by General Rangulself, and the Blizzard Army is led by General Odir."

"Are they good?" Ingrid asked.

"Olagson is big and strong like a bear and has experience. He's also good with the sword. Rangulself is the strategist of the three and the most intelligent. Physically he looks more Erenalian than Norghanian, although he's local. I haven't heard good things about Odir. He's said to be temperamental and reckless."

"Let's hope it's Rangulself who leads the action then," Ingrid commented.

"Yeah, that would be best," Nilsa joined her.

"Have you seen that the king doesn't command his nobles either?" Astrid said.

"He will as soon as his armies have the border under control," Egil said. "He'll call the Western league first and send them. Then he'll go with his brother and the rest of the nobles, those of the East."

"When will that be? Any guesses?" Ingrid asked Egil.

"Approximately one week," Egil replied.

"How do you know?" Gerd asked him.

"Because I heard that the army of Irinel is already near the border with Zangria from the east."

They all looked at Egil, surprised.

"Is King Kendryk coming with his army?"

"Of course, otherwise Thoran wouldn't dare to go against

Zangria. He's counting on Irinel's support," Egil commented. "They've signed an alliance, and besides, the attempt on Queen Heulyn's life was perpetrated by a Zangrian."

"Which gives the King of Irinel cause to go against Zangria."

"This is becoming most interesting," Viggo commented, smiling.

"Interesting isn't the word I'd use," Ingrid commented.

They watched the armies leave. And just as they had expected, the king and the Invincibles remained in the capital.

"Gerd, I'm going to need your help this evening," Egil said.

"One of your secret missions?" the giant asked.

"Irrefutable, my dear friend," Egil replied with a grin.

"Should we join you?" Astrid asked.

"It's not necessary. With Gerd's help it'll be enough. Better that you stay in the Tower in case the Queen calls suddenly," Egil told them.

"Fine, we'll do that," Astrid said.

"Where are we going?" Gerd asked.

"To see an agent with a good reputation."

"Good because he's trustworthy? Or good because he's good at shady dealings?"

"The latter," Egil said, smiling.

"Don't know why, but I was afraid of that," the giant shrugged.

Night was falling by the time Egil and Gerd arrived at the estate of a wealthy trader southeast of the capital. They went in at a gallop along the gardened avenue that led to an elegant keep in the Norghanian style, four floors high and with a steep-planed roof. It was lit up, and there were surly-looking armed men on guard in front of the door.

They were hailed.

"Who approaches?" a middle-aged guard armed with a short sword and knife called out. He was tall and thin with a scar on his chin.

Egil and Gerd stopped their mounts before the guards.

"We want to see Miroslav," Egil replied without dismounting.

"There's no one here by that name," the guard said, and four armed men appeared and stood close to Egil and Gerd.

"Oh true. In Norghana he goes by the name Mikolson. We want to see Mikolson, if you will kindly inform your lord."

The guard looked them up and down, studying them.

"My lord doesn't see anyone at this hour, and least of all without an appointment."

"He'll receive me," Egil said confidently.

"And who are you? You look like Rangers."

"That's because we are."

"My lord doesn't deal with the king's servants," the man replied and reached for his weapons. The other four guards did so too.

"Tell your lord that the King of the West is here and wants to see him."

The guard looked at him blankly.

"The King of the West? What King of the West? There is no King of the West."

"You don't worry about that, just tell your lord. He'll want to see me, I promise."

The guard looked at them again, this time with doubt in his eyes.

"Wait here. Don't dismount."

"We'll wait," Egil confirmed in an amiable tone.

The guard was about to go in when he said to the other guards as an afterthought, "If they try anything, kill them." Then he entered the big keep.

While they were waiting, they saw three other guards come out of the back of the keep. Egil and Gerd remained calm.

The veteran guard soon came back out.

"My lord will see you," he formed them.

"Thank you." Egil dismounted and Gerd did the same. They headed to the door as if they feared nothing, although the situation was dangerous. Those guards had an ugly look about them.

"My name is Iresten. Follow me," the guard they had spoken to said.

Egil, nodded and they went inside. Three guards followed behind them. If it was already obvious this was the estate of someone wealthy, what they saw inside the great house corroborated this. There were white bear skins on the floors, foreign tapestries on three walls, quality furniture from other distant kingdoms, and decorative objects that looked valuable.

They were led to a large room on the first floor. In it there were several velvet armchairs of different colors and three large armories of the kind used to exhibit weapons, not so much to keep them.

We wait here," Iresten told them. The three guards stood at the door.

Egil and Gerd looked at the weapons in the armories. There were swords of different styles in the first one. They all looked precious and well made. They were from different kingdoms—it almost looked like an exhibition of swords from all over Tremia. There were some from the Nocean Empire, Rogdon, Erenal, Irinel, and the distant east. In the next armory there were spears and pikes, also from different kingdoms and regions of Tremia. Some were huge and must weigh a ton, only manageable by warriors of Gerd's size.

If they liked the two first armories, the third one left their mouths open. It exhibited bows of all kinds of exquisite make. There were also several crossbows which caught Egil's and Gerd's attention, since they were little known weapons and only used in the east, in the city-states of the coast.

"Admiring my collection of weapons?" a shrill voice asked.

Egil and Gerd turned around.

"Magnificent weapons, impressive in fact," Egil said in a praising tone.

"They are. They've cost me a fortune," the man who had just come in smiled. He must be Miroslav. Nearing his sixties, he had kept himself in good health. He was not Norghanian, his features were more eastern. Tall and thin, he had a dangerous smile and his eyes were deep green.

"Some are exquisitely amazing," Egil commented, indicating one of the swords.

"Made by the best craftsmen. That I can attest to."

"You can tell by just looking at them."

Miroslav smiled.

"But I guess you're not here for my private weapons collection."

Egil turned toward his interlocutor.

"No, we're here for a delicate matter."

"I understand you're Olafstone."

Egil nodded.

"And I know you're Miroslav."

"I haven't used that name in a long time. Now I'm known as Mikolson. It's better for business," he smiled, showing well-kept white teeth.

"No doubt," Egil nodded.

"I was surprised you introduced yourself with your forbidden title. It's one only used in certain circles, and it's never done openly," Miroslav said.

"I figure that such a well-informed and connected merchant would be curious if I introduced myself with that forbidden title. Besides, I am in a bit of a hurry and I didn't want to waste time.

"I am curious indeed."

"I don't think that here, in this environment, my title poses any danger."

Miroslav smiled.

"No, it doesn't. In my house, everyone can negotiate, from kings to paupers, as long as they have gold. I will also say that honesty is appreciated in businessmen here too."

"That's what I had understood."

"So, how can I help the King of the West?" Miroslav asked, opening his arms.

"I need a name, and I've been told that you can provide it."

"Part of my business is dealing with names. What name are you referring to?"

"The one that hired a Zangrian assassin to kill the Queen."

Miroslav jerked his head back, no doubt surprised. And then he nodded repeatedly.

"What if I told you that deal never came through my hands?"

"Unfortunately I wouldn't believe you and we'd have a problem," Egil replied, dead seriously.

Miroslav's guards reached for his weapons. Gerd reacted, doing the same.

Egil and Miroslav stared into each other's eyes, their minds working overtime.

"Stay still," Miroslav told his guards. "I'm sure the Western League knows their leader is here. If anything should happen to him they would come for us, and they're a few thousand men."

"As well as the king's Royal Eagles," Egil added.

"True, I had heard. You have powerful and dangerous friends."

"But I've come to see you without them. I don't want a confrontation. I need the information. I know you took part in the deal and you have the name. I'd rather you give it to me instead of my having to take it by force."

"Which you will do if I don't oblige…"

"As I said, I need it. It's important."

"And if I gave you a Zangrian name?"

"I'd be very disappointed. We both know the hand behind the attempted murder isn't Zangrian."

Miroslav smiled.

"I had heard you were very intelligent. I can see why they say that and why Thoran will one day have a serious problem with you."

Egil shrugged and smiled.

"You and I, we're both businessmen. We can go on doing business in the future," Egil offered, smiling. "I'll need contacts and informers, which I know you have. I'll have the gold of the West at my disposal, and I pay my collaborators handsomely."

This proposal seemed to interest Miroslav, who remained thoughtful.

"Interesting. As I see it, I can kill you now and take my risk with the Western League and the Rangers, or I can do business with you now and in the future."

"And without taking risks," Egil pointed out.

"I'll need a gesture of good will," Miroslav demanded.

Egil nodded.

"I was expecting this." He put his hand in his Ranger's cloak and took out a bag of gold. He handed it to him.

Miroslav did not open it, he simply felt the weight in his hand.

"Very well. You have a deal," he said and offered his hand to Egil.

"It's a deal then," Egil confirmed, taking the hand and shaking it.

"The name you're looking for is Rolemus, a noble and spy of the Kingdom of Erenal."

Egil nodded.

"Where do I find him?"

"He's in the Zangrian border with Norghana, making sure the war happens. He's hiding on the Zangrian side, in the village of Murdol."

"It's a pleasure doing business with you," Egil told him.

"I can say the same thing. We will soon talk about more lucrative business."

"Absolutely. With your leave we must go back, important matters await us."

"Absolutely," Miroslav waved them to the door.

Egil and Gerd left the estate and rode back to the capital. While they were on their way Gerd could not resist asking Egil a question. He had many doubts about what had gone on.

"Do you think he's given you the right information?"

"He has. It's in his best interest."

"Do you trust him? You introduced yourself as the King of the West… isn't that too much of a risk?"

"Of course I don't trust him. He's a dangerous and intelligent man, with a great number of contacts. I gave him information he already had. There are agents in the shadows who know who I am and my title in the West."

"That's dangerous."

"It is, but no information can remain secret forever. Sooner or later it comes out. Sooner if many know it, no matter how loyal they might be."

"Then, it was Erenal who tried to kill the Queen?"

"Irrefutable, my dear friend."

"So, what are we going to do?"

"We're going to prevent a war and perhaps start another."

"That doesn't sound very good."

"I know, but it's all we can do."

The two friends rode on while the night enveloped them on the royal road to the capital.

Chapter 43

Camu, Ona, and Lasgol saw Dergha-Sho-Blaska leave and vanish into the inner cavern at the far end. The minor dragons began to give orders to the reptiles, which started to move. Only the humans remained still beside the thermal lake. Several scorpions started up the spiral ramp toward where they were hiding.

Lasgol motioned his friends to go up so they would not be seen. They went up silently, trying not to make any noise until they reached the upper lookout. Lasgol signaled to them and they sought an intermediate cavern, one of those used for food and storage, to hide in. The three sheltered behind some large water barrels.

Not long afterwards they saw several scorpions pass by toward other outer caverns. Lasgol considered their hiding place good, at least for the time being.

You've seen what Dergha-Sho-Blaska is plotting. What should we do? he transmitted to his friends, although he was questioning himself as well.

Go to cave and do justice, Camu messaged, along with a feeling of anger and rage.

That isn't a good choice, Camu. I know you're angry about Eicewald's death, but we can't confront Dergha-Sho-Blaska alone.

Yes, can, Camu insisted stubbornly.

Ona moaned twice.

Listen to your sister. She knows it's madness. We alone can't fight the Immortal Dragon, least of all when he has three minor dragons with him and all kinds of large reptiles in his service. They'd tear us apart in the blink of an eye.

We much powerful. I magic, you magic and bow. We power, Camu insisted.

The rage and anger you're feeling aren't letting you think clearly. I understand. I feel the same way. I also want justice for Eicewald and I'd like to finish off this Immortal Dragon. More so now that we know of his plans to enslave humanity and rule over the world. But we can't fight him and all his monsters. That's a terrible folly that would end with all of us dead. That way you wouldn't get justice or get rid of your feeling of rage. You'd only get us all killed.

Lasgol's words seemed to have an effect on Camu, who was left thinking for a while.

Not want all die for me, Camu messaged, along with a feeling of sorrow that reached Lasgol and Ona.

I know, don't worry. I only said that to make you see reason.

Have do something, he messaged, and the feeling of rage returned.

Yeah, that's what I'm weighing in my mind, whether to risk it or not.

Risk what?

Lasgol grimaced. *We can't fight the Immortal Dragon, and neither can we fight his minor dragons and reptiles. In fact, we're in no condition to fight anyone after the beating we received from the red dragon. And besides, they would all come after us if we dared to fight anyone. But I don't want Dergha-Sho-Blaska to keep the silver pearls. I'm thinking that, although it's very risky, we should try and take them from him. That way we'd thwart his immediate plans...*

Good idea. I like.

But it's very risky ...

No can let Dergha-Sho-Blaska succeed plans.

Yeah, that's what I'm thinking.

We steal pearls, Camu messaged, very sure of himself.

Doubt was killing Lasgol. On the one hand, he wanted to stop the Immortal Dragon from continuing with his plans of conquest and slavery at all cost. On the other, he had   the terrible feeling in the pit of his stomach that if he tried to go after the pearls he was going to end up dead. Worse than that, Camu and Ona might die because of him, attempting something crazy and not having better judgment.

Oh, I don't know... it's too dangerous... he transmitted, troubled.

I say risk worth.

Ona growled once.

Lasgol snorted and then sighed. He made the decision.

All right. We'll try to steal the silver pearls.

Okay! Camu messaged happily.

I only hope we don't end up dead, all three of us.

We do, you see.

I wish I had your optimism. Well, it's probably better I don't. I do need some common sense, although I'm beginning to think I'm slowly losing it.

Situation critical. Decision much critical. Always good.

Yeah... with that philosophy of life we won't even make it till tomorrow, Lasgol shook his head.

They waited a while before launching into the risky enterprise.

Several scorpions went by in both directions, some returning from the large cavern with the thermal lake and others going toward it. This was not good; they could discover them in the middle of the descending spiral. If that happened, it was going to be difficult to remain unseen. Lasgol decided to wait until night fell outside. Not because it would be any help regarding darkness, because the place was already dark enough and only the torches provided some light, but because he hoped the reptilian guards would rest. That would give them an advantage. Although they had no way of knowing whether it was night outside, they waited enough for it to be quite late into it.

They were prepared to try. They waited a little more to see whether any scorpion passed by. Seeing this did not happen, Lasgol decided to act.

Let's go, carefully. Avoid being found out.

Okay.

If we're found out, we escape. We don't fight, understood?

Yes, understood.

Ona growled once.

Camu used his Extended Camouflage skill and they left their hiding place. Slowly and alert to any sound, they headed to the largest cavern. They were about to arrive when they met the first obstacle. On the platform that gave access to the spiral that went down to the bottom of the cavern were two scorpions watching.

What do? Camu messaged.

The scorpions could not see them, and neither could they see their trail because they weren't leaving any footprints on the rock. The thing was, they were blocking their way.

I have an idea. Be alert. Lasgol bent over and carefully picked up a couple of pebbles from the rocky floor. He waited a moment and threw the two stones to one side of the platform, the farthest part that was in the shadows. He threw them hard, and when they hit the wall they made a suspicious noise.

The two scorpions turned at once toward the origin of the sound. They looked, but they could see nothing since it was pitch dark. Intrigued, they went over to check the sound with pincers and stingers ready.

Hurry up now! To the spiral!

The three moved fast, Camu setting the pace and Lasgol and Ona following him on either side so as not to leave the range of his camouflage skill that hid them. They started down the spiral at the same moment that the two scorpions, not having found anything out of place, were returning to their positions.

It worked, Lasgol transmitted with a soft snort.

We much good, I know.

Yeah, you know too much.

They went on down the spiral until they reached the lower part.

Let's stop to check, Lasgol transmitted, and they stopped. They went over to the rim and studied the situation. The first thing they saw was that the same groups they had seen before were still there: in one corner the scorpions with their leader, in the other the cobras with theirs. There were also two giant beetles by the water in the middle of the cavern. The humans, Defenders and Visionaries, were further away in another corner.

Lasgol had hoped there would not be so much enemy presence, that they would have retired to rest in some other cave, but that was not the case. They had not been lucky. The cavern was filled with servants of the Immortal Dragon, which would make the incursion difficult. He was beginning to feel that every time they had some complicated mission, luck was not in their side. Fortune was not always their ally, and today she certainly was not smiling on them.

Much guards.

Yeah, they're making it complicated for us.

We can.

Lasgol checked the cavern and traced a route that would take them from the spiral where they still were to the back cavern. He did it, considering where the cobras were, which constituted the greatest danger, since they could find them out by smell. The scorpions, beetles, and humans were not going to find them out if it was not by sound, at least that was what Lasgol was hoping.

We're going to go across. We'll go by the lake, as far as possible from the cobras.

By lake?

Yes, as close to the shore as we can. But beware of the cobras. Also the humans and scorpions. No sound at all.

Okay.

Lasgol tapped Camu's back and they started their descent. They reached the base of the spiral and stopped. They checked the cavern and its occupants. They seemed quiet, they were resting but at the same time watchful. The moment they had the least suspicion that something was afoot, they would all move and lunge at them. This is what Lasgol wanted to avoid at all costs.

They began to move forward, very slowly, step by step, all together. They headed to the center, to the lake. This part of the way was clear, at least at first. Lasgol was watching the four corners of the cavern and the different groups of enemies in them. With each step, the tension grew. It was like passing through a bunch of sleeping lions, which would eat Lasgol and his companions the moment they woke up.

Lasgol shook off the thought, although he knew they were all thinking the same thing. They had to be careful and move as one, or their plan would end badly. They stepped in unison, without hurrying, so as not to make any sound, one step at a time, slowly and in silence. It was complicated to achieve this. Since they did not see one another they had to move with Camu, and this was not easy.

Suddenly, the lead scorpion and the lead cobra shifted. They left their groups and joined in the middle of the cavern. Camu stopped, and with him Ona and Lasgol. They waited to see what happened. The leaders seemed to communicate somehow, although Lasgol was not able to see how. Since the leaders were in the middle of the cavern they were blocking their path, so Camu took the long way, going around behind the lake instead of in front of it as they had intended.

They began to go around the lake slowly. The tension increased since they could see their enemies right there, in front of them, and this made them nervous. Things became complicated quickly. At the back of the lake there were several crocodiles of great size. Lasgol, Camu, and Ona had not seen them because of the steam coming out of the lake. Camu stopped and they watched them. They seemed to be asleep. They were lying quietly by the water. The problem the crocodiles posed was that they would have to walk through the creatures, since there were two with half their body in the water and half out. They would not be able to keep bordering the lake.

We'll walk carefully between them, Lasgol transmitted.

Okay, was Camu's familiar message.

They reached the first croc, whose tail and hind quarters were inside the lake with the rest of the body and head out. With caution,

Camu maneuvered to pass by the crocodile without stepping on another one that was a little further right, also sleeping. They had to pass between them without touching either and also not be detected. Lasgol realized he was perspiring, and it was not because of the heat of the thermal waters. They stepped with extreme caution and avoided the first croc, passing the one in front very closely. The thing was that there was another crocodile with half its body in the water and half out, as well as two more in front of it.

With tremendous composure, Camu maneuvered through them. At one point they were in the middle of six huge crocodiles. Lasgol had the feeling that the creatures were going to wake up and the monsters' jaws were going to close on his legs in an instant and by surprise. Every step they took he felt this way, it was like treading in a forest filled with hidden traps. He would step on one, it would spring, and then when he tried to flee the rest would spring too. The crocs were going to tear them to pieces.

With every step they checked whether they had been heard or discovered in any way. The way became torture, not only for Lasgol, but also for Ona and Camu. They tread with such care that they only advanced a little bit with every step. With calm and serenity, little by little, they moved forward, slowly.

They made it around the lake without being noticed. They reached the higher part. From there to the back of the cavern there was not much, but it meant going out in the open with only their camouflage. The cover the lake provided had ended.

They went forward warily, alert to any movement of the enemy. The cobras were not far away, and this made them uneasy. If the cobras detected their scent, everything would be over in the blink of an eye. Lasgol could see it happening. The cobras would lunge at them, spraying them with their venom. Then the scorpions would be able to see them and would come for them, and finally the beetles, crocs, and humans would attack them. They would tear Lasgol and his companions apart. They would never get out of there alive.

Despite the ill omens, they continued moving toward the end of the cavern. The cobras did not seem to detect them, so they managed to cross the whole cavern and reach the end. The three felt as if they had performed an epic feat.

They looked at what was waiting for them in the back cave.

They were afraid of meeting Dergha-Sho-Blaska, but luckily he was not there. The cavern, which was colossal, larger even than the one they had just crossed, had no ceiling to the north, and they could glimpse the starry sky. The great dragon appeared to have left the cave through there. This gave them a breather. The absence of Dergha-Sho-Blaska was a relief. If he had been there, they would have had to leave at once. Lasgol snorted softly. This was good news.

If this perspective was good, the one in front of them was not. In the middle of the cavern the three minor dragons were resting. They were lying on the floor, appearing to sleep with heavy breathing. Behind them rose two pedestals made of silver, and on these rested the pearls, which glowed with intermittent silver flashes. On the first pedestal sat the Great Pearl, and on the second the twelve small ones. They were exposed like trophies, within arm's reach, only with three monstrous guards protecting them that were fierce, terrible, and terrifying.

As they watched the dragons, they realized the creatures were sleeping there precisely to protect their lord and master's pearls. No one could get close to them, least of all take them. That's what the three dragons were there for, to stop such audacity as the one which Lasgol, Camu, and Ona were about to try to commit. Lasgol knew instinctively that the dragons would sense any movement or fluctuation of power behind them. They were not going to be able to move the pearls easily.

No good, Camu messaged, guessing the problem.

No, it's not.

Have to do something.

Lasgol looked back and saw all the monstrous reptiles they had left behind. It was no time to give up, not after coming this far.

Give me a moment to think.

The situation was complicated. One false move and the dragons, and then the rest of the servants, would wake up and lunge at them. That was not what Lasgol wanted; they had to achieve their goal without this happening. The more he looked at the pearls, the more he felt that, if they touched them, the dragons would notice. He did not know how, but they would sense the intrusion.

He watched and thought. Surrounding the dragons posed no problem as long as they did not wake up. But how was he going to take the pearls without their noticing? He watched the dragons sleeping like three large bloodhounds. Lasgol knew they were regenerating energy the same way he and Camu did when they rested. When he thought about energy, power, he had an idea. It was risky, but it might work.

Camu, let's go toward the pedestals. Take a long detour, don't even go near the dragons.

Okay, I take a detour.

Slowly and carefully, hugging the wall to their left, they reached the two pedestals at the back wall. The dragons were left in the middle of the cavern behind them. They approached to almost touch the pearls.

Camu I want you to create an anti-magic protection dome, Lasgol transmitted to him.

I create, Camu created the dome, which covered the three friends and the pearls.

Now, I want you to send a lot of energy to the dome so that it cancels any magic inside it.

I cancel magic, Camu messaged, along with a feeling that he did not understand what Lasgol was asking of him.

Yeah, I know that the dome protects us from any magic that tries to penetrate it. What I want it to do is also stop magic inside it.

Not know if can.

Try. We lose nothing.

Camu shut his eyes and concentrated. He began to send energy to the dome, which was translucent but gave off a small silver glow.

I bet you can do it. You can cancel magic without any trouble, Lasgol transmitted encouragingly.

I can, you see, Camu messaged in reply as he sent more energy to the dome, which now not only prevented any outer magic from affecting them but also canceled the magic inside it.

Filter mental communication. Let it happen, or else we won't be able to communicate.

I leave mental messages, Camu confirmed.

I'm going to test something, Lasgol transmitted and then called upon his *Cat-Like Reflexes* skill. It did not activate. The green flash started but failed.

Good?

Very good, Lasgol confirmed.

What do now?

Now I'll take one of the pearls. With a bit of luck, the dome will not allow its power to move outward.

Not know sure.

I know. We'll have to risk it.

Okay. Take pearl.

Lasgol reached out and took one of the twelve Silver Pearls. He lifted it while he looked at the dragons out of the corner of his eye. They did not move. Very carefully, Lasgol put the pearl in his satchel. The dragons did not seem to notice.

It seems to be working. Keep sending energy to the dome.

I keep.

Lasgol picked up the twelve pearls one by one with extreme care and put them in his satchel. Every time he lifted one off its pedestal he looked at the dragons with dread. They were sleeping without noticing what was going on. His idea was working. Lasgol could barely believe it.

He finished putting all twelve pearls in his satchel, and the moment came to take the Great Silver Pearl from the other pedestal. He hesitated whether to do it or not. They already had the twelve pearls; they could leave and not take any more risks. But that would mean that Dergha-Sho-Blaska could still go on creating his army with the power of the pearl. He did not like the idea one little bit. No, he would not allow it. They were going to take all the pearls.

He put his hands around the pearl and began to lift it up.

The blue dragon shifted.

Lasgol froze.

The brown dragon shifted too.

Chapter 44

The border had not seen so much activity in a long time. On the Norghanian side, the three armies of King Thoran had taken their positions and set up their war camps—the Thunder Army in the center, the Snow Army on its right, and the Blizzard Army on the left. Thousands of soldiers waited, restless. They were ready, awaiting the order to start the fight.

King Thoran and his nobles had arrived two days before with the Invincibles of the Ice. Queen Heulyn was accompanying her husband, which was not normal on a war campaign, but the Druid Queen was anything but normal. Since she traveled with the King and the protection of the Royal Guard and Rangers, she did not require the Royal Eagles, although she had requested they come to the front anyway in case she should need them. This gave the Panthers some breathing space and placed them on the border with all the armies.

The King's retinue had camped behind the three armies. Thoran did not want to be too forward and become a target for Zangrian archers and assassins. The rearguard, well protected by the Invincibles of the Ice, was where he felt safer. The nobles of the East and their men stayed with the King and the Invincibles. The nobles of the West and their forces had come forward to stand beside the Blizzard Army, per Thoran's order. It was clear they would be the first to cross the river that acted as the border.

On the other side of the river, a league away, the Zangrian Army's forces were camped. Five regiments of infantry led by Zangrian generals of great worth, with between eight and nine thousand soldiers in each one. It was estimated that the Zangrian forces amounted to over forty-five thousand units in all. They were well-trained and fed. The colors yellow and black covered a huge expanse of land where the great army was camped. Caron, King of Zangria, led his armies and his tent with the command center was in the midst of them. The banners and size of the enormous tent left no doubt that the King was there. Together with his generals he was preparing for the battle that was already inevitable, although the war had not been declared as such by either side.

Not far from where the Zangrian armies were camped, Astrid and Viggo were approaching the village of Murdol from the south in the middle of the night. They had entered Zangrian territory, avoiding the border with Norghana which was plagued with soldiers, spies, archers, and assassins on both sides. Egil had drawn an alternative route, one much longer but safer. They had gone down south from Norghana until they had sighted the endless forests of the Usik. From there, they had gone east to enter Zangrian territory through an area watched, but less than the border with Norghana. From there they had headed north, to the village of Murdol, near the border but from Zangrian territory.

It had taken them days to follow that long detour to avoid the border, but it had been worth it. They were now close to their goal. They had left the horses hidden in a forest and were approaching on foot, avoiding surveillance posts of the Zangrian army. The village was well-lit and occupied by a hundred soldiers. Not far away, about half a league, was a war camp with over a thousand soldiers. If they were discovered, they would hang for spying. Escaping was not going to be easy with all those soldiers around.

They stopped to check the house. It was a country manor, a league south of the village. It had to be that one. They had looked around and eliminated two other houses of landowners in the area. They had not found their target in them. Astrid was in charge of slipping into the houses and searching them. Viggo followed in case any difficulty arose that needed to be eliminated. They were both wearing the black clothes of the Ranger Assassins and wore hoods and scarf covering their mouths and noses. Only their eyes could be seen.

"Guards around the house," Astrid told Viggo.

"Shall I get rid of them?"

"Only the ones under the back balcony."

Viggo nodded, confirming.

"Wait for my order."

Viggo nodded again.

They moved on. They came out from the vegetation where they had been hiding and carefully approached the two guards under the balcony. There were two others not too far away and then six at the front of the house, watching the entrance door. But the greatest problem was the patrol of four guards that went all the way around the house every short while.

At a signal from Astrid, they lay down on the ground among the tall grass. It smelled like a summer night. The air was a lot warmer in Zangria than in Norghana, and also the temperature was quite pleasant. The Norghanians were not used to it, for them it was too hot. It was the advantage of the kingdoms of Central Tremia, they enjoyed a mild climate. The two Assassins were enjoying the good weather though. For once they would not freeze on a mission.

The patrol passed in front of them. It was what Astrid had been waiting for. Once they had passed by, and running the risk of being seen, since the guards had not yet gone all the way around the corner of the house, the two Assassins moved on. They reached some decorative bushes in the back garden of the house and hid there. From where they were they could see the two guards chatting, leaning against the wall.

"Go ahead," Astrid whispered to Viggo.

Viggo shot out toward the two guards like an arrow. He ran straight toward them in total stealth. One of the guards saw a dark shadow coming at them like lightning and he squinted to make sure he was seeing correctly. It was indeed a shadow coming at him.

"What…?" he mumbled.

The other guard looked where his partner was looking.

It was too late. Viggo was already on top of them. He gave a tremendous leap and fell on the two guards like a creature from the dark. He hit their chins and temples with the butt of his knives to knock them out in the blink of an eye.

Astrid arrived a moment later and took out the rope with a hook she carried in her backpack. She threw it skillfully to the balcony and it hooked on at the first attempt. She pulled down to check that the hook was latched properly, which it was, and then began to climb up swiftly. Viggo followed her an instant later.

They reached the balcony and Viggo forced it open with his lock picks in a matter of moments. They entered the house silently. The room was dark and empty. Astrid went over to the door and, after listening for a moment, opened it a crack. Light came in from outside. She found that it opened onto a long corridor and that there was one guard posted in it. She lifted one finger for Viggo, to let him know, then pointed her thumb at herself. Viggo nodded, moved back, and let Astrid deal with the guard.

The door opened enough for Astrid to slip out sideways. As soon as her body was out, she hugged the wall and crouched behind a small table to hide. The guard was in the middle of the corridor and looked drowsy. An oil lamp on a small table beside him was all the light in the area. Astrid waited to make sure he was not looking in her direction and then poured a substance from a container in her Assassins' belt in a black scarf. She approached the guard stealthily and he did not hear or see her coming. With a lightning move, she covered the guard's mouth and nose with the scarf and pressed down hard. A moment later she left the guard unconscious on the floor without a sound.

Viggo came over.

Astrid indicated for him to follow her at some distance and she set off. She searched the area room by room. The target was not there. She went up a wide flight of wooden stairs to the floor above. Another guard was watching the landing. Astrid dealt with him before he could react and moved him out of the way so the guard inside the corridor would not notice anything. She did it so fast that it was as if a spirit had fallen on the guard without him even noticing.

Viggo watched from the stairs, lying on the steps.

The guard in the corridor was surprised not to see his comrade and headed to the landing. Astrid had moved the body of the guard to one side and was waiting with her back against the wall. As the guard came onto the landing, Viggo jumped up from the stairs and threw his knife at the man. He hit the guard in the forehead with the butt, and the blow and the scare made the guard's head jerk back. Astrid emerged on his left. With one hand she caught Viggo's knife in the air before it hit the floor, and with the other hand she knocked the guard out with the scarf.

She held the guard up so he would not make noise falling and put him gently on the wooden floor. Then she returned the knife to Viggo, who pushed the body to one side. Astrid continued her search, going into every room without making the least noise. She came to the end of the corridor and found a double door. She looked through the keyhole. There was no light, but it was a bedroom. She thought about calling Viggo, but she also had lock picks and knew how to pick a lock. It was necessary for any good Assassin. She might not be as good as Viggo with them, but she was good enough. She took her lock picks out and carefully opened the lock and entered the room.

She closed the door behind her and crawled along the floor like a black spider coming to bite anyone who slept in the bed there. She looked at the person sleeping in a big bed with a canopy. She could see him in the moonlight that came in through a window whose curtains were not fully closed. That man was not Zangrian. Short brown hair, hooked nose, and skin a darker shade than a Zangrian or a Norghanian, he was undoubtedly from the Kingdom of Erenal.

Stealthily, she came to his side and took out one of her knives. She put her hand over his mouth and the knife to his neck. When he felt the cold steel on his skin, the man woke up and opened his sleepy eyes. He saw Astrid staring at him, and the man's eyes opened wide as he realized what was going on.

"Listen carefully if you want to live," she whispered in his ear in a barely audible tone.

The man tried to speak, but Astrid had her hand pressed over his mouth.

"Are you Rolemus?" Astrid asked him and lifted the knife enough for him to nod or shake his head.

The man shook his head.

Astrid pressed the edge of the knife against his neck.

"In that case I'm not interested in you, I'll have to kill you," and she started sliding the knife across his neck to cut his throat.

The man tried to speak, his eyes nearly popping out of his head, desperate.

"What are you saying?" Astrid asked, removing her gloved hand form his mouth just a bit so he could speak.

"Yes… I Rolemus," he answered in a strongly accented Norghanian.

"I see you understand my language. You just said you were not Rolemus. I'd better kill you and keep searching."

"No! I prove!"

"Fine, prove it then. Silently, or I'll slit your throat."

Astrid let the man get out of bed without removing the knife from his neck. She followed him to a dresser, which the man opened.

"If you try to grab a weapon, that will be the last thing you do," she warned him icily.

"No…" the man denied as he moved his hand away from the drawer he was rummaging in and withdrew. He went to the rug on the other side of the bed, moved it back with his foot, and started to bend over.

"Very slowly, or you'll cut yourself," Astrid told him, not moving the knife from his neck.

With his right hand, he pressed on two wooden boards on the floor. One gave out a light *crack* and rose to one side. The man put his hand in and felt for something. He took out an object.

"Careful what you fetch from there," she warned him, pressing the knife against his neck.

The man showed Astrid his hand. There was a small notebook with worn-out leather covers in it. It was tied with a cord.

"Show me," Astrid told him while with her knife she pushed him back to his feet.

The man undid the cord, opened the notebook, and took out a folded letter, which he unfolded and showed to her. It was written in the language of Erenal, which Astrid could not read, but she did recognize something—the signature "Rolemus."

"All right, I believe you."

Rolemus breathed, relieved.

"Get dressed quickly, you're coming with me."

That he did not understand. So Astrid pointed at the closet and then at her cloak.

"Oh," Rolemus understood.

Astrid removed the knife from his neck and put it in the middle of his back.

"Quick."

The Erenalian nobleman got dressed fast. Seeing Viggo enter the room, his face showed the despair he felt. He could not escape and he knew it. They had sent two Assassins for him. He had no way out.

At midmorning Astrid, Viggo, and their prisoner left the Zangrian territory by the southeastern border. Four riders were waiting for them.

"Did everything go well?" Nilsa asked them, unable to bear the suspense.

"Smooth as silk," Viggo replied, smiling.

"You had us worried. You took longer than expected," Ingrid told them, looking at Viggo with joyful eyes, seeing him safe and sound.

"The first houses we searched were not the right ones. We lost a lot of time because of that," Astrid said.

"That's the trouble with not having the exact location of the target," Egil said in an apologetic tone with a shrug.

"You can't always have all the information," Astrid excused him.

"But in the end we found him, which is what matters," Viggo added.

"I'll look after him," said Gerd, moving his horse beside Rolemus. "If he tries anything, I'll club him on the head."

Egil looked at Rolemus with eyes half closed.

"There's no doubt it's him, is there?"

Astrid shook her head.

"I made sure it was him. You're going to like this," she said and, bringing her horse closer, handed him the notebook.

"Interesting. Is there anything incriminatory in it?" he asked Rolemus.

"I not talk," he shook his head.

"Oh, you will, of that you can be sure," Egil, told him. "I have a couple of friends   that will make you sing," he said while he leafed through the notes in the notebook and some of the letters folded inside.

"What are we going to do now that we have him?" Ingrid asked.

"Now we'll question him to make sure, although I'm certain the information we have is accurate. It was him who organized the murder attempt. I've already glimpsed a couple of interesting letters in this notebook of his."

"Then it was Erenal that tried to kill the Queen?" Nilsa asked.

Egil nodded. "Erenal would benefit from a war between Zangria and Norghana. What better way can you think of to make sure it happens, and also that the Kingdom of Irinel joins in the campaign, than murdering the Druid Queen? Her husband and her father would never forgive Zangria. They would destroy it."

"Is this because of the dispute between Erenal and Zangria over the territories of the Thousand Lakes?" Astrid asked.

"Because of that, and because Zangria and Erenal have hated

each other since time immemorial," Egil said. "It's what usually happens between neighboring kingdoms. Always in the middle of territorial disputes and blood feuds."

"The King will not believe us… he's convinced it was Zangria." Ingrid said.

"True. He believes the Zangrians not only tried to murder the Queen, but himself as well," Nilsa added.

"That's correct, Thoran believes the Zangrians are responsible for both attempts," Egil said.

"We can't clear up the first one…" said Astrid.

"No, no we can't." Egil nodded. "But we can use the second one and blame Erenal for both."

"Good idea, I like it," Viggo said, nodding enthusiastically. "We blame it all on Erenal."

"It might work, yeah," Astrid joined in.

"I still think the King won't believe us," Ingrid insisted. "He wants it to be the Zangrians, and he's already convinced. The same goes for his brother Orten."

"Then we'll use our secret weapon," Egil said, smiling.

"Secret weapon? What secret weapon? Do we have one?" Nilsa asked out loud while the others wondered the same thing, staring at Egil.

"Irrefutable, my dear friends," he smiled at them.

Chapter 45

Lasgol was watching the dragons out of the corner of his eyes in the middle of the cavern. He had the Great Silver Pearl in his hands. He was trying to steal it and put it in his satchel where he had already put the twelve Silver Pearls he had previously taken from their pedestal. The blue and brown dragon seemed to have noticed, because they had shifted in their sleep.

Watch out, dragons move, Camu messaged the warning.

Are you still maintaining the anti-magic dome?

I maintain.

Then they shouldn't notice anything.

Pearl much power, perhaps come out.

True. We have the twelve small pearls. Should we leave it at that and run?

No, we take all.

Are you sure?

I much sure.

Lasgol was not at all sure. The two dragons had not woken up, but the fact that they had moved was not a good sign. Perhaps Camu's dome was not containing all the power of the pearl and a part of it was leaking out and that was what they were feeling. On the other hand, he did not want to leave the Great Silver Pearl there. He knew Dergha-Sho-Blaska had used it to create minor dragons, and from what they had heard this was part of his plan to conquer the world. Who knew what the Immortal Dragon might do with it. Whatever it was, it would not be good for humanity. He decided to risk it and not give the dragon the chance to do whatever it was he was planning with it.

Very slowly, he started moving the pearl toward his satchel.

Once again the blue dragon shifted.

Watch out... Camu messaged in warning. He was not taking his eyes off the dragons.

Lasgol froze like a granite statue.

None of the three moved. They barely breathed, and they did so without a sound.

The blue dragon opened its eyes and looked toward the entrance of the cavern. It seemed like something had bothered its rest.

Stay still, don't even breathe, Lasgol transmitted, terrified to be discovered.

The dragon gave out a strange internal grunt, to which the brown dragon replied to with a similar sound.

Lasgol did not know what to think, but he certainly did not like that.

Suddenly, the blue dragon began to turn its head. It was going to look directly at where they were. In a quick movement, Lasgol put the great pearl back on its pedestal where it had been. Then he stayed totally still.

The dragon looked at the pearl with sleepy, half-open eyes. He glanced over it and looked back toward the entrance of the cave.

It had not realized!

But Lasgol knew he would notice something odd. The twelve minor pearls were not there. It would not miss that detail. Quickly he took the pearls out of his satchel and put them all back on their pedestal. Just when he had finished, the blue dragon's head whipped its head back to look at the pearls.

Ona, Camu, and Lasgol stood still like frozen statues.

The dragon looked at the great pearl and then at the twelve small ones. It blinked hard and its reptilian eyes seemed to recognize that everything was in its place. A moment later it looked back toward the cave entrance.

Lasgol waited to see what the dragon would do next. It finally shut its eyes, lowered its head, and continued sleeping.

Lasgol wanted to let out a snort of relief but did not just in case.

Dragon asleep again, Camu messaged.

I'm going to take the pearls again, keep a lookout. Carefully and without the least sound or abrupt movement, Lasgol took all the pearls and put them in his satchel. They weighed quite a bit, and for a moment Lasgol wondered whether it would hold them all, so he put some of the minor ones in his Ranger's belt pockets.

I bad news.

Not a good moment for bad news.

Not energy left.

That's terrible news.

That' why I tell.

Lasgol realized that if Camu ran out of energy, the dragons not only would feel the power of the pearls, they would also see them, they and every other reptile and human in the other caverns.

We have to run out of here at lightning speed.

Yes, much running.

We'll go the same way back in the opposite direction. Quick, Lasgol transmitted.

He tapped Camu's back twice and the three began to withdraw. They were hurrying, careful and tense. Hugging the wall, they went around the three dragons. Lasgol did not take his eyes off them, terrified they would wake up at any moment and surprise them.

They reached the entrance to the cave with the lake. They went in fast and followed the same tactic, retreating over their footsteps but a lot faster. Camu led them along the same route, only three times faster. He was running out of energy.

As they were bordering the lake, passing through the crocodiles, one of them moved unexpectedly and blocked their way. Camu had to stop short and Ona's right leg was revealed when she took one step further and came out of the range of the camouflage, which seemed to be shrinking because of lack of energy.

Ona back! Lasgol transmitted in warning when he noticed.

The panther reacted with lightning speed and her leg vanished again. But one of the crocs had seen something. It moved to take a closer look, and it was followed by another.

Quick! We have to go around, they're going to see us!

Camu moved sideways, hugging the wall on his left and moving away from the water. Their original route had become impracticable. The two huge crocodiles were sniffing the spot where they had just been. Camu led them to the wall and they followed along it.

Humans ahead, Camu messaged in warning as he headed straight to them.

Don't worry. Of all the creatures here, the humans are the ones with the least possibility of detecting us.

They passed by them and watched them sleep. The snoring of some of them was quite loud, which was good news.

Camu, we can be seen!

No energy left, he messaged urgently.

Don't use it all or you'll faint, and this is no place for that!

I save little. No worry, not faint here.

We have to reach the spiral and start climbing. We're visible already, Lasgol transmitted, realizing that Camu's and Ona's tails were visible. He felt as if all the cobras and scorpions had seen them. In a moment they would all lunge at them just before Camu ran out of energy and they were left in the open, bodies exposed to all those eyes.

He looked back and except for three of the crocs, which did seem to have picked up their trail or essence and started moving toward them, the rest of the cavern's occupants were still sleeping with only a few watching, but it did not seem like they had spotted them yet. Although that was going to change very quickly.

Quick, the crocs have picked up the trail! Lasgol transmitted urgently.

They hurried, seeking the darkest area to get to the spiral. When they reached it they hugged the bottom and climbed two loops at a fast run before Camu had to stop his skill before completely running out of energy.

No more energy to use.

Now we're visible. Be alert. We hug the walls and stay in the dark.

They reached the platform at the last stage of the spiral. Lasgol could not believe they had managed to cross both caverns without being seen. It had been close. But their problems had only just begun. On the platform were the two scorpions they had fooled before, but now without camouflage it would be a whole different story.

Two scorpions on watch duty. What do? Camu messaged.

I doubt we can fool them again.

Fight?

We're in no condition to fight. We're wounded and you've got no magic. Fighting is not an option.

Then what do?

Flee.

Flee? How?

We're going to run out of here as if we were being pursued by the Immortal Dragon himself.

Work?

No idea, but we don't have any other option, so fleeing it is.

Okay. Flee.

Lasgol adjusted his satchel and Ranger's belt. He did not want to lose his precious cargo during their flight, and they were going to have to run for their lives. Then he grasped Aodh's Bow and nocked an arrow.

Ready?

I ready.

Ona put her right paw on his leg to indicate she was ready too.

Very well. We'll run onto the platform and head for the way out. I'll distract the scorpions. You run.

Sure? Camu was not convinced.

Sure, I still have some energy left. I can use the bow.

Okay.

Go now!

They climbed onto the platform and were left visible and unprotected. The scorpions saw them. They ran toward the exit, and as they were running Lasgol released an Earth Arrow, which exploded in the mouth of the first scorpion already lunging at them. The arrow blinded and stunned it.

Ona reached the exit and Camu was close behind her. Lasgol was running as he nocked another arrow and released. It was another Elemental Earth Arrow, which hit the other scorpion on the head. He was only trying to buy them some time to escape, not to kill the creatures—that would demand too much time, and besides, the alarm would be given and they would have every creature after them.

They left the cavern, leaving the two scorpions stunned and blind. They would recover quickly, but Lasgol and his companions were already running as if the hounds of hell were after them. Ona was in the lead and running quite fast given the wounds she had sustained. Camu was a tad slower, also because of the beating and because he was not as fast as the panther. Lasgol's wounds hurt as well, especially the burns on his legs and his bruises, but there was only one thing on his mind: getting out of that place. That made him not feel the pain.

They went through a couple of supply caves which fortunately were empty. From there they headed to one of the larger caverns where the prisoners were digging for fossils. They crossed them along an upper passage. Below everyone seemed asleep, at least the humans were. There were scorpions and snakes on guard, but their purpose was to watch the prisoners and not pay attention to who crossed over their heads several feet above them.

Don't stop, keep running!

Come behind?

Lasgol glanced back and saw several scorpions in pursuit.

Yes, they're coming. Run!

They went on as fast as they could. Lasgol released behind them every now and then to stun the leading scorpion and try to slow them down. Being so large, they moved fast.

They crossed another catwalk above a cavern full of slaves, and at the end they met two cobras on watch.

Cobras ahead! Camu messaged in warning.

Coming! Lasgol took over for Camu and released at the first cobra with an Air Arrow. The electrical charge left it puzzled, and Ona seized the chance to get to it and, gathering momentum, lunged at the cobra and threw it off the catwalk with a powerful shove. The cobra fell down to the floor of the cavern amid hisses of terror.

The other cobra attacked Ona, who jumped back to avoid its fangs and the injection of its deadly venom. Lasgol released another Air Arrow, and the charge stunned it. Camu instantly took advantage of the distraction to deliver a blow with his tail that threw it over the catwalk.

We keep going! Lasgol transmitted as he continued releasing against their pursuers, trying to slow down their progress.

They reached the third deep cavern where the slaves were sleeping and started to cross the catwalk as fast as they could. Ona was beginning to feel sore from the beating and Camu was not doing too well either. He lost his footing every now and then and Lasgol began to worry. Racing away was a good idea if they could all run and were well, which was not the case. The three were wounded, bruised, and might even have some internal bleeding. They could not keep up this breakneck pace.

He looked back and saw that they were now being followed by scorpions and cobras. They moved too fast due to their great size, and that was not good for Lasgol and his companions. Lasgol released behind every now and then, but he ran out of arrows. Their escape was not going well. Their enemies were gaining on them. They could not go any faster, and they were feeling the effort of the run. In case that was not enough, Lasgol had run out of arrows, which made his bow and many of his skills useless.

Don't stop, we have to get out of these mountains! Lasgol urged them on encouragingly.

They came to the end of the caverns and Ona was able to locate the corner of the wall they had come in through, but she could not cross it. For her there was a solid wall of stone, and no matter how much she wanted to think it was not so, she could not. But that was not Camu's case.

I cross, you come with me, he messaged to his sister, leaving half his body in the cavern and passing half to the room on the other side.

Ona moaned but, gathering courage, she climbed onto Camu's tail along his back and crossed to the other side, passing over her brother.

See? Easy.

Ona growled once and Lasgol ran in after them.

I've run out of arrows and we have to cross the entire city to escape from here. Go on?

Yeah, half the mountain is after us, Lasgol transmitted in confirmation.

Run.

As fast as you're able!

They left the palace they were in as fast as they could and came across the dead body of the red dragon and the two scorpions they had killed. Lasgol looked at them out of the corner of his eye as they passed by. If their pursuers were already furious, once they saw this they were going to be even more so.

They came out to the streets of the city and took the first avenue that went south. They kept running with all their will. They could hear the hissing of the cobras and the strange grunts of the scorpions behind them that were hunting them. Lasgol glanced back and counted over twenty pursuers, all huge. They could not stop, or else the creatures would catch up and massacre them.

Turn left at the next street!

Ona took the street to her left and Camu followed. Lasgol followed right behind them. They followed east for a while, with Lasgol looking back and measuring the distance that separated them from their pursuers.

Turn right! Lasgol noticed that the giant scorpions and cobras had trouble   turning, and since they were in groups they bumped against one another and stumbled among themselves. That was why he was ordering abrupt turns every two streets. With this tactic they managed to gain a little advantage which they badly needed.

After two more left turns and then right, they faced another avenue that headed south. They ran down that with their tongues out, exhausted from the escape.

We're almost there!

Almost where?

Outside the city.

Onto desert.

Lasgol realized Camu was right. He had not thought that far. Once they escaped the city, they were going to go headlong into the great desert. It was not a good prospect, especially when they were being chased by dozens of massive scorpions and snakes.

They left the city and, as Camu had anticipated, before them stretched the great desert.

We keep going south!

Okay, Camu messaged, along with a feeling of exhaustion.

Climb that dune. We'll hide behind it! Lasgol pointed at a high dune in front of them that could hide them from their pursuers who still had not come out of the city.

They ran to the dune, which was considerably high and could hide them if they managed to climb it. They had almost no strength left. It was not going to be easy. Ona was climbing and Camu was trying to follow her. Lasgol was a few paces behind them, glancing back. They had managed to gain the right advantage—they might make it after all. They just had to take cover behind the great dune.

Suddenly, the dune started to move. The three fell down in the midst of strange tremors and quakes under their feet.

And then Lasgol realized.

The dune was not actually a dune.

It was the great crocodile camouflaged!

Chapter 46

Ona moaned.

Hold on, it's the giant crocodile! Lasgol cried as he held onto one of the bony ridges on the side of the giant reptile.

Camu managed to adhere to its side with his soles. Ona, on the other hand, had to climb up the side using her claws. Once on top, she crouched on the colossal back of the monster, trying to dig her claws into the tough skin.

The giant beast rose and roared, opening its long snout. It shook its tail and then its head from side to side. But it could not move its body so well.

Lasgol quickly realized this.

Get on its back!

Camu started up. It was easy for him since he could adhere to almost any surface with the soles of his paws. For Lasgol though, climbing up the side of the monster was like climbing a great mountain with his bare hands. He held onto the bony ridges of the monster and sought for footholds for his feet in order to climb.

The croc started to shake harder. It was aware of the three strangers trying to climb onto its back. The shaking was powerful, and Ona and Lasgol had to hold on hard so as not to fall off. A fall from that height would not kill them, but it would doubtless leave them very sore.

Camu got to the top with Ona, who was holding on as best as she could. She even bit down on one of the bony ridges of the monster's scales to hold better and not fall down. Lasgol was struggling with the shaking and the height. Climbing onto the monster had seemed like a good idea, especially so it would not eat them or crush them with its legs or colossal body.

But now he was not finding it such a good idea. He was losing his footing with every shake, and he almost fell to the ground. He held on with his hands and was left hanging. He clenched his jaw and held fast while the monster shook hard again. It wanted to get rid of those parasites on its back. Lasgol was trying to find a foothold. At the same time he was keeping an eye on his satchel. If it fell off he would lose the great pearl. And if he lost his Ranger's belt he would lose several of the small pearls nestled inside it.

The situation was most complicated. And to make it even more critical, out of the corner of his eye he was able to glimpse their pursuers coming out of the city and approaching fast. He breathed in the torrid air of the desert and kept climbing. The most important thing now was to get to Camu and Ona. He had to deal with one problem at a time. Trying to solve them all at once would only lead him to failure. He focused on climbing.

You can, Camu encouraged him from above.

Coming. Hold fast.

We well up here.

Lasgol continued climbing amid the enraged shaking of the crocodile and its fearsome grunts. The downside of this improvised strategy was that, even though the reptile was so gigantic it could not reach its colossal back, although sooner or later it would find a way to get rid of them.

Lasgol finally reached the top.

Let's go to the head, he said. He had noticed that right between the head and the beginning of the back there was a space where they could shelter between the head ridges and the beginning of its back.

They reached the spot and held on for dear life.

What do? Camu messaged.

Lasgol looked at the giant monster and then at the two dozen pursuers that had already reached them and were around the monster, and he snorted.

I'm very open to suggestions. Any suggestions.

Ona moaned.

Not know what do?

Lasgol shook his head.

Never in my life did I ever think I'd find myself in such a situation.

No good.

Very bad…

Suddenly, the giant reptile lay down and started rolling on its back on the sand. It had guessed how to get rid of the annoying vermin on its back.

Hold on!

Crocodile crazy, Camu messaged, feeling the reptile roll over in the sand.

Not crazy, it's trying to get rid of us!

Luckily, Lasgol had chosen their shelter well. They were rolling and the sand was falling on them, but not when the monster got on its back. They were inside the crack between two bony mounds and it could not crush them.

Hold on! It can't crush us!

Lasgol and Ona were holding on with their hands, feet, claws, and teeth so as not to fall off. Camu was relaxed—all the rolling in the world was not going to knock him off.

The scorpions and the cobras were watching the giant reptile rolling in the sand without coming too close, since it might crush them.

Suddenly, the three friends had another problem almost worse than being crushed to death. The monster stayed on its back with its back in the sand. The three found that they could not breathe. They were half-buried in the sand.

No... air...

Lasgol was digging with his hands, trying to open a way for air while the monster continued lying on its back with its belly in the sun. It started to scratch, and everything became a nightmare of sand for Ona, Camu, and Lasgol. They were buried in the sand, which shifted with every rub of the giant reptile. It was trying to squash them, but it was going to drown them in sand instead.

It moved to one side and they were free for one moment. They breathed in deeply, filling their lungs, and at the next moment it buried them again. The feeling of being suffocating in the sand was horrible. The monster was on top of them. Its back pushed them against the sand and submerged them in it.

The lack of air made Lasgol desperate for some way of getting out of this mess at once. He tried to stab the back of the croc with his knife, but its scales were too hard and he could not penetrate them. If he wanted him and his companions to get out alive, it would have to be with his magic. But how? Would he be able to? Were they all going to die here? He felt tremendous pressure falling on his shoulders.

Hold on, he transmitted to Camu and Ona.

Lasgol mentally searched through his skills one by one, seeing which one he could use in this situation that might help. He dismissed the archery ones, since he could not use the bow without

389

arrows. The defense ones would not help either, since he would suffocate. He had to make the colossal reptile turn over so they could get free and breathe. But how? Time was running out. How to make the giant crocodile turn over?

Lasgol did not know how to make it do what he wanted. But he could try to communicate with the giant creature as if it were just another animal. After all, that was what it was, only a giant one. He did not stop to think, there was no time. He was beginning to suffocate from lack of air. He called on his *Animal Communication* skill so he could see the croc's mind aura. Something surprising happened. He picked it up, but it was very small compared to the monster's huge size. The aura was no bigger than an apple, and it was sort of brownish in color.

He wasted no time and tried to communicate with the monster's aura.

Listen to me, he transmitted to it.

There was a flash in the brownish aura, so Lasgol guessed he had been successful. The giant crocodile stopped scratching against the sand, although it did not turn over. Yes, it must have received the message and was wondering where it had come from and how it was possible. Lasgol decided to test his luck and transmit something else and see whether it listened.

Turn over.

Once again there was a flash in the reptile's mind's aura, so Lasgol knew it was receiving the transmissions. It was a different thing whether it would do as told. In fact, it did not have to. Lasgol was not its master, and this beast most likely only responded to the wishes of the Immortal Dragon.

Regardless, Lasgol needed it to obey, to turn over. He had no more air and was going to suffocate. The three would die if it did not flip over. And in the midst of his despair, an idea came to his head. He had one skill which he had used only on a couple of occasions but which might work here. It was *Animal Domination.* He remembered he had used it to scare away an ogre and some bear in the past. It was not a skill he had mastered completely and the thought of using it on this monster made him hesitate. He was not sure he could do it. On the other hand, he had no other options. This was all he had. It was desperate, but desperate times called for desperate measures.

Lasgol gathered a large amount of energy from his inner pool and called on the *Animal Domination* skill.

Flip over. Now! He transmitted the order with authority. There was a green flash in Lasgol's head and another strong one in the aura of the great reptile.

And something astonishing happened.

The crocodile obeyed the order.

It turned over onto its belly with its back to the blue sky.

Lasgol, Ona, and Camu breathed, free of the sand that had been suffocating them.

Breathe! Good! Camu messaged joyfully.

Ona moaned once and lifted her nose and mouth to the sky to better inhale the desert air.

Lasgol filled his lungs with the precious air. He could barely believe what he had just done.

The giant crocodile started to move.

Lasgol immediately used the skill again. There was a flash and the skill activated.

Stay still. Don't move.

The reptile stood still as Lasgol had ordered.

Camu realized it was Lasgol who was dominating the monster.

You command crocodile?

Yes, and it seems to be working.

That be much impressive.

Yeah, well, I'm surprised it's obeying me.

Be Drakonian power.

You think so?

Be sure. Drakonians dominate with mind.

I guess so, yeah…. because of the part of my magic that is Drakonian… anyway, its mind isn't very big to be honest… that must help.

Dominate more easy.

Yeah, that's what I'm thinking too. Whatever it is, we're saved and that's what matters.

While the three were recovering, the scorpions and cobras seemed to realize that something was not right. They did not understand why the giant reptile was not attacking the three strangers. They started closing in aggressively.

Problems, Camu messaged.

Lasgol saw them and almost instinctively ordered the crocodile,

Stand up!

The giant reptile did so, putting them out of reach of the scorpions and cobras, which were beginning to surround it, wondering whether to attack it or not. It was an ally, and yet it was not letting them get to the three enemies.

The scorpions and cobras began to utter hissing sounds and odd grunts. They seem to be talking to the crocodile. Lasgol did not like that at all.

Don't listen to them! he transmitted to the croc.

Seeing that the crocodile did not respond to their demands, the cobras started slithering up its legs while the scorpions did the same up the long tail.

Coming for us, Camu messaged in warning.

Lasgol had already realized.

Shake off the cobras and scorpions! Lasgol transmitted the order to the giant reptile, which obeyed at once. The cobras flew off its legs as it shook them powerfully and the scorpions were thrown in several directions when it shook its tail hard.

Better escape, Camu messaged.

Ona growled once.

Yeah, let's get out of here. The minor dragons will soon come out to see what's going on and I don't want them to find us.

Lasgol calculated the situation and ordered the giant crocodile.

Take us south. Fast!

The giant reptile started walking on its huge legs with slow steps. Lasgol could barely believe he was commanding this gigantic being, but it was working. As they escaped, the scorpions and snakes started attacking its legs so it would not go away.

Defend yourself from them! Lasgol transmitted.

The crocodile stopped for a moment and with its tail and jaws it attacked the scorpions and cobras. Some died in its mouth and others were thrown off, and the unluckiest ones were crushed by its legs. It was not long before it had gotten rid of them all.

Keep going south! Lasgol ordered.

As the giant crocodile marched away and their enemies and the city were left behind, the three friends felt invincible riding on the back of the impressive creature.

We much good, Camu messaged proudly.

This time I have to agree with you. The truth is we've done quite well.

Ona growled once.

Lasgol could not believe they had managed to enter Dergha-Sho-Blaska's hiding place, discover the dragon's secret, steal the pearls from him, and get out alive. And most of all, to escape riding a giant crocodile.

Course? Camu messaged.

Lasgol thought for a moment. *We'll go east.*

East? Not go south, great city Zenut?

Lasgol shook his head.

To get home from Zenut we'd have to get a ship and go halfway around Tremia. It'd take forever.

That little good.

That's why we'll take a shortcut.

Shortcut in east?

The Mountains of Blood lie to the east.

I remember mountains.

And do you remember what's in those mountains?

Camu nodded.

In mountains tribe Desher Tumaini.

And what does that tribe guard?

Ohhhh… I know. Great White Pearl. Portal.

Exactly. We'll take the portal in the Mountains of Blood and go back home to the Shelter.

Much good idea.

I'm glad you like it.

Ona growled once.

All happy dance, Camu messaged and started dancing, flexing his legs and wagging his tail.

Ona joined in the dance.

Lasgol smiled and had no choice but to join them too.

If it was already a sight to see a monstrously gigantic crocodile crossing the desert, seeing one with the three of them dancing on its back made it unbelievable. The desert dwellers who sighted them would be telling the story for generations.

Chapter 47

King Thoran's war tent was busy that morning. With him were his brother Orten and a number of nobles of importance from the East: Count Volgren, Duke Uldritch, Duke Oslevan, and others. There were no nobles of the West who, although at the war camp, had not been summoned to the war meeting. They were all dressed in their best, with armor as expensive and shiny as it was good for fighting.

Who was present was King Kendryk of Irinel, accompanied by Reagan, First General of his armies. They had arrived by sea the day before with a small part of their troops. The majority of the Irinel Army had arrived by land to the Zangrian border from the East. King Kendryk had left his son, Prince Kylian, in command, and he was awaiting instructions to invade Zangria from the East.

The two Kings were discussing the course of the military action, placing and moving wooden pieces on a large map of the bordering areas and a great part of the Kingdom of Zangria, which rested on an oak table. The pieces represented the different armies and militias of both kingdoms involved in the conflict and the positions they were currently occupying according to the latest information.

The outside of the tent was guarded by Royal Rangers and some of the Invincibles of the Ice. Inside, Thoran's Royal Guard watched everyone present. The Commander of the Guard, Ellingsen, and First Ranger Raner were making sure that security was uttermost. Thoran was not going to suffer another murder attempt, neither him nor the allies under their protection.

The King had summoned the three generals of his army to report. They did not take long to appear.

"The Generals of the Army of Norghana!" an officer announced from outside the war tent.

The three Generals walked in through the heavily watched door of the tent.

"Report!" King Thoran ordered as they bowed to show their respect to the King.

"The Thunder Army is ready to cross the border and clear a path,

Your Majesty," General Olagson informed.

"The Snow Army is ready to follow the Thunder Army," General Rangulself informed.

"The Blizzard Army has archers ready all along the river. The light cavalry will cross the river as soon as the order is given," General Odir confirmed.

"Any trouble?" Thoran asked his generals.

"None. Everything is ready, Your Majesty," said Rangulself.

"Have the enemy positions changed?" Orten asked.

"The scouts and spies we have on the other side of the border have informed us that the Zangrians maintain their position," Rangulself reported.

"I find it somewhat strange," King Kendryk said. "They have all their forces amassed here," he pointed on the map, "before your armies," he told Thoran. "Yet, my son could come in through the East and attack their troops along their flank."

"They must not want to divide their forces on two fronts," King Thoran reasoned.

"If they don't oppose resistance, my son's forces could even come down South and then attack from behind their back," King Kendryk commented, puzzled.

"Bah, that's because they don't know how to organize a proper defense!" Orten boasted.

"Don't underestimate the enemy," his brother told him.

"We have their best general in the dungeons, I bet the others aren't any good," Orten replied.

"Excuse me, but we know that the Zangrian generals are optimal military leaders," General Reagan of Irinel intervened.

"Rangulself? What do you think?" King Thoran asked.

"I think like the distinguished General Reagan. The Zangrian militaries are cautious and well-trained. We can't afford to underestimate them."

"Nonsense! I say we attack now and gut them all like fish!" Orten brayed.

Thoran meditated this.

"How many forces do you have?" he asked King Kendryk.

"About thirty-five thousand soldiers, the best of Irinel. Five thousand here with me and thirty thousand with my son."

"Added to our forces, that gives us a very important numeric superiority," Thoran reasoned. "Even if they have the advantage of knowing the land and their soldiers are fighting to save their country, they won't be able to stand up to such a superior force."

"We'll destroy them! We'll take Zangria in a week!" Orten cried feverishly.

"We shouldn't count on it. We must act with prudence," General Reagan intervened.

"Do you suspect anything?" King Kendryk asked him.

"I'd guess, from what our spies have found out, that King Caron of Zangria is buying the military support of other kingdoms."

"Which are those kingdoms?" Thoran asked, frowning.

"We know he's been talking with Queen Niria of the young Kingdom of Moontian."

Thoran and Orten looked at each other blankly.

"Why would Moontian support Zangria? They're not allies, nor do they have common interests," said Thoran.

"Let's say it's not good for Queen Niria if Irinel becomes a military and economic power," King Kendryk said.

"They have territorial disputes?" Thoran asked.

"Several. Stagnant. Since a long time ago," King Kendryk admitted.

"Irinel and Moontian don't have cordial relations," Reagan explained.

"And they don't want you to conquer Zangria and become more powerful, because they know they'll be next," said Orten.

Reagan nodded.

"No king wishes a rival to prosper," Kendryk commented.

"That you can swear in blood," Thoran said.

Orten laughed with loud guffaws.

"Even so, if the Moontians send forces they can do nothing against our combined armies,"

"They could get the support of the Masig tribes," added General Rangulself.

"Of those savages of the prairies? Humbug!" Orten gestured incredulously.

"Let the General speak, Brother," Thoran snapped.

"No one hates the Norghanians more than the Masig. If we go to war, there's a good possibility the Zangrians will ask the Masig for help."

"Those tribes are savage and they're not organized, they have no leader to speak for all of them. In fact, they have hundreds of tribal chiefs," Thoran commented.

"The fact that they've never united doesn't mean they can't do it. It's a possibility to consider. It might also be that only a part of the hundreds of tribes of the Masig nation would join Zangria."

"They might attack us from the back while we're attacking the wings of the Zangrian forces," argued General Olagson.

"Do we have any evidence that this alliance is formalized? Has there been any troop movement?" Thoran asked.

"No…" Reagan started.

"Not yet," Rangulself replied.

"Because there won't be any!" Orten cried. "Let's attack and destroy them!"

At that moment the officer at the door announced another figure.

"Attention! Here comes Queen Heulyn of Norghana!"

The Druid Queen came into the war tent, to the clear surprise of all those present. Some of them forgot to shut their open mouths and others to deflect their curious gazes.

"My King," Heulyn courteously greeted her husband with a slight bow of her head.

"My Queen," Thoran replied coldly and frowning.

"Father, you look good in your war armor."

"My child, it always cheers my heart to see you but perhaps this isn't the best time and place…" King Kendryk suggested. He did not think it was his daughter's place to be in a war tent.

"This is no place for the Queen," Orten snapped, looking annoyed at the interruption.

"On the contrary. This is the exact place and moment where I need to be."

Several murmurs of protest were heard among the nobles.

"Wife…" Thoran, who did not want her there, started to say.

Heulyn silenced them all by raising her hand and waving it cuttingly.

"I'm here to prevent Kings, Nobles, and Generals from making a great mistake."

"And what would that mistake be?" King Thoran demanded to know as he looked at the Queen, displeased.

"Attacking the Kingdom that did not commit the murder

attempts."

"What on earth are you saying?" Orten said as if she were crazy.

"Zangria was the Kingdom that tried to kill you," Thoran assured her.

Heulyn waited patiently for the murmurs, cries of incredulity, and other complaints to subside.

"I have proof that it's the Kingdom of Erenal who is behind the attempts and that they did so in a way that the blame would fall on Zangria, precisely to achieve what you are about to do—attack Zangria."

"That's complete and utter nonsense!" brayed Orten.

"Measure your words, Orten, don't forget I'm the Queen of Norghana," Heulyn threatened him with her finger.

"We all know it was Zangria, you're wrong," Thoran said.

"You all believe what Erenal wants you to. As you well know, the greatest enemy of Erenal is Zangria. And here you all are, plotting how to destroy her. I'd say that the one who stands to win from the fall of Zangria is Erenal, and they will do so without shedding a single drop of blood of their forces or spending one gold coin from their treasury. Meanwhile, you will lose thousands of soldiers and thousands of gold coins if you attack Zangria, which will fight to the end since their King Caron had nothing to do with what you accused him of."

"What you're saying is true, but you're wrong about Caron, he is guilty," Thoran insisted amid new murmurs and whispering from the nobles.

King Kendryk moved to his daughter's side.

"Do you really have proof of this conspiracy?"

"I do, Father," Heulyn confirmed as she gestured toward the door.

Astrid and Viggo came in holding Rolemus, who had his hands tied behind his back and was also gagged.

"Who's that? What does all this mean?" Thoran asked, more and more puzzled.

"This is the agent for the Kingdom of Erenal who hired the Zangrian assassin who tried to kill me. I have him here, and I have his letters from a nobleman close to King Dasleo, Marchius, in which they prepared the plot," she said and produced the notebook with the letters. She held it up to show them.

"I don't believe it!" Orten protested.

"I'll let you question him later, I'm sure you'll get all the information you need out of him with your methods and they'll corroborate what I just told you all."

"If this is true, it's Dasleo whom we have to execute, not Caron," King Kendryk said as he leafed through the notebook and letters.

"It's true, and I want Dasleo's head on a silver platter," Heulyn demanded with fiery eyes.

Thoran went over to Heulyn and Kendryk and started leafing through the evidence.

"I don't know the language of Erenal. Bring me a bloody interpreter!"

"I'm telling you, it's as I've explained." Heulyn insisted.

"I'll draw my own conclusions," Thoran replied.

They waited for Irakurteson, an Erudite who spoke several languages and always accompanied the Royal Retinue.

"Read these letters out loud in Norghanian," the King ordered him.

Irakurteson did so. The letters detailed the order to hire a Zangrian assassin and the gold available for such an operation, the reasons and need for the attacker to be Zangrian. One sentence was repeated in all the letters: blame Zangria. A clear goal appeared in all the letters: cause a war between Zangria and Norghana to weaken both and for Erenal to take over Zangria afterward.

Once he finished reading the letters and several notes in the notebook, there was a tense silence in the war tent.

"How did you find out all this?" Thoran asked Heulyn.

"I have my means."

"I want to know how!" Thoran demanded.

"My protectors found out for me."

"My Royal Eagles?"

"That's right. They discovered the intrigue and presented it to me so I could bring it to you."

Thoran looked at Astrid and Vigo and seemed to recognize them.

"Orten, question that pea head. Now!" Thoran said. "Don't let him die!"

"I'll be delighted," Orten said, grabbing the man by the neck and leaving with him.

"We'll wait until my brother comes back. He won't take long."

"It's more than clear," Heulyn said.

"It makes all the sense in the world, and considering the evidence…" King Kendryk told Thoran.

"I won't make a decision until I'm fully convinced," he said adamantly. Thoran did not want to admit he had made a mistake regarding Zangria.

They waited, and while they did they started discussing. Heulyn was speaking to her father in their language. Thoran was not talking and neither were his Generals.

It was not long before Orten came back. He did not even bother to wipe the blood off his hands.

"What did you get out of him?" Thoran asked.

"It's as the Queen said," Orten admitted, looking annoyed.

Thoran nodded.

"Is he alive?"

"Yes, he's alive."

"Keep him that way."

Orten nodded.

"What are you going to do now, King of Norghana?" Heulyn asked.

"We can still take Zangria," Orten intervened. "We can act if we did not have this information. The other kingdoms won't be able to blame us for this war."

"I would also like to squash Caron and his kingdom. He's done nothing but pester me all this time, and he's a rival," Thoran said.

"That wouldn't be a good idea," Kendryk told him. "We might take Zangria, but it would weaken us both. You heard, it's what would benefit Dasleo. In a year he'd attack us, when we're in the middle of recovering from the fray, and would take Zangria off our hands."

"Besides, this outrage demands satisfaction. We have to go for Dasleo and Erenal, not for Caron and Zangria," Heulyn said, enraged, her hands making fists.

"I want them both dead!" cried Thoran.

"We must be intelligent at this time," King Kendryk told him in a pacifying tone. "If we want to avenge this outrage, our best ally to go against Erenal is none other than Zangria."

Thoran and Orten looked at the King of Irinel.

"You're not saying…?" Thoran asked.

"Why not? We explain what's happened to King Caron, how Dasleo has played him, and we offer our help to finish off Erenal," Kendryk said.

"And it will be Zangria who will take the brunt of the war's wear and tear...." Thoran was beginning to see the picture.

"Exactly. Once Erenal falls, the one at a disadvantage will be Zangria," Kendryk helped him reason.

"And then we can take Zangria besides Erenal," Thoran saw the light and his eyes lit up.

"As long as you bring me Dasleo's head, I agree with this. I won't oppose this strategy," the Druid Queen said.

"General Rangulself," Thoran addressed him.

"Yes, Your Majesty."

"Have all our armies withdraw to Norghanian territory. Two leagues inside the border."

"Yes, Your Majesty, at once."

"Kendryk, you and I will send messengers to the Zangrian army asking to parley. We'll speak to Caron, we're going to make him a tempting offer."

"To conquer Erenal?" Kendryk asked.

"To destroy Erenal, and then destroy Zangria."

King Kendryk nodded.

"Let's hope he takes the bait."

"Oh he will, I'm sure. There's nothing Caron wants more than to see Dasleo fall. He hates Erenal a lot more than he hates Norghana. We'll offer him a unique opportunity, and one with motive. He won't be able to turn it down."

Kendryk smiled.

"This alliance of ours will go far."

"Ah... don't you doubt that. Tremia will be ours. Kingdom by kingdom," Thoran smiled insidiously. "Now, let us begin."

Chapter 48

Three days later, Lasgol walked into the Panthers' room in the Tower of the Rangers. It was the wee hours of the morning, and he found them all asleep. The light of the moon came in through a window and lit up the silhouette of the sleeping bodies lying on the bunks. Gerd's snores echoed along the walls rhythmically.

"You shouldn't sneak into the Royal Eagles' room at night," an acid voice which he recognized at once as Viggo's said. The Assassin already had his throwing knife ready in his hand.

"You know I like trouble," Lasgol replied with a smile.

"Lasgol?" Astrid asked between fearful and hopeful as she recognized his voice.

"Yours truly, and still alive and kicking," he said with a smile from ear to ear.

"Lasgol!" she cried, jumping out of bed into her beloved's arms, knocking him down with her momentum.

"Have you missed me?" Lasgol asked her, laughing with his back on the floor as she showered him with kisses.

"Where have you been all his time? We had no news from you! Do you want to kill me with worry?" Astrid chided him. "I've had my heart in my throat all this time!" she said, hitting his shoulders with her flat hands in scolding.

"As well as all of us," Egil joined her. "You must've had an interesting adventure to have taken so long to come back and not sent any news."

Nilsa got up and lit one of the oil lamps.

The rest of the group woke up from all the noise.

"It's so nice to be back," Lasgol said, his face lit with the joy he felt at being back. "And yes, it's been a complicated adventure."

"The weirdo had to make one of his entrances… he couldn't wait until morning and let us sleep in peace," Viggo complained, but he could not help smiling at Lasgol, seeing he appeared to be all right.

"As soon as Astrid stops smothering him, I'd like to give him one of my bear hugs," Gerd said, already spreading his arms open.

"Don't be offended, big guy, but I prefer Astrid's hugs," Lasgol replied, unable to erase a smile from his face.

"Let the lovebirds enjoy their reunion," Nilsa said, giggling.

Astrid went on kissing and hugging Lasgol for a long while until she finally stepped back and helped him to his feet. Then she let the others greet him, but without letting go of his right arm. She did not want to lose him again.

"I'm glad to see you. You look tired, but you have a good color," Ingrid told him, patting his left shoulder. "Where on earth have you been to get so tan?"

"By the color I'd guess quite south, am I right?" Egil asked, him giving him a heartfelt hug.

"You are rarely wrong, my friend. I've missed you sorely in this mission. You would've been so useful…"

"Yet you're here and you look well, so you've been able to manage on your own. Ona and Camu? Are they all right?"

Lasgol nodded repeatedly.

"Yes, they're both well. I've left them taking care of something."

"I so want to see them!" Egil said.

"I don't. I'm glad you didn't bring the bug and kitty," Viggo told him with a wink, and taking Lasgol's left hand they bumped shoulders by way of greeting. "Welcome, weirdo, I haven't missed you at all."

"I don't believe you," Lasgol smiled back at him. "You must've been bored out of your mind without me and my troubles."

"I'll agree to that, a little."

"Tell us all," Ingrid asked. "We also have important news to tell you."

"It's a long story. I'll tell you once I've rested a little. I'm worn out, and I know you'll have hundreds of questions as soon as I tell you what we've been through."

"In that case, rest first and we'll talk in the morning," Egil accepted.

"If possible after breakfast," Gerd suggested. "Since it'll be long… you know…" he said, rubbing his stomach.

"But how can you be such a glutton?" Viggo chided while the others laughed.

His friends' laughter was like a healing balm to Lasgol's soul. Being here back with Astrid and his friends was the best thing in the world. It healed everything, even the anxieties of the uncertain future.

They let Lasgol rest for the remaining of the night. Astrid did not leave him for a moment. It seemed to her as if she were going to lose him again during the night.

The next morning, after breakfast, they all sat on their bunks and the time came to explain everything.

"Shall I go first, or do you want to?" Lasgol asked them.

"Perhaps it'll be better if we tell you our news first," Ingrid said.

"Okay. What's gone on during my absence?" Lasgol asked. "I'm dying to know."

"Better if Egil tells you," Ingrid said.

"You're going to love it," Viggo told him with a face that meant he would not.

Egil told Lasgol everything that had happened in Norghana during his absence, focusing on the Queen, the political events, the training for Royal Rangers, and the discoveries they had made.

Lasgol listened attentively without missing a detail. Once Egil finished telling him everything Lasgol was silent for a moment, and then he spoke.

"First of all, my congratulations for becoming Royal Rangers. It's a great achievement," he said with a big, proud smile.

"Thank you, it is an honor," Ingrid replied proudly.

"I feel bad for you, you should be one too," Gerd said.

"Don't worry, big guy, I'm sure there'll be an occasion later on."

"Don't think it's anything to write home about. We're nothing but glorified nannies," Viggo said, dismissing it as unimportant.

"And secondly, great job discovering the plot of Erenal," Lasgol said.

"It's what comes from being so incredible," Viggo said as he wiped off imaginary dust from his shoulders.

"I'm absolutely sure of that," Lasgol laughed.

"Don't be so vain, my numbskull," Ingrid said to Viggo, and he blew her a kiss.

"Then are we going to war with Erenal?" Lasgol asked, concerned.

"That's what it looks like. War has still not been declared. It seems that Thoran and Kendryk are negotiating with Caron an alliance against Erenal," Nilsa commented, "so far General Zotomer and all the Zangrians have been released."

"Well, they're making all the moves to get themselves a deal,"

Lasgol said.

It won't be easy for them to agree. If they do, and they very well might, we'll be drawn into a tough war. Dasleo is a good military king. Erenal has skilled armies and a great tradition, as well as allies," Egil explained.

"We can always stop this war too," Gerd said in a lively tone.

"Look at the optimistic giant, as if it were that easy," Viggo mocked.

"Let me remind you that we've stopped the war against Zangria," Gerd replied, making a face that meant it was not impossible.

"A great achievement," Lasgol agreed.

"We'll see what we can do…" Egil said in a mysterious tone.

"Another important person the King has released is Gondabar," Nilsa said suddenly.

"He has?" Lasgol had been waiting for this anxiously.

"He has. When he came back from the border. On the condition that if he hears the least mention of a dragon, he'll hang him," Ingrid said.

"Our king and leader, always so charming," Astrid said in a disappointed tone.

"At least he's free and back at his post, right?" Lasgol asked.

"Yes. He's here in the Tower, in his own chambers. He'll want to talk to you," Egil said.

"Good, I'll go later."

"He'll be pleased to see you," Nilsa told him.

Lasgol nodded and was thoughtful. "What happened to the two prisoners you rescued before they could fall in Orten's hands?" Lasgol asked.

"Yeah, I'd also like to know," said Gerd, looking at Egil with a face that showed he was not happy not knowing.

"You haven't told?" Lasgol asked, surprised.

"He's been very quiet these past few days…" Viggo said. "Which isn't usually a good sign."

"I did not want to press you, but I would like to know what happened to them," Ingrid said.

"Even if it's not good," Astrid added. "You know we're with you."

"Always with you, no matter what," Nilsa promised.

Egil nodded and took a deep breath.

"I'll tell you, you have a right to know. I questioned them with Ginger and Fred's help. You know they're almost infallible when it comes to drawing the truth out of someone."

"Well, rather you by using them," Gerd corrected him.

"Yeah, that's it," Egil agreed. "I questioned them for two days in a row. Thank you for covering for my absence."

"Don't worry, the Queen did not give us much trouble. One outing to the forest with the Druids, and the other day she was shouting with the King all over the castle," Viggo said.

Egil smiled.

"After questioning them, I reached the conclusion that what happened in Rogdon wasn't that they were found out by Orten's agents. What happened was that they managed to escape from their guards, and when they were trying to leave Rogdon they were found out by Orten's agents, who were looking for them."

"Why did they escape? They were safe and protected," Nilsa asked.

"Because men are like that. They appear to have great ideals and that they'll keep their word. But then reality hits and their life doesn't convince them, and they take the wrong path. They decided to escape and not keep to what they had agreed upon. They were supposed to spend one year in Rogdon in hiding until it had all blown over and then they could choose another destination. That was the agreement. But they had gold in their pockets. Gold of the West, for the service rendered and the risk taken. The gold was burning a hole in their pockets, they wanted to spend it and have a great life. The guards prevented them from doing this because they'd draw the attention of the agents looking for them. They already knew all this and it had been gone over with them, but they gave in to greed. Men with little integrity."

"Wow..." Nilsa said wondering.

"Weak of spirit," Ingrid said.

"Gold is hard to resist," said Viggo. "Especially if you have it with you."

"They were supposed to do it for the cause, not for the gold," said Astrid.

"Yeah, that's what it was supposed to be for," Egil nodded. "The cause wanted to reward them and also buy their silence, hence the gold."

"It didn't work…" Lasgol said.

"No, in the end it did not."

"So what's happened to them?" Gerd asked, afraid of doing so because he had already guessed the answer.

"The West can't afford such a problem. They solved it."

"Solved it forever?" Astrid asked.

Egil nodded.

"Thoran won't be able to get any information out of them. No one will."

Viggo made the sign of passing a knife along his throat.

"Not a good development," said Lasgol.

"I told them that trying to murder Thoran was a bad idea. Now they're reaping what they sowed and they were lucky we intervened. They could've ended in the gallows."

"Well, one less problem," Viggo said, waving it aside.

"I'm sorry to have involved you in it," said Egil.

"The Panthers are together in everything always. In everything. For better or worse," said Astrid.

"And evil," Viggo added with a mischievous grin.

"Now tell us what you've been through," Astrid begged Lasgol.

"Very well," Lasgol told them calmly everything that Ona, Camu, and he had been through and what they had found out. When he finished, the looks of disbelief and shock on their faces were almost comical.

"What an adventure! Thank goodness I wasn't with you this time!" Viggo said, looking serious.

"But you've crossed half of Tremia!" Gerd cried.

"The central part of Tremia, to be precise," Egil corrected him. "What an interesting expedition, I would've loved to go on that journey with you."

"I would skip the part in the desert. Too much suffering, and with my skin…" Nilsa made a horrified face.

"That's what I call an adventure, the rest are trifles," Ingrid said, nodding, impressed.

"You shouldn't have taken so many risks, not without us to help you," Astrid chided. She was not at all happy with what she had heard.

"I had no choice but to take the risk," said Lasgol. We have to look on the bright side. We've found out that Dergha-Sho-Blaska isn't only very intelligent, he's also wise."

Egil nodded.

"He's a powerful creature with a wisdom and intelligence spanning thousands of years. That explains why he didn't act as soon as he was reborn and why he hasn't lunged to conquer the world yet. It's because he has a secret plan, one which he's carrying out cautiously and without raising suspicions. He won't be hasty. We must understand that for a millenary creature time is a lot more relative than for us. He doesn't think like we do."

"That's right," Lasgol agreed. "He was not in a hurry. After all, he's thousands of years old and also immortal."

"One which, come the time, might go on living just by changing bodies. If he gets in trouble, he could be reborn in another," said Astrid.

"Then he's carrying out some kind of secret plan, and he does it without taking any risks so that nothing and no one might stop him," Ingrid said.

"We will stop him," Viggo said confidently, folding his arms on his chest.

"It seems that way. Now he has more followers, not only humans but monstrous reptiles that serve him now and will be loyal when he rules over the world," Nilsa said with a shiver just thinking about it.

"He's not going to rule the world. We'll stop him," Gerd said with conviction, nodding repeatedly.

"Well, it's not going to be at all simple," Lasgol said.

"Lasgol is right, but at least we've found out his secret," said Egil with a thoughtful look on his face. "Instead of facing the whole of humanity alone, he's opted for creating an army of monstrous reptiles and minor dragons who will assure victory, minimizing the risk. It's a brilliant plan, if you think about it."

"Brilliant for him, bad for us," Viggo said.

"Very bad," Gerd joined in.

"If we all join against the dragon and his armies, we'll win, I'm sure. The kingdoms of Tremia have armies with thousands and thousands of soldiers," Nilsa said.

"That would be the ideal thing, that all the kingdoms, that all of humanity would unite against him. But, do you really believe they will? I don't," Astrid said quite pessimistically.

"I'm with Astrid on this," Ingrid joined in. "That two kingdoms unite against a greater enemy is something that seldom happens. That all of humanity unites? I find it impossible."

Egil raised his hands.

"Let's not get carried away by ill omens. We need to focus on what's important. We've found out his secret: we know where he is and what he's trying to do. That gives us an advantage."

"Especially because Lasgol has stolen the Silver Pearls," Astrid added, sounding incredibly proud of him.

"Without the pearls he won't be able to continue creating his reptilian army," said Nilsa. "That's good news."

"Not only that, but from what you've told us, he had some other plan for the Great Pearl and that's why he was looking for the smaller ones. You've also thwarted that plan," Ingrid said,

Lasgol nodded.

"I think so... although I don't know what this other plan is, and that has me worried."

"What's important is that we've been able to thwart his plans. For now at least, which gives us an opportunity," Egil commented, looking as if he were turning the matter over in his mind.

"Are the pearls safe?" Astrid asked.

"For now. Camu and Ona have them. Camu is using his skill so that the power of the pearls can't be picked up. But we need to find a container like Eicewald had, one more powerful still to keep the pearls in, so poor Camu can be free of that responsibility."

"In that case, this should be our priority," Egil said. "We can't let Dergha-Sho-Blaska recover the pearls."

"Besides, it puts Camu at risk, as well as Ona," Astrid added, worried.

"I agree that the container has to be a priority. We have to deny him the possibility of getting the Pearls of Power back," said Ingrid.

"There's another matter we should also pursue..." Lasgol commented.

"What matter? Another of your troubles?" Viggo asked.

"Something like that," Lasgol replied. "We have to seek and find the weapons with power that can kill dragons. What was said about Aodh's Bow has turned out to be true. The Bow is capable of killing dragons, which means that some of the other weapons might be too."

"That's an idea I like," Ingrid agreed.

"Me too," said Astrid.

"One thing, mischief-maker, didn't you say that in order to make the bow work you used your own magic?" Viggo asked.

Lasgol nodded.

"Yes, I suspect it uses part of my magic, the part that isn't Drakonian …"

"Then it's no good for us, we won't be able to use them," Viggo shook his head. "We don't have the Gift."

"Maybe the other weapons don't need magic to work. We don't know that," Gerd said, always the optimist.

"Or that there's another way of activating them," Astrid commented.

"We could also arm magi with them," Egil suggested.

"Yeah, with how well we get along with the Ice Magi and their new leader, that's a great idea," Viggo said ironically.

"It's not ideal, but it's an acceptable solution," Egil said firmly. "There are different possibilities for the weapons. I think it's important we get them, and the sooner the better."

"Then let's make this clear. We have to find a magic container for the pearls, discover more anti-dragon weapons, and kill Dergha-Sho-Blaska and his dragons and monstrous reptiles, is that it?" Viggo asked.

"While we go to war with Erenal," added Ingrid.

"And we put up with the Druid Queen and her new magic," Nilsa noted.

"And we make Egil King," Gerd said.

"True, how forgetful of me, I had left those two trifles out. It all sounds too easy, like child's play," Viggo said ironically and started making crazy faces as if it were all madness.

"Whatever it may be that we have to get, together, all of us, we'll get it. That I know," Lasgol told them.

"For the Panthers!" Nilsa said, raising her fist.

"For the Panthers!" they all joined in.

The adventure continues in the next book of the saga:

Note from the author:
I really hope you enjoyed my book. If you did, I would appreciate it if you could write a quick review. It helps me tremendously as it is one of the main factors readers consider when buying a book. As an Indie author I really need of your support.
Just go to Amazon end enter a review
Thank you so very much.
Pedro.

Author

Pedro Urvi

I would love to hear from you.
You can find me at:
Mail: pedrourvi@hotmail.com
Twitter: https://twitter.com/PedroUrvi
Facebook: https://www.facebook.com/PedroUrviAuthor/
My Website: http://pedrourvi.com

Join my mailing list to receive the latest news about my books:

Mailing List:
http://pedrourvi.com/mailing-list/

Thank you for reading my books!

Other Series by Pedro Urvi

THE ILENIAN ENIGMA

This series takes place several years after the Path of the Ranger Series. It has different protagonists. Lasgol joins the adventure in the second book of the series. He is a secondary character in this one, but he plays an important role, and he is alone...

THE SECRET OF THE GOLDEN GODS

This series takes place three thousand years before the Path of the Ranger Series

Different protagonists, same world, one destiny.

You can find all my books at Amazon.
Enjoy the adventure!

fb882bea-569a-4a05-ae8b-88b5c6efcfbfR01